THE
DOMINION
OF
WYLEY
McFADDEN

Scott Gardiner

The **Dominion** of **Wyley McFadden**

A NOVEL

VINTAGE CANADA
A Division of Random House of Canada Limited

VINTAGE CANADA EDITION, 2001

Published in Canada by Vintage Canada, a division of Random House of Canada Limited, in 2001. First published in hardcover in Canada by Random House Canada, Toronto, in 2000. Distributed by Random House of Canada Limited, Toronto.

Vintage Canada and colophon are registered trademarks of Random House of Canada Limited.

National Library of Canada Cataloguing in Publication Data

Gardiner, Scott, 1959-
   The dominion of Wyley McFadden

ISBN 0-679-31105-X

I. Title.

PS8563.A6244D64 2001   C813'.54   C2001-930122-7
PR9199.3.G37D64 2001

The publishers have generously given permission to use extended quotations from the following copyrighted works. From *The House in Paris*, by Elizabeth Bowen. Copyright © 1961 Alfred A. Knopf, Inc. Reprinted by permission of Alfred A. Knopf, Inc. "The Rat is the conciset Tenant" from *The Poems of Emily Dickinson*, Ralph W. Franklin, ed., Cambridge, Mass.: The Belknap Press of Harvard University Press. Copyright © 1998 by the President and Fellows of Harvard College. Copyright © 1951, 1955, 1979 by the President and Fellows of Harvard College. Reprinted by permission of the publishers and the Trustees of Amherst College. From "A History of Rat Control in Alberta" by Michael J. Dorrance. Copyright © 1989 by Alberta Agriculture, Food and Rural Development. Reprinted by permission. From H. B. McEwen's Foreword to "Rat Control in Alberta" by J. B. Gurba and C. F. Barrett. Copyright © 1983 by Alberta Agriculture, Food and Rural Development. Reprinted by permission. From "Summary of Fur Management Regulations" by the Ontario Ministry of Natural Resources. Copyright © 2000 Queens Printer Ontario. Reprinted by permission. "After the Rats," from *Poems for All the Annettes*, by Al Purdy. Copyright © 1968 by Al Purdy. Reprinted by permission of the author.

Text design: Scott Gibbs
Cover design: CS Richardson

www.randomhouse.ca

Printed and bound in the United States of America

10 9 8 7 6 5 4 3 2 1

IN MEMORY OF MY FATHER,
WHO PUT PEN IN MY HAND, PAD ON MY DESK,
AND THOUGHT IN MY HEAD.
AND MY MOTHER,
WHO TOOK CARE
OF EVERYTHING ELSE.

In all this reasoning I favour
myself – when I impute
rats, and cannot prove
at all they really did and do exist.
Except each morning I see
myself lessen, diminish . . .
Frantically I cling
to heart tissue, tightly hold
the intangibility located
in my head where thoughts rush
out and charge and change and die.
It's curious. One would not think
habit of belief, custom of thinking,
syllogism, paradigm of me could
disappear and some other me
replace me, some other silly mannikin
enact again my whole personal painful
joyful unique personality:
but I expect soon
to be sitting in a tavern drinking
beer contemplatively, and one by one
thirstily the other beasts enter.

—FROM AL PURDY
"AFTER THE RATS" (1959)

*. . . we can look
with pride and
satisfaction on the
fact that Alberta is
still basically rat-free.
However, the price
of continued
freedom is continued
vigilance . . .*

H. B. McEWEN
DEPUTY MINISTER,
ALBERTA AGRICULTURE
MARCH 1983

W hat McFadden is now is a trapper, or more precisely, an urban trapper, but he has put that profession aside for the moment to enjoy the fruits of his labour. He and his truck have just passed the town of Wawa, off the eastern flank of Lake Superior. Greenish ponds and beaver dams slide by the windows, now the big lake itself has disappeared, and miles and miles of conifer and aspen. Peering at the mirror and the wobbling road behind, McFadden sighs, then shifts into a lower gear. There is a girl by the wayside, and Wyley McFadden is slowing down to pick her up.

Between gears it occurs to him that he hasn't taken on a hitchhiker in years. These days most drivers don't risk it. Then again, these days most people don't hitchhike. McFadden has always made a habit of picking up female hitchhikers. It seems to him neglectful – negligent, even – to leave a woman standing at the side of the road. As the distance shrinks, he calculates the implications, meditating outcome, analyzing risk, and then again absolves his conscience. He'd have stopped for this one anyway, regardless of consequence; it's been obvious from half a mile she's under serious attack.

Although McFadden is a trapper of the urban variety, he prides himself on maintaining the same level of skill as his bush-dwelling colleagues. It is habit for him always to scan his surroundings for signs of game. So far he has spotted two bear and a moose, though this is no keen feat of woodcraft since all of them were just hanging around the side of the road looking miserable. For strategic reasons McFadden has timed his holidays to start in early June. Early June, on the northern reaches of the Great Lakes, is the beginning of the height of mosquito season. It is also, coincidentally, the tail of the blackfly season, so on a good day, a warm, calm day after rain, both mosquito and blackfly will rise in equal numbers. The bear and the moose were keeping to the cleared verges beside the highway, hoping for a breeze to blow the bugs away.

Judging from the motion of the girl up ahead, there is no such breeze to be had.

From a distance she appears to be performing some exotic dance. A little closer reveals that, if this is a dance, she is not the best of dancers. Mostly she's hopping from one foot to the other, bending in oddly rhythmic intervals and waving her arms. Occasionally a thumb shoots out to indicate that she is hitch-hiking.

Wyley McFadden's cargo is delicate. He has no intention of jolting his load just so he can stop a little faster. He slides smoothly down the gears and taps the brakes only just a little. As he eases closer, the dance resolves itself into a pattern.

Starting off on her right foot, she brings her left one up to pass behind the other, high up as she can get without falling. At the same time she bends and swipes a hand along the leg she's standing on, then unbends everything, changes feet and does the same on the other side. In the pause when both feet are on the ground, she brushes her arms, face and as much of her back as she can

reach, and briefly performs the hitchhiking signal. She is outfitted in what appears to be tennis whites, and McFadden decides
she must be an idiot.

He rolls up beside her and leans for the door latch.

Before the truck has stopped, she is running for the passenger
side, batting at the cloud around her head. Without a word she
dives for the seat, shaking her hair and sending a swarm of insects humming through the cab.

At such meetings on the road there is usually small talk:

"Morning. Where you going?"

"Hi! Just up the way to Hornepayne."

"Well, I can see you as far as White River."

"Great. Thanks."

There is none of this. Within seconds McFadden's own skin is
punctured a dozen times. "Get moving!" she says, but McFadden
is already pumping the clutch. Gravel flies beneath the wheels
and the truck shudders sideways onto the pavement. The gears
groan in acceleration.

The girl levers down the window as they pick up speed to
blow the attackers back outside, and begins with ferocious intensity to destroy any still attached to her skin. McFadden slaps
his neck, his cheek, and bears down on the gas.

"Jesus," he says.

For a while he too is preoccupied with scratching and slapping. Most of the mosquitoes are soon killed or blown out, but
the smaller, thicker-bodied blackflies continue to creep in numbers across the windshield. The girl is methodically crushing
them with her thumb. Bloody fingerprints dot the glass.

"So," says McFadden, rooting for a Kleenex, "where are you
going?"

The girl turns to look at the road ahead. Her left eye has
swollen partly shut.

"That way," she says, motioning with her head, then leans
across him to squash a bug on his side of the screen.

– – –

There is a fetish that comes over people in the presence of blood-drinking insects – a universal and feverish compulsion. It is, perhaps, a primordial response; an obsession on the part of the psyche, having been delivered from torment, to turn on its tormentors in savage retribution; a terrible and pitiless desire to obliterate the enemy, to annihilate it absolutely. McFadden and the girl dedicate the next several minutes to a silent and bloody operation of seek-and-destroy.

With one hand on the wheel McFadden patrols the area forward of the steering column; the girl ranges throughout the rest of the cab. McFadden targets anything immediately ahead, the girl deals with whatever is beyond his reach. When a humming tells him a mosquito is circling in an eddy behind his head, it is the girl who turns and reaches from her knees to seek it out. And when a blackfly crawls from where it had lodged unfelt in his hair, it is she who pinches it from the lobe of his ear to crunch between her fingers. He hands her the Kleenex when all is done, knowing that in the thickness outside she will have breathed some in.

"Thanks," she says, and blows her nose.

They drive for miles in silence.

As the country rolls by, he makes excuses. He fiddles with the radio, adjusts the air vent. Twice he changes gears for hills that do not warrant change of gears. These little motions afford the opportunity to look. He sums her up with tiny glances, ascertaining her condition. It is easiest to see her legs, and these are bad. Mosquitoes pierce the skin and pump for blood; blackflies gorge out little holes until their heads embed, feeding as they go. One incurs dilatation, the other scrobiculated lesions.

She is wearing pink-and-white running shoes, badly scuffed, and low-cut socks with pompons. Otherwise her legs are bare. On closer inspection he sees they *are* tennis whites – or were – now stiffened with a starch of mud and mashed mosquito. Her arms are in the same condition as her legs.

McFadden remembers that she must be an idiot.

"Why are you hitchhiking?" It comes out unthinkingly. "Don't you know how stupid it is for women to hitchhike?" He's about to launch into the perils of blackfly season too, when abruptly he stops.

Turning to lecture, he has seen that her ear is raw with blood. The auricle, warm and exposed with capillaries so near the surface, is the blackfly's darling. McFadden sighs and begins moving the truck onto the shoulder.

"What are you doing!"

The edge in her voice has nearly caused him to accelerate again.

"Why are you stopping?"

"I have some alcohol," he says, "behind the seat."

"I don't want to drink!" She is glaring, practically ablaze. Her eyes flee to the window, take in the muskeg, the dwarfish spruce and miles of nowhere. *"I don't want a drink at all."*

"Rubbing alcohol," he says gently, and points to her ear. "For the blood." He has brought the truck almost to a standstill. "Why don't you roll up your window," he says very softly. "We don't want any more coming in."

When the truck has stopped, he reaches over the seat to the storage compartment, fishing for his first aid kit. He opens it on his lap and removes the plastic bottle and several cotton swabs. Before he passes it over, he wets a swab and does his own ear and several punctures on his forearm where the blood is still tacky. He wants her to perfectly understand what this is all about.

When he has finished, he discards the swab and passes the bottle and unused cotton to the girl. She takes it, but reluctantly. With his hands free he starts the engine again and eases back onto the highway. Not a car has passed. He will not ask her how she has come to be on the side of the road. Wyley McFadden has an understanding with history.

"I'm a doctor," he says, though he has not said these words in years.

– – –

This is day two from the city.

Everything has been ready for weeks. The expedition itself is a paradigm of system and strategy. At each step it has been crucial that there be no delays; it has also been vital that nothing be rushed. Yesterday was the day he was scheduled to leave, and yesterday he left on schedule – in the morning, after ten o'clock and before eleven, between rush hour and the buildup again around noon. Wyley McFadden has been anticipating this excursion for a very long time.

Designing the truck was the biggest challenge. He is no draftsman, and found it a painstaking and tedious chore to make effective use of the space available. He is amazed at the amount of copper he managed to fit, to say nothing of the soldered joints, which so far seem to be holding, and very pleased with the neatness of his wiring. Installing the a/c was no treat either. Accommodating these intricacies, and the load, of course – and provisions – cost him hours of frustration. The cargo itself he'd been accumulating for the better part of a year. McFadden is by nature a planner. When circumstances call for action, he embarks with a wilful attention to detail.

The morning of departure he was up, as usual, hours before dawn, most of the transfer already seen to, provisions stowed, water tanks filled, propane containers checked again and bolted to the tailgate. From the outside the truck looks remarkably like any ordinary camper van, including the various stick-on silhouettes of elk and ducks, as well as flags from several provinces indicating to all the world the owner of this recreational vehicle is a woodsy, travelled sort of fellow. As a final touch, McFadden added the bumper sticker: *HONK IF YOU'RE HORNY.*

By 10:30 a.m. he was on the Don Valley Parkway. By 11:00 he'd exited the 401 to the 400, heading north. By 1:00 p.m. he had passed through Barrie, Orillia, and crested the great shield of granite over which he is still travelling today, with his plans already in tatters.

McFadden has underestimated the size of northern Ontario. On the map it seemed much more manageable than it has been on the surface. His calculations have failed to take into account the highway's grade. Since the Soo the road has been one long hill and then another, the truck creeping along at half anticipated speed. Although the scenery is beautiful, he's already far behind schedule, grinding up another endless slope in the company of a passenger who fits his itinerary absolutely nowhere.

– – –

There has not been conversation for miles.

In some ways this suits McFadden. He is no longer accustomed to conversation. In other ways it is difficult: he is not used to company either. In his mind the two go together. The reason he has had so little conversation, these past years, is that he has had very little company. Yet here he has been – for more than an hour – in the presence of company, but without conversation.

He had tried, earlier on, shortly after the misunderstanding with the alcohol. There was a can of Coke in the truck. He had obtained this Coke somewhere south of Sturgeon Falls when he stopped for gas at a service station built to resemble a Hudson Bay trading post. So far he has passed several dozen of these ersatz stockades and their commercial reproductions of the north woods log cabin: bearskins on the wall, moose heads by the door and a teepee or two in the parking lot. McFadden suspects that the native peoples from this area would never have used this type of structure, since the buffalo skins that presumably covered them were unavailable until the other side of Lake Superior, a thousand miles or so away. Be that as it may, there is an authentic demand for Indian moccasins, as well as cassette tapes of loon calls with wolf-howl backbeats for travellers wishing to re-establish their connections with nature.

This particular trading post was giving out a promotional can of Coke with every fill-up. McFadden does not particularly like soft drinks, but it goes against his nature to turn down something free, so the can of Coke has sat beside him since Lake Nipissing.

The silence that's descended after the alcohol incident is a markedly different kind of silence than the one he practises himself. McFadden's customary silence is an orthodox one, a self-contained silence that is as it should be. *This* silence is distinctly unnatural. It is an improper silence in that it exists merely because people who should be talking are not.

He rummages to find the Coke. "Alcohol-free," he says, handing her the can, and smiles to let her know he is telling a joke. Long ago he has learned that humour is the antidote to many uncomfortable situations, and that the effort of expression – in the telling of a joke – is often more important than the joke itself.

She takes it, pulls the tab and drinks. But there is no smile in return to acknowledge his attempt. She drinks the Coke and looks out through the window at the muskeg rolling by.

After a while McFadden tries the radio. But now they are on a part of the highway with low rock hills on every side. All he gets is static. They drive on through black spruce and Jack pine.

In time they pass a sign saying *Marathon, 32 kilometres*, reminding him that it is time to start thinking about water and lunch. But first he has to offload this passenger. He is about to ask her where he can drop her when she beats him to it.

"How far you going?" she says.

He is startled after such quiet, and answers truthfully. "Alberta." Then, taking the opportunity, "Where can I let you off?"

She looks at him.

"Alberta," she says, "will be fine."

– – –

He simply cannot believe the astonishing depths of his stupidity. McFadden is still groping for a way of taking back Alberta and replacing it with Marathon when she touches his elbow and points across the dash.

"Look, a bear."

For the moment both Marathon and Alberta disappear as both of them peer through the windscreen. McFadden's professional and predatory nature is instantly awakened by the presence of game, particularly big game. As an urban trapper he never gets to deal with any genuinely big game, and the prospect of sighting another bear, even his third since Toronto, temporarily overrides his thinking in other directions. She is pointing to the ridge of an outcrop thirty feet above the shoulder.

It is indeed a bear, a fully grown male by the size of him, a three-hundred-pounder. The bear is sprawled, headfirst to the wind, lying flat out with his paws across his snout.

"He's up there for the breeze," says McFadden, unable to resist the opportunity to show off his understanding of wilderness matters. "This is a pretty good stretch of road, open enough for the air to move . . . Back in the bush, where there's no wind at all, the bugs would be driving him nuts." He looks at her and grins, trying again for conversation. "This time of year it's hard for them to decide which is the biggest threat – flies or people."

"I know the feeling," she says. Somehow he is made to feel singled out.

– – –

Marathon is now behind them, and McFadden is beginning to experience the ripening of guilt.

Guilt works at maximum efficiency when operating from more than one direction. A simple, unilineal guilt may actually be satisfying at times: there is always the positive pleasure of doing whatever is causing it. However, when conflicting guilts evolve in tandem, they combine to outweigh the comforts of mitigation. On one hand McFadden is definitely past the time when he should stop and tend his cargo. On the other, in order to safely do so, he must first ditch this girl.

The equation itself is straightforward. Clearly, he is faced with the choice of dropping her somewhere defenceless against bugs, bears and other men in pickup trucks, or keeping her – and imperilling the whole point of his expedition.

McFadden contemplates the double-pronged dilemma.

There are those who believe, and Wyley McFadden is among them, that guilt was invented as a spur to the imagination. Wherever there is guilt, there is also the challenge of devising ways to alleviate it. Human achievement is measured in degrees of guilty circumvention. McFadden opts for ingenuity.

It is essential to his overall strategy that he avoid towns and people. (Of course this isn't always possible – he has to stop from time to time to fuel the truck – but his general plan is to keep contact to the barest minimum.) The well-being of his cargo demands that he stop very soon. It is necessary, however, that this not be in a public place. It is furthermore imperative that he keep the girl away from the back of his truck.

Clearly, he has no choice but theatrics.

McFadden cocks his head. "Did you hear that?"

Naturally, she has not.

He tilts his ear the other way. "There it is again!"

The girl is puzzled. She's heard nothing, but she is involved now, turning her own head to catch whatever mechanical mystery disturbs him. He purses his lips and looks troubled.

"I'll just stop and have a look. It's probably just something come loose in the back. Nothing serious, I'm sure," he adds in case she *is* worrying there is something to worry about.

For the last several miles McFadden has been scouting for a spot. He doesn't particularly want to be bitten any more than necessary. So, remembering the bear, he has been on the lookout for a high, windy place off the road. Up ahead he sees a loading area one of the timber companies has cleared for stacking logs. The bush has been cut back in a circle off the roadway.

"I won't be a minute," he says, pulling in, and jumps out of the cab. Immediately he slaps himself behind the neck. "Stay here," he shouts through the glass. "The bugs are bad."

Unfortunately, the bugs *are* bad. A ten-foot stack of logs has cut the breeze to nothing. There is a stagnant ditch to one side, breeding mosquitoes by the thousands. Several hundred appear to have found him already. The girl is showing not the slightest inclination to follow. He scurries to the back, unlocks the door and hustles inside.

Things are a little worse than expected. It takes some time to restore order and see to the plumbing. A flying entourage has entered with him and he must take care of these before going out again. It's several minutes before he drops what needs to be dropped into the ditch and scuttles back to the cab.

"Where were you?" says the girl. *"What were you doing back there?"*

McFadden is busy rolling up his sleeves to check that nothing has crawled underneath. He has not noticed her hand on the latch or the tone of her voice.

"Things came loose," he says. Satisfied his arms are bug-free, he rubs his fingers through his hair to dislodge any possibilities there.

"I don't know what you're thinking," she says, "but if you've got a bed or something back there . . . if you're thinking anything like that . . . Just don't. Don't."

His shock subducts itself to indignation. "Listen," he says, and begins to remind her whose truck this is and whose expedition, and who is the driver and who is the hitchhiker he didn't have to pick up in the first place, and how these sorts of gross assumptions are exactly what's strangling civility as it is meant to be practised . . . but when he looks up at her now, what he does see is fear. He sees her hand on the latch and her eyes rolled to scan the landscape for someplace to run. He also registers a nipple, hardened in stress against the fabric of her shirt.

McFadden sighs and looks out over the steering wheel.

"I stop," he says, "every few hours to check the load. That's what I do." He puts on his seat belt. "I'd appreciate it if you put yours on too. It's an eighty-dollar fine."

He lets out the clutch and pulls out of the landing and onto the highway. He is looking straight over the steering wheel and down the road ahead. After a while he hears the click of her doing up the passenger belt.

"What have you got back there, anyway?"

"Cargo," says McFadden, concentrating on the highway.

- - -

"Sorry."

They have driven a long way without further exchange. McFadden has found a local broadcast of a CBC talk show. The guest appears to be a Dutch zoologist studying a colony of chimpanzees transplanted to an island off the coast of Holland. McFadden was not aware there was an island off the coast of Holland with a climate mild enough for chimpanzees. He's fascinated: chimpanzees have always interested him, particularly in their genetic similarity to himself. McFadden has long held a theory that the main evolutionary difference between chimps and people is that *Homo sapiens* got out of the trees and into the open where the harsher living gave their brains a chance to grow. It's a defining characteristic, in his opinion: the constant human drive to seek out someplace less pleasant than where you are already. At the moment the zoologist is discussing chimp sexual practices and McFadden is intrigued to discover that certain chimpanzees have sex for the sake of pleasure alone. Furthermore, so this scientist suggests, they actually practise a form of oral sex that appears to have no function beyond what it suggests. McFadden turns the knob to increase volume. If this is true, it's further proof of his belief that animals and humans are much more similar than otherwise.

He wants details. Who initiates this behaviour? The male? The female? But the interviewer is squeamish and diverts the conversation to a pointless exchange about the zoologist's publisher. McFadden knows from experience she is much more comfortable with gossip than science; this is not the first time she has disappointed him. He listens to her show often, on his rounds, and deeply resents these bouts of intellectual truancy. He is contemplating scanning for another station when he becomes aware the girl is saying something.

"I beg your pardon?"

"I'm sorry," she says again.

With so much of his own company, McFadden tends to let his mind wander. He spends a great deal of time in his truck, quite a lot of time in his workroom, and listens to the radio. Much more often than not he chooses talk shows, being on the whole more enamoured of words than of other kinds of sounds. Often something said will spark a train of thought he allows to carry on as long as it wishes. When the girl speaks, he is a little slow in shifting mental gears.

"What?" he says. "Sorry for what?"

"That back there when you stopped . . ." She is scratching the bites on her knees. "I thought . . .well . . ." A hollow laugh. ". . . it wouldn't have been the first time."

"Don't worry," he answers, quite at a loss. "Not to worry."

Strange, he thinks. In a separate part of his mind he is truly curious about this girl and how she came to be alone in the middle of nowhere without so much as a handbag. At the same time the prospect of disclosure appalls him. He wants to know but doesn't. A more practical thought intercedes.

"Listen," he says, "is there anyone you want to call, or . . . ?"

"No." Her tone is neither flat nor sharp. After a pause, "No, thank you."

The atmosphere in the cab has changed from uncomfortable to distinctly embarrassing – at least so far as McFadden is concerned. He can feel himself beginning to warm. There is something here he wants no part of.

"Lunch!" he says, delighted with the inspiration. "Have you had lunch?"

Of course she has not had lunch. But his relief at having

found something else to talk about has shot his brain a jolt of oxygen. "I forgot all about lunch!"

The truck is equipped with a small on-board refrigerator, into which McFadden has packed all the food he hopes he will need for at least the outward stages of his journey. When he stopped for the watering, he had intended to bring back something to snack on, but in all his cunning forgot. The girl's reaction, and his chimpanzee program, had knocked it out of mind.

"Are you hungry?" His obvious pleasure at being back on safer ground makes the girl smile too.

"Yes," she says, and then more emphatically, "Oh God, yes."

"Good." He pauses. "I'll have to stop again, though," he says and hurries on. "The food is in the back, but I'll only be a minute."

"It's OK." Her smile this time is a real smile and increases McFadden's own. "I said I was sorry."

"It will only take a second."

But he has thought of a problem. In McFadden's opinion there are only four beverages fit to be consumed with food: wine and beer on the side of alcohol, milk and water on the other. He has a case of lager in the back as well as a crated selection of decent-enough wines he knows will travel. There is no milk, though. He is not at all keen on the thought of having only water to drink with his lunch. Nevertheless he is leery about proffering anything else, after the alcohol incident.

"Umm . . ." he says, then changes his mind. They have rounded a bend and the lake has reappeared. For the last hour or so the highway has departed from the shore; now it has rejoined it. The truck has crested another hill and Lake Superior lies massively below them, glittering darkly like some Bergmanesque reversion of an Adriatic vista. A laneway leads downward to a rocky beach, dotted here and there with picnic tables and posted signs advising campers not to feed the bears.

McFadden swings the truck and stops in a spot overlooking the water. There are no other cars. "If the bugs are bad, we'll just eat in here," he says. "If it's OK outside, we can sit at one of the tables." He is opening the door but pauses. "Umm . . . What will you have to drink with lunch?"

He hurries on so it seems natural. "I have some cold beer, some wine and of course water. Sorry, but I didn't think to bring soft drinks or anything like that."

"Oh, whatever is fine," she says, confused now that this has become a production. "I'll have whatever you're having."

"Fine," he says. "Just wait here. I won't be a minute."

The first thing McFadden feels, after relief at being out of the truck, is wind – a soft, warm wind, straight in off the lake and smelling of water and the wetness of life within. McFadden lifts his nose and holds his arms outstretched. Not a bug lands.

He moves to the back of the truck and unlocks the box. All is well. With just a glance to double-check he steps directly up the centre aisle to the refrigerator. McFadden has decided on pigeon. Before leaving the city he had roasted a dozen or so, gently cooled and wrapped them individually in wax paper with a double sheath of tinfoil. Unless something goes wrong with the fridge, he is confident they will last for several days. McFadden removes three, considers, and lifts out another. By the look of her it's been a while since she has eaten.

The bread is perhaps a little on the hard side but will do. He has not stocked much in the way of tableware, but locates two forks, two knives, a couple of plates and his pepper grinder. Life without fresh pepper, for Wyley McFadden, would not be worth the effort.

Before setting out this morning he had selected for chilling a very young Côtes du Rhône rosé, in the hope that the weather would match it. He is exceedingly pleased with his choice. There is a plastic bucket stored in a cupboard; he lifts it out, sniffs to check for relative cleanliness, then drops in the pigeons, the cutlery, a roll of paper towel for serviettes and a small jar of flavoured olive oil. (Despite his contempt for health-food fanatics, McFadden has recently given up butter.) Pocketing the corkscrew, and with the plates tucked under his arm, he locks up again and makes for the nearest table.

The girl has disappeared.

She is not at the picnic table. She is no longer inside the truck. McFadden scans the shore, but there is no sign of her. He begins to call but realizes he does not know her name. Shrugging, he goes to the table and unpacks the meal.

In a few minutes he hears the sound of a closing door and turns to find her emerging from an upgraded wooden outhouse. "There's hot water," she says, "if you're interested."

McFadden was not interested, but now he supposes he had better go and wash his hands. "Excuse me," he says, unobtrusively checking his pocket to be sure he has the keys, and removes himself to the facilities.

When he returns, he finds the girl has set the table. The bucket is empty now, so he takes it and goes to the lake and dangles in a finger. The water is surprisingly cold; not ice-cold, but cold enough to keep the wine much cooler than the air. Filling it, he disturbs a school of minnows. Minnows have always fascinated McFadden. He wonders if they belong to a species that stays small like this or if they are the hatchlings of some larger fish. He can't tell; sunlight and water have skewed perspective. They could be trout, but for that matter they could be anything. He wonders if there are trout in this part of the lake. He has brought fishing tackle, but there will be no time for fishing on the outward trip. Perhaps on the drive home, when he'll have all the time he wants.

"These are the skinniest chickens I've ever seen."

She has unwrapped the pigeons. McFadden is about to be truthful again but checks himself. People have unreasonable prejudices. These particular birds have come from the elevators on Cherry Street, where they have fed exclusively, or almost exclusively, on spilled grain. Factory-farm chickens, by comparison, coagulate against the tongue like parboiled polymers.

"They're squabs," he says, deciding to be truthful after all but picking a word he believes she will not recognize. "Very much like chickens, only better." Enjoying his play at head waiter, he opens the wine with a little flourish and pours.

"Whatever they are, they smell great."

McFadden had wrapped each bird around a sprig of rosemary and the aroma has reached his nostrils too. Pleased, he passes her the bread and they begin to eat. After a moment he rips off a square of paper towel each and tucks them under the pepper pot so they won't blow away, then washes down another mouthful with a sip of the rosé.

Although the bread is hard, the birds are moist, and the meal is very good. The girl is famished. Already the first bird is a ruin of bones and skin and she is mostly through the second. He pours more wine and excuses himself to go back to the fridge for another bird, chiding himself on the foolishness of this tiny pleasure. It's been a long while since he has watched someone eat food he has prepared.

Her concentration on the food is so total he can watch her openly. The visit to the bathroom has both improved her appearance and worsened it. She has wet her hair, and pieces of it curl, sticking to her cheek and ear. The dabs of crusted blood and smashed mosquito are washed away, but the process has aggravated the swelling. One eyelid is distended and partly closed. Bites cover most of the skin he can see, and probably much of what he can't – but so far no sign of serious allergic reaction. She will be sorely itchy for the next few days, but by the end of the week she should be fine. It occurs to him that she has not complained, though she must be in genuine discomfort. A couple of Tylenols should lessen that a little. For the moment, though, the taste of food has wiped out everything else. He wonders how long she has been without. She could do with fresh vegetables, and absently he wishes he had some to give. Radishes go perfectly with pigeon, and would have been so easy to store.

The folly of this line of thinking reminds him that it's time to start seriously considering how to get rid of her. It's still fairly early in the day, but he must be absolutely shed of her by dark.

She has devoured her third pigeon. The wine is down to the heel of the bottle; he divides the last of it between them. The girl pushes her plate to one side and swings her legs beneath the seat. "Wow," she says. "That was so good . . ."

She is holding both hands over her stomach and smiling. It is a primal smile, a primordial smile, a smile of animal contentment – a smile like the smile of a dog with a ball, or a purring cat. It is a smile utterly impossible not to smile back at, and McFadden does.

He had been just about to tell her that at the next town, or the town after that, he will have to let her off. With an effort he wills the smile away and draws a breath to get his mind on track.

"What did you call them?"

"I beg your pardon?"

"The little chickens." She smiles at a leg bone, to illustrate.

"Oh." He very nearly says pigeon, but stops himself. "Squabs," he says, and takes another breath. "Very much like chicken . . ."

She laughs. "Only better." And laughs some more.

The sun is shining and McFadden is finding this difficult. He takes a third breath, but a rumble of gravel cuts it short. He looks up to see a Winnebago lurching into the lot, swaying on its massive springs.

"Time to go."

"I'll wash the dishes," she says.

"Don't be silly!" Even to his own ear he sounds absurdly like a hostess at a dinner party. "I'll do them later."

The girl observes him, her smile receded to an echo. McFadden stands and begins scraping the remains of the meal into a garbage container. The girl is loading the dishes and utensils into the bucket of lakewater. The empty bottle has gone into the trash.

"It will only take a minute," she says, and before he can stop her, she disappears into the Ladies' side of the public toilet.

McFadden reminds himself there is no cause to be nervous. Nevertheless he has the motor running when she reappears and hands him up the pail. The girl arranges herself in the cab.

"Thanks for lunch," she says.

"My pleasure."

He backs around and eases the truck out of the lot. She's still watching him in a way he's begun to find annoying.

He had intended to get out a map while they were stationary, and consult her about where she would like to be dropped. Nipigon, he knows, is still an hour or two ahead, Thunder Bay about the same again. He plans to stop overnight somewhere before Dryden, but perhaps there is another location she would prefer. Whatever her decision, Thunder Bay is as far as he will take her.

He's already determined that he has no choice but to give her money. Women carry their money in their purses; this one has no purse – therefore it follows that she must also have no money.

How she came to be on the side of the road with no purse and no money is none of his business. He must contend only with the fact that, at present, she is in his cab and has eaten his food, and by the laws of common civility he cannot simply set her down and drive away. He tries to calculate how much he should give. She will need bus fare to wherever she is going – he has not the faintest idea what buses cost – and money for food and perhaps a night's accommodation. He has no intention of bankrolling a trip to the Rockies, but she'll need enough to get her somewhere civilized. This adds up.

A figure of one hundred dollars comes to mind and is instantly rejected. It's possibly not even enough, but as far as he is concerned, it's too much. Make it fifty. Is fifty sufficient? He does not really know what a bus from Thunder Bay costs, but factoring in meals and sundries, fifty doesn't sound like much. Thunder Bay is a long way from anywhere. If she has to stay somewhere overnight . . . Not enough.

All right then. One hundred.

Having decided, McFadden feels better. There is a certain satisfaction in largesse, though he would have preferred to enjoy it to a smaller degree. His conscience is bought off, at any rate. McFadden is content with the arrangement. This means he will have to access his reserves – he had not quite budgeted for this – but so goes life on the open road.

"Listen," he says. "It's not possible for me to take you to Alberta." He has his eyes fixed on the lane ahead and does not look at her. "I can take you as far as Thunder Bay, if you like. You can get a bus or something from there."

He pauses. The unpleasant thing about charity is the embarrassment attached to either side. "If you need it, I can give you some money to see you home all right, if you need it . . ."

He waits for her answer. In the silence an interval of sound begins to reach his ear: a tiny whirring purr that stops, waits a beat, and begins again.

She is curled with her face against the window, arms hugged beneath her breast, mouth open just enough for the female little snore.

With one hand on the wheel he unbuckles his seat belt and reaches across her to be sure the door is safely locked.

McFadden drives the next two hundred kilometres alone.

– – –

Though, of course, not alone.

For the first hour he is careful not to wake her. A man who sleeps but fleetingly himself, he has a postulant's appreciation of its virtue. He has switched off the radio, and steers as gently as he can over dips and roughness in the pavement.

She does not wake. Indeed, she hardly stirs. He finds himself more and more inclined to watch her, taking his eyes off the highway for moments at a time, flicking back and forth between the road and her.

There is something in the pose of sleeping women. Something soft and slight and slenderly surreal. He understands why painters are so often challenged to attempt them, and why so seldom they succeed. It must exceed the scope of canvas – the implausibility of rendering motion within rest. She is deeply asleep, immovably asleep – and yet she moves. Tiny spasms quiver her legs and tug her fingers. Lips purse to open, part, then softly close again. Dreaming eyes agitate the surface of their lids. Hands resting on her stomach rise and fall in rhythm with the pulse that ticks along the valleys of her neck. Even bespeckled with bites like this, there is a beauty to this girl and in this pose well beyond the scope of two dimensions.

He feels a twitch between his legs and almost laughs. "So!" he says, enjoying the absurdity.

McFadden's sense of humour leans to the absurd. Despite his background – or perhaps because of it – he is a lover of irony, a student of the paradox. The notion of this girl is . . . clearly as paradoxical as paradox can get.

Oh well.

She is certainly asleep.

They pass above a canyon with water swirling far below; house-size boulders dot the flood bed. Then endless forests of green and black, receding by the mile into the afternoon. The day is waning. Soon the sun will be in his eyes. He decides it is time she started to think about becoming conscious.

A road sign reads *Thunder Bay, 89 kilometres.* Just over an hour. There is a buckle in the pavement and McFadden aims for it deliberately. The truck jolts. He winces for his cargo, but the girl does not stir.

After a moment he turns the radio on and craftily escalates the volume. He fiddles with the tuner. Static crackles between wails of cowboy geldings; a rapper chants a bar and is mercifully extinguished; someone on a local buy-and-sell is offering a used refrigerator. He has it loud enough that it's definitely irritating him, but still she shows no sign of waking. As he adjusts the band, a familiar voice leaps from the speaker and, by force of habit, his fingers pause and tune it in. Tom Cheek is explaining, in measured baseball cadence, that despite a count of 0 and 2 the batter is a threat to knock the next pitch out of the stadium.

"Who's up?" asks McFadden, and twists the volume to a comfortable level. The pitch comes in; the unknown batter strikes out. "Damn," he says, and loudly thumps a palm off the steering wheel. The girl does not stir.

Even so, he wants to know the score. Like most of the rest of his city, Wyley McFadden has fallen off the baseball bandwagon. In bygone years he'd been an avid fan, especially for those two World Series. But the players' strikes have jaundiced his opinion, to say nothing of the Jays being eight games back this year already. It makes for an interesting tutorial on the subject of loyalty. McFadden himself can't decide if he should feel guilty on account of being such a fickle fan or if the guilt derives from having squandered his affections on something so trivial in the first place. On balance he isn't too worried one way or the other. Last year they were gods, this year just a bunch of greedy Yanks. Such is the nature of human evolution.

But he misses baseball. It's the eurythmy of the game, the almost episodic structure. He could turn on a baseball game and instantly grasp the plot and recognize the characters, know exactly what to expect from any given episode except perhaps the ending. He's always assumed that's why people watch soap operas. Baseball is the perfect radio game. Television, to McFadden, is a dangerous drug, and a dull one at that: if Dante had lived to see it, he'd have made Limbo a place of eternal network programming. McFadden does not own a television or ever allow himself to watch one.

Radio is different. Radio allows the mind to participate yet wander on its own. It's the ideal medium. Like baseball itself, it's mobile; it keeps him company while he's busy doing something else. He has long ago decided that baseball is not a sport; it is a game, and with the virtue of a game moves from beginning to end according to the pace set by those who play it. In baseball there is time to daydream. McFadden listens to the radio, and daydreams as he listens.

But today he can't afford to daydream, and anyway the Jays are trailing six to one. He fiddles some more with the tuner, playing with the volume, maximizing the crackle between stations, but the girl is showing no reaction. He is actually contemplating physical intervention when the word "federalism" jumps like a spark into his ear. McFadden is diverted. It's a political discussion, and Wyley McFadden has a special interest in politics.

It soon becomes apparent that the speaker is a separatist of some stripe, female, a name unfamiliar to McFadden, and that the voice representing the federalist side is deeply frustrated. As McFadden listens, his own indignation begins to quiver. In minutes he is shouting at the radio.

McFadden often talks to his radio. He recognizes that, as a form of dialectic, this has its limitations. However, he assures himself that his complete awareness of this fact cancels out any psychological implications. On this occasion he can furthermore argue that he is deliberately raising his voice in order to rouse his passenger, though so far to no effect. If the truth be known, he is genuinely angry. It is the moderator who ought to be yelling at this dangerous person, not Wyley McFadden from the other side of Lake Superior.

The central theme appears to be an analysis of what, precisely, Quebec wants – though it is clear from the start that the answer is obvious. The real question is, why? The question has been put a dozen different ways and still has not been answered. McFadden at first is patient, urging the discussion along several different tacks – economic, cultural and so on – and the moderator, surprisingly, obliges him with detailed and well-reasoned demonstrations of how, on every point, the province's position is demonstrably stronger within Confederation than without. What's irritating the federalist representative, and what is driving McFadden to distraction, is that the Péquiste is not bothering to answer, or rather is so shamelessly ignoring the objections that it's polemically embarrassing. Her position is that her province will simply be better off on its own, and that's what's going to happen. Neither motive nor consequence is relevant.

McFadden is barking out his indignation. Bad enough *La Presse* is operating like a francophile incarnation of Tass without anglophone radio hosts doing it too. It strikes him what a microcosm this is of national events, and it offends him. He wants the other side to let blaze so this stupid person at least will understand that contempt begets anger. The only answer to passion is passion, and the hapless federalist is keeping his far too righteously in check.

"Reason is a form of language!" he shouts, and the sleeping girl beside him barely stirs. "It only works if both sides understand the grammar!"

But thumping the steering wheel is having no effect on anything.

– – –

They have passed already through the malls and fast-food phosphorescence of Thunder Bay. McFadden is silently and earnestly rebuking himself. He really should have taken care of this by now.

Somehow all the traffic lights and exit lanes, after so much lake and forest, took up more concentration than he would have thought, to say nothing of that damn Péquiste. Anyway, before McFadden has really registered the transition, Thunder Bay is behind them and they are back among the timber. As if to illustrate the point a convoy of tractor-trailers thunders by, loaded with logs en route to some pulp mill to be processed into toilet paper. Their back stream buffets his truck and recalls to mind his cargo. The day has gotten long.

He can't believe she's still asleep. In fact, he's become a bit concerned. The route through Thunder Bay involved lots of starting and stopping. That kind of driving is usually impossible to sleep through. He has not, after all, been terribly careful about noise. She should have been showing at least some reaction.

McFadden peers at her as closely as the road allows. Has she lost colour? The physician in him snaps to alertness. He jabs the radio off and listens to her breathing – more shallow than it should be.

"Miss?" he says, and clears his throat loudly. "Hello? . . . Hello!"

She remains inert.

He veers the truck off to the shoulder, talking to her all the time but getting no reply. Rapid deceleration like this would rouse most sleepers, but the girl is undisturbed. Gently he takes hold of her shoulder. No response. He shakes harder and she moves, and turns her head, but does not surface into consciousness.

Her skin is warm to touch. He places a hand to her forehead and finds it feverish. Her pulse, too, is accelerated.

"Leave me alone!"

Suddenly she is awake and flinging her arms. *"Get away from me!"*

"It's all right," he says, "I'm –"

She has vomited.

"You're safe," he tells her, very calmly. Wyley McFadden has been vomited on before. "I am a doctor," he says, for the second time today.

She breathes for several seconds. "Oh," she says. "Oh." Her teeth have begun to chatter. "Please leave me alone." She is trying to hug herself.

"Right," says McFadden. "Just relax. I'll be back in a second."

He slips out through the driver's side and around to the back of the truck, unbuttoning as he goes. Inside he finds a blanket, the roll of paper towel and a clean shirt. He also notes that his incautious driving has taken its toll. He will have some caretaking back here once the mess up front is sorted out.

McFadden sits for a moment on the tailgate. The next big town is Dryden – but that's still three hours at least. Another option is to head back to Thunder Bay.

Better first to get a firmer read on her condition. This time he approaches from the passenger door, knocking on the window to let her know he's coming through. She is sitting up.

"I made a mess," she says in the forlorn voice of the helpless and the ill.

"It's all right." He tears off some towel and wipes what he can. The girl's teeth are chattering, but she takes the towel from him and attempts to clean herself. "Wrap up in this," he says, and tucks the blanket in behind her shoulders. She's trembling.

He leaves her for a moment, walks around the hood to the driver's side and takes his first aid kit from behind the seat. As first aid kits go, it is better stocked than most.

"How are you feeling?"

"OK."

He has long been accustomed to this ridiculous and automatic answer. Nevertheless it is a helpful sign.

"Good. I am going to take your temperature."

He has a thermometer in his hand and briskly places it beneath her tongue. While she is docile, he reads her pulse. Fast, but not dangerously so. Her temperature too is up – but not alarming.

In a moment he is satisfied that he has now assessed her status – and aghast that it is mostly due to him. Fool, he tells himself. Imbecile. It is reasonable to assume she suffered some form of trauma before he found her, alone and nearly naked at the side of a deserted highway. Fool. She is covered in insect bites; a first-year med student would be concerned about reaction. She was standing in the sun when he found her. Covered in insect bites and standing out under the sun. How could she fail to be dehydrated?

And what does he do? What is the medical response of Dr. Wyley McFadden? Ex-doctor, he reminds himself, and no bloody wonder. He feeds her half a bottle of wine. Oh yes, and a can of Coke.

There is a reservoir of water in the back and he draws off a glass. It is not especially cold, but it is pure enough.

"Try to drink this," he says.

She has no problem swallowing, and this too is reassuring, though her eyes are closing again as he takes the glass away. He has, at least, come to a decision. He has been absurdly stupid throughout, and his tolerance of stupidity tends toward the minimal, particularly as it applies to himself. She's not sick enough to need a hospital. That is some consolation. But certainly she isn't well enough to simply drop someplace. McFadden arranges the blanket and collects the soiled towel. He starts the engine, checks the mirror and turns the truck around to head back the way they have come.

The girl is asleep again. The cab reeks of gastric fluids. McFadden lowers the window a crack to circulate some air, but only a crack. She's shivering; at least he can see to it that she doesn't risk a chill.

Five or six kilometres along the road he finds it. He had noticed it in passing, one of those places that seem to grow out of nothing into nowhere. He turns into the drive and parks at a distance from the office.

"Sit tight," he says, though she is sleeping, and walks to the aluminum screen door and the hand-painted sign saying *Vacancies*.

– – –

The Conibear Motel is the kind whose existence defies the laws of economic probability. It has no neighbours. There is no other building for miles. It overlooks no intersection. There is no view. A bulldozer has come and pushed aside the spruce and the aspen, and in the cleared space someone has built a motel. The sign by the highway, on cracking four-by-fours, promises every room comes with heating and a colour TV.

There's one other car in the parking lot. McFadden assumes it belongs to the proprietress, who is staring at him as if he has descended from space. She is working hard at a mouthful evidently presenting something of a challenge.

"I would like a room," he says.

The woman's eyes bulge, head bobs and throat constricts as she forgoes chewing and swallows. McFadden winces with her.

"Yes," she says, releasing a bubble of gas. She moves from behind the desk and passes him a registration card. Folds of skin wobble beneath her arms. "Just sign it . . . And I'll need a credit card imprint."

McFadden is unprepared for this. "I'm paying cash," he says.

The woman stares. The side of one cheek bulges and recedes as she roots beneath the gums. "Always need an imprint . . . for security." She enjoys the savour of the word, and repeats it. "Security."

"Ah." McFadden reaches for his pocket. "What is the rate for a double room – one with two beds?"

"Forty-nine, plus tax."

McFadden consults his wallet. He removes five twenties and puts them on the table. "My card is at the limit," he tells her with a look he hopes is sheepish. "Here's a hundred on deposit. You can give me back whatever I don't owe in the morning."

He is filling out the registration as he speaks. The address he puts down is a London apartment he lived in as a student. He pauses for an instant over the space requesting his plate number, and scribbles the seven so it looks like a one, and changes the nine to a six. Across the top he writes "$100.00 – deposit," dates it, and hands her back the card.

"I said you only had to sign it." She considers for a moment over her rack of keys. "Fourteen," she says, and passes him the ring.

"Thank you." McFadden turns to leave.

"Checkout's at eleven."

"Thank you again," he says through the screen.

The room is at the opposite end of the building. The girl is asleep, sprawled beneath the steering wheel. He has to move her head so he can drive. "Wake up," he says, shifting her so he can reach the pedals. He has cranked down both windows; a rancid stink pervades the cab.

The proprietress is peering at him through her louvred blinds. McFadden reverses the truck and backs to the door of number fourteen. He can unload the girl from the passenger side without too much being seen. "Just a minute longer," he tells her, though she is showing no sign of impatience.

The room itself is a surprise. There are curtains at the windows, framed prints on the walls. The bedding appears thick;

towels in the bathroom are frayed but clean. He wonders again how this place survives.

He has left the door standing open. Between the truck and the nearer of the beds is a distance of only five or six steps. McFadden does not particularly wish to be seen carrying an unconscious girl into the room of a roadside motel.

"All right," he says. "Time to move."

When she does not respond, he takes her by the feet and pulls. Now she's lying on her side, her legs sprawled over the seat. "Come on!" But she shows no inclination to assist. He changes his grip to the elbows and pulls again. Slowly the rest of her body eases toward him. He readjusts her knees, steering by the elbows, until she is sitting, facing him, her feet dangling just above the running board.

"Good. Can you walk?"

"No." Her voice is slurry but more adamant than he might have wished.

"I'm sure you can." He takes her by the wrists again and pulls. Her arms stretch compliantly toward him, but the rest of her has slumped the other way. McFadden shifts his grip to her elbows and pulls harder. Slowly her body comes toward him. At the point of equilibrium he slides his hands beneath her hips and hoists until she's standing, propped against the fender, hands against his chest.

"No," she says.

"Yes," says McFadden. "Now you can walk." He slips his hand around her waist, keeping hold of one elbow, and steps away from the fender. Her feet move with his.

"No," she says again.

"Oh yes," replies McFadden.

In a moment he has her in the room. "Do you need the bathroom?"

"No."

"Fine," he says, and stretches her out on the bed.

The Rat is the concisest Tenant.
He pays no Rent.
Repudiates the Obligation –
On Schemes intent

Balking our Wit
To sound or circumvent –
Hate cannot harm
A Foe so reticent –
Neither Decree prohibit him –
Lawful as Equilibrium.

EMILY DICKINSON

McFadden has never quite made up his mind about Timothy Findley. He flattens the book on his chest and stares at the ceiling, trying hard to decide. There is a touch, somehow, of Robin Leach, a regrettable fascination for pomp and nonsense. A little too much of the Hollywood. McFadden suspects the soul of a frustrated courtier, born into an age of insufficient ceremony. On the other hand his plots are ingenious, and his characters reliably intricate. So far he is not as taken with this one as he's been with its predecessors, though he approves its setting. It's good to hear stories told from home.

He sighs and squares the book again, thumbing its spine to keep it open. The girl is snoring. It is a reedy, slender sort of sound, like the girl herself.

Her temperature is down to normal now; this is the sleep of simple exhaustion. He wonders again how she has come to be here, and again pushes speculation from his mind. He does not wish to think of her.

It took the better part of an hour to disinfect the cab, and another repairing the damage in back. One of the watering tubes had ruptured; a sluice of bilge needed draining before he could even begin with everything else. Luckily, no harm had come to the cargo. With the line repaired and the water cleared away he was able to confirm, to his great relief, that there had been no losses. More by good luck, though, than good management. He opened the ventilating system to full – running off auxiliary batteries he will now have to find some way of recharging – and blew the dampness, and most of the odour, out into the atmosphere.

The rankness of the cargo hold was nothing compared to the stench *inside* the cab. McFadden's still uncertain the upholstery will be dry by morning. Through it all, the girl slept.

He'd left her where she lay, sprawled on the bed. Throughout his comings and goings she hardly moved – except perhaps to curl a little tighter, an awkward reminder of yet another problem: though the truck might now be clean, the girl herself was not. In fact, she stank. Their room was soon as pungent as the cab.

He tried everything – wheedling and reasoning, cajolery and threat. Twice he took her by the shoulders and pressed until he feared his fingers might leave bruises. Her only response was to shrug him off and burrow deeper in the pillow, though once she raised her head and cursed him with a venom that backed him physically away, then instantly dropped off again.

In the end he'd had no choice. The smell was awful. It had seeped into every corner of the room. Opening the windows had no effect; the longer it lingered, the more acrid it grew. He was concerned, too, from an epidermal standpoint, about infection; insect bites are nothing less than lesions. Bacterial contact of this magnitude virtually guaranteed a problematic healing.

On the other hand, this was an era of judicial enmity between the sexes. No one should be more aware of this than him. It took very little, these days, to land a man in trouble. But it was weak, he told himself, and vapid and stupid and morally corrupt to fear the consequence of doing what is right. Besides, the room was unlivable.

"Listen," he said, standing by the foot of her bed. "If you don't get up, I'll have to do this."

The girl made no response. She was lying on her side, face down against the pillow.

"All right, then . . . " Drawing a breath, McFadden took an ankle in each hand and lifted. With a twist of one, a steady pull with the other, he turned her so she was lying on her stomach. Her legs, from the knees down, trailed from the edge of the bed.

"Can you do this yourself?"

No reply.

"You're sure?"

Still no answer.

"Then here we go." Leaning over, McFadden shifted her arms until they lay outstretched above her head, then pulled the girl's shirt over her head and away. He crumpled up the material, took it to the bathroom and threw it in the sink. In his absence, she moved her arms to lie against her naked ribs; otherwise she made no motion.

"Can you do the rest?"

It was when the skirt came off that he found them. A line of bruises trailed along the buttocks, precisely where they met the thighs, a tidy pattern of purple on pink, carefully, artistically arranged. There was no explanation but the one confronting him, even as he held himself suspended, one hand pressed against the mattress, the other dangling the garment. His mind, for the moment, refused to take him in any direction.

"All right."

He heard her speak into the mattress. It was a voice neither awake nor asleep. A voice from far away beyond the present.

As McFadden leaned above her, his mind as rigid as his body, she turned beneath him and rolled onto her back.

"All right," she said, with closed eyes staring at the ceiling. And opened her legs to him.

– – –

By his watch seven hours have passed. It's now after three in the morning. The Findley novel rests, cracked-spined upon his chest. He doubts he has had an erection like this since he was seventeen. Certainly not of such duration.

It would be too simple to say that McFadden is overwhelmed with self-disgust. His disgust is of an infinitely greater magnitude. Disgust, for that matter, isn't even quite correct. There is probably no word, or none he can think of, to encompass the amplitude of what he feels, the panoply of chaos enveloping his mind. *Chaos?* Something related to chaos. And confusion. No shortage of conflicting truths in the life and times of Wyley McFadden.

What he wants, more than anything, is to be away from here. To be gone from this room and this girl, to blend them back into the past and leave them. McFadden is seized with an adolescent longing for things to be otherwise, to rewrite history and change it for the better. In his edited version he lets himself drive safely by. He does not let her into his cab. Or better still, there is no girl. Someone else has picked her up. He never knows of her existence. Or she *is* there and he *does* pick her up, but he drops her off in Marathon and continues on in ignorance. There is no lunch. No wine. No illness and no motel.

No piece of chattel trained to serve.

In the solitary hours of his journey home he'll wonder how his insight came to be so clear. Though even now he understands that it was there from the beginning, the omnipresent urgency – that keen awareness of precisely that. Is it possible he'd felt it from the start, from the instant she stepped into his cab? It might explain . . . No matter. What is clear is that the girl is trained to sex.

He has not the slightest doubt his abstract is correct; it's the clarity itself that makes McFadden shiver. It's also clear that she has fled from this – or tried to flee. And when again she's taken up and forced into a room and laid upon a bed, it is inescapable even in sleep, the thing she must do.

"Then do it!" whispers a voice in the darkness.

McFadden closes the book and moves it to the table by the bed, gets up and crosses to the sink for another glass of water. His erection has abated only somewhat. No matter.

Since he left her, the girl has hardly moved. Her sleep, he believes, is a relatively healthy one, though deeper than any he has seen without the aid of medication. She must have been awake a very long time.

He feels himself stiffen again and clucks his tongue – wishing he could relent, just this once, and allow himself to watch the television. But Wyley McFadden is a man of principle.

This makes him smile.

There is a chair by the mirror and he draws it to the corner of her bed. McFadden sits with his glass – a very small glass of water with a much larger presence of Scotch – and watches the girl in the moonlight.

It is a deceptive light, a decidedly complicated light, coming in from more than one direction. On one side of the room it filters through the window; this is the light of the moon. But from the other side the yellow glow of the bathroom bulb spills through the crack where the door is hinged, only just reaching the bed. The two lights shade the room in opposite directions. Her chest rises and falls in this uncertain darkness. One breast is covered by the sheet, the other is not. A single nipple casts two shadows.

He draws his chair a little closer.

Angling to the left is the shadow of the moon. To the right slants the taller shadow from the bulb, slightly sharper against its own more yellowed slope. With every breath the shadows rise and open, like the blades of scissors, then close again upon the fall.

McFadden is fascinated. The duality appeals to him. He draws the whisky through his teeth and toys with imagery. The moonward side, of course, must stand for flesh. In this light he bathes in the curve of hip and bend of knee, the parting and closing of lips, and moistness and heat. This is the light of the groin.

Yet the bathroom bulb reveals another side. By its yellow light he sees the jaundice, the sores and the bruises, the naked signs of illness and neglect. This will be the reasoned light of science.

He remembers the cartoons of his childhood. When the hero was confronted with moral dilemma, miniature figures would appear at his shoulder, arguing for good behaviour or bad. McFadden is taken with the concept of an angel and a devil crouched at either ear, one in a lab coat, perhaps wearing a stethoscope, prescribing professional solicitude, the other sweating in the moonlight, hissing "Fuck her!"

He acknowledges the sweaty side, but there is no doubt whose argument will win the day. Moral quandary is merely shadow boxing; debate just a way of passing time. Life, for Wyley McFadden – or human life, that is – is defined as simply the business of reconciling opposites. Or if not reconciling, then at least negotiating a workable détente.

His erection, only moments ago showing signs of retreat, has returned with new insistence. But McFadden understands this has no bearing on the rest of him. He has always taken a philosophical approach to his desires.

So it is not properly disgust he feels, certainly not as it might apply to himself. There is nothing wrong with his wanting this girl. There would only be something wrong if he allowed himself to have her.

On the other hand, he is seething with much more than disgust at whoever has done this. If Wyley McFadden had the power, he would prescribe death to the architect of those bruises. He swirls the whisky in his glass and reflects upon the Hippocratic oath by which he is no longer guided – if indeed he ever was.

There is of course the argument that desire of this sort must necessarily be wrong, because it's that which drives whatever forces have brought her to this. If men did not lust for the thralldom of women, there would be no profit in bruises. Though this is like saying if only people stopped hating one another, the world would wake to peace. It's a specious argument, grandiloquent in its own simplicity. Lust itself is no sin – only how one chooses to pursue it.

His glass is empty, but he decides for the moment he will not refill it. These flights of speculation are a joy to him, though fickle. He knows he's in a groove. Now he's landed on sin, his mind will wander there all night. Sin has always been a favourite.

McFadden has come to view the entire concept as a product of theatre, not theology, a form of drama scripted by prehistoric admen, later taken up by Hollywood. Sin is the fodder of sitcoms and second-year psychology students. There was that American president – was it a president or one of their televangelists? McFadden can't remember now – who confessed on television to having sinned many times in his heart. Theatre.

Sin is only sin if it is permitted to impose itself on others, and McFadden – in *this* circumstance, at any rate – has imposed on no one, rather has been imposed upon. His hard-on, safely out of harm's way in the folds of his pyjamas, is not a sin. It is merely an embarrassment.

The night is perfect in its silence. The only sound is the rhythm of her breathing; the only movement the rise and fall of that single breast, opening and closing its articulated shadow. There are two or three hours left until dawn. McFadden knows he will not sleep.

He places his glass on the table and quietly slips his trousers over his pyjamas. Soundlessly he moves to the bathroom and switches off the yellow bulb. Now there is only the moonlight.

Smiling, he lets himself out of the room.

Outside, a cat, almost at his feet, patrols his truck in the pale white glow. It pauses in its enterprise, then slips away, mewing once into the darkness. He unlocks the back and steps inside. Most of the dampness is gone by now; the air is fresh. He settles

himself in a corner and empties his mind to the presence of life. There is no guilt to contemplate among his cargo. Merely life. No morality – or sophistry to frame it.

Only life.

– – –

But by noon McFadden's perspective is rather less benign.

The morning's shot, ruined, destroyed, utterly gone — and where is he? He has been up for many, many hours. He has cleaned the truck again, both inside and out. He's checked the oil and all the fluid levels. He's refilled both water tanks. He has, in the small hours after dawn, recharged the on-board batteries with an extension cord surreptitiously plugged into an outlet at the back of the motel – though they are nearly dead again already. It's hot today. The truck is standing in the parking lot, under the sun. He has moved it twice to spots of shade, but it's still too hot. He's had to run the air conditioning unit or his cargo would broil. If she doesn't wake up soon, he'll have to leave the engine running just to keep the air on.

If it were possible to pace, McFadden would be pacing. He's tried pacing outside, but the bugs on this breathless day have driven him back, and it's pointless to pace in a ten-by-twelve motel room. The Findley novel, begun back in the wee hours, is nearly done. It's gotten good, the moment when it all explains itself approaches – still he can't concentrate.

Several times he has hovered at the doorstep, keys in hand, one foot straining for the other side. He has the privilege. He deserves the privilege of leaving. And yet he stays. What would she do when she wakes? He has contemplated putting money where she would find it on the bureau. Perhaps the hundred he had decided to give her earlier. Perhaps a little more. But there is something somehow sordid in this, something too closely connected to payoff and guilt. Though why he should feel guilty, for the life of him he can't understand.

He stays.

Twice someone has come to make up the room and twice he's had to send them away. It's nearly noon and McFadden has gone back to bed to soldier on with Findley. The ironic thing is that now he is tired. He has not slept; his eyes are closing. The book keeps tilting down toward his chest. He opens his eyes to find the book fallen from his hand. The second time he lets it lie. It is pleasant, shutting out the light. But only for a moment.

– – –

He feels her presence, though he is not yet nearly awake.

Somehow she has entered his consciousness before it has switched to the part that governs waking hours.

"So," she says. *"Feeling better now?"*

She is watching from the corner of the room. McFadden has opened his eyes, although his lids are partly stuck. He closes them again. After a second he turns his head to look at the window, but he can't see. It takes him a moment to realize that they are covered with steam. He looks at the girl again. Her hair is wet. She has showered. McFadden understands that both of them are now awake.

"Was it good? . . . Did it help you sleep?" She is wearing his shirt.

He turns the other way and looks at the clock on the bed stand. The Findley novel spills over from the bed onto the floor. It's after two. He isn't sure which side of midnight this relates to.

"What?" he says. It is all he can think of to say.

"What do you mean, what?" Her eyes are blazing, but she has not moved from the corner. "You know fucking well what! Humping me in here . . . wherever *here* is . . . and doing your little thing . . ." She is gazing fiercely about the room, darting her eyes from the bed to the bureau and the dresser by the window. *"Asshole!"* She whirls and goes back to the bathroom. He hears the door slam.

McFadden does not move. He attempts to raise his left arm, then his right. They respond. He curls and uncurls his fingers and watches them do as they've been told. So his brain and his senses are synaptically linked. He tries to remember what has just happened, but his mind prefers to remain wherever it was before.

Can she possibly . . .

The door opens again. He hears her rooting through his toilet case. Something lands with a crash on the counter. All that he is thinking now is that he could have left. He should have left. He should have left hours ago. This is too absurd. He should have left.

He can leave right now.

McFadden tears off his pyjama top, but his shirt is in the bathroom, on the girl. His pants are where he left them, folded on the chair. A thought strikes and he jumps out of bed. His wallet is still safely in the pocket. He flips through the billfold: everything intact, even the hundred he had earmarked for her earlier. She's still banging around in the bathroom.

He needs to use the toilet.

He could take off right now and just leave her his shirt. But he needs to use the toilet.

McFadden wrestles out of his pyjamas and pulls on his pants while she's still out of sight.

"Oh?" she says. She has suddenly appeared again. "Going so soon? Don't want to stay around for seconds? . . . Or maybe *conscious* girls are a turnoff."

She is speaking through a mouthful of toothpaste. Her face assumes a leering grimace as she reaches around to scratch a spot between her shoulders. The shirt falls open and she looks at herself.

"I am covered in mosquito bites," she says. "Every inch of me. Everywhere. I look like some kind of leper." Her gaze shifts back to McFadden. "But maybe you're into lepers. Maybe you just like to fuck unconscious lepers." She pauses, toothbrush poised. "Never heard of that one yet."

McFadden is simply staring. It occurs to him that the toothbrush she is using is his. He can't take his eyes off the toothbrush.

"Oh, pardon me. Oh, I beg your pardon! You don't want me using your toothbrush. You can fuck me while I'm sleeping, but you don't want me using your toothbrush. What a guy."

"I did not fuck you!"

It bursts out of him, like the forlorn wailing of a child, so ludicrously that he closes his eyes and covers his face with his hands.

He hears her spitting in the bathroom. He hears the tap running. There are footsteps coming back toward him.

"It's all right," she says. Her tone is softer. "You're probably healthy . . . strange, but most people are. Maybe we can work this out." She looks at him, wiping her mouth with the back of her hand. "Tell you what. We'll do a deal." She's suddenly quite conciliatory. "Whatever's done is done already, right?" She has crossed to the bed and stands before him, almost between his knees. "What do you say we do business . . . ?"

There is a cluster of bites around her navel. For some reason McFadden is reminded of a constellation. He thinks it is Orion.

The girl bends a little so their eyes are even. "The deal is this," she says. "Take me with you. You can do me all the way to Cowtown, or wherever it is you're going, just take me with you." She smiles again, holding out her hand. "Get me out of here and I'm your toy for the trip."

In her other hand she's holding out the tennis skirt and top. McFadden sees they are still damp. He washed them in the sink last night, and hung them in the shower stall to dry.

"Only just try to wait till I'm awake, OK?"

"Excuse me," he says. "I have to use the bathroom."

McFadden is sitting on the toilet, pants around his ankles and holding his head, when he remembers the truck.

The girl is doing something to her hair with his comb. He startles her, rushing by. The air conditioner has died, he has no idea how long ago. There is a whoosh as he opens the door, and a wave of hot, thick air. To his immense relief there have been no fatalities – though conditions are decidedly fetid. He opens the screened windows and jumps up to the cab to turn on the engine and get the fan and the air conditioner going again. This could have been disaster.

The girl is standing at the doorway, his shirt partly done up with a button. She is peering at the back of the truck, trying to see inside. McFadden closes it quickly and replaces the lock. He is poised between the truck and the girl – trying to decide what to do – when a movement shatters his already fragile train of thought. The woman from the office has stepped out onto the sidewalk and is staring, hands on mountainous hips. The girl, covered with welts and naked under his shirt, leans against the door frame, staring back.

"Just checking out," says McFadden, smiling his waiting-room smile.

– – –

Miles go by again in silence. McFadden, for his part, is too aghast to speak. The odious fatwoman too had all but asked him if he'd had a good time.

"You're three hours over," she'd said. "But I'll only charge the one night. You look like such a happy couple."

At least he got away with stealing her hydro.

"Travels light, don't she," she'd said, watching the tennis skirt climbing into the truck. It was evident to both of them there was nothing underneath. "You take care now."

McFadden climbed into the seat, turned the truck back onto the highway and has not spoken since. The girl has made no move to break the silence, but he catches her watching, from time to time, and looking away.

It's absurd. It is unbearably embarrassing. He feels as if he is floating somewhere above the cab, screening this as if it were a movie. Priority one is to get rid of her. The sooner the better. The only thing that needs discussing now is where. But he also knows, as soon as he tells her he's letting her off, she'll accuse him of having his way and then dumping her. He knows this.

Giving her money will only confirm it. On the other hand, if he *doesn't* give her the hundred, he'll be truly abandoning her.

He has to, in some way, make it absolutely clear that he did in no way touch her; that yes, he did take her clothes off, but that was for reasons pertaining strictly to medical hygiene; that there was never anything carnal in any of his actions at any time.

A billboard on the right says they have just reached the Arctic watershed, at 1,652 feet above sea level. All the rivers from this point drain northward to the Arctic Ocean. For a moment he allows the drama of this to resonate, but it doesn't last.

There's still the cargo to think about. This should have been his first priority. This is the reason he is here, after all. So, before anything else, his responsibility is to tend to his cargo.

It would be great, though, if he could first ditch this girl.

"Would you hand me the map, please?" A neutral way of breaking the silence. "In the glove compartment, just in front of your seat."

"I know where to find a glove compartment." She pushes the button and the door swings down. "Which one?"

"I beg your pardon?"

"Which map? It's full."

McFadden carries road maps of each of the four provinces he will be visiting, as well as a thick stack of municipal directories.

"Oh. Sorry. Ontario, please. It should be on top."

The girl hands it over.

"Thank you," he says.

"My pleasure."

He has no way of knowing if this is intended to be sarcasm.

As he fumbles, trying to unfold the map and drive at the same time, the girl reaches over and takes the wheel. McFadden hesitates, then lets go. The truck stays between the yellow lines. "Thank you," he says.

"My pleasure," she says again without expression.

The map tells him nothing he doesn't know already. The next big town is Dryden; after that, Kenora. Then it's Manitoba. Dryden is still at least two hours off – probably more – and he can't afford to leave it that long. He has no choice but to pull over again and find some way of keeping the girl in the cab.

He folds up the map and hands it back. "A couple of hours till Dryden," he says. "And then another hour or so, and then Kenora."

He lets this hang a while, hoping somehow she will say it would be wonderful if he could let her off in Dryden. She says nothing.

"I'll have to stop soon," he says. "To check the back."

Still she says nothing.

McFadden has sighted a transmission tower of some sort, in the hills ahead. Perhaps there will be an access road. He knows she is watching him.

"So what is it you do back there, anyway?"

He looks, and he is not mistaken: from her tone it is clear that she has given the question a sexual dimension. It occurs to him that of course she thinks this is a camper van, with fold-down tables and beds and perhaps a kitchenette in back. The fact that she is evidently making game of him doesn't make things any easier.

She is waiting for his answer, moving her hands up and down her legs, unconsciously scratching.

"I think I have some calamine lotion," he says, "packed away somewhere," and nods at her legs. "That should take some of the itch out."

"Oh . . ." Now it is her turn to be chastened. "Thank you."

"My pleasure."

He says it before he can stop himself, and glances quickly to see her reaction. She holds his gaze, probing his own expression.

McFadden looks away, back down the highway. They have driven past the tower. There is no access road.

A mile or two go by.

"I was joking, you know," she says.

"Joking?" He tries to remember. "About the calamine lotion?"

"No, not about the calamine lotion . . . About last night."

"Last night?"

"I was only joking."

"Joking."

"Well, at first I wasn't joking – at first I thought you did. I just figured you did. But then later I thought about it and I realized you didn't. So I was only joking after that. Not that it would have mattered, really."

McFadden wonders how many times on this trip things are going to turn around on him. "Umm . . ." he says. And after a while, "What wouldn't have mattered?"

"Whether you did or you didn't. I was overreacting."

"I see."

"I was so out of it."

"Yes."

"So you didn't, then, right?"

It is her uncertainty that brings him back. The McFadden floating above the truck and the McFadden driving it reunite upon the solid ground of moral validation.

"No," he says. "I did not."

The girl nods, thinking things over. She has clearly lost the initiative, though McFadden has the impression she is quietly regrouping. He suspects she is about to renew her offer, despite the change in circumstances. This he most definitely does not wish her to do.

"Are you feeling better?" Distraction is the essence of medicine. "You were very ill last night." He can hear his voice assume the timbre of practical detachment. "You vomited several times."

She has gone quiet, perhaps even downcast. He studies her carefully, feigning professional concern. "Has the nausea returned?"

"No," she says like a little girl. "I'm feeling fine this morning, thank you."

"Morning! *Morning?* We didn't get out of that hotel until well past *morning*. It's nearly three p.m.! The day's half over. I should be through Manitoba by this time."

She is silent. McFadden is actually feeling a little ashamed of himself. He hadn't meant to let his indignation out like that. They pass a sign announcing the town of Raith, which he feels is somehow appropriate.

"Sleep," says the girl. "What I needed was sleep." McFadden nods with studied sympathy. "I can't tell you how good it was to sleep." She has folded her hands and is looking down at her feet. "They wanted me awake. Weeks and weeks, I think. Maybe months. They never let you sleep."

She is looking at her feet with a voice so hollow McFadden loses track of the road. The truck bumps along the shoulder until, cursing, he has brought it back onto the pavement. "Sorry," he says, though it is not his driving he is speaking of.

They pass a truck stop with a dusty line of rigs in the parking lot. This must be Raith.

"And food," she says. "You have no idea what you'll do for food." She looks up at him, changes her mind and assumes a smile. "Will you buy me breakfast?"

– – –

Most of the tables are empty. It's the quiet time between lunch and dinner. A clutch of truckers sits near the counter, discussing routes and loads and the general dimness of dispatchers everywhere. They stop talking when McFadden and the girl walk in, then ease back into it.

The place is done in varnished cedar and linoleum. Carved wooden signs dot the wall behind the register, backwoods epigrams zoologically inspired. *The cut worm forgives the plow*, reads one; *A busy bee has no time for sorrow*, says another.

McFadden is surprised to find himself diverted, and stands a moment reading. *The crow wished that everything was black, the owl that everything was white.*

"These aren't bad," he tells the girl, who ignores him utterly.

The air is infused with the smell of frying bacon. She has gone directly to the nearest table and taken a seat.

A middle-aged waitress emerges and hands them menus. "What can I get youse?"

"Coffee –" says the girl.

McFadden cuts her off. "One coffee," he says, scanning the menu. "For me. My guest will have a large glass of tomato juice, vegetable soup and toast. I see you have oatmeal." He pauses and looks to the waitress, who nods. "One bowl of oatmeal, then, please." McFadden's mother had brought him up on oatmeal and the subsequent weight of medical evidence has only reinforced his high opinion. "I'll have the bacon and tomato sandwich," he says.

He closes his menu and hands it back. The waitress looks at the girl for confirmation, but the girl is staring at McFadden. He takes the menu from her hands and passes it over. The waitress isn't sure if she is finished.

"I am not eating oatmeal."

"Well, you're not drinking coffee. It's acidic, and a diuretic on top of that. Thank you," he says to the waitress, who lowers her pad and disappears. "Look, you were sick yesterday because your system rejected what you ate. If you're not careful, it will just happen again."

"I was sick because you got me drunk. And what were those things . . . ?"

"Squabs. It was not the squabs, they were perfectly wholesome. And you don't get drunk on two glasses of rosé."

The waitress comes, fills his coffee cup and goes away again.

"In another few hours you can tackle a larger meal, once your stomach has dealt with this one. But I really think, for now, you should take my advice."

She has placed both hands palms-down on the table. There are thick bands of calluses below each knuckle. McFadden leans forward, repositioning the pepper shaker. He has no idea what could have caused this.

"You're thinking you could eat a horse right now, I know," he says. "But ten minutes after you've finished, you will feel full. I promise." He stands up, takes his sunglasses from his pocket and sets them on the corner of the table. "You can eat again in a few hours." He pushes his chair so it is tucked away beneath the table. "I'm just going to organize things in the truck. I'll be back shortly."

In ten minutes he is finished. There is a commotion at the table by the counter, which stops as he walks in. The waitress is bringing out their meal. The girl is looking out the window. McFadden puts his keys beside his glasses on the table. "Go ahead," he says, still standing. "I'll just go wash up."

The walls of the men's room are decorated with more of those wooden signs. *The cistern contains* – he reads while soaping his hands – *the fountain overflows*. McFadden is smiling as he returns to the table.

There's an unmistakable buzzing going on among the truckers –muffled spurts of laughter, furtive observations. The men are looking over at the girl, and McFadden's smile disappears. He crosses the room and moves his chair so there's nothing in between them, and stares at the truckers. Most of them look elsewhere. He places his hands on the table and steadily drums his fingers, melodically, each finger striking out a separate note. If one of them looks up, McFadden is staring, drumming with his fingers. One or two stare back, then elect to concentrate on sorting out their peas. They have stopped laughing. In a short while they have stopped talking.

McFadden does not address his own meal until each has paid his bill and left, trying not to look but watching through the corners of his eyes. He will have to think about this, he knows; later, when he's by himself, he will have to give his conduct here some thought. The waitress walks by and catches his eye.

"I like your signs," he says.

"What? Oh." She glances around at the walls. "They're for sale, if youse're interested. My husband does 'em up out back."

"I expect he uses a router." McFadden had been speculating as to the mechanics of sign manufactory.

"Yeah . . ." she says. "I guess." But now she's smelled an interest, she has come around to stand beside the table. "He does them custom, you know. He could do one while you're eating. It's not like he's busy."

McFadden takes a bite of his sandwich. It's cold, but he doesn't mind the coldness. The girl has been observing the encounter with an abstract lack of interest, her attention absorbed in the food. He'd seen her, though, as he turned the corner from the men's room. He had watched the composition of her face at the arousal of the truckers, her expression inscrutably, unconditionally torpid – as oblivious as it is just now. But in another of those unpleasant stabs of insight McFadden understood how precisely she had read his own response.

He puts his sandwich down and asks the waitress for her pad.

"What?"

"I don't need the whole thing. Just a piece of paper, and your pencil, if I may. I'd like to place an order."

McFadden writes in neat block letters, and hands pad and pencil back. "Can your husband carve me one that says that?"

The woman holds the paper out and squints. "Is that some kind of word?" she asks, and then, "Yeah, I guess. I'll go see."

Smiling again, restored, McFadden opens the halves of his sandwich and sprinkles them with pepper, then squirts a little dab of ketchup on the side. He's always had a weakness for ketchup, he tells the girl by way of conversation.

"You were wrong."

The sandwich pauses, midway to his mouth. "Wrong?"

"I'm still hungry."

She has finished her food, even the oatmeal, but the glass of tomato juice is still mostly full. McFadden reaches over and speckles the surface with pepper. "It's not so great for your stomach," he says, "but it improves the taste." He smiles again and dips his sandwich in the ketchup. "You're looking better already."

She is indeed. Her hair is washed, her colour has improved. He is contemplating some elaboration when the waitress reappears.

"He says he can do that one up in fifteen minutes, if youse're interested."

"We're interested," McFadden says. "Tell him that will be fine." He returns to his sandwich.

"You don't even want to know what it costs?" the girl asks.

"I beg your pardon?"

"Your sign. You didn't ask how much it costs."

He had, in fact, been considering this omission. But McFadden is pleased with his purchase and does not wish to appear crass. Also, he's been wondering how best to mount it on the metal panels of his truck.

"Quite right," he says. "I should have asked."

"Serves you right if he charges an arm and a leg."

He continues to chew his food in silence.

"But now I think you're right about the other thing."

"What other thing?"

"I'm full. I can't believe it." She's rubbing her stomach. "I thought there could never be enough, but I feel full. How did you know?"

"I'm a doctor," he tells her again. Three times now, by his count. "Or at least I was."

— — —

McFadden is leaning at a forty-five-degree angle, arms outstretched, toes digging into the pavement.

"How long did he say I should do this?"

"Five minutes. Minimum."

Even from his perspective it's clear how ridiculous he must look.

"I'm going to go sit in the truck."

"Go ahead," he tells her, relaxing his stomach muscles now the girl is out of sight. But in a moment she is back.

"It's locked."

"Of course it is."

The girl is waiting. McFadden contemplates the situation, which he would not hesitate to describe as delicate.

"Can I have the keys?"

"Um," he says. "They're in my pocket."

"Which pocket?"

He isn't sure. He can't remember if he put them in the back or in the front. They're somewhere in his pants, at any rate. McFadden is beginning to regret the purchase of this sign. The problem is with getting it stuck.

He's never been completely satisfied with the camouflaging of his vehicle. He'd achieved a certain folksiness, true; but all along McFadden has sensed that the overall impression could somehow be folksier. It had come to him – the moment he'd walked into the restaurant – that what his truck needed was a name. Like what fishermen paint on their boats, or those monikers stencilled on the sides of dump trucks.

And then the name itself had come, in a flash – just like that – a deeply satisfying twinkling of inspiration. McFadden has never been much interested in names; ideas suit him better. Yet here was an appellative that captured the essence of abstraction itself. He'd felt he had reason to be pleased.

The man had brought the sign up to their table just as they were finished eating. Even the shape was pleasing: a smooth, thin tablet of cedar, barely eighteen inches in length; rounded letters neatly carved and blackened with a torch. The girl's nose crinkled at the smell of new-burnt wood.

"What's it mean?"

But McFadden's mind was occupied with the technicalities of adhering the sign to the side of his truck.

"Can't screw her on," the carver agreed, thoughtfully considering McFadden's paintwork and scratching himself through his coveralls. "Let's see what I got out back."

While McFadden paid and thanked his wife, the man had rummaged in his workshop and returned with a tube of something resembling glue. "This ought to do her," he'd said, and then they'd all tramped out into the parking lot. The man squeezed out dollops of the tarry substance, and squinted as he read the instructions on the back of the tube. "It says here 'apply pressure for a minimum of five minutes, to ensure a proper bond.'" McFadden had nodded in a show of technical comprehension.

Which is how he has come to be leaning at this uncomfortably acute angle, careful not to jiggle the adhesion while maintaining a uniform pressure . . .

"Can I have the keys please?"

He can't tell if the blood is rushing up into his head or down into his legs. But already his shoulders are aching. He wonders if it has been a minute yet. The angle of his forearms makes it impossible to read his watch.

"I told you the guy would stiff you."

"What!" McFadden is indignant. "Twenty-five dollars? – no GST or PST – I think that's more than fair."

"Your money." She has moved uncomfortably close. He can actually feel a tendril of her hair against his ear. "Where are they?"

"Where are what?"

"The keys."

". . . They're in my pocket."

"Which pocket?"

". . . I'm not exactly sure."

Whereupon the girl begins to pat him down. For McFadden the experience is distinctly unsettling, though he is awed by the matter-of-factness with which the girl herself conducts the procedure. His alarm intensifies when she withdraws his wallet, but apparently this is only to canvass the area more completely. He can feel her fingers probing. Once assured the pocket's empty, the billfold is replaced as briskly as it had been removed. Her mouth is barely inches from his ear. The air between them stirs with tiny exhalations as she twists to reach around the front. McFadden finds himself immoderately grateful that his present posture tends to flatten what he's certain is an inappropriate reaction on his part.

"Aha!" she says. "Here it is!"

He is fiercely aware that he's blushing, but takes comfort from the fact that this too can be put down to his evidently isometric disposition.

"See you . . ." she says, waving the keys, and disappears around the front of the truck.

McFadden has elected to fix his sign against the driver's side, just to the rear of the cab. He hears the passenger door open. Her face appears as she rolls down the window, vaguely smiling, and then disappears again. He begins counting steamboats.

McFadden has always believed that if something is worth doing, it is worth doing properly. Although his shoulders are truly aching, he holds his place until he's reached a full five hundred – then very nearly buckles when he tries to straighten up.

He can't stop himself glancing to see if the girl has observed this, but there is no face in the window. She must be out of sight on the passenger side. McFadden walks in little circles, swinging his arms to renew the circulation. When he opens the door, he is surprised to discover that the girl is not there. He reaches for his keys, out of habit.

It's only now that he starts to feel a little nervous. He waits a minute, then forces himself to wait a few minutes longer. She is probably just in the ladies' room. When a decent interval has passed, and still no girl, he hurries back into the restaurant.

McFadden paces up and down before the women's washroom, wondering how to deal with this, and jumps when the waitress goes by.

"Have you seen . . . um . . . the girl I was with?"

The woman smiles kindly – sympathetic with these little misadventures. She nods toward the window.

McFadden turns. It's one of those moments that seem to take place outside of time. He looks out through the window, and there he sees the girl – framed precisely like a photograph – unlocking the back of his truck. He watches, transfixed, as the door swings open . . .

"Don't!" He whispers, but of course this has no effect.

Calmly as he can, he leaves the restaurant. The girl is standing, staring through the open tailgate. Calmly as he can, he takes the door and closes it. The girl, quiescent, stands rooted by the bumper, staring. He takes her by the hand and leads her to the cab, and hands her up into the seat.

When he is safe behind the wheel again, he puts his palm out for the keys, which still dangle from her fingers.

"You have rats," she says.

– – –

One thousand three hundred and seventy-six, to be precise, he tells her. Unless more have been born in the last hour, which is unlikely since to his nearly certain knowledge none are due for seventeen days or more. He'd left the city with 1,378, but two died the first day out. Since then there have been no losses. Considering all that has gone wrong since, McFadden takes a certain consolation from this. It helps to keep things in perspective.

They have pulled out of the lot, back onto highway 17. The girl is sitting cross-legged in the seat, her back against the door.

"Buckle up."

"What are you doing with a truck full of rats?"

McFadden looks out his window and beeps the horn twice. "Vacationing," he says.

She repeats the word, moving her lips without sound.

"Holiday," he says. "Holiday-*ing*. Excursioning. Buggering off

. . ." He pauses. "Fucking the dog." The part of his thinking in charge of speech can't seem to come up with anything better than prattle.

"Why are you taking a holiday with a truck full of rats?"

"Right . . ." he says. "Most people prefer sunscreen and Stephen King." He beeps the horn again. "To each his own."

She is still staring. There is a frankness to her, an openness of expression that has reduced his flippancy to nonsense.

"Put your seat belt on, please."

"Are you going to tell me?"

McFadden is caught in a moment of understanding. Something informs him that, if the answer is no, she will drop it and they will drive along into another silence. The surprise is how fervently he wishes this not to be.

"I'm taking them to Alberta."

"Why?"

"Why?"

"Yes, why?"

"Because Alberta doesn't have any."

"Right."

He glances across the cab. She is staring back, an icon of seriousness, though now that she has her seat belt fastened she has to turn her head to do it. The silence lingers. He knows the girl has decided she has asked enough. The incentive is his now. He does not quite know where to begin.

"It's a long story," he says.

"You have a long time."

McFadden nods. He understands he has surrendered. An independent segment of his mind wonders what he has surrendered to, but McFadden himself is more concerned with when. Was it only now? Only in these last few minutes? He doesn't want to think it coincided with her offer back in the motel, but a part of him admits this must be true. Of course there is the very valid reasoning that now that she has seen his cargo, it would be wiser to keep her near. Safer.

Whatever the reason, he knows that he intends to take her with him. The nice thing about causality is how easy it is to spread around.

"It's a long story," he says again, measuring the now-alarming possibility that she might change her mind.

3

But fate is not an eagle,
it creeps like a rat.

ELIZABETH BOWEN,
THE HOUSE IN PARIS

yley McFadden became an urban trapper shortly after his disgrace, divorce and quiet resignation from the College of Physicians and Surgeons. His interest in rats evolved later.

It began, as many *magna opera* do, as something quite apart from all that it eventually became. Something like an accident. He had found himself, when everything was said and done, cut off from friends and family in both the social and economic sense of finality. He had certainly lost his profession.

There was McFadden, completely adrift from all of life's anchors. His wife had not merely sued for divorce but obtained a court injunction specifying that, if he came within one hundred metres of her person, he could be arrested, or possibly shot – though this was something of a legal afterthought as McFadden, by this stage of events, was widely assumed to have fled the country. Financially he was, or should have been, in ruins. There was not the slightest possibility of his practising medicine; he should count himself lucky not to be walking a cell in Kingston Penitentiary. Every visible asset ended up with someone other than himself. They even took away his Instant Teller card.

But Wyley McFadden has always had an ear for ancestry, and this is what preserved him. A long and sturdy line of genealogy had marched unfailingly toward him, secure in the wisdom that the safest highway to the future rests on careful paving of the past. *Hoard at harvest* – his very genes advised – *and eat in winter.* McFadden had an understanding with his chromosomes.

His own harvests, to be honest – in terms of year-end balance sheets – had always been good. But blood is thicker than fortune. Even at the pinnacle of his earning power, in those flush years when OHIP billings were generously augmented by his patients in cash, McFadden had by force of habit extracted a portion of his income and hidden it. Tithing, he called it, with respect to his Presbyterian progenitors, though to a less than congressional authority he paid it.

By the time of his transition McFadden had salted away a considerable sum, in the form of Maple Leaf gold coin (with a few odd krugerrand for diversity's sake), and buried it. Simply buried it, in a hole in the ground in the garden – or rather, several holes here and there as topography suggested. Neither his wife nor her lawyers, nor Revenue Canada and theirs, nor any other of the hostile forces lined against him and his equity had the slightest notion of this bounty. Wyley McFadden was pleased to keep them in ignorance. When the last of them had finished plucking the tendons of his fiscal corpse, when the adjusters had adjusted and the liquidators liquidated, when the erstwhile Mrs. McFadden had retreated with the car and the cottage to a slightly smaller house in north Toronto, and the lesbian mothers had signed off on their share of the cut – there was more flesh left on the bones of Wyley McFadden than any were ever to know.

And McFadden disappeared. Or so it was supposed.

Another sort of man might simply have taken the money and run. Indeed, McFadden gave some thought to Mexico, or even

California – but how could he live among people raised without the benefits of winter? A form of escape, to be sure; but so too was lobotomy. The Mediterranean seemed a little more appealing: an island in Greece, a timbered *gîte* in France, a seaside villa somewhere on a cliff in Portugal.

Perhaps later.

His own country beckoned like a memory from childhood. Wilderness brooded in his blood. McFadden's temperate soul yearned for the forest. He considered homesteading in British Columbia. He thought of building a house on a rock on a Labrador outport and living off codfish and caribou. Of sail and snowshoe and spruce bark and sealskin. He also thought of the Vintages outlet on Queen's Quay and his season's tickets to the symphony. He thought of Kensington Market and Philosopher's Walk in the fall. And here his thinking paused. He knew he'd be starting over; that part was certain. It was the notion of doing it somewhere other than home that seemed so unappealing. Seven generations of his family had lived and bred and built and died in the ice-bound winters and typhus summers of Muddy York. McFadden was reluctant to leave it now that there were so many nice restaurants.

If not paradox, then at least dilemma, and a pretty one at that. On one hand, McFadden's contrarian soul yearned for a northern adventure; on the other, he had not the slightest intention of leaving home to achieve it.

It has never been quite clear to him precisely when a whisper of the urban trapper first began to breathe into his ear. He wonders if it might have been in Panama, or perhaps a little earlier. Sometime, at any rate, during the performance of his disappearance.

There wasn't time to plan it quite as finely as he might have liked – and he remains a little awed with how comprehensively it worked – but McFadden is proud of his achievement. The plan itself was the essence of simplicity: leave a clear trail of departure but none at all of return.

He bought a one-way ticket to Bolivia with a credit card he had – for the sake of verisimilitude – lifted from his wife. Air Canada passenger manifests indicate that he boarded his plane in Toronto and deplaned in La Paz. According to records still on file with the Canadian department of Citizenship and Immigration, Wyley McFadden visited Lake Titicaca and vicinity before descending the Andes to the swampy region near the border of Brazil, where he took an interest in inland navigation, eventually disappearing by boat somewhere in the Pantanal do Rio Negro, and has never been heard from again.

If truth be told, McFadden quite enjoyed his stay in South America, though on the whole he found the living a little on the easy side. Once he was satisfied that everyone was certain he was gone for good, he set out on his way back home – by routes much more circuitous this time – taking comfort from the knowledge that, although he still had no idea how he'd undertake his new profession, at least he had decided what that profession was to be.

– – –

Another moose appears at the side of the road, this one right at the verge, so McFadden has to brake hard in case it decides to cross. In moose country each year there are hundreds of fatalities. Moose are intensely stupid creatures, often standing still until the very last moment then stepping out like subway suicides. Truckers on the northern runs weld heavy iron grates across the noses of their rigs.

This one is a yearling cow, all ears and knobbly knees, and holds her ground until they've passed. Neither the girl nor he offer to exchange a word: she is waiting for him to speak, McFadden is wondering where to begin.

He lets his mind wander – free association. Perhaps this will get him going, though he knows it won't. For some reason he keeps coming back to squirrels. Occasionally pigeons, but mostly to squirrels. An absurd parallel has only just this moment struck him. He can't decide whether the absurdity lies mostly in the parallel itself or in the fact that it has never occurred to him before. In any case he has perceived an analogue between the evolution of his marriage and his relationship with *Sciuridae carolinensis*. Both had started sweetly enough, and both had shared the inclination to go sour over time.

"What are you smiling at?"

"Sorry?" he says, glancing at the speedometer.

"You were smiling."

"Was I?"

"Yes."

"Oh."

He's still cruising nicely at just under eighty clicks per hour.

"Are you just going to shut up and smile for the next two thousand miles?"

"It's not quite two thousand miles . . ." he says. "Probably closer to twelve or thirteen hundred." Another calculation. "That works out to just about two thousand kilometres, though."

The girl blinks and speaks no more, waiting for him to say something worth the necessary breath.

McFadden drums his fingertips along the ridge of the steering wheel. "Have you ever eaten squirrel?"

"*Squirrel?*"

"Yes. Have you ever eaten squirrel?"

The girl leans back in her seat and presses her hands into the upholstery. "Jeez," she says. "I haven't had squirrel in *years*."

This is not the reply he'd been expecting.

– – –

McFadden estimates the squirrel population of Metro Toronto at somewhere between four and five hundred thousand. He has based this mostly on his own field observations, balanced cautiously against data from the Ministry of Natural Resources, the

Department of Forestry studies and a scattering of post-graduate work uncovered during the academic segments of his research. Half a million squirrels is a lot of stew.

In those early days he delighted in every new dish: baked squirrel, broiled squirrel, squirrel fried and fricasseed. Squirrel cacciatore. Squirrel tetrazzini. Peking squirrel and squirrel *à l'orange*. Indian squirrel; Mexican squirrel; Portuguese squirrel and squirrel in Kentucky batter. Squirrel pie, squirrel puffs, squirrel pinwheels, and squirrel pâtés. Sweet and sour squirrel, and brandied squirrel with chanterelles. Squirrel supreme, squirrel satay, squirrel Dijon – squirrel *véronique*. He was tempted, for a time, to experiment with squirrel tartare but decided against. The flesh of *carolinensis* is much like rabbit – perhaps a little gamier – which in turn is like chicken, only drier. It lends itself to sauces.

The Toronto grey squirrel, so far as McFadden is concerned, has two defining characteristics: one, it tastes good; two, it's incredibly stupid and easily caught. At first he saw the latter of these qualities merely as a pleasant bonus to the former. But as time went by, his attitude changed. McFadden now understands pleasure mostly as a function of its brevity. He now regards *carolinensis* with barely qualified contempt. He still eats them, of course – in fact they remain a staple of his diet – but with nowhere near the satisfaction he used to. It's their idiocy that has got the better of him.

In terms of population density, Toronto squirrels are five or six times thicker on the ground than they have any excuse to be. City living has made them soft, scruffy, and astoundingly dense in both the physical and figurative applications of the word. They're so easy to trap, it's embarrassing.

This of course is good for business. Though in all honesty, the process of disenchantment began before there was truly a business to speak of.

During the early phase of his life as a trapper, McFadden set his sights deliberately low. At first he aimed solely for an achievable level of self-sufficiency. Set against the wider scale, this goal was relatively artificial; there was money enough in the kitty to keep him going for quite some time regardless. But this was not the point. McFadden intended to be a trapper, not merely some trifling dilettante. It had to be a viable business or the whole point of it was lost.

As with any other entrepreneur guided by a realistic business plan, McFadden was reconciled to operating under deficit for the first quarter or two – while he learned the ropes. During this, his self-imposed apprenticeship, he restricted himself to trapping only for food. Commercial opportunities, he hoped, would develop later.

– – –

Now it's his turn to be shocked. How can she leave a statement like that just hanging?

"You mean you eat *squirrels*?" He hears the incredulity in his voice, though he does not intend it.

"There's nothing wrong with squirrels!"

There is already a defensive edge. The irony here is more than he's willing at the moment to appreciate.

"Anyway, it wasn't really squirrels. It was more like . . . prairie dogs."

"Prairie dogs!"

"That's what I said. Prairie dogs. Only not the little kind . . . the bigger ones." She glances out the window. Perhaps a prairie dog will pop up so she can show him. "I've never seen one here. I don't think you have them in the East."

"Groundhogs?" says McFadden, trying to be helpful.

"No! Not groundhogs. Smaller than groundhogs. About the same size as your Ontario squirrels, but with smaller tails, and I think a little fatter." She pauses. "They live underground, like prairie dogs. Only they're bigger."

"Ground squirrels!"

"That's it!" she says. "Ground squirrels! That's why we called them squirrels, I guess. Sounds better than prairie dogs."

"Richardson ground squirrels, I bet," he says, showing off.

She gives a look indicating she is unimpressed with the finer points of rodential taxonomy.

"You *ate* ground squirrels?"

"So!" she says. "So what? So we ate ground squirrels. You're the one who brought it up." She is now definitely hostile "Just because we ate ground squirrels is no reason for *you* to get on your high horse."

McFadden is so bemused at having discovered someone else at least marginally familiar with *Sciuridae* cookery that he brushes this aside. "How do you cook them?"

She glares at him.

"Did you fry them?" he says. "Did you bake them? Did you ever try them *dijonnaise?*"

"First of all you get me drunk. Then you try to fuck me while I'm sleeping. And now you want to laugh at me." She has taken hold of the door latch. "Pull over!"

McFadden's astonishment is genuine. "Hold on!" he says. "I wasn't . . . and you know perfectly well I didn't . . . "

"You wanted to."

"How would you know? You were busy throwing up." He feels he's scored a point with that one.

"Only because you got me so drunk it backfired."

He sucks a breath and counts to ten. "I will not be drawn into this," he says, exhaling. "We have been through this before."

The girl is studying the roadside.

"I apologize if I've offended you." His words are as dignified as he can muster. "I was not being facetious. I was merely curious." He clears his throat and looks down the highway. "I'm something of an aficionado of squirrel cuisine myself."

The look she gives him is decidedly unfriendly.

"I've cooked a squirrel or two myself, in my day," he says, unable to withstand that barren gaze. "But not ground squirrels. I've never even caught a ground squirrel – unless you count the odd chipmunk, which of course is too small to eat anyway . . . I guess like your prairie dogs. Tree squirrels – that's what I'm talking about. The black ones and the grey ones. You know, the ones you see in every park. They're Toronto's civic mascot. Did you know that? Most people don't even know that."

McFadden is aware he is providing unrequested information. He looks at his watch.

A little while ago they crossed the time zone. On the left-hand side of the road, in the middle of nowhere, a surprisingly tall sign emerged from the bedrock to inform them that they'd just passed from the Eastern Time Zone into the Central one, and that they should now change their watches. But McFadden hasn't quite caught whether it's meant to go backwards or forwards. Time zones have always befuddled him. Aware of his weakness, he's been careful to make allowances for error. But now he can't remember which way the allowance was intended to go.

"When we passed that sign back there," he says, "did it say we gained an hour, or lost an hour?"

"We lost an hour."

"We lost an hour, oh." He raises his watch to cue this visually. "So five o'clock becomes six o'clock?"

"No. Five o'clock becomes four o'clock."

"Then you mean we *gain* an hour."

She looks at him. "When five turns into four, it's losing, not gaining. Where did you learn to count?"

For some reason these things have always confused him. "Yes, but we are gaining an extra hour of daylight, aren't we?"

The girl looks out her window.

"I just want to get this straight. My watch should now read quarter to four, not quarter to five?"

"Yes," she says, turning her head to face him again. "It's always earlier out West."

"Well, that's good news then! I mean, we get an extra hour of daylight. There's a whole extra hour before we have to worry about it getting dark."

"Turning into a pumpkin?"

McFadden is not so easily diverted. "If it's only four o'clock," he says, "not five, then that means we can drive another hour before we stop to eat." He takes his eyes off the highway to examine her. "Your system should be ready for another meal by then. What would you say to a good thick stew of squirrel, with carrots and peas?"

She has been watching him back, and smiles that sudden smile that seems to flash like klieg lights when the circuits click. "Weird," she says. "That's exactly how my grandfather used to make it."

"That's all I was asking!"

"What was?"

"Back there when we were talking about squirrels, that's all I was asking, how you cooked them."

"Oh. Well, I don't think we used peas. Does yours have potatoes?"

"Of course it has potatoes. It has to have potatoes. Potatoes are mandatory, as are peas . . . I'm sure your grandfather would have also used peas."

"How would you know that?"

"I *don't* know. It's just that it's a very standard recipe – more traditionally with chicken or rabbit – and it always calls for peas. Dried peas or maybe lentils, which is why you have to start it early, to give them time to soak."

"Well, I don't think my grandfather ever used peas."

"Well, fine then."

After some minutes it becomes evident the topic is exhausted. McFadden is mulling over this unexpected bit of information. So the girl is from the prairies. It's the first thing he knows about her.

"Are you going to tell me about the rats?"

He is silent for a moment, squaring his shoulders and drumming his palms along the steering wheel.

"I know," she says. "It's a long story."

– – –

Generally speaking, McFadden does his homework.

Before setting foot in the field, he visited the Reference Library at Yonge and Bloor and applied himself in earnest to a detailed study of present-day trapping. As a measure of seriousness, he adopted, in all its rigour, the well-acknowledged Harvard School of Business case-study approach. He was diligent. In due time he assembled, piece by careful piece, a comprehensive analysis – a full-scale feasibility report – allocating probabilities of success.

From the outset he admitted that his plans were tinged somewhat with romance. He could never help picturing the trapper's life as something from a Krieghoff canvas: toboggans and snow, Hudson's Bay blankets, dogsleds, bearded men in smoky seats and long clay pipes. These were the images that seduced him in the first place. He was perfectly aware of this – McFadden has always kept an open eye to his seductions – and fully prepared for his inquiries to render a much more pragmatic picture. Even so, reality surprised him.

He began by looking into licensing. McFadden was fairly certain that trappers would be licensed, like plumbers or dentists, or any other potential source of governmental revenue. He imagined the process as something in the nature of applying for a fishing permit: filling out a form and sending in a cheque. He did not expect he'd have to go to school to qualify.

He found a pamphlet published by the Ontario Ministry of Natural Resources, artfully titled *Summary of the Fur Management Regulations*. As well as the expected schedule of licensing fees and a breakdown of open seasons on fur-bearers, the booklet contained a disconcertingly long list of regulations couched in the kind of language they teach at Osgoode Hall. But what truly startled was a passage near the bottom:

> Persons applying for a trapping licence are
> required to complete the Fur Harvest, Fur
> Management and Conservation Course. The
> course is given by Ministry-licensed instructors,
> and students are required to purchase the *Fur
> Harvest, Fur Management and Conservation
> Course* manuals. Following the course, each
> student will be subjected to a written and prac-
> tical examination.

McFadden read this over several times. Unless he was mistaken, it was telling him there was actually such a thing as trapping school. He read it one more time and decided the only way
to find out was to call. It took fifteen minutes getting past the
voice mail, then another fifteen tracking down exactly who had
the authority to answer questions, but eventually he had an appropriately designated human being at the other end. Yes, the
course existed. Yes, there was space available. McFadden was so
bemused he didn't have the presence of mind to order the *Fur
Harvest, Fur Management and Conservation Course* manuals and
had to waste another quarter calling back.

But it was worth it. He was beginning already to suspect that
he'd be operating under circumstances never imagined by the
Fur Harvest, Fur Management and Conservation authorities.
But McFadden was delighted with the prospect of attending an
academy of his peers, though admittedly, at the outset, a little bit
nervous as well.

In his years as a clinician he'd attended dozens – if not hundreds – of seminars, as new procedures passed in and out of
favour. He'd presented quite a few papers himself. McFadden was
no stranger to the lecture hall. But this was something else
again. It was so far out of his experience, he wasn't sure even
how he should dress. Long ago he'd mastered the rules of clothing: function *a* equalled outfit *b*, like working by a slide rule.
Somehow he couldn't imagine a roomful of trappers showing up

in jackets and Milanese ties. On the other hand, it was foolish expecting bowie knives and coonskin caps. In the end he went with a plaid shirt and jeans (the same thing he was wearing most days lately anyway), which was more or less what everybody else was wearing too.

On his first day of class McFadden was uneasy. It wasn't as if visions of *Deliverance* were dancing through his head – just that he felt a little bit uncomfortable. His own motives were clear enough, those of the others far less so. As it turned out, though, they were just what he should have expected: decent enough people, hunters and farmers, looking to a supplemental income. Perhaps not the most grammatical, but friendly. There was good humour, stories and jokes around the coffee urn at break time, but McFadden struck up no lasting friendships during his internship among the fraternity of trappers – no leaning up against the pickup truck, scuffing shoes and shooting breezes. The urban trapper must of necessity be a breed apart.

The months went by productively. For McFadden it was time well spent, though if there was a lesson to be learned above all else, it was that this whole thing was going to be a lot more complicated than he'd led himself to believe.

– – –

They are seated by a fire, he on a stump of log, she tucked into a folding chair he has carried down from the truck; it had not occurred to him that he would need more than one of any item on this trip. The fire changes with the breeze, wafting smoke sometimes into his face, sometimes into hers. It's a problematic fire, forever on the verge of going out, demanding fuel, then blazing into sudden furies – drawing them closer, then forcing them farther apart. McFadden has heated their meal on a Coleman stove, also carried from the truck. It's the girl who's insisted on the fire, which is consuming at least as much of her attention as him. In the middle of a sentence she will get up and disappear into the trees, dragging back another branch of deadwood and bringing with her fresh clouds of mosquitoes, which the smoke from this fire is intended to be driving away.

"There," she says, arranging another log above the embers. "That should hold it."

She has pulled her legs up in the chair, parting her hair with her fingers and leaving smudges of soot. McFadden is amazed at the speed of her recovery, awed by the resilience of this girl. Her second bowl of stew lies empty by the chair; there has been a confrontation already at his refusal to let her have a third. He is aghast at how willingly she exposes herself to the mosquitoes. This place they have found is at the elbow of a largish stream, with a flood plain around them wide enough to let a breeze blow down through a fairly open valley. Here the bugs are minimal, but whenever she steps into the stillness of the trees they attack in gravitating hordes. The girl does not seem noticeably phased.

Her colour has bloomed and much of the swelling receded. She's still wearing his shirt, which falls to the middle of her thighs when she stands. Stepping over boulders and fallen timber, picking her way through the bracken, there is a sway to her hips now, a fully female swing, that was not present in her movement before.

"I'm amazed," he says candidly, "how well you are recovering."

"The bugs?" she says. "There were bugs enough where I come from. I'm sure in my life I've been bitten a million times." She mops her brow with the tail of his shirt and extends the smudge. "I think you just get used to them. When I was a kid, I never even swelled up. I guess this time was just too much."

Two questions present themselves: Where *does* she come from? and, more cautiously, *what* was too much? He decides to begin with the lesser.

"And where was that?"

"Where was what?"

"Where was it you grew up?"

She tugs the shirt to smooth it and crosses her legs. "You'll find out," she says. "You're taking me there."

McFadden breathes a moment. "But where, precisely, is that?"

"Stop trying to change the subject. It's *your* story we're doing. Save me for some other time."

The problem, he finds, is that her smile is impossible not to smile back at.

But now she is serious. "I still don't understand a thing you've told me, you know. If I hadn't seen the rats" – she pauses to look up at the truck, dimly visible through the trees a hundred yards or so above – "I wouldn't believe a word of it. Urban trapper! I mean, what kind of crap is that? You make it sound like it's a job, like you've got a union or something." She pauses again and levels her gaze. "And anyway, didn't you say you were a doctor?" She is sitting up straight, hands on knees, shooting McFadden a positively disconcerting look. "Or was that just another trick to get my clothes off?" Evidently this is some prevailing form of humour.

He gives the matter a moment's thought but can't come up with a satisfactory retort, and so elects instead for understatement. "I *was* a doctor," he says. "Of the medical variety. Now I am a trapper."

"What do you mean you *were* a doctor? How does somebody stop being a doctor?" She narrows her eyes, focusing perhaps a little more critically than is comfortable. "You're old," she says, "but nowhere near old enough to be retired."

"Thank you."

McFadden stands and pokes the fire, redistributing the coals until they flame again. When he returns to his log, the girl is still staring.

"So which is it, doctor or whatchamacallit?"

"I've told you, an urban trapper is exactly the same as any other kind of trapper, except he does his trapping in a city."

"Bullshit."

"I am a first in my field."

The girl is as amused with his attempts at comedy as he is with hers. She pushes at the bowl with the tip of her toe. "And you are honestly telling me that this was made from squirrels."

"East end squirrels, to be exact. But you should recognize a squirrel stew when you taste one. *You're* the one who says your grandfather used to make it."

"Stews all taste the same. That's why people who can't cook make them."

McFadden contends this hotly. "I can assure you that one kind of stew is entirely different from another. Squirrel stew is completely different in flavour than, say, beef stew . . ."

"Beef!" she says, looking up. "What's this about beef? You mean you actually go to the supermarket? No, wait. Don't tell me – you're a cattle rustler too! You rustle cattle off ranches in Scarborough."

McFadden has not been the object of sarcasm for quite some time. Again he takes refuge in established fact. "Didn't you say you liked the peas?"

"Peas?"

"The peas in my stew. Remember? The dinner you were clamouring for second helpings of? Before that, you were complaining because you didn't think you'd like the peas."

"I didn't say that. And what makes you think I liked yours?"

"You ate two helpings! And you would have had more if I'd let you."

"You're a cheap asshole, you know that?"

"You know perfectly well . . . " But he has seen that she is joking again and lets the sentence trail away.

"And anyway," she says, "that wasn't dinner. That was lunch." She has shifted her gaze to the river. Flood waters have left a wash of granular deposit along the bend, like a narrow pebbled beach. She leans forward and rearranges McFadden's rearrangement of her fire. "This is nice, though," she says. "This is very nice . . . I wish we had some marshmallows."

"Christ!"

"What?"

McFadden is staring at his wristwatch. "It's nearly eight!"

He has been secretly monitoring the time. Although he has been tracking it, mindful of its progress, McFadden is still surprised how much of it has disappeared. His reaction is not entirely counterfeit.

The girl takes a stick and pokes the fire.

Summer solstice is only weeks away. These are the longest days of the year, longer still in these latitudes. It won't be dark until nearly eleven. If they get moving now, he still can log another two or three hundred kilometres before calling it a day. On the other hand, this *is* a truly pleasant spot.

"I'm going up to check the cargo," he tells her.

At the truck, everything is in order. All 1,376 of his charges appear in perfect health; there is no indication of anything at all that should concern him. He putters for a time, changing water, freshening the feed, cleaning the bottoms of his cages one by one. When he returns to the fire, it is getting on for half past the hour.

The girl is naked in the river.

She has wedged herself into the centre of the channel, arms afloat behind her, legs downstream and spread into the current. The water is shallow, perhaps two or three feet, the river slow and potent. As he watches, she lifts her chin, arches her back. Her knees break the surface, splitting the current off to each opposing bank. McFadden is transfixed with the image of it entering and flowing on through her. He collects himself and clambers up the slope. It is getting cool; she will need a towel.

He makes a point of being gone for several minutes. Walking down, he whistles and crackles the brush with his feet – though it is unlikely, above the babble of the stream, that she will hear his circumspection. She is wading out as he arrives. First hips, then thighs, and now her knees appear above the ripple. Droplets catch the falling sun and swirl away beneath her. She has seen him and so he waits for her – holding out the towel.

The bottom is uneven and she picks her way deliberately, placing one foot carefully before the other, hips rolling left, then rolling right. There is nothing for McFadden to do but wait. The girl lifts her arms to wipe the water from her eyes, wringing it back through her hair with her hands. It is the ancient posture of sexual display: hands behind the head, back arched, breasts trained and presented. He cannot honestly judge if this has been intentional.

"Thank you," she says, accepting the towel.

They return to their seats by the fire.

The sun is setting; it's getting late. The temperature too has dropped. There is nothing said between them and soon she is shivering. The towel cannot cover all of her at once. He places more wood on the fire. Smoke rises and slants in his direction. The girl pulls her chair closer to absorb the fire's warmth, her bare feet steaming on the rocks McFadden has piled to either side. Water droplets trace a path from thighs to knees, then sizzle in the embers.

"Cold," she says. "But God, it feels good to be clean."

McFadden excuses himself and again wanders to the truck. He has made one decision at least, perhaps two, though one of them was made some time ago.

It takes a moment to rummage through his belongings and find a pair of cotton sweatpants, the only article he can think of with which to cover up the bottom half of her. The top is easier. He locates a pullover, with a hood, and a bulky woollen sweater.

"Thank you," she says. "Again."

She stands, folds the towel and hangs it from the back of her chair, then pulls the top over her head. Still standing, she inserts herself into his sweatpants. McFadden has returned to his log and watches her until it occurs to him that this is just what he is doing.

He is – or was in former times – professionally accustomed to the nakedness of women. She, according to the evidence so far, appears equally at home with being naked. By all standards there should be some neutral kind of parity to this, and of course there is. Yet he finds himself gripped in an adolescent struggle not to stare. It is a thing of awe to him, what change a day can bring. Stripping the clothes from her only yesterday, he had missed entirely the girl he sees today: this slim voluptuousness, this spare abundance. Perhaps beauty of this kind truly does require motion. But of this there can be no doubt: the girl is beautiful.

He is staring out across the river, hoping for some timely piece of flotsam to justify his gaze. Surely by this time she is clothed. McFadden is thinking of the bottle of Macallan he has laid in for the trip, though now he is nervous of anything at all to do with alcohol.

"Well," she says with what to his ear is a genuine sigh of regret, "we'd best be going."

Now he can turn his head.

"We'll be staying here tonight," he says.

— — —

All along he's planned to camp.

He has carried with him from the city a nylon tent and sleeping bag, an air mattress and pump, his Coleman stove, his cooking utensils – all the necessities of a properly outfitted camping expedition. It's cheaper, and much less risky; the inquisitiveness of that woman at the motel has already proven as much. Though granted, it was the girl who provoked that, not his rats.

Nevertheless, it only makes sense to stay away from people. The truck has been carefully set up to generate most of its own electrical needs. From time to time he might require an emergency hookup, like this morning – was that only this morning? But this is to be the exception, not the rule. Except that something has happened to the rule. This stop today was meant to be for food, yet somehow the fire had got itself going, somehow the lawn chair unfolded, and the day – somehow – drifted away. It's now after nine. Technically, it would still be possible to log in some miles. But by the time the fire's put out, and the dishes washed, and everything loaded back into the truck, they'd be barely on the highway again before he'd have to start looking for another place. And the girl is right – this is a lovely spot, though she may not have had camping in mind.

"What do you mean we'll be staying here?"

"I must ask you to stop repeating my statements as questions."

"What do you mean, we'll be staying here?"

McFadden has suddenly realized he *enjoys* seeing her disconcerted. He also realizes – and this too is something he will have to think about – that it's because so far it has been so much the other way around. He had also better face the fact that all day long he's been avoiding telling her.

Several times today – no, many times today – he reminded himself that he should probably let her know about his plans. Yet somehow, each time the thought sidled into consciousness, it more quickly danced away again. The simple truth was that whenever his thinking touched the subject of where to spend the night, it leapt instantly into contemplation of *whom* he would be spending it with. He tried to rationalize. He reminded himself that it was her idea to come along in the first place, that surely she must know you can't drive all the way to Alberta without stopping to sleep. But of course she knows; her offer in the motel room made that clear enough.

And here the darker thought condenses – the one he's been dodging all day; the one the angel at his shoulder is forcing him to contemplate, the one the devil on the other smirkingly conceals. Or is it the other way around? In either case he can't escape the fact that he has practised subterfuge; that if he had informed the girl earlier he was expecting her to spend the night with him alone – and completely alone, in a forest in a tent – if he had told her this, she might have had the opportunity to change her mind.

"Listen . . ." he says, his voice sounding strained even to his own ear. "I can take you someplace else . . ." Caveats are crowding in too fast for declaration. "I mean, if you don't feel comfortable, I can drop you somewhere else. There's absolutely no reason at all for you to have to stay here."

She is watching, puzzled. "What's got into you?"

"Sorry," he says. "I just feel stupid I haven't explained everything."

"You mean there's *more*?"

"Well, I mean about the camping, and . . ." He is embarrassed, ashamed of himself.

She smiles again. There is a distinctly vulpine cast to this girl when she cares to display it. He is certain she has knowledge of what he has been thinking. Did her eyes flick deliberately where he thinks they did, or has he truly turned fifteen again?

"What do you mean we'll be staying here? You can start by explaining that."

"I have told you," he says. "We're camping."

"Camping?"

"Will you stop doing that!"

"You're the one with the ants in his pants."

McFadden stares at the river. This time a piece of something does float by – a stick, he guesses, heavier at one end than the other. It bobs and spins and sinks, then pops back to the surface. He watches it disappear.

"I have a tent," he says. "And a sleeping bag, and a groundsheet, and all the other equipment which, when assembled together in a wilderness setting, defines camping. And that is what we are doing – camping. Though as I've said, it's no trouble dropping you somewhere else first." A mosquito has landed in the hollow of his neck and he slaps it, lending a certain natural resonance to the point.

"What kind of tent?"

A pause. "A nylon tent," he says. "A two-person nylon pop-tent." McFadden is trying to remember what it said on the box the tent came in.

"Does it have a fly?"

He is about to be annoyed when he remembers that tents do indeed have flies, though he is not absolutely certain about his. Some weeks ago he set it up for practice in his backyard. It went up smoothly, though it was next to impossible getting all the parts back into the tiny nylon bag the whole thing was meant to go into. If memory serves, he got it on sale at Canadian Tire – not among the most expensive, but not the cheapest either. He is confident it will suit his needs, but for the moment he can't recollect the details of its fly.

"Of course it does."

"Good." The girl is eyeing the treetops. "It might rain."

This startles him. He cranes his neck. The sky is still a basic blue, some clouds in the distance – quite far away, really – their bellies lit up with the setting sun. "Oh," he says, "I don't think so."

"What about the sleeping bag?"

Another mosquito buzzes by his eye. He bats at it, misses and tries again. This is the question that's haunted him.

"What *about* the sleeping bag?" He's still looking at the river.

"What kind is it?" she says suspiciously, and when he does not answer, "How big is it? Is it the mummy style or one that opens up on all three sides? . . . Well?"

McFadden can feel his ears turning colour. All afternoon he's been pondering the implications of having brought only one sleeping bag.

"It's a standard type," he says, and clears his throat. "With a zipper. It's good to twenty below zero. Centigrade."

The girl's mouth is not smiling. "I guess we don't have to worry about freezing."

McFadden busies himself with the fire. The girl has not removed her eyes.

"If those rats are coming in," she says, "I'm walking."

In a moment McFadden will ponder, also, the implications attached to the profoundness of his relief. But he *is* relieved. So immensely relieved he loses syntax.

"Oh no!" he says. "Oh no no no. No, those rats stay in the truck. They're all set up there. They're perfectly fine. Yes, you see I've set it all up so it's self-contained. Everything they need – except sometimes water, of course – is right there for them. Oh no. The rats don't leave the truck until we get there."

"And then what?"

"*What?*"

"What happens when they get there?"

"Oh," he says, not quite coming to grips. The circuits of his brain are completely overwhelmed with the understanding that she has changed the subject. The maze in which he found himself has vanished. His mind stands blinking on an open plain. A mosquito – two mosquitoes – buzz above his eyelid.

"Well," he says, aware that something must be said and, waving his hands in the space before his eyes, "didn't I tell you?" At present he cannot remember what has been said, and what left unsaid.

The girl's silence indicates the negative.

"I'm letting them go." McFadden scratches his scalp. "I thought I'd told you." He can feel the cells beginning to respond. "That's the whole point, you know." He waves an arm toward the truck, notices a mosquito engorged on the back of his wrist and splatters it, crimson, among the dusty pores. He turns up his collar, hunches his shoulders and squares his body to face her. He is fussing with rolling down his shirt sleeves.

"I have predetermined the locations," he says, "concentrated within specific quadrants of south and central Alberta." The button on his right cuff is annoyingly stiff. "In each of these locations I intend to introduce clusters of selected breeding specimens – depending, of course, upon on-site verification of habitat viability . . . and . . . um . . . harbourage availability, and so on . . ." He has paused again to remove a bug intent on crawling up his nostril. "The goal is to establish genetically self-perpetuating colonies in locations they are likeliest to flourish, given the proper food supply and, you know . . ."

She stops him, holding up a hand while shaking her hair with the other. McFadden is aware that the air around them is filling with movement, though the leaves and the treetops are perfectly still. There is a little silence, or what would have been a silence except for the hum of many hundred thousand whirling wings.

The girl and McFadden have communicated without speaking. He's already on his way to the truck.

"I hope your tent is bug-proof," she says.

– – –

The other thing about squirrels is that they're not even fur-bearers. McFadden acquired this information his very first day of class. It surprised him. He remembered, or at least he was fairly certain he remembered, seeing women in squirrel coats. Certainly the squirrels themselves wore fur, but this was a point apparently lost to authors of the Game and Fish Act, which describes the North American grey squirrel as a *game* animal – in the company of deer, moose and pheasants – rather than a fur-bearer, which are those animals sought by trappers. The distinction, as he was to discover, was more than moot.

To make matters more confusing, the Act further subdivides its categorization of squirrels according to *species*. There are two kinds of squirrels in Toronto. One of these is the grey squirrel (which is the same as the black squirrel, the one being merely a colour-morph of the other – this McFadden *did* know); the other is the red variety, now nearly vanished from the city.

Game animals, he discovered, are defined as animals that *hunters* are licensed to pursue; *fur-bearers* are those species allotted to *trappers*. According to the Game and Fish Act, red squirrels are classified as fur-bearers while black squirrels are listed as game. Trappers could harvest red squirrels for their fur, but not black ones; hunters could shoot grey squirrels for their meat, but not red ones. Looking back, there must have been something in this equation that triggered his imagination, but at the time it brought nothing but compounded gloom.

Prognosis, no matter how he skewed his business plan, seemed increasingly dim. Not only was production thick with legislative barriers; not only was marketing controlled more tightly than conceivable; but sales themselves were at an all-time low. McFadden wondered how *anyone* in trapping made a living.

From beginning to end the industry was incredibly scrutinized. It seemed to McFadden it had more rules of ethics than the medical community. Certainly there were more regulations applied to trapping than there were, for instance, to driving a car. The Game and Fish Act is longer in substance than the Highway Traffic Act, and this was only provincial legislation – on top of which came the federal and municipal governments weighing in with sanctions of their own.

Open seasons on most fur-bearers were incredibly short. These turned out to be established not only according to each species' breeding cycle but also by climatic conditions affecting the primeness of pelts. (The theory and practice of determining prime was itself a study of Cartesian complexity.) McFadden applauded the conservationist spirit underpinning the Act; he just hadn't realized how tiny a window it actually left open. Quotas were strict, not just imposing maximum harvests but also setting minimum numbers as well.

One regulation stated that trappers needed written permission from every owner of private land they trapped on. Another forbade trapping in public parks. This might have made sense farther north, where traplines were generally granted over crown land, but presented quite a disincentive to the urban practitioner.

He liked the historical parts best. In the old days a trapline was just that – a string of traps set out in a line, usually shaped like a loop, which ended where it started so the trapper could finish his rounds where he began. In modern meaning a trapline refers to a region, a designated block of geography within whose boundaries the licensee is permitted to harvest according to strictly set controls. The present-day trapper is considered the custodian and manager of his region, responsible for its biological health and well-being. The laws impose strict quotas for most species, but also demand that these quotas not be *under*-harvested. As top predator of his territory, it's the trapper's responsibility to ensure that no population imbalances occur.

McFadden admired the theory, but a downtown practice . . . ? Here again, though, a little bell was quietly starting to ring. On one hand, the city suffered a serious overabundance of several discernible species. On the other hand, a complex tangle of laws seemed to be preventing this population imbalance from being in any way sensibly redressed.

Despite the odds, McFadden was hooked. He applied himself to his studies, and also to the monitoring of his nascent trapline, which at this stage was mostly a matter of looking through the kitchen window to check the box trap tactfully concealed behind a rhododendron. He continued to expand the thresholds of *Sciuridae* cuisine. McFadden kept his nose to the grindstone. His Harvard School of Business Case Study and Feasibility Plan was telling him that no one worthy of the program would even begin to contemplate embarking on a scheme of such commercial madness, which was nice. It was the only thing, lately, cheering him up.

– – –

He's not quite sure how this happened, but the girl has taken over his campsite.

The first hint was the countermanding of his tent location. They got everything ferried down from the truck: his little red pop-tent, the groundsheet, an orange tarpaulin he bought because he thought it might be useful and which the girl immediately commandeered, his sleeping bag, his propane lantern, and the neatly balanced little steel axe he fell in love with at Canadian Tire and has been itching for a chance to use ever since. The girl helped carry everything down from the truck.

By this time they have lost the breeze. It dropped and dropped, unnoticed, while they were seated by the fire, then died away entirely. Not a blade of grass bends or leaf stirs. Nothing moves but the bugs, and these are moving now in masses. With his hands full of equipment, McFadden learns the trick of jutting out his lower lip and blowing air across his face to discourage them from landing. It works – sometimes.

He'd thought the ideal place was by the river, on the smooth and level surface by the pebbled wash. But the girl quite correctly pointed out that if it rains, the river might flood. McFadden acceded to the wisdom of this, though there's still hardly a cloud in the sky and the stream bed – now that he's had a chance to look around – is definitely the only level landscape in the general vicinity. She picked instead a spot among the trees, where he hadn't looked, and he admits that it is fairly flat, except that there's a ten-foot sapling growing in the middle of where the tent is supposed to go.

"You have an axe," she says.

He also has a shovel. One of those green army-surplus varieties with a folding blade small enough to carry strapped to the back of a knapsack. McFadden uses his folding shovel to dig back the earth away from the base of the tree; he is disinclined to dull his new axe. While he is shovelling, the girl disappears, but returns with an armload of evergreen boughs. Spruce, he thinks, but they could be hemlock. She has taken his axe.

The excavation is finished, but she won't give back the axe until the pile of evergreen is nearly as high as her waist. The bugs have gotten very thick.

"There," she says, depositing her final armload and running a hand through her hair.

McFadden very nearly amputates his foot, trying to flail mosquitoes and chop at the same time, but in short order the tree is down and he can backfill the cavity around the stump. The girl has got hold of his axe again. This time she's trimming all the branches off the little Jack pine he's just felled. She seems to have a thing for branches.

In a moment McFadden has the space levelled to his satisfaction, with the mix of earth and pine needles spread around
more or less evenly. He is keen to get the tent up because the
bugs are murderous. The equipment was piled near the fire
while they scouted for a place to put the tent, and McFadden
hurries over and fetches the groundsheet. But now the girl is covering the ground he has just prepared with layers of spruce
boughs. She places them carefully, one at a time, with all the ends
pointing in the same direction, overlapped and intertwined so
they fit together in a springy weave. McFadden slaps mosquitoes
and fidgets. He would very much like to get this tent up.

Finally he is permitted to spread the groundsheet, though he
must first go with her to the river and bring back several stones
to anchor its edges. The tent itself, bless it, takes only minutes,
and soon is staked securely on every side. McFadden has to
admit that the pile of boughs beneath has given its floor a pleasant spring, however redundant once he gets the mattress filled.

But the girl has found fault with his fly.

"What's wrong with it?"

"Too thin," she says, fingering the nylon. He can see the outline
of her hand beneath. "Not waterproof."

"What water?"

But she has vanished once again into the brush. He shrugs and
busies himself with his mattress. There is the sound of more
chopping, but McFadden can't see what because he is now inside
the tent – a surprisingly roomy and perfectly dry tent – trying to
unfold his inflatable mattress. Proper bedding, he knows, makes
all the difference between a comfortable outdoor experience
and a thoroughly unpleasant one. McFadden is pleased with how
big this tent feels from the inside, but still, once he gets the mattress spread out, there isn't much floor space left over. This
only means it's a big mattress, which is also fortunate in light of
recent developments. No wonder it's taking so long to fill. The
tent has come equipped with a mesh screen at the door which
he has zipped shut to keep out the bugs – a lucky thing, because

the battery-operated air pump isn't working right. It keeps un-coupling from the valve; he has to hold both parts together or the air blows out instead of in where it's supposed to go.

From time to time the chopping stops and he hears the sound of dragging. Occasionally the tent walls move when something touches from the other side. He can't go and look because the mattress is only half-filled; if he lets go now, all the air he's got in it so far will leak out again.

There is the sound of hammering. More chopping, more thumping, and a lot more rustling.

"What's going on out there?"

But the girl doesn't answer. McFadden tries to calculate how much more air this thing will need. She must be off into the woods again.

By the time he has finished, the noises have ceased, or at least altered. He hears crackling now, and smells smoke. So the girl has moved the fire closer to the tent. That makes sense. It also explains the chopping.

But when he crawls out, he sees that his tent has doubled in size, and changed colour. She has built another one on top of it. A businesslike frame of saplings lashed together – she must have found the coil of rope he keeps behind the seat – supporting a central ridgepole over which she has stretched and pegged the orange tarp. He puts a hand against the structure and leans. Nothing moves.

"Top one keeps out the rain," she says. "The other one is for the bugs." McFadden has not even heard her coming up behind him.

"Impressive."

He means it, and is rewarded with one of those smiles. She is all covered in twigs and pine needles, and smells like Christmas.

"Now," she says, "where's the food?"

"Didn't we just eat?"

"That was ages ago."

McFadden looks at his watch; it's well after ten. This whole day is a confusion. He has to keep reminding himself they didn't get on the road until the middle of the afternoon. And then there was that time change. His sense of continuity has vanished.

The girl is drumming her fingers against the side of her new tent.

"Let me see what I've got," he says.

– – –

His duck is turning nicely crispy when the wind starts picking up again. At first it's just a hint of breeze, then a little stronger, then a little stronger still. Now the smoke is running flat along the ground, disappearing with the wind into the night. McFadden is particular about his duck. In many ways it represents the transformation to his present lifestyle. Geese too, for that matter. He has a special interest in waterfowl, which predates any urge to take up trapping.

Toronto ducks have always bothered him. He finds their slothful indolence offensive, their brazen disregard for what should be the hazards of *ferae naturae*. The fact is, city ducks have no business being classified as creatures of the wild. On the other hand, they've managed to avoid the downside of domestication. What they do get is the best of both worlds, while at the same time avoiding the unpleasanter sides of either. In short, they have their cake and eat it too – which is, as far as McFadden is concerned, an admirable goal from the philosophical perspective. But ducks don't philosophize. McFadden believes that only those minds capable of coming to terms with a rationalization should be permitted to enjoy its benefits.

His research has indicated that the city's goose population triples every decade. What particularly irks him is that now they don't even bother flying south. Why should they? Local industry heats the lake up so it's cozy even in the dead of winter. Old ladies visit every morning with bagfuls of baked goods to float upon the pleasant pools of their existence. He was incensed to discover that the Toronto Humane Society actually sets aside a portion of its budget every year for waterfowl relief.

According to his calculations there are more erstwhile migrant geese among the piers and parking lots of Lake Ontario than nesting on the mud flats of Hudson Bay. As far as he's concerned, the city has sufficient problems coping with its human over-population. It's frustrating enough to hear the food banks crying for donations without these feathered bundles of web-footed pro-tein gobbling up the handouts as well.

So it was only natural that waterfowl should have ranked among his earliest quarry. The problem with ducks, though, is that they're hard to catch. It isn't that they're any more intelli-gent. He rates squirrels and ducks about par in terms of brain space; Canada geese might seem a little more imposing, but that's only because of their size. McFadden has yet to invent a trap suit-able for ducks. The problem isn't practical, it's procedural: he could build one – he just wouldn't be able to hide it.

The toughest part of urban trapping – and this McFadden has learned the hard way – is trap concealment. A trapper must bal-ance the necessity of maximizing his trap's attractiveness to its quarry against the even greater need to minimize the likelihood of its discovery by people. He still writes off twenty to thirty per-cent of his equipment annually to human depredation. In the early years, before he learned the ropes, the numbers were worse. A found trap is a lost trap; that's the rule of business in McFadden's one-man field. His units for squirrels are designed for camouflage, and also, squirrel sets can be tucked away into nooks and crannies where people don't look. But a box trap large enough to hold a duck would be impossible to hide.

The other thing about them is how loud they are: a trapped duck is a noisy duck, and noise is anathema to the urban trapper. So for a time his catch was limited or almost non-existent, in terms of waterfowl – until the day McFadden experienced the first of his brainstorms.

He was walking up Yonge Street, as it happened, passing one of those techno stores, the kind whose windows are completely

taken up with TV sets and video screens. McFadden cheats
sometimes, and watches from the sidewalk. There were dozens in
this one, banked in rows, and all of them flashing the same vi-
brant image of a man standing waist-deep in turquoise water,
casting a net that spread across a crimson sunset before splashing into coral sea. The man was supposed to look like he was
fishing, and the tourist board he was fishing for turned out to be
Bermuda's, or the Bahamas', or one of those islands people fly to
in February to touch up their melanomas. But it got McFadden
thinking.

He went out that day and bought some netting and rope, and
little lead sinkers and reels of heavy fishing line. He spent hours
cutting and splicing, and hours more practising in his backyard. It was surprisingly difficult, and he nearly gave it up before
he got the knack. But after that it was only a matter of planning
– and cautious execution. The next morning found him on a
lonely dockside by the Metro Pumping Station with his pockets
full of breadcrumbs. He got there just at dawn, when the waterfowl were waking and most people still in bed. McFadden fed the
ducks until a proper flock of them had gathered. Then he simply
waited for his moment and cast his net.

He went home with half a dozen mallards and a largish
goose.

This, he's discovered, is the advantage of working in a city so
culturally removed from its port. McFadden seldom passes beneath the suppurating belly of the Gardiner Expressway without
a nod of gratitude. It might as well be the wall to his private
game preserve. There are a hundred spots off Lakeshore he can
throw his net with hardly a second thought to concealment.
There's just never anyone to see him but the odd tugboat crew,
who couldn't care anyway. Which is a good thing, because a net
full of mallards can make a noise to wake the dead.

McFadden has come to think of this as fishing, which may be
something of a misnomer except for the fact that from time to
time he actually does land a fish, invariably a carp. He's pulled

them in upwards of forty pounds. In several oriental cultures the carp is a talisman of luck; and McFadden is happy to take his luck where he can find it. Certainly, there's always a market – so much so, he's tempted to fish for them deliberately, especially during off-seasons, when time weighs heavier on his hands. But always he reminds himself he is a trapper, not a fisherman, and that diversifying is one thing, but foolhardy expansionism is something else again. So he contents himself with his squirrel and his raccoon, his pigeon and his duck. Though with duck, admittedly – at least with respect to its cookery – he's a little on the sentimental side.

Ducks are treated with unassuming seriousness in the kitchen of Wyley McFadden. And he's not terribly happy with the way this one is going.

"This," he tells the girl, "is a disgraceful way to treat a duck."

"So I hear. When's it ready?"

McFadden is carefully browning the breasts, fussing and turning each so it sears but doesn't burn. The procedure would be much more elaborate if he were doing this at home, but here he's making due with an iron skillet, a bag of potatoes and a tin of mushroom soup. It's to be a one-dish dinner, and McFadden is embarrassed at its crudity.

He has laid in only frozen breasts – there is no room for the rest of the bird, and breasts are the best part anyway – all neatly packed in layers, like stacks of frozen hamburgers. They take up hardly any space in his tiny on-board freezer.

At first he is pleased at the wind's revival. He has his Coleman stove set up just beyond the tent, and a lantern hung for light. The girl has wondered why he bothers with the stove when she has laid out a perfectly good fire. But McFadden doesn't trust a naked flame. They are prone to fluctuation, cooling too fast and heating too quickly. Campfires are inappropriate to haute cuisine. He has decided that at some point in the future he will try to roast something for her on a bed of open coals – she seems to delight in the embers and the smoke – but not his duck.

Now that the breeze is up, it's blown away the bugs. He had moved his propane stove as close as possible to the fire, to take advantage of the smoke. It helped to keep the insects off, but there was also the possibility that a stray spark would reach the propane and blow them both to kingdom come. The breeze is a blessing.

McFadden is finished with the duck and transfers the pieces to a plate. The girl eyes the meat, but McFadden warns her off. Now he browns the potatoes. These will take a little longer. He would like to have parboiled them first, but so be it. While the potatoes are cooking, the weather picks up. This is precisely why he's cooking with a proper stove instead of on the fire: the wind's now licking flames all over the place, blowing the heat diagonally instead of permitting it to rise. It would have made a mess of his duck.

Once the potatoes are done, McFadden shifts them from the pan. He carries the hot skillet to the river, along with his spatula, and dips in some water. A little white wine would have been better, but he still has not made up his mind about the wisdom of this. The water hisses on the hot iron, and McFadden scrapes the bits of duck and burnt potatoes up into the liquid, working the blade back and forth across the bottom of the pan. The girl watches from the shadows, folded in her chair beside the fire. She seems to find it not at all remarkable to see him cooking at this hour.

With the pan back on the flame, turned low, McFadden opens the soup. He's had to make a separate trip back to the truck for the can opener and his halogen flashlight. The soup goes in, a little at a time, stirred until it thickens. McFadden shakes his head and clucks his tongue. This is no way to treat a duck. But it will taste just fine.

Now it's only a matter of stirring the potatoes and the meat back into the pan, adding the necessary seasonings and letting the whole thing simmer.

"How long?"

"Oh," he says, "an hour. Maybe a little less." He is surprised he's not more tired than he is.

"An hour!"

She is looking at the sky. McFadden can't help noticing an expression of discontent.

"Did you say you had another tarp?"

He has to think. There is a second tarp, folded up behind the driver's seat.

"Yes," he says, and when her eyebrows tell him she is expecting more, he tells her where to find it and passes her the flashlight. "Wait a minute." She has started up the hill, but pauses. "As long as you're going up, you might as well bring down a bottle. A Pinot Noir, I think, would do nicely."

"A what?"

"A wine," he says. "A red. It's in a crate just before the cages, left-hand side. You may have to pull a few bottles before you find it . . . oh . . . and the corkscrew should be in the cabinet above."

The girl has not moved. She looks up at the truck, looks back at McFadden, lifts a foot, puts it down again. It occurs to him suddenly that she might not like the thought of all those rats. They have that effect sometimes.

"You know what?" he says. He has gotten to his feet. "Why don't I go with you?"

Her look of uncertainty is touchingly endearing. As if McFadden needs endearment.

When they reach the truck, he hands the girl her tarpaulin and loads her with the wine, the corkscrew and a couple of glasses, which she accepts with an expression he cannot read. "I'll be down in just a minute," he says, and puts the light into her hand.

His rats have surprised him, how well they've taken to the road. All appear robust and healthy, in a condition as good as or better than when they left the city. Fresh air must be good for them, too. He's developed an undeniable affection for these ingenious rodents, something almost like pride in the way they have adapted. He sends a silent wish – not quite a prayer, but its agnostic cousin – for their chances once they get to where they're going. This is very much how his own ancestors made it to the New World, crushed into the steerage of a pitching ship. Though come to think of it, conditions here are more wholesome.

McFadden putters, changing litter, freshening water, distributing treats he knows he shouldn't be giving. Both cab and box have in-board lights so he can see. There's nothing here to require his attention. He switches off the lights and picks his way in darkness back down to the river.

He's been gone no more than ten or fifteen minutes, but in his absence the tent has been transformed again. There is an awning now, stretching out above the doorway, like the kind that shelter footmen at entrances to the better-class hotels. One corner extends just beyond the firepit; smoke rises and curls around the edge, backlit against the starker, whiter beacon of his kerosene lamp. McFadden's outdoor kitchen has acquired a roof.

"You'd get rained out, otherwise," she says. There is an oddly guilty tone, and a certain smacking of lips that leads him to believe she has been sampling his duck.

McFadden cranes his neck. Somehow, with all the cooking, he has failed to take into account these clouds, this purple spread of bruise enveloping the stars.

"Well, I'll be damned," he says.

– – –

The rain begins, and then it rains and rains, sheets of it – but they are dry beneath the awning. Even the fire is snug, and now the evening takes an oddly cozy turn.

The girl adored the duck, rhapsodized about it once she'd finished licking clean both plates and the cooking pot as well – though he's certain he could have fed her sawdust stewed in Bovril and she'd have eaten it. Her appetite is like nothing he has seen. He knows this to be the effect of some imposed starvation. McFadden believes it is important, now, that he try to learn the details. His plan is to ease toward it, gently. He believes that he can get her talking – that she herself would like to talk – but that the whole of it is bound in something so repugnant she is loath to start. Yet he's sure that if he can only get her going, she will open up.

And it is going well.

The rain drums against the awning and runs – sometimes gushes – off the nylon roof. The food was good, the fire warm, tucked just beneath the awning, where the water cannot reach. She has stacked a pile of fuel beside it so there isn't any danger of it running out. The girl relaxes in her lawn chair, feet propped against the woodpile. She still has on her sneakers, and those tennis socks with pompons. The nearer one, he sees, has snagged a burr.

When it rains hardest, water pours off the canopy so fast it falls in nearly solid sheets. The tent is behind them, the fire in front, and these undulating curtains shutting out the rest. The effect is of enclosure, of walling out what lies beyond.

McFadden has decided it's time for the burgundy. There's nothing available for decanting, of course. And he should have set the bottle aside a little while to give the grape a chance to breathe. But he is feeling thirsty. In his mind the atmosphere has called for drink. No need to stand on ceremony.

Events of yesterday should have warned him, but McFadden has thought this over and decided there were too many factors involved to attribute her illness to alcohol alone. He also believes the advantages in this case might well outweigh the risks. Besides, people's weaknesses should not prevent others from enjoying theirs.

He pours, just a little in the bottom of her glass – not to offer would be rude – and hands it over. She accepts. He pours himself an equal measure and places the bottle carefully on the ground where she can reach it or not, according to her wish. The rain rains, the fire crackles. Otherwise . . . silence.

McFadden breathes, and sips his wine.

A little time passes and the girl now has the bottle in her hands, asking without speaking if he would like some more. He thanks her, holding out his glass.

"You're welcome," she says.

They talk of little things. How long the rain might last. How nice the bugs are gone. McFadden wonders where they go when the weather turns like this. She frowns, then says she doesn't know; maybe in behind some bark, or hiding out in all the leaves. McFadden confesses how impressed he is with her construction, how well it keeps out the rain. She shrugs. Nothing, really.

And so it goes. He hopes that if he drops enough allusions to her camping skills she will tell him where she learned them, and this will be a place to start. But somehow this does not happen. There is no reticence – nothing in her words to show conceal-ment. It's simply that the conversation remains at the level it began, and goes no deeper.

But she is drinking. Not in gulps, not in any way deliberately, but steadily, a mouthful at a time. She has filled her glass, then filled it up again. In a little while he sees the wine is finished.

McFadden still has half a glass and nurses it, uncertain what to say. He places some wood on the fire and pokes the charcoal with a stick. The rain drums on. He says something about leaving the dishes till morning and she nods. Maybe it won't be raining then, he says. He's wondering how to put this night behind them when she speaks.

"What's your sign mean?"

"My sign?"

"Your *sign*," she says. "The one you got at that restaurant." She is shaking her head with something he's not quite sure is amuse-ment. "The one you went to all that trouble sticking on."

"Oh," he says. "That sign." He'd forgotten. The reminder cheers him. "Paradox," he tells her, smiling. "It says *Paradox*."

"I know that. I can read *that*. I was there, remember. But what does it mean?"

"Oh." McFadden has to think. "It's not an easy word. It's a little bit hard to explain." He has to take a drink to jog his thinking. "It means," he says, "when things are opposite but true."

It's always been McFadden's favourite word, but he isn't ready to do it justice. He tries to think of some examples, but for some reason nothing comes.

He's still gazing in his wineglass, wondering why his brain has left him in the lurch like this, when she stands and smoothes her hair. He looks up, but she is studying the rain. Then she turns and lays her hand against his neck.

"Let's go to bed," she says.

This has of course been with him since they parked the truck, but he has kept it in the background. He has kept that part of it at bay. For a moment McFadden's mind is blank, then he masters it, smiles – at least he thinks he smiles – and tells her he's just going to finish up his wine.

The girl stares, then disappears into the tent.

McFadden finishes his wine.

Then he rinses his glass in the water running off the roof. He does the same with the rest of the dishes, and fills up the cooking pan to soak it overnight. He banks the fire, scraping ashes overtop in hopes the coals will still be going in the morning. He moves things away from the edges of the awning.

When all is covered up and stowed securely, McFadden takes off his clothes and puts on his pyjama bottoms. He rolls up his pants and his shirt and his underwear, and stuffs them into the end of the bag he keeps for whatever needs washing. Then he gets out a few fresh things for tomorrow and places them by the doorway, where they will be handy in the morning. He finds his toothbrush and brushes his teeth, leaning into the water and splashing his shoulders and chest. The towel the girl used earlier has been hanging by the fire. He rubs himself dry. He takes off his wristwatch and lays it on top of his trousers. It's coming up to midnight. He uses his pocket flash to light his way into the tent.

The girl is asleep.

McFadden crawls in on hands and knees. It's hard getting through without bouncing the mattress. He has to turn to do up the mosquito net and zip the door shut all the way around. He can't help jostling a little. The girl stirs but does not wake. Her breathing is profoundly rhythmic; this is no pretended sleep. She is nearly dead centre on the mattress, but it is big enough that there is still some room for him. Unzipped, the sleeping bag is more like a duvet. Crawling in beside her, McFadden cannot help but see that she is naked. But this he was expecting. After all, she was expecting him.

It was cold outside, washing himself in the rainwater. But now it's warm beneath the cover. It's been a long day; a long, long drive without much sleep. He lets the muscles of his neck relax. He is aware of the naked girl beside him, but this awareness lacks its former urgency. He feels a yawn and lets it come. McFadden folds his hands across his chest and allows his eyes to close as slowly as they want. The breath goes into him and out. People never know they are asleep until the sleep is over.

– – –

But now the sleep is over. Oh yes, McFadden is awake, every bit of him, and cursing whatever might have done it. A falling tree? A blast of thunder? There was thunder, earlier. But now the rain has stopped and the thunder with it. He listens to the random dripping, the rhythmless tapping on the tarpaulin stretched above them. So it must have been the girl. Of course it was the girl.

What was it they used to call this? *Blueballs.*

He has always identified the term with the back seats of those large and now extinct automobiles, and those girls – those girls who should have been statistical anomalies but who seemed to find him every time – those girls who'd go for anything at all so long as it was done to them and not to him. He remembers definite orgasms – theirs, of course. Panties down, fingers flicking;

blouses open, bras unhooked; gasping mouths and heaving hips – the whole extravaganza just so long as *his* zipper stayed securely closed. A strange take on morality, in retrospect, but re-productively prudent, he supposes. And to be fair, he was always willing; it was always him who brought them to it. He can still remember that feeling, though, like any second his pants would burst for sure.

Blueballs. Strange to be experiencing it again at this phase of life.

The girl is sleeping. In her sleep she seeks him out. Evidently she's attracted to his warmth. He moves away and she follows, like some heat-seeking missile. A snoring Exocet. Though the sounds she makes, when she makes them, are something quite apart from snoring.

He's run out of room. He is completely off the mattress; not only off the mattress now but driven up against the wall. His face is mashed against the nylon. There is nowhere left to go. Her hand is palm down on his chest, with her cheek against his throat. This itself is not so bad, except that strands of hair keep creeping up into his nostril. What's worse is how he's pinioned at the hips.

She has thrown a knee across and trapped him. There is nowhere he can go and so it waves there, only inches – some-times less than inches – from that central part of her which he will swear is several degrees warmer than the rest. He is certain that the back of his hand is much warmer than the front, though he daren't move in any sort of test.

McFadden lifts his head and cranes his neck. He still can't see. Her head prevents him and it's too dark anyway, but even if it weren't, he knows what he would see: a broad expanse of empty mattress. An uninhabited continent; an empty sea. He yearns for this space like Franklin must have yearned for open water. *That's it! Think of ice! Think of cold. Think of being locked in ice, encased in cold cold ice and howling snow on every side.* McFadden concentrates for several minutes, but it doesn't work. Already in his mind the ice is melting and washing down his thigh.

He has to sleep.

The girl sighs and moves some more, and McFadden twists a little from the waist. He is very grateful for the spruce boughs. This would be worse with a tree stump in the middle of his back, but they have cushioned him against the ground. It's actually almost as soft as the air mattress. He thinks he would probably be comfortable if he wasn't folded up like this.

Also he suspects that it has kept them dry. It's rained for hours and there is not a drop of moisture in the tent except whatever may have percolated out of him. He wouldn't swear to it, but he's fairly sure he's heard the sound of water trickling below them. This was when he was sleeping, or maybe just about to sleep, so he can't be sure. But he suspects that the combination of ground-sheet above and that layer of evergreens below has let the water flow right underneath the tent, never touching them.

Clever girl. He wonders how she knew.

He can smell her. Not perfume or musk – she has none to wear – or for that matter even soap. This is unadulterated woman, this smell, distinct from any other. McFadden tries to think of it in terms of simple chemistry: pheromones, blind receptors. Strictly clinical.

Whatever it is, it's painful. There is a breast in direct contact with his rib. At least it would be, except for his pyjama top. Thank God for pyjamas, even if the bottom half has let him down. He can definitely feel a nipple, though. In his mind it feels as taut as his.

It's true that all he really has to do is move. Push her back a little, shift himself to match, shuck off these pyjamas and there you have it. Bob's your uncle. It isn't like she's not expecting it. Probably wonders what has taken him so long.

McFadden moves his hand. He lifts. Her legs part softly on their own, slipping up and out in want of invitation only. She makes another of those strangely glottal sounds, the rhythm of her breathing changed already. A little more pressure, a little gentle push, and he has her on her back. There is room now to lift. Her breathing has quickened; McFadden can feel the rise and fall of ribs and belly. There is space to manoeuvre. He readjusts the sleeping bag, bunching it off to one side, and now he is astride, kneeling overtop of her, filling up the place between her legs. He allows himself to linger just a moment – and then one more mighty push and he's away. Safely over on the other side.

She's still asleep. He's fairly sure she's still asleep, although her breathing has clearly altered. So has his. Jesus, so has his.

McFadden tugs the sleeping bag so she's covered up again. It takes him several minutes in the darkness, fumbling to find the ties and zippers that have sealed the nylon flap. Eventually he gets it open and crawls out, headfirst, into the night. A man whose grasp does not exceed his reach.

It's much cooler, much wetter outside. But the rain has stopped, the stars are out. He fills his lungs and exhales hard; it isn't cold enough to see his breath. Too bad.

McFadden drags the lawn chair back toward the fire and tries to get it going. He fans it with the frying pan, wafting ash into his face. It doesn't catch, though he can see some living embers glowing underneath. He finds his stick and stirs them, feeds them twigs and bits of birchbark. He gets down on his hands and blows. This is hard work, even for a smoker now twenty years reformed, but in time he is rewarded with a tiny lick of flame, and this he stokes until it's grown into a fullfledged blaze, spitting sparks around the cuffs of his pyjamas.

Now what?

The bugs are starting to find him. It is bug-free inside the tent, but he doesn't want to go there. Thinking makes it worse. McFadden scratches his belly and settles into the lawn chair, listening to the fire and the chatter of the river down below.

He pictures the girl wading out, water dripping from her hips, sunlight captured in the droplets. He is unaware, of course, but the image has bloomed already as an icon of his private eucharist – a moment caught and nevermore surrendered, wading out of memory now and then until the day he dies.

At present, though, it puts him in mind to take a dip himself. Maybe that will help. McFadden takes off his pyjamas and picks his way down toward the water. There is starlight enough to show him where to put his feet. The river is high, much higher than this afternoon. He sees the girl was right: if they had built their camp down here, they'd be awash by now. She certainly has her practical side.

It's cold, but not enough to chase him back to shore. He steps his way in deeper, careful not to let the current push him over. He can feel the water mounding up around his calves. By the time he's in up to his thighs, he has to lean against the stream or risk his balance. There's a lot more water than there was this afternoon. He's deciding it may be wiser to postpone this swim, when something gives beneath his foot. McFadden's legs shoot out from under him, and in a moment he is spinning with the other flotsam, heading fast downstream.

At first he's merely cursing, furious with the idiocy of this. But by the time he's sorted up from down, it's clear he's in some danger. He can't stop. He tries to find the bottom but only ends up spun around again. The first rock hits him hard along the ribs. He sucks in water and, gasping, hits another. He's more ready for the third, but he's completely lost his equilibrium. For a while he has no notion where the surface is. By the time his head breaks free, he is in a bad way for want of oxygen. But his chin stays up, and now the focus is simply on keeping it there.

There are no rocks in this stretch, or if there are he misses them, so he has a chance to get himself positioned in the current, riding along feet first with his arms stretched out like sweeps. His nose is out of the water. He has a growing fear of driving up against something, being split in two. He tries to squeeze his legs together, so his feet will take the impact, but this makes navigation much more difficult, and he's forced to concentrate on just keeping the water out of his lungs. He wonders about waterfalls.

McFadden bobs along for quite some time. His thoughts are scattered: his rats; the girl in the river – this river? He catches glimpses of many stars above. There's Ursa Major. So that must be the North Star. Does that mean he's heading north or south?

Something bumps against his arm, but he can't grab hold. Then something else. This time his feet have brushed the bottom, and he tries to use his heels to brake but ends up spinning sideways. Now his hands are touching bottom. He digs his fingers hard, but nothing holds. He is moving slower, though, groping with hands and feet for anything to drag against. He is definitely going slower. The water is less deep. There's a floor beneath him suddenly, and he thrusts with everything he has – and stops. But the pressure pushing from behind is still enormous. Every time he moves, he slips. It takes discipline, teaching himself to breathe in little snatches, minimizing his resistance. The current wants to push him onward, but he's making headway. He finds a rock and braces, and now he knows he's going to be all right.

There is a moment of the utmost terror when he tries to stand, slips, and falls flailing back into the river. But this time the current moves him into shallower water, his hands and knees solidly on the bottom.

A shaking McFadden crawls out onto a pan of gravel less than a kilometre from where he started, though he is certain he has travelled miles. He sits with bits of stone dimpling his naked buttocks – glad to be alive, and alive enough to curse himself with passion. He has no idea where he is. It takes a while even to determine which bank he's on, but eventually he works out that he's landed on the right one. Thank God, at least he doesn't have to try to cross the river. He is bruised severely; here and there he's lost a flap of skin. But no cracked or broken bones, as far as he can tell.

It is a long walk, though, longer still not knowing how far he has to go.

By the time McFadden makes it back to camp, he is registering signs of hypothermia. The fire has burnt down low and he very nearly walks right by it. He was certain it was farther. The vision of himself stumbling downstream, barefoot, naked – with the camp getting farther and farther behind – brings on even fiercer chills. He can barely feel the wood he's piling on the fire. Everything from the shoulders down is numb.

He knows he's been severely eaten by mosquitoes, but he doesn't feel it. Only his feet. He pulls the lawn chair up so close he has to back it off again when his nose tells him the hairs on his legs are starting to singe. There's just enough light to see. His feet don't look as bad as they feel. There are lacerations – a deep one in the middle of his left instep – but nothing too ugly. He walked in shallow water where he could, to spare them. Splashing along, ankle deep, the current was much less formidable than its full force in the middle of the stream.

All in all, this could have been worse.

But he is still shaking with cold. He should get some disinfectant on his feet, he knows, but the thought of walking up to the truck is just too much. They'll do until tomorrow.

By now the fire has taken off the worst of the chill. The injured parts of him are starting to sting. His feet hurt worse hobbling the few steps to the tent than they did the whole way back. He is perfectly aware that this is psychological. But still they hurt.

Getting the tent flap undone is an effort. His fingers are slow and clumsy – even more so doing it up again in the dark from the other side. Bending over and crawling like this hurts in more places than he can really think about. But the pain is distant; he's so cold and tired, he hardly feels it. The sleeping bag is like a warm, soft sea.

The scream's so sudden it blasts away his sense of balance.

"Get away! Get away get away get away!"

It has shot him completely off the mattress. He winds up tangled in the sleeping bag, somewhere off against the far side of the tent.

She's still screaming. *"Get away from me! Get away. I won't! I won't! I won't . . . I won't . . . I wonnn't!"*

He can't see, but he feels the mattress rocking. A gasping, ragged breathing fills the tent – though it could be his own he's hearing. It takes him several seconds to find his voice and control his heartbeat.

McFadden eases himself away from the wall. "It's all right," he says, then tries again because no sound has come out. "Nothing's going to hurt you."

"Who's that!"

"Shhh. It's only me. You were dreaming."

"Who's that?"

"It's all right," he says. "It's all right. You had a dream. No one's going to hurt you." He is gingerly attempting to lever himself right side up.

"Ohhh . . . oh."

He's not certain yet if she's awake. "Can you hear me? It was only a dream. Everything's OK."

Silence.

She seems to be breathing slower. He has his own lungs more or less in order. Christ.

"Try to take a breath," he says. "Don't be afraid, it's just me moving. I woke you up, I'm sorry. Look. It's only me getting back onto the mattress."

"Oh," she says. "Sorry. I'm sorry. That was . . . oh."

"Shhh. Shhh. Go back to sleep. It was only a dream."

He is terribly cold. Terribly cold. He has to get himself back beneath the blanket. He's just not in a frame of mind to deal with this right now.

He hears her exhale, long and ragged. "Yes," she says. "OK."

He is now under the sleeping bag, hugging himself.

"I'm sorry."

"Go to sleep."

He feels the mattress shifting as she settles. He has tucked his legs up as far as they will go, hugging the bedding beneath his chin. His back is to her. A little spasm takes him as the warmth begins to penetrate.

"You're shivering."

McFadden curls a little tighter.

"Your teeth are chattering." The mattress undulates beneath him. He feels her closer. "You're *freezing*!"

Her hand touches a spot on his arm where some skin has torn away. He flinches.

His reaction in turn has startled her and sent her scuttling back over to the far side of the tent. This would almost be funny if he could only get warm.

"Sorry about that . . . I mean, it's all right. Don't worry, I had a little accident."

"What kind of accident?"

"I fell into the river."

"What?"

"I went in for a swim and the current was too strong and I got swept down the river. It was . . . oh, I don't know. A long way." This is as much as he intends to say. Chattering teeth make syntax an effort.

She has crept beside him again. "Why were you swimming?" The tone strangely reminds him of his mother, though the similarity holds no fascination at this time.

"I don't know." He doesn't care about elucidations either.

But the girl is not demanding explanation. She has wrapped herself around him, so gently that he hardly feels her – an arm across his shoulder, a leg around his waist. He trembles and she trembles with him. McFadden dimly recognizes what this should be doing to him. But he has no appetite for irony, at present. It's warm.

He feels her breath behind his neck. He has stopped shaking.

"Go to sleep," she says.

Is it his imagination or is he being rocked?

"Go to sleep."

But McFadden already is.

4

Surprisingly, overland transportation of rats has not been a major problem, with no more than eight infestations reported in any one year. Most infestations within the interior of Alberta consist of a single rat transported by truck . . .

MICHAEL J. DORRANCE
A HISTORY OF RAT CONTROL IN ALBERTA
PRINT MEDIA BRANCH,
ALBERTA AGRICULTURE
1984

He wakes inside a womb.

It takes a little time, of course, to arrive at this analogy. At first he's not alert enough for anything so esoteric. He is conscious only of redness, of heat, and thick, thick moisture. He is very hot, he is very damp. Wet, in fact. But oddest is this colour, this strange, translucent, glowing pink – like looking out from inside something live. He blinks, but the redness doesn't go away. He moves his head, but it won't move with it. He is slick with sweat. When he lifts his arm, the mattress shifts and partly drains a puddle that has collected in the trough beneath his chin.

His shoulder hurts, and this begins to bring him back into the present.

It occurs to him in time that what he's feeling is condensation. The rubber coating of the mattress has gathered it in tepid lakes. It's like a steam bath in here.

This light is just too strange. But he's awake enough now to make connections: it's the sun shining through the orange tarp, then filtering a second time through the carmine ceiling of the tent. The effect is very strange. Corpuscular, like he's stuck inside a giant blood cell.

It must be body temperature in here. There's a squelchy sound whenever he tries to lift his leg. A drop of sweat trickles down into his eye. So this is what it's like to live inside an artery; there should be giant ventricles pumping somewhere in the distance.

He is not enjoying this. It reminds him of lava lamps and all that psychedelia people played with in the seventies. He thinks he would like to get out from inside this tent now, but he hasn't quite worked up the nerve to do it because he's been discovering how many parts of him hurt.

He can't believe the change in temperature. There's a spot on the ceiling that looks oranger than the rest; it makes his eyes sting if he stares too long. So this must be the sun. He wonders what time it is, but he isn't wearing his watch.

He sticks a leg up – which hurts not only the leg but several other parts as well – and examines the damage. A bit of bruising, a glistening lesion or two, but really not all that bad. If it hurts this much, it should look worse.

"Oww," he says aloud, and feels better for it.

The door flips back.

"So, you're still alive."

It is not a modest pose he's striking. He tucks up his leg and clutches at the sleeping bag.

"Too late, I checked you out this morning. What were you doing last night – dancing with bears?"

"I fell in the river."

"So you said."

"I did?" He doesn't remember.

"How can a little river like that do all this damage?" She is lifting up the sleeping bag, probing underneath.

He pulls it back and winces. "It was flooding."

"Flooding? It can't be more than three feet deep. Though I

admit it *is* above the spot you wanted us to put the tent." She seems to be in awfully high spirits for having almost found him dead and missing.

"Hold on a sec." Before he can say anything, she's disappeared.

But she's back in a minute, pushing his first aid kit through the door ahead of her. "First things first."

He still has not quite come to terms with this morning, and before he's really had a chance to take stock, she has flipped away the sleeping bag and is daubing antiseptic on a raw spot by his knee. It stings. He jumps.

"Baby."

This is ridiculous, but now he is actually biting his tongue in a determined effort not to yelp.

"Oh, by the way, I fed your rats."

"Christ!" he says. "The rats!" McFadden struggles with the sleeping bag.

"Don't worry. I fed them. They're fine. Some of them are actually kind of cute. As long as you don't get your fingers too close."

"Jesus, this heat will be killing them!"

"It's only hot in here, under all this plastic." She has hooked his elbow out from under him and bounced him back onto the mattress. "Outside it's fine."

"What did you feed them?" He is groping for his pants, but they are nowhere to be found.

"Squabs," she says, and giggles. "What do you think I fed them? The same little pellets I saw you giving them yesterday, two scoops per cage in each little dish . . . Someday, you know, you'll have to honestly tell me what you're doing with them."

McFadden has no recollection of her watching him feed the rats, but these are the correct proportions. He settles back into the mattress. "Water too?"

"Of course water too."

He contemplates the brighter patch of orange on the ceiling. "What time is it?"

She flicks her head to brush the hair back from her face and glances up at the patch of ceiling he's been looking at. "About three, I'd say."

"*What . . . p.m.*? It can't be."

"Turn over."

"Why?"

"Turn over."

McFadden turns over. He feels his buttocks clenching as she does a spot near the outside of his thigh.

"Ooh." She must be referring to a particularly nasty cut. "Turn back over."

McFadden does as he is told.

She is humming to herself, examining her handiwork. She seems to be paying particular attention to a spot below his pelvis, dabbing coyly with a fluffy piece of linen.

"So . . ." she says, in a voice that would have warned him if he wasn't warned already, " . . . what exactly was it that made you want a swim last night?"

"What are you doing?"

"I was just wondering . . . um . . . what got you, you know, *up* like that? I mean, why you couldn't sleep?"

"*Get out of here!*" he roars, dragging the sleeping bag back over.

"Fine." She's scooping up the cotton balls, backing out the exit. "I think I'll take a little dip myself." The door flap closes and she zips him in.

Evidently his injuries have not been entirely debilitating.

– – –

McFadden was far and away the best skinner in his class. Not merely skinning, of course, but fleshing and boarding as well. This at least was some consolation; all those years at med school had to translate somehow. His specialty was never the scalpel-wielding end of things, but still, he has good hands.

They began with muskrat. The instructor brought in a bag-
ful, one for each student, which he'd stored up in his freezer.
McFadden finished his before anyone else at his table, and was
clearly reckoned to have done the neatest job. Muskrats were
not among the species he would likely be pursuing once he
started full-time trapping. There wasn't much of a muskrat population in Metro, and they're only worth a dollar or two anyway,
even in a good year. But they were satisfying practice.

The real test was raccoons, and here again McFadden shone. A
properly pelted raccoon represents no small effort. First there's
the skinning itself, which isn't all that difficult so long as the
blade doesn't nick the gut. Then comes the laborious business of
scraping the fat (particularly thick with downtown individuals, as
McFadden was to learn to his profit). This is the hardest part.
Extreme care must be taken to remove all lipids, which might
otherwise mould and hinder drying, while at the same time not
to scrape too deeply and disturb the leather. All this must be
accomplished without loosening the delicate guard hairs. Nor
must the scraped-off fat be allowed to grease the fur. Failure in
any of these results in downgrading of the pelt, with accompa-
nying diminishment in value – a significant loss with pelts
worth so little in the first place.

McFadden completed his first raccoon in expert fashion,
though the whole process was surprisingly time-consuming,
and depressing in the knowledge that even an XXL, number one,
dark silver prime, wouldn't fetch more than forty dollars, the
market being what it was.

There was simply no escaping the fact that McFadden had
chosen to enter the Canadian fur trade in the period of its sorri-
est decline. Fur belonged to fashion; and fashion, in these recent
years, had turned its back. There were pockets here and there
around the world that kept the trade alive, and scattered individuals aloof to the collective. But the sequinned moguls of
haute couture had some time ago decreed that, while it was acceptable and elegant to sport the skin of an animal with the hair

removed (particularly if it was dyed a shiny black to set against the matching boots), it was manifestly not acceptable to wear it with the fur intact. Leather was in and fur was out, and an immensity of difference was reckoned between the two. A Danier suede still earned the world's caress, but to appear in public wearing mink was to invite the worst.

In those days the anti-fur crusade was at its peak, international trade sanctions very much in place. Gory promotions kept passions over the Atlantic coast seal hunt high, though the hunt itself was largely dead. Friends of Bambi still lurked in stairwells from Vienna to Bombay, eager for their chance to scrawl morality on the backs of passersby with cans of blood red paint. McFadden himself encountered such a one in the cultural heart of his very home.

It was a performance of *Madame Butterfly* – was it *Madame Butterfly* or that disappointing *Carmen*? In any case, the opera was finished and he was making his way back to his truck in a lot a few streets over from the O'Keefe. It was now habit with him to park in distant corners whenever possible – an acquired caution. An older couple were a few steps ahead. McFadden was loosening his tie and fishing for his keys when an explosion of breath stopped him dead in his tracks. A figure had sprung from the shadows and, as God is his witness, was blasting the woman with a spray of aerosol paint. It took a moment to make himself believe what he was seeing. This, after all, was Toronto.

The human mind is an instrument of strange efficiency, processing random thoughts in astonishing sequence. McFadden's own response took place over tiers. In the upper level his reply was academic, perhaps even scientific. As a physician he feared for the woman's heart; she had recoiled into her husband, who in turn was sprawled across the hood of someone's BMW, the woman thrashing on the pavement, shielding her face with her hands while her attacker aimed and fired from above.

At a second level his reaction was something closer to political: he had recognized the statement being made, and had identified it as belonging to the camp of his opponents.

But at its deepest and most elemental stratum, his reflex was transcendentally testicular.

Even so, things might have been different.

McFadden has often placated a skeptical conscience with assurances that, if only the attacker had retreated in some other direction, all might have been otherwise. But the attacker did not. With a final sweep along the woman's coat he lowered his arsenal, lifted his heel and sprang straight into McFadden's chest. Wyley McFadden is not a narrow-chested man. The spray-painter was taller and younger – quite a bit younger – but McFadden is not so easily unbalanced, and his hands are the hands of his forebears. One of them found itself wrapped around the throat of this lunatic. The other, somehow, got hold of the spray paint.

Over many solitary hours since, he has analyzed his feelings about the events as they occurred. McFadden is not ashamed of what he did – at least so he tells himself – but he is not proud either. Or is he? This niggles both his conscience and the colder part of thought he likes to think can operate above emotion. Would he do the same again? He truly doesn't know, but then again, why should he? Whatever else, he would surely have preferred the whole thing never to have happened. It was a night of many casualties: he ruined a new and quite expensive overcoat. He had to throw away his season's tickets with five productions still to go; and he took away a young man's eyesight.

At least he thinks he did. It is by no means certain that actual blindness resulted, or if it did, that it was irreversible. McFadden believes it is possible – he is no ophthalmologist, mind – but he cherishes the hope that, with prompt attention (and after all, they were only blocks from St. Mike's), at least partial vision might have been restored. Though aerosol paints are known to be extremely toxic, and the force of their spray from such a distance is likely quite destructive to ocular tissue. He did not let go until the can was empty.

The incident was never mentioned in the news. He combed the papers and hovered near his radio for days, but there was nothing. Perhaps all parties were too traumatized to file complaints. For his part, McFadden had simply dropped the boy and walked away.

The next day he came back at rush hour in a wide-brimmed hat and retrieved his truck. For many months afterwards he avoided the whole theatre district. A man in his position can't risk brushes with the law. As to the final outcome, he simply doesn't know. McFadden prefers not to think about it, though of course he does. How wrong was he? How right was he? He has never honestly made up his mind. Justice is a funny thing.

Be that as it may, it was a terrible time to go into trapping. The industry answered public pressure with still stricter controls. Licensing was further tightened. By the time McFadden entered the profession, every pelt required stamping by a government inspector before it could legally be sold. Meanwhile, prices continued to decline. As an urban (thus, illegal) trapper, McFadden was effectively cut off from his market, even if its bottom had dropped out some time ago.

Yet instinct kept him optimistic, something teasing at the corners of his mind. McFadden never lost the feeling that there had to be a way around this – an angle, somewhere, he hadn't yet turned. Though inspiration took its time in coming. It was quite a stretch before The Big Idea struck, one of those first fine days in spring just a week or two before winter admits the season's lost, the sparrows beginning to nest, the pigeons at their loudest, and McFadden, gazing through the plate glass window of his favourite noodle shop on Spadina just a little up from Queen, finally putting two and two together.

He'd just spent the morning out on the islands, poking here and there on foot, inspecting the quieter backwaters as potential trap sites. In the end he'd had to conclude that the logistics of transporting everything by ferry would overcome any benefits, unless he bought himself a boat – which so far was not at all an economic proposition.

Still, it was a pleasant morning. There are bits and pieces of Old Toronto still lurking on the islands, mossy hints of former days. McFadden allows himself a visit or two each year in early spring, always on a weekday to avoid the mobs. Too bad it couldn't work that way with ducks. He wonders if anyone has ever done a head count of the ducks on the Toronto Islands. There have to be thousands. Wherever he went, the ducks were there before him, assailing him for handouts, muddying his shoes. It always seemed he left a little sooner than expected, mostly on account of the ducks.

He caught the ferry back to the dock at the foot of Yonge Street and strolled north to Queen, with Chinatown in mind for lunch. McFadden has always been in love with Chinatown. His own great-grandfather ran a trapline up what is now Spadina back when it was still a cutpath, and probably poached it at that. It pleases him to think the same geography now plays such a vital role in the interests of yet another trapping McFadden. *Plus ça change, plus c'est la même chose*. Though his progenitor could scarcely have imagined the transformation from harvest place to market.

Most days he'll start his walk at University, where Queen starts getting interesting, heading west – browsing the bookstores, watching women stomping by in miniskirts and steel-toed boots designed to repel the bites of rattlesnakes. On Queen Street this is not implausible. When he reaches Spadina he'll head north, into the upper reaches of what they call the Fashion District, which to him is mostly banks of warehouses with cutrate stores at street level. He always tells himself he should actually go inside one and see what's there, but he never does. The whole point of this stretch is that it's out of doors. Up the street is Chinatown, and a different air.

McFadden adores the feeling of solitude amongst the throng. The street here is so busy, so bustling and packed – and yet as he moves along with the crowd, his impression of aloneness is never more intense. He is joined and yet disjoined. It's a very oriental frame of mind, as far as he's concerned, and he approves of it. He feels invisible in Chinatown, yet also wholly indivisible – a single cell within its private wall of plasma, yet linked with all the others in their complex multicellular collective. This is the substance of an organism and, for him, the substance of a city. Chinatown is city living at its best. What's more, he loves the food.

This street has always been his antidote to disinfectant. He used to come down here on weekends just to cleanse his palate. The foetor, the ferment; the yeasty, reasty opulence; the must and fust and frowziness – these compound smells of Chinatown have always acted as a catalyst upon his sleeping salivary. A place of germination even in the dormancy of winter. In his days as a clinician he never got here often enough. Now he stalks the place at will.

At one time or another he has sampled the menu of probably every food purveyor in the district. As Toronto's population grows, so too does its bill of fare. If there's ever been a better argument for immigration, McFadden has yet to taste it. Still, he has his favourites.

One of the things he adores about the Chinese is their tradition of displaying food for inspection by the eye before consignment to the belly. He likes this too about those Greek rotisseries along the Danforth. Far too much cuisine is done up out of sight.

He was standing at the window, examining the duck. Although McFadden seldom orders the barbecued duck, their hanging presence there at storefront – the crinkled orange skin, the beads of salty oil – never fails to jangle his taste buds. The sun must have been hidden, for there was no reflection on the glass.

Absentmindedly he scratched at the beginnings of his beard, studying the duck. Perhaps a door inside was closed, perhaps opened; perhaps a patron came or went. In any case a draft must have been created, building from the back of the establishment, moving up toward the front, rushing for the door. On its way it sidled by the duck and gave a gentle nudge; only just a hint of motion, the tiniest rotation along the axis of its two webbed feet. As the duck's head turned, McFadden caught a glint in its eye – or that was what it felt like at the time. Of course it probably was just a vesicle of grease, a tiny prism of oil refracting the sunlight, which just at that moment must have chosen to come out. But it was enough to spark the dawn of recognition. A gleam passed from the eye of the duck to the eye of the man. But that gleam was all that was needed. The corner was turned.

Within a month McFadden had more orders than there was time in the day to fill.

– – –

He's decided to stop in Dryden. The girl doesn't know this – McFadden hasn't told her – but it is clear to him she's due for shopping. He has been trying these last several miles to come up with a delicate way of suggesting as much. There must be things she needs, as a woman – feminine hygiene products, for instance; she's been wearing the same socks three days now at least. He should really have thought of this yesterday. It has also occurred to him to wonder how the women of his former life would have survived this long without so much as a hairbrush. His ex-wife, cut off from her makeup table, would certainly have lost her sanity and died.

The problem, though, with respect to these matters is that McFadden is completely in the dark. As a former specialist in female reproduction it would be fair to say he knows more about the *insides* of women than most women do themselves; but he has never been much of a hand at the outside, cosmetic side of things. What he does know is that this stuff is expensive. His wife was forever railing about the Great Insult: how diabolic that women's ware always costs so much more than men's – a sure conspiracy. He pointed out that markets reflect only whatever prices buyers are willing to pay, and that if there was conspiracy among Italian fashion designers, it was unlikely to get much beyond their plastic surgeons. But of course his arguments never carried any weight.

Be that as it may, he has absorbed a strong conviction that the things women need don't come cheap, though in terms of actual dollars he hasn't a clue. Harder still is deciding how to launch the topic.

He steals a glance at the speedometer. The girl has a tendency to drive too fast if he doesn't keep an eye out. He's had to remind her twice already that she's been speeding, and both times draw her attention to how unwise it would be – bearing in mind the nature of their cargo and the evident fact that she is not in possession of a driver's licence – how downright stupid it would be to get stopped for something so pointless as speeding. She has agreed, absolutely. Nevertheless, the speedometer keeps creeping up.

She catches him looking and points to the dash. The needle is poised exactly on eighty.

"Congratulations," McFadden sighs, and settles his foot back against the gearboot.

"How is it?"

"Better, I think." Though he's not really sure if it is.

His foot is why the girl is driving. He is a bit worried about this foot. Not really worried – concerned, a little, about infection. Also about how much the damned thing hurts. He'd got it nicely disinfected – at least he thought he had – and sutured closed and neatly wrapped in bandage, but it has started swelling. McFadden now thinks that with the extra bulk of the bandages his boot simply got too tight. In retrospect, he should have stayed off it altogether. But he won't admit this to the girl.

He had insisted on doing his share of breaking camp, lugging things up to the truck, overriding her objections. It ended in a sort of compromise – she did at least two trips to his one – but he came away with a credible show of having done his best. He is, by nature, unable to do otherwise, or so he tells himself. McFadden remains a member of that generation that believes it is the business of men to discipline their hurt, to contain it as best they can unto themselves alone. He is skeptical about the entire concept of equality, even in mathematical terms, but certainly in its application to human beings. It is clear to him that women suffer pains of which men, by the nature of their physiology, remain ignorant. It is quite enough, as he sees it, for them to bear their own without having to shoulder men's complaints as well. Thus it is the obligation of every man to do his suffering in silence. To McFadden this has the nature of an eternal law, like gravity. More importantly, he knows that women know it.

There are two commandments McFadden believes should be branded backwards on the forehead of every man so he can read them in the mirror while brushing his teeth: One, *Never strike a woman*. Two, *Never let a woman hear you whine*. Both are cardinal. Though in his years of practice he has seen the first much more readily forgiven than the second.

At the same time a more cynical part of him knows he gained something, in the girl's estimation, while she watched him sewing up his foot. It was not as tricky as it looked, though in plain truth it hurt like hell. But he was cavalier enough about it at the time. McFadden is proud of himself on his own account; that the girl was present he counts only as a bonus.

He watches her driving. This is the first time he has been in the truck's passenger seat; the experience is distinctly odd. His back is against the door (which he has twice checked to be sure it is locked). His foot is propped against the gearshift. Two hands on the steering wheel, she's intent upon the road ahead. She knows, too, that she is being watched. It strikes him that the most intriguing aspect of this whole theatre is that – dramatics aside – it was all above-board and necessary.

He was cut. It was neither prudent nor possible to go to a hospital. He needed stitches. Left ankle firmly held across right thigh; toes pulled back with one hand, forceps manipulated with the other. Eleven sutures neatly thrown while the girl sat perched in her lawn chair, watching. Never a word – not a sound throughout – watching his hands and watching his foot. Watching his face. Every silver lining has to have a cloud around it somewhere.

"It's still swollen, isn't it?"

"Not too bad, really," he says. "It's fine."

He's had to back off a little in the bravado department. By the time they'd finished packing and seen to the rats and fired up the truck, his foot was truly throbbing. He has to admit it was affecting his driving. If you're going to be at the wheel of this kind of vehicle, you really should be prepared to use the gears. It hurt every time he touched the clutch, so he avoided shifting. Whenever he had to change, he found himself delicately depressing the pedal with the side of his toe. He is now willing to admit that this was not very effective. They were going round a curve, and his attention must have wandered, because suddenly, dead ahead, a huge bird with a wingspan wide enough to fill the cab was lifting off the highway. McFadden caught a glimpse of something brown and gory, and tried to swerve around it; then that disconcerting jolt as the wheels passed over. He hit the clutch compulsively, gearing down, but he must also have jammed the tender spot – a sky white flash of pain made him miss the gear completely. The engine whined, the truck almost skidded, and they ended up coasting most of the way around the bend in neutral before he gingerly found his gear and got them back onto their side of the highway.

"What was that?"

"An eagle."

"I know *that.* It was a bald eagle, *Haliaeetus leucocephalus,* scavenging that roadkill. But what was the roadkill?"

"Beaver."

"A beaver?" McFadden was professionally embarrassed that he'd failed to identify a species as obvious as this, though to be fair, downtown trappers don't see a lot of beaver. Furthermore, his foot was still sending spasms up and down his leg. "I would have thought beavers were too intelligent to let themselves get killed like that."

The girl lifted a shoulder. "Nothing especially smart about beavers."

"Well, they're smart enough to regulate their own environment."

"Not this time."

McFadden was oddly vexed. "What makes you such an expert on beavers?"

Even as the words came out, he heard the secondary connotation. He glanced over quickly, then too quickly tried to look away. There was no doubt, in the arching of her eyebrows, that she had caught it too. He felt himself beginning to stammer.

"Want me to drive?"

"What?"

"You heard me. Do you want me to drive?"

"Umm . . ."

It was, in all honesty, not an option that had even occurred to him. And he was still unsettled about the beaver thing.

"I don't know . . ." he said. "It's a standard shift . . ."

The girl made one of those sounds of air blowing over lips. "So?"

"Well . . ."

Not that he's given the matter much thought, but it has been an assumption on McFadden's part that women tend to drive cars with automatic transmissions. His former wife, for example, had regarded the ability to drive a standard shift as being right up there with taxidermy in terms of useful skills for people to possess.

"What I mean," he said, "is that you have to know how to shift gears, and . . ." Already he was having a bad feeling about this.

"You think I'm too stupid to drive?"

"I didn't say that! I only meant that I didn't know you knew how to drive a *standard* shift, that's all."

"Oh."

McFadden was looking straight ahead, but he knew the girl was staring.

"*Standard* shift," she said. "You mean like pushing the engine up to forty in second so you can skip third altogether. *Standard*-shift driving like that? Like almost putting us into the weeds because you're looking at your foot instead of at the road . . . I guess that's the kind of driving you mean?"

"I was not looking at my foot!" Though it was true he may have skipped a gear or two. "Umm. Well . . . Do you have a driver's licence?"

"Right, right. I must have left it in my other purse." She opened her arms to display the sum of her possessions. "Look, if you want to drive, fine by me. I was only trying to help. I guess I just didn't realize that *standard*-shift driving was only for smart people who say they're doctors and collect rats and go walking around barefoot in rivers in the middle of the night. That's all."

– – –

Now that he is starting to get used to it, it's really not bad. The girl has turned out to be reasonably competent. It's actually almost relaxing. He hasn't been a passenger for years. Being a passenger is better for thinking, and what he has been thinking about, these last several miles, is Dryden.

They have just passed a mile sign, so he knows they'll be there soon. There is no shortage of bona fide reasons for stopping: he wants to get some fresh vegetables, the propane tanks need topping up, and so on. Groceries and gas are easy enough to pass off as routine. It's the other part that makes him nervous. He can't begin to picture himself following her up and down the aisles of a drugstore, carrying her basket. Same with clothes: the idea of some little sales clerk wondering if he's her father while he stands around waiting for the girl to try things on is just too grotesque to contemplate. He hated that even when he was married. The influence a man has in the decision-making process is so close to nil anyway, he might as well be killing time with a newspaper on a quiet bench someplace. At least then he wouldn't have to feel like some sort of vaguely tolerated Peeping Tom.

The problem, of course, is the money end. It boils down to him either stalking around in her wake with a shopping cart, just so he can be handy when it comes time for the cashier, or simply giving her the money and arranging to meet her whenever she's done. The second option wins hands down in terms of personal preference, except that he has no idea how much she needs. It would obviously be counterproductive to give her too little, to say nothing of embarrassing; but it would be just as embarrassing to fork over too much, like some vulgar . . . Well. He is not prepared to examine himself in that light either.

Meantime, what he should be looking for is one of those malls, preferably the kind with a supermarket. Every town has one, hulking over treeless acres amid the tracts of car lots, fast-food chains and self-serve gas bars. McFadden has managed to organize his life in recent years so he never actually has to go inside one. But for the sake of convenience he supposes he'll have to today. One good thing is that their parking lots are always so vast, he should have no trouble leaving the truck someplace inconspicuous. With a little luck this shouldn't take too long.

"My grandfather was a trapper," she says out of nowhere.

"What? Sorry – I beg your pardon."

"My grandfather was a trapper."

It takes a moment to assimilate. He is not really sure what sort of reply he should make. Also he's noticed the speedometer is well above eighty, but he will ignore that for the time being. This is the first time she has volunteered any piece of herself.

"I remember there were always skins hanging off the logs of his cabin. Coyote, I guess, and badger. And a lot of smaller ones – I don't know what they'd be . . ."

"Muskrat?" mumbles McFadden, despite himself. Muskrats are by far the most-trapped fur-bearer of North America, except in Toronto.

"Yeah, maybe muskrat. It was always dark, and kind of smelly. Like at a butcher shop except with smoke. Come to think of it, I don't remember any windows. I guess there must have been windows, but I don't remember any. Even the door was tiny. I was little enough so I could walk right under it, but my grandfather and all the older people had to bend over to get through. I used to think he made it that way just for me."

She is silent now. McFadden has made small noises to indicate that he is listening – nothing big enough for interruption.

"Where was this?" he says after a while.

"Oh –" She stops. "You know . . . I don't know. Weird, but I really couldn't tell you. It was way out in the bush. Way out somewhere. I could take you there, I bet, even now; but I couldn't ever tell you how to find it. When there was snow, you had to take a snowmobile. I remember riding around the cabin checking rabbit snares. It was in the foothills; the mountains always looked so close. And it was on a lake, because my grandfather used to come home with boatloads of fish and he would smoke them in this metal box. And we used to take some home with us when we left, because I remember all the white people on the bus turning their noses and sniffing like they didn't like the smell . . ."

"White people?"

She looks at him. "White people. You know, like people who aren't Indian."

"Right."

He's astounded. But he shouldn't be, because now he sees it. The oval eyes, the cheekbones. To cover himself, he tells her she is speeding.

"Oh, yeah."

The speedometer drops by seven or eight kilometres. The girl is talking.

"If the booze ran out, my mother used to tell him he was living in the past, trying to go on like that. Nobody made a living trapping any more, you did a lot better on welfare. But I guess he made it OK . . . How do *you* do it?"

"How do I do what?"

"You said you were a trapper. How do you make a living?"

"Umm . . ." he says, not willing to change the subject yet compelled somehow to honesty, "I cheat."

"What do you mean, you cheat?"

But he has seen the mall, coming up on the left – a giant billboard advertising all the businesses inside, and a Loblaws Superstore off in the corner. This must be Dryden.

"Turn here!"

"Here?"

"Yes. Right up here on the left. You'll have to get over into the other lane."

"Why are we stopping here?"

McFadden has rolled down his window and cranes his head to see behind. "You're all right after this Honda . . . OK, *now*." The girl signals and changes lanes, and gears down for the entrance. "Good," he says, "there's a gas station too. Why don't you park over there behind that trailer."

"Why are we stopping here?"

– – –

They are parked in the shadow of an eighteen-wheeler, up on blocks and separated from its tractor. McFadden assumes it's been there awhile. The girl and he are in the back, seeing to the rats. McFadden works the left side, down the line of cages, filling up the feed trays. The girl dispenses water on the right. When they reach the end of their respective rows, they switch. The cages themselves are already cleaned. He continues to be amazed with how these rats of his acclimatize. It bodes well for their future. The girl, for her part, seems to be adapting too.

"I thought you said we're supposed to stay away from towns."

"We are."

She looks through the rear at the cars pulling in and out of the lot. "Doesn't look that way."

"There are just a few things we need."

"Like what?"

"Like gas," he says. "And groceries."

"You could get stuff like that somewhere more out of the way than this."

"Yes, we could." He has finished with the feed bin and is now making adjustments to the ventilator. The girl has put the watering hose back into its housing. McFadden lifts the bag of debris and steps out of the truck onto the pavement. The girl comes out after.

"I've been thinking," he says, "that you might need some things." His back is to her while he scouts the lot for likely garbage bins. There is nothing immediately in view, so he turns to her again, still dangling the garbage. "Some clothes maybe and, you know . . ." his free hand makes a vaguely swirling motion, "female things." He finds it's better looking elsewhere, so he scans the parking lot attentively, taking in a sum of nothing.

The girl is simply standing, her arms hanging loosely by her thighs. She turns her hands slightly, opening the palms toward him. It is an eloquent gesture, acknowledging all she does not have, declaring what she does. But McFadden does not see it. He can't bring himself to look.

After a moment he turns and hands her the bag. "Hold this," he says, and climbs back into the truck. "Wait here."

McFadden keeps a fund of money carefully concealed in the interior. Crouching, he removes the baffles and counts out several hundred. He glances to the doorway, but the girl is standing where he asked her to, out of view. In just a few seconds he has restored everything to its original position.

"I'll carry the bag," he says, stepping down off the bumper.

The girl is still standing. He reaches across her and takes the bag from her hand. "Come on. The sooner we see to this, the sooner we're on the road."

She follows without speaking. It's a longish walk, several hundred yards of asphalt. McFadden limps toward the glass-fronted entrance. He's just had another brainstorm.

As usual with inspiration, it is rooted in the physical. When McFadden let himself down from the back of his truck, he did so having forgotten all about his foot. Indeed, this last little while, his foot has bothered him hardly at all. He could feel it now and then if he shifted weight, but the swelling must have subsided during the drive because even walking up and down just now, he was barely conscious of discomfort – at least until he jumped off the back of the truck.

Now it hurts. McFadden has remembered a quote from some-where – perhaps Clausewitz – something to the effect that only the ablest general succeeds in turning his disadvantages to strengths. Maybe Machiavelli. In any case it has just occurred to him that he can use this limp to his advantage.

"It's still sore?" The girl has found her tongue.

"Not bad, really." He has to hide the smile of his chicanery. It does hurt, but not enough for a limp like this.

"Why don't you let me carry that?"

"Don't be silly. It's not heavy." He is really feeling very clever.

They make their way in silence to the entrance. There is a garbage container by the door; McFadden deposits his burden there. Inside, he peers at the floor plan.

"This way," he says. Full of cheer, but limping.

Down several promenades and around several corners they find it. McFadden has remembered the law of mall shopping: the store you wish to visit is always geographically farthest from whatever point you enter. On the way they have passed several drugstores and clothing outlets; he's fairly certain she will find whatever she needs. He takes command of a shopping cart and wheels it first to the vegetable section. The cart has let him take a little weight off his foot, which, with all the irony of life, has started genuinely hurting.

McFadden has become a method actor.

"You like beets?"

The girl, after the slightest pause, gravely shakes her head.

"Yams, then? Sweet potatoes?" She nods and McFadden piles

some into his cart. "I think we have plenty of white potatoes still in the truck."

There is no reply to this, and he has not expected one. He moves the cart a little farther down the aisle.

"Leeks?" Again she nods, and again McFadden tosses several into the bottom of his cart. "Asparagus?"

This time the response is strongly negative.

"Hard to keep anyway. We'll make do with beans." McFadden picks methodically, sorting the tender from the dry. Those he intends to keep – both the yellow and the green – he has placed in a pile by themselves to one side of the bin. The girl hands him a clear plastic bag, which he cannot open. She hands him another she has opened for him. "Cursed things," he says.

While he is filling his bag, she tears several others from the roll, and puts into them the yams and leeks spilling loose around the bottom of the cart.

"Waste of plastic." But the girl seems not to have heard.

Next he chooses carrots. He pauses, speculating, by the lettuces, considering the endives, hefting the romaine. "Not feasible," he decides, moving over to the fruits.

When they have finished with the produce section, McFadden's cart is far too full. His eyes, he tells the girl, are bigger than his storage space. They have to reverse direction and put things back. Some of the yams are returned to their box, as well as the peaches he has decided in retrospect would not travel well anyway. The girl has encouraged him to do the same with the Brussels sprouts, but he has kept the Brussels sprouts regardless.

"Folic acid," he tells her. "Vitamins A, C and E6, as well as pretty good levels of iron. Not to mention roughage. Now on to the meats."

McFadden has been giving the meats some serious consideration. There is very little room in his freezer – more than when he left Toronto, true, but still not enough to be frivolous. While he ruminates, the girl has sauntered to the far end of the counter.

"Can we get some bacon?"

"What?" His mind is taken up with the pros and cons of sirloin tip. "Fine."

In the end he opts for pork, a one-kilogram roast, which reminds him that perhaps he might want to get some applesauce as well. Applesauce, of course, is fifteen aisles from where they stand.

When the jam section is found and several tins of niblet corn likewise obtained, and when a half-dozen eggs and a litre of milk are thrown in for a campfire breakfast, McFadden no longer has to pretend he is limping.

By the time they've finished with the checkout, a cartload of goods has been transformed to several surprisingly heavy shopping bags. His foot is providing a virtuoso performance all of its own. There is a coffee shop not far from the market. McFadden aims for it.

They find a table and he orders. The girl is surprised that he has not intervened again against caffeine, though he himself is too distracted to remember. He has not been looking forward to this moment. But his foot is throbbing and he is embarrassingly tired. Somehow the delicacy of the situation has greatly diminished.

McFadden reaches into his pocket and pulls out a fistful of bills. "Here."

"What's this?"

"I meant to take you shopping." He is trying to sound apologetic. "But my foot is killing me." He shrugs. "Buy some clothes . . . and things . . . to get you wherever you're going. I meant to go with you, but . . ." He shrugs again. "So you'll just have to go on your own." She starts to speak, but he puts a hand up. "But I'm going to need a favour."

"What?" It is a tone that understands the nature of these things.

"You have to go get me a newspaper."

"A newspaper."

"Yes. But it's got to be a *Globe*. I'll take a *Star* if I have to, but under no circumstances will I be reduced to reading the *Sun*.

Sorry to ask, but I just don't feel like walking any more right now." An unpleasant thought has struck. "You would think they'd get the *Globe* up here, wouldn't you? I wonder . . . Sometimes these smaller places are funny."

He is glancing around the coffee shop, perhaps looking for confirmation that *The Globe and Mail* is indeed available north of Richmond Hill, when he sees – right there on the counter, still folded – the very thing itself.

"Well, will you look at that!"

He almost forgets to hobble, but his foot reminds him well before he gets to the counter.

"Son of a gun." He lifts the paper and scans the masthead. "Look at this – it's the Saturday edition! Is today Saturday?"

The waitress confirms today is Saturday. How could anybody not know when it's the weekend?

McFadden beams. "Then I'm all set."

His pleasure is not entirely feigned. McFadden truly does enjoy a quiet hour with his paper. It is a daily ritual – the only one, in fact, he has sincerely missed since going on the road.

He has folded the Sports page out onto the counter. He likes to check the box scores first before moving on to the real news.

"I guess it could be worse . . ."

The girl is still at the table, holding the bills in both hands. "This is a lot of money."

"What?" McFadden hasn't raised his eyes from the page; it annoys him that the playoffs run so late into the summer. "Oh. To be honest, I really don't know how much those sorts of things cost. If it's too much, just bring back the change."

He has flipped back over to the front section.

"Thank you," she says.

"Take your time; get whatever you need. I'll be here."

Naturally, he's been following the provincial elections. There seems to be a lot of swing in politics, these days. McFadden is a passionate follower of politics, but as *persona non grata*, no longer a participant. This only serves to make his interest keener.

He hears the chair scrape, though his eyes stay down.

"Thank you," she says again.

"I'll wait."

He does not permit himself to look. Only when he knows she must be nearly to the door does he lift his eyes and watch – for an instant, before she disappears – wondering if this will be the last of her.

McFadden lurches to the table and applies himself to his paper.

He is comfortable, to begin with. With the pressure off, the pain is gone. He's tired, though, and wishes he could just stretch out somewhere. It's a fairly decent edition. Some days the news is full of things that interest, others there's so much rubbish it might as well be *The National Enquirer.* Today's is somewhere in between, though a little slimmer than he would have expected for a Saturday. Maybe there are pages missing.

McFadden seldom reads the paper in any given order. After a quick look at the Sports he usually skims the rest, seeing what's there. Today there are a handful of articles that look promising, an assortment of in-betweeners, and the usual no-news fillers he wouldn't normally bother with but may be forced to today, depending on how long he's willing to wait.

A lot of the front section he sets aside for later, because it's mostly pre-election stuff that's all been analyzed already. The Focus pages are filled with the usual horrors out of Africa and a long analysis of the sorry state in Russia. This is better. McFadden has become increasingly convinced the world will soon be regretting the collapse of the Soviet Union, and he's human enough to enjoy seeing his predictions coming true. For the life of him, though, he can't understand how these silly-ass Americans are still congratulating one another. But that's the nature of ideology: it's at odds with intelligence. If he were running the State Department, he'd be quietly sending the Russians all the help he could give, on the assumption that it's better dealing with a familiar Kremlin than a bunch of former apparatchiks selling nuclear secrets to any Third World despot with ready ruples.

The next piece is strongly critical of Canada's peacekeeping efforts. This one he agrees with. McFadden has never had the slightest faith in the United Nations: you can't stop wars by committee. And any soldier stepping out of his barracks in a baby blue helmet is only asking for a punch in the nose.

He has put his paper down, and wonders – as he has wondered many times on many Saturdays – why so often people close their eyes to what they see is true in favour of truths existing only in their heads. What they *see* is an age of terrifying weaponry, and within it, nearly fifty years of peace. What they *believe* is that this force, by definition, is antithetical to peace; therefore peace will be ensured if we do away with it. As logic goes, he has to admit it's seductive. The problem with the equation is that we already *have* peace – or as close to it as the world is ever likely to get. But everybody seems to overlook this. McFadden hopes he's wrong, but he is convinced the next quarter-century, without a cold war, is going to be a lot bloodier than the last twenty-five years, with. Schools should give up on social studies and teach paradoxy classes instead.

Paradoxy. He likes that. If it isn't a word already, it should be: the science of upholding opposite truths. For example, it would on the whole be a good thing if this girl decided to keep the money and run. He knows this. On the other hand, it would be awful.

Paradoxy.

He wishes he'd thought of something like this back when she asked about his sign. A practical example would have helped. Not that this one's all that practical, but then again, it's not a practical subject. That's why he likes it – which is itself a contradiction in that he's such a practical person. He wonders again if the girl is gone for good. McFadden rubs his eyes and returns his thoughts to the paper.

He feels the waitress staring. Have his lips been moving? He catches himself sometimes. Maybe she just doesn't like it that he has his foot up on the seat.

There are of course a slew of articles about Quebec. *La Belle Poule des Provinces*. McFadden has never really blamed Quebec, at least not until recently. You can't fault historical conditioning. Everything Canada has done over the last forty years has conditioned Quebec's feeling of uniqueness. It's always been the odd child of the Confederation. Quebec is just different, and everyone's always known it's different. A child shouldn't be culpable for how it's been reared. French speakers the world over are obsessed with their uniqueness; it's an ethnographic quirk. They have conventions every year to get together and pat themselves on the back because they've come up with their very own word for *hamburger*. There are millions more French-speaking people in the world than there are Dutch, or Danes. But the Dutch don't seem to worry. Or the Danes. It's only the French who need to obsess about their culture; other people just get on with theirs.

Québécois are the same. The climate here has toughened them a little, but every time they've wanted recognition as being wonderful and special, the rest of Canada has obligingly dished it up. And this is how it should be. They *need* it. What does it cost? They're family. At least that's what they're supposed to be.

What really irks him is the other nine. The grown-up provinces. The ones who should know better. He likes the anecdote about the household with ten children: one of them is born with a limp, but the other nine can't stand it that their sibling is getting the attention, so they all start limping too. Constitutionally, the danger has never really been Quebec, it's the rest of them. Though it always seems to start with Alberta.

The waitress is staring again. What's her problem? He looks around the room. Only two or three tables are occupied. There's a young thug in the corner, all done up in leather with tattoos and something metal in his nose, and that Auschwitz-style hairdo. He looks like he's just dying to get to Queen Street, if only he hadn't blown his bus fare on the boots. The funny thing is that the girl he's with looks normal: a mousy little thing with printed flowers on her smock and hair done up nicely with a curling iron. The angle's wrong, but she may even be wearing a skirt. She must think the leather boy's a poet.

Idiots.

Now he's got himself worried about curling irons. He didn't even think about curling irons. She'll probably need one. Did he give her enough for a curling iron? How much *are* curling irons?

The waitress is still looking. Maybe she's one of those people who think of their workplace as an extension of their home. Chastened, and somehow vaguely resentful, he shifts his foot back to the floor. His coffee cup is empty anyway, and he's been eyeing the doughnuts. McFadden makes a point of limping on his way over. Step, wince – look brave. Step, wince – look brave. Lean heavily on the counter, wince a little more.

"Oh, dear," she says. "What's happened to your foot?"

"Wolverine."

"What?"

"Can I have one of the chocolate ones, please, with the cream inside? And a refill."

The waitress insists on carrying everything back to his table. Now she feels just terrible. He hauls his leg back up on the chair.

"Can I get you anything else, dear?"

"No, thank you."

Thinking about Quebec has got him thinking about Alberta. And thinking about Alberta has him worrying about the rats. This is the excuse he needs to look at his watch. Not even twenty minutes. He is very disappointed with this doughnut. Fake cream. Probably just as many calories.

McFadden believes that Canada should build a Court of the Star Chamber.

The Court of the Star Chamber, if he remembers his English history, was used by the monarchy – Tudors seem to ring a bell – in order to examine the conduct of barons charged with destabilizing the central government. As McFadden envisages it, the barons would stand – chained, he likes to think – in a blinding shaft of light beneath a tall and twinkling ceiling, answering charges directed from on high. It entertains him immensely to think of the provincial premiers, past and present, similarly trussed and blinking.

Newfoundland, did you or did you not accept millions of federal dollars in order to grow cucumbers in a place where cabbages cannot even take root, a thousand miles from any markets, and did you not all the while rail to your electorate about the unfairness and indignities of Confederation upon your erstwhile colony?

"Well, moy Lord, if we'd only got more by the way of transfer payments, ye see –"

Silence!

Poor Newfoundland. They've killed every fish in their ocean, but of course that was all Ottawa's fault, and now they don't know what to do about getting in their ten weeks of work every year to qualify for pogey. The solution, of course, is to throw out the whole concept of employment, put them all on a giant allowance, and keep them down home whittling puffins so American tourists can drive up in good weather and take pictures. Now he's read there's a new scheme afoot to tow icebergs into St. John's and turn them into vodka. At least this time there's sure to be a local market.

He supposes Newfoundland should really fall into the same category as Quebec: expensive, but quaint enough almost to be worth it.

It's the Westerners who really irritate him. Especially the Albertans.

Alberta, you stand accused of jumping up and down and threatening to separate just because Quebec is too. What have you to say?

"The people of the West, Your Worship, have long suffered exploitation, usurpation and alienation at the hands of an insensitive East –"

Silence! Alberta, please tell the court the amount in your province's Heritage Fund, and what you intend to do with the money.

"Well, Your Worship, that's kind of a secret –"

Silence! Bring in British Columbia.

It's probably not fair, singling out Alberta. All of them do it. Even Ontario holds Ottawa responsible for its own election of Bob Rae. But Alberta has raised it to an art form. The cradle of protest, from Tommy Douglas to Preston Manning. They don't care if it's from the left or the right, so long as it comes out from under a Stetson.

McFadden taps the tabletop and stretches his neck. Albertans must know that Quebec's tactic of threatening to leave Confederation in order to get more from confederation is in fact harmful to Confederation. Of course they know it; they're always telling everyone how much they hate it. And yet they do it too, because it works.

Inconsistent with reason and yet true: paradox.

Logically, then – if he himself approves of paradox, and he does – he should also approve of Alberta's paradoxical approach in its application of the principle. McFadden looks up at the waitress, whose back is to him, and smiles. That's why he's taking rats.

The woman turns in time to see his smile abruptly disappear. He's just remembered that Tommy Douglas was from Saskatchewan, not Alberta. Well, they still wear Stetsons. McFadden shoots the waitress a wink, and then feels guilty when she scuttles off into the kitchen. Talk about your paradox. He's worse than the lot.

"I wasn't sure you'd still be here."

He actually jumps. He hadn't heard her coming.

"Who? Me? What do you mean *I* wouldn't still be here . . . It's . . . Never mind."

He has got himself under control, seizing the paper, ardently engrossed. The girl is putting parcels down beside him. He has

managed to get his foot off the chair more or less inconspicu-
ously, head down in the editorials, casually asking if she's found
everything she needs.

"Oh, yes."

The way she has said it nearly brings his head back up. But he
masters this too. "Good," he says. "Good."

A wad of money materializes by his elbow.

He acts surprised, pushing part of it back to her side of the
table. "Get us both a coffee, why don't you. You must be thirsty.
I'll just finish up this article." But he has noticed there's a lot of
money left. He hopes she has thought of everything. "Did you get
a curling iron?"

He's really a little pleased that he has remembered an item she
apparently has not. Something in the silence makes him lift his
eyes.

Her smile has vanished. "I'm sorry . . . I didn't know that's
what you wanted." She had been just about to sit, but now she's
standing still behind her chair. "I guess I should have asked about
the colour too. Do you want it different?"

The posture tells him she is waiting for an answer. He simply
doesn't understand the question.

"I can get some bottled stuff. It's not as good as a salon job, but
it only has to hold a few days, doesn't it? . . . I'll need a sink,
though. What do you like?"

McFadden is still trying to understand what she is talking
about.

"A lot of guys go for blond, but I'll be honest, it doesn't work
with me. Red's OK, though. How about red?"

"Oh God. No." It has come crashing in what she's been saying.
"Oh, no . . . I didn't mean . . ."

He actually has to pause and give himself a shake. "I don't
want you to change your hair. I can't tell you how beauti– I never
meant that you should change it. I only meant that you might
want to *have* a curling iron. Like . . . I don't know . . . a toothbrush. In case you wanted one."

A current of confusion has spilled around the table. The girl's still standing. They stare at one another, sharing the awareness that their purposes have crossed, wondering where the error lies. From the corner of his eye McFadden notes the studded creature at the other table leaning back to see what's happening.

"Listen," he says, an analogy has come to him. "My wife would hardly leave the house without a curling iron – certainly never pack a suitcase. I just thought –"

"You're married?"

"*No!* Jesus. No. I haven't been married in years. Look, just order us some coffee while I finish up this article, will you." He can't remember what he was reading. "And get a doughnut – though I can't vouch for them. Your hair is just fine like it is."

She shrugs and saunters to the counter. McFadden takes the opportunity to aim a savage glare at the table in the corner, and is rewarded with a hasty backswing of shaven head. This mollifies somewhat. While the girl is gone, he puts away his paper. He wonders what's inside the bags.

"Cream?" she asks.

"Oh. Yes, please."

"Sugar?"

"No, thank you."

She sits and primly folds her legs.

"The other night," he says, "when you were asking about the sign on the truck –"

"It wasn't the other night. It was last night."

"What? Last night? That was only last night?" He can't believe what's happened to his sense of time. "All right," he says, "last night –"

"What about last night?"

"I've been thinking about how to explain it."

Her eyes flick up from her cup. "Explain what?"

"My sign, for Christ's sake."

"What about it?"

"What it means."

"You said it means when two things are opposite but still true."

"Er, yes," he says, "I did." He's surprised she has retained this; it's not the most accessible of concepts. "But what I wanted to explain is what it means."

She has pulled out his Entertainment section and is squinting at a picture of Madonna. "I know what it means." She shrugs and turns the page. "Like when a guy wants to fuck you, then hates you for it after."

He is instantly defensive. "Or when women tell you all they want is Mister Nice Guy, then dump you the first time you send flowers."

The girl leans forward in a way that somehow makes her presence intensely immediate – McFadden has only just now noticed she is wearing a different top – and brushes his beard with the paper.

"You don't hit me as the flower type."

"Very nice." He knows she's not sure what he's talking about. "The blouse," he says. "It's very nice."

Now that he's observing, it *is* nice. More of a T-shirt than a blouse, he thinks, or some sort of hybrid of the two. It seems to have more detail, though it looks like it's made of the same sort of material. And the neck is completely different, with a lot of shoulder showing. From the point of view of physics, he's not quite sure what's holding it up.

"Thank you," she says. "It wasn't expensive."

"It's lovely."

"*Thank* you."

"How's your doughnut?"

"Good." She says this on the bite, and a little piece falls and lands perched, just below the neckline. She retrieves it, smiling, and puts it in her mouth.

McFadden looks away.

"Did you get everything you need?"

"Oh-h yes." There is a decided slyness to her tone. She is watching him above the doughnut.

He looks away again. "Good."

The waitress is scowling again as they leave, though McFadden doesn't know now if it's him or if it's her.

– – –

They have been driving into the sun. It's a low, reclining sun, filling up the cab with yellow evening warmth. McFadden's head keeps nodding. He is glad the girl is driving. It feels like he aches in ten places at once, starting with his foot. Worst is this steady, throbbing fatigue, centred right between his shoulders and rippling out from there. Another yawn, but he fights back this one too. He is glad the girl is driving.

They haven't spoken much. She's been strange since they left the mall; at least he thinks it's her. But then again, it might be him. He's too tired for talk. Amazing that a little shopping trip could wipe him out like this. Shopping's always done that to him, though – shopping and looking at pictures too long at the art gallery. It felt like miles back to the truck. His adventure in the river last night seems to have taken its toll. God, he still can't believe that was only last night.

This time the yawn escapes before he can prevent it.

"Where do you want to stop?" she asks.

McFadden's been thinking about this too. He's not at all looking forward to setting up a camp or, for that matter, cooking. He scrunches down a little and looks out the window. Maybe it will rain.

"You-hoo! Where would you like to stop?"

"A motel," he says. McFadden lifts his arm and waves, by way of elaboration, toward the setting sun. "It's getting late."

The girl says nothing, only nods. It seems a nod not so much of agreement as of confirmation, but McFadden is beyond interpretation. They have just passed Kenora – or was it Keewatin? He leans a little to open up the glovebox, and unfolds his map.

"Manitoba must be coming up. You'd think there would be a motel somewhere between there and here. And hopefully a restaurant."

The girl moves her head again that way, almost like she's smiling, but not. "Sure."

"Fine." McFadden puts away the map and folds his arms, looking out into the evening sun.

He's asleep when they arrive, or close enough to sleep that he hasn't noticed they are slowing until they've nearly stopped. The wheels bump, the seat beneath him bounces, and McFadden raises his eyes to the spectre of the Border-Line Motel.

"Wakey wakey."

The Border-Line evidently represents, for travellers en route from Upper Canada, a final chance to stop, rest, replenish and prepare before setting out onto the plains. The terrain on one side appears in every way identical to the terrain on the other – the same black spruce and aspen they've been driving through for days now. McFadden assumes the distinction to be psychological. Even so, he is glad of it. The chief advantage to its being on the Ontario side is simply that they've got here sooner. All he wants is a pillow and a place to close his eyes.

The girl rolls to a stop in front of the registry office. McFadden rubs his chin, blinks and sucks some air in hopes of waking up. His back has seized.

"We're here," says the girl, in case he has missed this fact.

"Home sweet home."

McFadden climbs down from the truck. The girl follows. For some reason this surprises him. He had expected her to wait in the cab. He doesn't know why he is surprised, or why he would have preferred her to stay outside. He just would have.

A man in a vest is standing at the counter.

"A double room, please." McFadden stifles another yawn. "One night."

"Very good, sir." This clerk has obviously taken a hotel management course.

McFadden appreciates it. "Payment will be cash."

The clerk nods discreetly. McFadden fills out the registration card and slides it back across the counter.

"Will that be one key, sir, or two?"

"Oh." This has caught him unprepared. "Umm . . ." He finds himself looking at the girl.

"One's fine." She says it before he's had a chance to decide. "Is there a restaurant in this place?"

"To the left, miss." The clerk has handed her the key. "Your room is at the back of the building. Just follow the driveway."

"Thank you."

"Yes," says McFadden, "thank you."

The girl is already out the door. From habit, he starts toward the driver's seat, but the girl is there ahead of him, jangling the keys. He stops, and crosses to the passenger side.

"*Double* room?" she says before he's all the way in.

But McFadden is mid-yawn, and doesn't hear.

– – –

The room is surprisingly spacious. There is the usual plate glass window, closed off with a curtain, the customary television and two twin beds a yard apart. The bathroom has one of those red lights built into the ceiling that turns the room a glowing orange. For a roadside motel, the Border-Line is upscale.

They've brought their luggage in – McFadden his suitcase, the girl her assortment of plastic shopping bags. He has opened his case and lifted out his pyjamas, his toothbrush and a black plastic comb. McFadden is now as unpacked as he will need to be. The girl fusses with her parcels, going into the bathroom and coming back, going in again and closing the door behind her. He sees that she has bought a lightweight carrying bag, like a gym bag with pockets. Clever thing. Whatever other purchases she has made have now evidently gone into this. He is mildly curious, but is prevented absolutely by gentleman's code from peeking inside.

McFadden lies back on one of the beds, feet still flat on the ground. After a time he is aware she is back in the room. He opens his eyes, and shakes himself awake.

– – –

The meal, despite its queasy texture, takes its time.

The Border-Line's restaurant facilities are a model of their type. Tables are Formica white and stainless steel, the floor a brownish tide of tread-worn carpet. The waitress is blond and padded. McFadden orders a double Scotch. He would have skipped this meal entirely if he were on his own, but he knows how much the girl needs nourishment. "I'll have a chocolate shake," she says.

They order food. McFadden requires only toast and a bowl of minestrone; the girl is getting everything on the menu. He asks for another Scotch while she deliberates between fried or mashed potatoes. Is it his imagination or has she gained back a little weight already? He continues to be amazed at how her looks compound with every day. Biology is truly a marvellous thing. McFadden has caught himself wishing for the first time in years that he were younger, but it's only because he's tired. This whole trip – all the planning and preparations – has obviously taken more out of him than he'd reckoned. And of course the girl, and all the delays, and falling in the river – he hasn't had a proper sleep in days.

The waitress brings the milkshake and his Scotch. The girl tastes hers, then applies herself in earnest to the straw. That new top is certainly flattering. From what he can see of her shoulders, which is quite a lot, the mosquito bites have almost vanished. Amazing.

"Bless you," she says.

"Bless me?"

"You yawned – I said bless you."

"You only say bless you when people sneeze, not when they yawn."

"You can say bless you whenever you like. There you go again! Bless you."

"All right then." He picks up his glass. "Geshundheit."

"But I didn't yawn."

"Geshundheit means health. In Germany they call medical clinics Geshundheit-houses."

"All right." She raises what's left of her milkshake and aims the straw into her mouth. "Geshundheit," she says, and sucks.

McFadden drains his glass. It's a tumbler. He cannot fathom how anyone could serve Scotch-over-ice in a tumbler. Ordinarily he would have sent it back and made whoever's tending bar pour it into a proper glass. But today he can't be bothered. It's doing its job: he can feel the muscles in his back beginning to loosen. Though the foot still throbs.

"Stop yawning!"

"I can't help it."

They've now been brought their dinners, and the girl is hard at it. First course appears to be chicken, fried in batter. Very greasy. A little dribbles down her chin, but she stops it with a finger and licks it up. McFadden spoons his minestrone. He should have encouraged her to order something more digestible, but he doesn't have the energy. Tomorrow he'll see she eats some vegetables. There's a slushy puddle of peas beside her french fries, but he reckons these as less than nothing in terms of nutrition.

She catches him glowering, and smiles. "When are you going to tell me about your rats?"

This reminds him that he still has to clean out all the cages and see to feeding and watering before he can go to bed. The thought is not a happy one.

"Didn't I tell you already?"

"No."

"Yes, I did." He tries to think. "Yesterday. At the campsite, yesterday." He still can't wholly grip the fact that that was only yesterday.

"No, you didn't. You said some stuff about colonies and breeding populations, and stuff like that, but you never said why you were doing all that in the first place."

"I didn't?"

"No."

"Oh."

His minestrone is almost finished. So is his toast. The girl is tapping her plate with a fork.

"Well?"

McFadden sighs. He's not much up to chronicling, this evening. "All right." He has put down his spoon and reaches into his pocket for his wallet. Inside is a folded piece of newsprint, perhaps two inches square. He passes it over and goes back to his soup.

The clipping is from the *Globe*. He thinks it's from the *Globe*; it's the sort of little ditty they like to run on the last page of the front section. But then again, it might have been some other paper. He honestly doesn't remember. It's been hoarded in his wallet for quite some time.

The clipping quotes an unnamed source in Alberta's Ministry of Agriculture, stating there are no rats in the province. It does not explain how Alberta has come to be devoid of rats, nor does it offer any statistical or zoological interpretations. It merely states, in phraseology that can only be described as smug, that Alberta, as a province, is rat-free.

McFadden's interest was aroused enough to clip it out and put it in his wallet. There it might have stayed until the next time he tidied up his billfold, but soon afterwards he happened on a second, even stranger snippet.

This time he was in a bookstore – one of those second-hand shops along Queen Street where he likes to pass the time of day. He was leafing through a volume, enjoying the smell as much as the text itself, when he became aware of a radio somewhere in the background. He must have caught the word "Alberta" and then "rats" – together in the same sentence. At least he thought he did. It was enough for him to close the book and cock his ear.

Someone must have come in just then. The doorbell jingled, floorboards creaked and there were voices. McFadden lost track of whatever it was he was hearing. The interview seemed to be with someone whose job it was to patrol a border, eradicating rats – or so it sounded. He was sure he heard the word "Alberta," and the subject of the discussion was certainly rats. Could it be that the government of Alberta actually hired people to protect its rat-free status?

McFadden forgot his book and hurried up the aisle. It was difficult pinpointing exactly where among the shelves the radio was stationed. Precisely at that moment the proprietor waylaid him, and by the time he got himself more or less politely disengaged, the interview was over. A Beatles song was playing.

Later on, he wished he'd asked what frequency the thing was tuned to; he might have been able to write the station for a transcript. But it seemed such a silly request at the time. At that point, too, he had no idea how the matter of rodential inequalities would come to occupy his thinking.

Still, the whole thing might have passed into oblivion had not McFadden only days later acquired the first of his rats.

It was not, of course, the first rat he had ever caught, but it *was* the first rat he'd ever been inspired to keep. Now and then McFadden will find a rat in one of his sets. Rats have much the same diet as squirrels and are attracted to similar baits, but squirrels are much more common in Toronto – at least on the surface. So he's always slightly startled when he checks a squirrel trap and finds a rat instead. Usually he can guess where it has come from; he will spot a nearby sewer pipe or a subway grating. If he happens to be trapping down around the lakeshore or near the stockyards he might even expect a rat or two. But the rat this day had come from Rosedale – very near the back garden, in fact, of a former prime minister. Something about this gave him pause.

Rats, of course, have no commercial value. Whatever their neighbourhood of origin, neither fur nor flesh of this species has any hope of market. McFadden therefore had no cause to kill this rat. He thought about simply opening the door and letting it go. The concept of a Rosedale rat amused him. He could well imagine the furore this one rodent would cause if it was spotted, scuttling across the flagstone paths, nosing the euonymus – wrinkling its whiskers at the edge of someone's granite pool.

This is what restrained him.

If this rat were ever discovered, its existence – and perhaps more than just that – was in jeopardy. New Age pest exterminators claim to be target-specific, hitting only what they're contracted to eliminate. In military language this is known as the surgical strike. McFadden, mindful of the terminology and a reader of the foreign news columns, is skeptical. Not that he would accuse his opposite numbers of intentional carpet bombing, but he worries about collateral damage. Efforts to exterminate this one rat might well have deleterious effects on the wider populations of squirrels and raccoons, so favoured by his clientele. And that would be bad for business. Rosedale raccoons are particularly noted for their plumpness.

More significantly – and honestly – McFadden found himself liking this rat. He had been tending toward disenchantment, of late, with the incredible stupidity of squirrels. Even raccoons, whatever their reputation, seemed to him unbearably dim-witted. He couldn't help perceiving a disturbing inversion of Darwinism spreading out across the urban landscape: the softer the living, the softer the brain.

As part of his research during those early days as a trainee trapper, McFadden went through the Yellow Pages checking out the pest-control outfits and wildlife removal services he fully expected to be his major competition. It was the high point of his learning curve. To his surprise and great delight he discovered that, far from representing competition, these operations were perfectly symbiotic with his own endeavours. According to their advertising, not only did they guarantee never to harm their evictees, they also promised not to inconvenience them.

Posing as a homeowner with a raccoon in his chimney,
McFadden telephoned several and asked them to explain their
services. He was informed that for a fee of between two and
three hundred dollars, depending on the circumstances, they
would come to his house, catch his raccoon, fasten a wire mesh
across his chimney so it couldn't get back in again – then let it go.

"Interesting," he'd said. "And where, exactly, would you let
it go?"

"Naturally, that would have to be there on the property, sir.
Otherwise the animal would suffer dislocation."

In case his mind was not fully at ease on this point, McFadden
was further advised that, since his raccoon was already established and familiar with the neighbourhood, he needn't worry at
all; it was sure to have no trouble finding somewhere else to stay.

"Like, for instance, my next-door neighbour's chimney."

The reply was deadpan. "If your neighbour hasn't dealt with
us already, sir, that would be a possibility."

"God bless you," said McFadden, and meant it.

Follow-up calls established that the same philosophy applied
also to skunks, squirrels and even pigeons. But not to rats. Rats,
he discovered, were classified as vermin – in the company of
roaches, termites and other such creatures falling on the far
side of whatever mysterious line separates good biology from
bad. He learned to his surprise that there are two tiers in the
world of pest removal. Homeowners with squirrels in their attics
are directed to one kind of company, whose job it is to ease them
out as gently and as kindly as ever they can. People with rats call
a different number. Rats, it turns out, get poison and gas.

Even from the beginning McFadden couldn't help seeing this
as somehow – *unfair* would not be quite the proper word – *ill-
considered*, perhaps. Not from any impulse toward sentimental-
ity, but as an affront to the prerogatives of logic. A good paradox
is one thing, zoomorphic bigotry something else again. Especially
as all local evidence points to squirrels as being by far the
greater nuisance. McFadden seldom even *saw* a rat – and it

wasn't because they weren't around, only that they were clever enough to keep out of sight.

So McFadden's attitude with respect to this Rosedale rat tended to benevolence. Not so the rat. It watched him with a hostility so intense he found himself actually backing away from the trap – an embarrassing admission for a practitioner in the familiarity of his chosen field. There was little doubt that this rat made the connection between him and its predicament. It had given up fighting the trap, having reduced all other options to zero, and was now composing itself for battle with *him*. To McFadden there was something inherently admirable here. For some reason he was reminded of the football adage about the best defence being a good offence, which in turn put in mind his own ancestors at various tight corners in history. McFadden did some not-too-rapid calculations, staying well back from the trap, and came up with a ratio of roughly 400:1. This was how many times bigger he was than this rat. Still the rat had him nervous.

Professional demeanour keeps McFadden at a distance from the vagaries of sentiment. Nevertheless, he found himself loading the rat into the back of his truck and taking it home. He would keep it just a day or two, for interest, then let it go somewhere more hospitable.

That was the better part of twelve months before the present McFadden, seated at a table in a motel restaurant on the threshold of the Prairies, spoons his soup and contemplates the rising brows and plunging neckline of this other strange creature across the table.

"Pass the butter," she says, as he stretches a tired shoulder to oblige.

– – –

The next time he caught a rat, he kept it too. And he built a cage for it, beside the first one, in his basement. In time there came another, and then another after that. He learned to be careful how he housed them; rats have a lethal way of sorting out their differences. Looking back, McFadden is still not certain if by this time he was already clearly thinking about Alberta. But the notion must have germinated, started sprouting roots.

How quickly they learned to make the best of things, assimilating the routines of their new environment, learning from their own mistakes. He himself soon learned never to handle them without first putting on a pair of metal-mesh butcher's gloves and then some leather gauntlets overtop. No wonder rats and humans live so close together: the two of them represent the most aggressively adaptive species natural selection has yet to produce – at least among mammals. If Alberta truly had no rats, this must be a misfortune for Alberta. The whole framework of Confederation, after all, was supposed to be based on equality of assets.

By the time McFadden produced the first litter in what was to become a full-scale breeding program, there could be no doubt that Alberta had clearly become, in his mind, a place in need of rats – though it was still mostly a matter of whimsy. But that winter was a long one, in both the meteorological and political climates. Reading his paper, McFadden was becoming more and more disgusted with the assaults upon a political tradition those same papers showed him was the envy of a barely civilized world. The United Nations routinely listed his country as the world's best place to live, while the nigglists at home did their level best to pick it to pieces.

At some point in the long chill of January he decided what he needed was a holiday. Like any careful traveller, he paid attention to his itinerary. Once again McFadden found himself spending evenings in the library. Then he started making phone calls. The archives of the Alberta Ministry of Agriculture seemed the sensible place to begin.

It is probably safe to say that if McFadden had discovered the whole thing was fiction – if his inquiries revealed that the province of Alberta sheltered just as many rats as any other standing member of Confederation – then matters would have stopped right there. He would have brought his rats up from the basement, packed them off to Scarborough and wished the lot of them a fond farewell.

But this is not what happened. Alberta was definitely, positively, ratless. And proud of it.

In short order he collected all the proof he needed: documents issued by the provincial government itself, the whole history of Alberta's rat prevention program spelled out for all the world to see. He felt like a Cold War spy tuning in to CNN, but there it was: the how, the why and the wherefores, right down to geographical considerations and procedural techniques. The quantity of evidence was simply overwhelming. McFadden was turned.

From time to time he still feels a little guilty about picking on Alberta. As a source of constitutional paralysis, Alberta isn't really any more to blame than Saskatchewan or New Brunswick or any of the others – though the rest of them, so far as he knows, have plenty of rats already. By rights he should be taking this load to Quebec. But he's willing to concede Quebec its special status, and anyway, it's hard to tell with rats if they're anglophone or allophone. Besides, Quebec still has a hefty population of its own, despite its immigration laws.

And really, the whole thing was only a joke. He has to admit, though, that it's been quite a lot of effort for what amounts to not much more than an experiment in the malleability of humour, especially when it's nobody's humour but his own. On the other hand, if this actually works, he'll have spread the mirth across a rather grander audience. He has taken quite a lot of pleasure, on his solitary rounds, speculating outcomes if his little trick succeeds: Will Alberta accept its loss of rat-free status, and join the march of zoologic confraternity? Or will it fight this twist of evolution tooth and claw? At least now he can share the punchline with the girl.

She has handed back his scrap of newsprint.

"Let me ask you something, seriously. Are you crazy?"

McFadden folds the slip back into his wallet and thinks about it. It is not the first time his sanity has been called into question. "I don't know," he says. "You decide."

"If I get this right, you're taking a truckload of rats all the way from Toronto to Alberta because this piece of paper says Alberta doesn't have any."

McFadden opens his mouth, but there is really nothing for him to contradict in this assessment, so he closes it again and nods.

"Two things," she says. "*Are* you crazy? And how can all of Alberta have no rats?"

"You said you come from Alberta, didn't you?"

"Yeah . . . I lived there when I was a kid."

"I thought everybody in Alberta knew about the rats. I was under the impression it was a high point of their public school curriculum."

"Not where I come from."

"Where's that?"

"A reserve. You never heard of it."

"Really?" This interests him. "Where?"

"Don't change the subject."

"All right," he says. "So you lived in Alberta. Did you ever see a rat?"

The girl pauses.

*"Musk*rats don't count. They're different."

"I'm sure I must have . . ."

"Come on! Think about it."

"Wait a minute! Hold on. I lived for two years in Toronto too, and I never saw a rat there either."

"You lived in Toronto? What part?"

"Stop that! So what about it – I never saw a rat in Toronto either, but you've got a whole truckload of them. So just because I didn't see any in Edmonton doesn't mean there might not have been lots of them there too, hiding."

"Edmonton? I thought you said you lived out in the woods on a reserve."

"My job tends to take me to the cities."

This quiets him.

He has to admit she has a point. He can't properly refute it without going into all the background, and right now he's not up to it. He is mumbling something to that effect when the waitress intervenes.

"Dessert?"

"No, thank you," he says, and covers up another yawn. The soup has made him sleepy.

The girl asks for a double chocolate cheesecake with an extra side of ice cream. "And coffee," she says. This is spoken with a look of defiance.

"Tea for me please," replies McFadden fastidiously.

When the waitress has cleared away their plates, the girl puts her elbows on the table and leans forward. "What about the other part?"

"What other part?"

"Are you crazy?"

"I guess I must be," he says, blinking, and yawns.

– – –

Despite his heavy eyes, they linger. The girl requires a second slice of cheesecake and several coffee refills before she declares herself full. While she eats, he talks. At first it's an effort; he's just too tired for this, but too tired also to succeed in clumsy efforts to stall the conversation. And there is no denying that once she has him going, he carries on all by himself. A year of solitary scheming is a lot to bottle up.

The girl is a good listener. Once he's launched, she's silent, shaking her head at the greater absurdities, hiding her smile at the smaller ones, never disguising the fact that she's amused.

It has been a very long while since McFadden has enjoyed the pleasure of amusing. He succeeds on his own account quite often, but sharing this with someone else, even someone who is not necessarily laughing in the same direction, is a strangely heady thrill. She has asked about the rats, so he starts there; the rats are quite a story on their own. But reconstruction of events requires illustration; anecdotes are pointless in the absence of their history; references demand an explanation; footnotes serve only to confuse without the subtext of the text itself. Before he knows it he's getting clinical, and McFadden calls a halt. He's just too tired. He is rubbing his eyes and twisting his neck, wondering if he can simply tell her that his batteries are dry.

"Let's go back," she says.

"That would be great."

The yawns have begun again before the waitress carries back his change. They walk in silence. McFadden opens the door with his key. "I have to go and see to the, um – cargo," he says, standing at the threshold.

She smiles. "I'll help."

With the two of them it takes hardly any time at all. He does one side, she takes the other, working their way down the rows. The truck is parked near the highway beneath a stand of aspen. The Border-Line Motel is crowded, but all its guests have conveniently parked beside their rooms. McFadden is sure his rats will spend a quiet night.

"Thanks," he says, holding out his hand to help her off the tailgate.

"My pleasure."

He unlocks the room again, and steps to one side to let her in. They pause a moment in the middle of the floor. "Do you want the bathroom first?"

"No," she says. "You go ahead."

McFadden's pyjamas are laid out already. He takes them with him and closes the door. The Arborite sink is now surrounded with an assortment of tubes and bottles. So she's bought some makeup. It occurs to him as he turns the tap that this may in part explain how she has looked so good this evening. The science of makeup is a mystery to him; the only time he ever really notices is when someone's done too much of it. It did not seem to him that she was wearing any. Then again, her cheeks *were* redder. This must be an example of its effective application. Still, part of it at least has to reflect an improvement in overall health.

He gets a shock when he takes off his shirt. He is bruised from thigh to shoulder. McFadden probes and winces, but the scrapes seem to be healing over and his stitches look clean enough. No wonder he feels so battered. It's consoling.

The water is wonderful. He has got it up hot, hot as he can stand it; swaying under the nozzle with his head bent, both hands pressed against the tile. McFadden leans against the shower wall until his knees begin to wobble. God, he's bushed.

After a while his skin is pink and wrinkled. He is dizzy for a moment, reaching down to shut off the tap, bracing himself against the shower rail, watching the water swirl away around his feet. The room is like a steam bath. Rivulets of condensation trickle down the walls. A full-length mirror hangs on the door, but it's white with fog. Just as well.

There are four good-sized bath towels. McFadden uses only one. Women, he knows, need more towels than men. He contemplates trimming his beard but decides to save that for the morning. The advantage to wearing a beard is that for days on end you can ignore it. It's too foggy in here anyway. That orange light, though, is definitely speeding up the drying process. McFadden hangs the towel on the door handle. By the time he's finished brushing his teeth, he is dry enough to put on his pyjamas. A cloud of vapour spills out with him around the door frame.

"Holy PJs," says the girl. He doesn't know what she is talking about. "Are those little hockey players?"

There are, in fact, miniature hockey players in the pattern of McFadden's brown pyjamas. He must have known this at one time, but he's worn them so long he's forgotten. He walks by her to the other bed and sits, as she is, facing the television.

The girl gets up and hands him the remote control. "I hope you like mine as much as I like yours."

On the television, a pickup truck with wheels like mutant doughnuts is driving over a row of parked cars. It has chrome smokestacks bristling out along its fenders, and begins to bounce as the roofs of some cars cave in more thoroughly than others. The announcer's voice rises in excitement, because now the truck appears to have wedged between a rusted Datsun and some sort of Chrysler K-car. Suddenly the picture changes. A man holding a crash helmet is talking. He is dejected. McFadden assumes it is the driver whose monster truck got stuck halfway over his row of cars.

He pushes several buttons on the remote control until the picture tube goes black again. The girl has disappeared into the bathroom.

The bed he has chosen is the one farther away from the bathroom. This way she's closer if she needs to go there in the dark. It is most unlikely that anything will wake him. Already he's beginning to feel that pleasant weightlessness, that sense of falling but not worrying, never worrying about landing, just enjoying the fall. The covers are tugged up under his chin, the pillow is moulded to his head and the mattress is falling away beneath him. He can hear water running in the bathroom, but the sound is far away.

In the space of merest heartbeats, McFadden is asleep.

He has peculiar dreams.

– – –

At first McFadden dreams a sound. It's a glottal, groping kind of sound, irregular yet musical, rhythmically discordant. He understands that this sound has changed the pattern of his sleep.

As his breathing alters, he begins to feel a movement. It's not him, but he knows he's connected. Something outside of him keeps moving, and it seems he is moving with it. His body needs more air, his head is sinking back to let his jaw gape, and now there is smell: a sweetish, pungent presence, tugging in his brain. The trail of this has drawn him upward, outward – now to touch, now warmth. No, not warmth – heat. Something slides along his cheek and in his ear and down his neck. His own hands are moving, twitching, reaching out for this. When it runs along his upper lip, the whole of him responds.

His eyes are open.

The room is blue. And moving. Blue light flickers on the ceiling and the walls, and these liquid, grinding sounds are pulsing with it. Shadows flash and groan about the room. Something brushes his face and he closes his eyes, but everything is moving around him, tugging from the bottom of his spine, quivering his senses.

The television's on. The television is making these lights and these sounds, and when he looks the girl is there between his knees. The shadows blink again and she is smiling, lowering her mouth to him.

Then his shoulders sink down and down into the mattress, and his heels and ankles too, but at the waist he's straining for the ceiling and a voice so far away says *no* – but it's a muffled voice and throttled by the pure white flash that sears away the others, and by the burbled chorus welling out of him to mingle with its echoes in the room.

Then McFadden is alone again.

Alone again, although the blue still flickers from across the room while the mattress, damp beneath him, shifts and settles, and a blaze of yellow light assaults his eyes then goes dark again. And then the sound of running water.

McFadden breathes and closes his eyes and breathes some more.

But the dream is over.

*. . . (very few rats enter
Manitoba from Ontario)*

DAN A. HARVEY,
PEST MANAGEMENT
SPECIALIST
*RAT CONTROL ON
THE PRAIRIES*
SASKATCHEWAN
AGRICULTURE
1985

He wakes to find the girl in his bed. The sun is cutting planes of brightness at the edges of the curtain. Motes of dust particulate, drift, and disappear again. McFadden reaches out a hand and passes through it, like slicing through a wall – into the light from the shadow and out again the other side.

It has cast, this light, a narrow band along his chest and hers, cutting almost straight across the bed, bisecting bottom from top. With his fingers he can play with shadows, moving them up, then down toward the girl, like a spider lowering its thread. Little Miss Muffet unlacing her tuffet, stroking his curds and his whey; along came the spider and crept up inside her, and now little Muffet . . .

His hand withdraws so he can lift the sheet. Yes. A camisole, perhaps a negligee. Garter belts and crotchless little panties. He can smell perfume now, too. The whole ensemble. Dryden must have had it all.

The TV's still on. It's too early for programming, just those bands of colour with their dormant hum. She must have fallen asleep with it still on, though he supposes the movies were mostly meant for him. Pick-a-porn programming; they'll show up on his bill at checkout time, he knows – an extra measure of embarrassment. McFadden tugs and draws the sheet a little higher, to cover her.

So this has happened, after all.

The irony is, he wouldn't mind another crack, now he's conscious enough to participate. He can feel the stiffening, a little harder every heartbeat. McFadden tiptoes out of bed. He still has on his pyjama top, but the bottoms have disappeared. There isn't much to merit shyness at this juncture, but he doesn't want her seeing him this way, so he creeps, sideways, along the wall and into the bathroom.

She's still asleep when he edges out again, legs and limbs jumbled in the bedding. Quietly he dresses and quietly slips to the door. He makes it out into the air without detection.

The morning is intensely bright. It's that pristine hour when the night is well and truly over and day itself has earnestly begun, but not quite. Dewdrops still sparkle in their independent multitudes; every spider's web is perfectly intact. It's too early yet for breeze. The air is still and moist enough for McFadden to lift his chin and see his breath. In the coolness, mosquitoes haven't yet begun to air their wings, though an early bird or two is giving throat. McFadden realizes he is hungry. Nothing like a blow job to sharpen up the appetite.

The sign on the door says the restaurant doesn't open for half an hour yet. There is a stack of newspapers though, freshly delivered and bundled up in plastic twining on the sidewalk. He is startled to see it's the *Winnipeg Free Press* – though of course they are much closer now to Winnipeg than Toronto. Does this mean he's making progress? It's a Sunday edition. Yes, it is Sunday; it has to be, since yesterday was Saturday. Amazing. Five days and he's still not out of Ontario.

It will be good, though, to have a paper with his breakfast. The *Globe* doesn't publish Sundays, so one day a week he is reduced to reading the *Star*. He wonders how the *Free Press* compares, then looks at his watch. Still half an hour to go. Well, he can put the time to good use seeing to the rats.

Cutting out across the lawn, he leaves a trail of footsteps, boot-sized ruptures in the silver mat of dew. The tailgate is slippery with it. Wherever he touches the surface, vertical puddles appear for just an instant, then twitch and roll like spilling beads behind the bumper. No surprises this morning: everyone bright-eyed and scaly-tailed. He takes his time – emptying the litter, topping up the food trays, cleaning out and filling up the water tubes. Eyes watch him from behind the mesh, then turn about their business. He has caught himself from time to time tapping the wire, talking to them.

McFadden is back outside the restaurant well before his thirty minutes have elapsed. He cups his eyes and presses his nose to the glass: no signs of activity, not even lights. The bundle of newspapers is heavier than it looks, reminding him again that his back is still sore, but he gets it heaved over so it's flush against the wall. Another look around for witnesses, then he cuts the twine and takes one.

Of course, it isn't really theft. He'll pay up whenever someone bothers to show. In the meantime he is going to sit down on this stack of newspapers, lean his back against the wall and study up on how the world has changed since yesterday. An awning above has warded off the dew. This wall is facing east; it's warmed up nicely with the rising sun. All in all he's cozy, dry and almost comfortable. Perhaps, when they come, he will ask them to bring him his first coffee out here. A pleasant way to start what is bound to be an awkward morning. He has no idea what kind of fallout he should be expecting.

McFadden has worked his way through the sports pages. He has dealt already with most of the headlines and is midway through a surprisingly thoughtful analysis of matters in Kuwait when a crunch of gravel tells him someone is coming up the drive. He assumes it is a member of the motel's staff, hopefully the cook. It has lately been McFadden's habit to practise non-chalance with strangers; he does not look up until the footsteps have nearly reached the door.

The girl is walking out of the sun.

At first he doesn't realize it's her. She is wearing a dress. Later he will identify this as one of those wispy summer items that have been in fashion since the days of Lucy Maud Montgomery, except that Lucy Maud would surely have insisted her characters wear something underneath. What he sees right now is fire – tongues and sheets of it, clinging and flashing all around the outline of this figure undulating from the sun; legs and arms and body silhouetted in incandescent light, catching in the fabric and the hair, alternating colours like an infrared photograph, orange and red at the perimeter, yellow farther out.

Then he shades his eyes and she is standing there between his legs with the sun streaming all around her. And he opens his mouth because he probably should say something, but she is bending with a hand against his neck, and kisses him.

Then the door swings open to the restaurant and she is leaning there against it, slapping a hand on her hip, smiling, shading her eyes as she smiles. "Hurry up," she says.

McFadden has the paper rumpled out between his hands, like a hopeful sail.

"Come on!" She is actually stamping her foot. "You can finish reading inside. I'm starving!"

For some reason it's the door that baffles him. He stands, blinking, while she takes him by the elbow, hustling him in. "If you're not awake yet, what are you doing out of bed?"

It is a mystery to him how this door has come to be unlocked. A waitress is standing by with menus. Where has this waitress arrived from? The door sighs closed behind him, and the girl is pulling up a chair, one for him as well. McFadden sits. She smiles and holds out both their coffee cups while the waitress fills them to the brim.

He can smell the coffee now and the girl is smiling, brushing her hair from her eyes. "Good morning," she says.

"Good morning," replies McFadden.

It had simply not occurred to him it might be.

− − −

They are now in Manitoba.

He is still chuckling about the billboard they passed at the border: *DON'T GIVE ZEBRA MUSSELS A FREE RIDE!* Huge block letters, sponsored by some department of the Manitoba government. He has to wonder what they'd say about a truck full of rats. "Let me get this straight," she's saying. "You took out an ad in a Chinese newspaper . . .?"

"The *Jia Hua Weekly*," he says, looking out the window to conceal his mirth.

"Whatever. And you got some Chinese chick to translate it into Chinese so that only Chinese people could read it . . ."

"Mandarin," he corrects her, "not *Chinese*. There are probably a hundred different languages in China. Mandarin's just the one most widely recognized, sort of like Latin in the Middle Ages." He is deliberately ignoring her irritation. "A lingua franca, if you will . . . though come to think of it, that one was more likely Italian, so why they call it French is a bit of a puzzle."

McFadden is in tearing spirits. If he wasn't driving, he'd be rubbing his hands and cracking his knuckles. He can't seem to keep the grin off his face, though he knows it's unseemly.

For some reason his attitude annoys her. "So how do you know she translated it right? How do you know she didn't just give you back something that said, like . . . I don't know . . . 'Confucius say white men fucking idiots'?"

Here McFadden laughs so hard his eyes tear up. He has to take his hands off the wheel and thump himself in the chest, trying to catch his lungs up with the rest of him. The truck's trajectory has deviated somewhat out of true, and though his efforts have kept them on the pavement, it is nevertheless a fact that they are occupying rather more of it than strictly necessary.

"For Christ's sake!" She has taken hold of the wheel. "What's wrong with you this morning? Pull over. You're not fit to drive."

He thinks this a splendid idea. The foot's still hurting a little. More to the point, he's delighted with the prospect of freeing his narrative from commonplace distractions. "You have no idea," he says between hiccups. "You have no idea how dead-on you just were."

McFadden's first attempt at intracultural liaison was not so much a dismal failure as a brilliant farce. Oscar Wilde would never have dared so ridiculous a script.

The first stage was hiring an answering service, or rather what they now call voice mail, so he could retrieve his messages by remote without fear of being traceable. That part was simple enough. Next he went through the Yellow Pages and found an agency off Broadview on Gerrard that specialized in Chinese translation. McFadden elected to put on a jacket and tie, and conduct his business on a formal footing. He had with him a brown file folder in which rested a single sheet of paper. Printed carefully, in his best block letters, was the four-sentence advertisement he wished translated into Mandarin so as to be readable by the widest possible spectrum of Toronto's Chinese-speaking population.

He should have been forewarned by the reaction of the woman at the desk, though at the time he was only impressed. She was a grandmotherly type with wrinkled eyes and cross-hatched cheeks, comfortably plump. McFadden explained that he wanted the following four sentences, now in English, translated into Mandarin or perhaps Cantonese, whichever would reach the larger audience. He then intended to run this translation in the classified section of the *Jia Hua*, hopefully next week. The woman smiled and nodded, outlined a fee schedule and asked to see the ad. McFadden passed it over.

It seemed to him that, as she scanned it, her throat did something like a swallow. He could tell she was reading it more carefully a second time, which made him nervous. It was an unusual piece of writing, to be sure; he had no idea what was going through her mind. Was she suspicious? He tried to make himself look matter-of-fact, but what he felt was just plain shifty. Maybe he shouldn't have worn the sunglasses. Was it his imagination or was she avoiding his eye? It was a relief to see her straighten her shoulders, nod her head and very carefully place the paper on her in-tray.

"Anything else?"

"No," he said. "Thank you."

Now she was definitely looking anywhere but at him. McFadden wasn't sure what to think. This could be trouble. On the other hand, it might be just a case of oriental inscrutability. That steadied him. The more he considered, the more this made sense. She was merely being professional.

"You can pick this up tomorrow," she said to a spot of light above his shoulder.

And that was that. He left the building pleased with its aura of restrained propriety. Too many offices are far too chatty. The last thing a customer wants is casual questions from clerical staff.

So he was much more at ease when he returned in the morning, much more his usual self. This time it was a man at the desk, who nonchalantly handed him a sealed envelope with an invoice attached by a paper clip. The man registered no trace of surprise, tallying the bill, and McFadden paid up. A routine matter satisfactorily transacted.

Outside, on the street, he opened the envelope, though what he was looking for he couldn't have said. Certainly there was nothing he could do in the way of proofreading. His English original was stapled to a page bearing a small block of exotically impenetrable Chinese characters. When he compared the two, the one seemed a little longer than the other, but having not the slightest idea of sinitic sentence structure, he could make nothing of this.

McFadden replaced the folder in his briefcase and proceeded to his next stop. He had done a bit of research on the various Chinese-language newspapers presently serving the Toronto region, and decided that the *Jia Hua* would best meet his needs, having, so far as he was able to determine, the most effective circulation. Its offices were out in Mississauga.

"I would like to run this advertisement in your newspaper," he said, after being shown to the person in charge of classifieds.

Here again he was in doubt of his reception, owing to the unusual nature of the service he was proposing to deliver. McFadden had given a great deal of thought to his four short yet punchy sentences:

```
Wild  Game  available  for  discreet  clients.
Any  Quantities.  Reasonable  Rates.  Please
leave msg @ . . .
```

This at least was how it went in English. Again he thought he witnessed a reaction – a brightening of iris or a flickering of brow – but again he wasn't sure. If the man had any reservations, he kept them to himself, and named a figure – quite a lot higher than expected – which McFadden paid in cash.

From this point forward it was merely a matter of biding his time until the paper came out. When the first copies reached the stands a few days later, McFadden was waiting. He had trouble even establishing which pages were the classifieds, and he didn't know if he was meant to start the paper from the back or from the front. But eventually, by dint of laborious cross-referencing against his original, he was able to confirm that a series of characters exactly like his were present on page seventeen, and there was the telephone number – so his ad was run. Now it was merely a matter of waiting for someone to call, or not.

McFadden had prepared himself psychologically for the possibility that no one would respond. Only the truly entrepreneurial would rise to a bait like his, and who knew how many of

those were out there or, for that matter, how many would see his
ad. He made himself wait a full twenty-four hours before dialling,
holding his breath while the fibre optics hummed, straining
his ear to catch the mechanical voice at the other end informing
him that he had . . . twenty-two messages. *Twenty-two!* He
nearly panicked and hung up.

With a mind slightly reeling, he pressed the buttons necessary
to play back his recordings, only to encounter the magnitude of
his mistake: *Chinese.* Everything was Chinese. All of it. He didn't
understand a word – not a sentence or a syllable; just a lot of
chortling and chuckling and raspy exhalations punctuated occasionally by coughs, which were the only thing he *could* recognize.
The rest he presumed to be Mandarin, or maybe Cantonese. It
might have been Mongolian for all the meaning he was able to
extract. The only thing that struck him at the time was that every
voice seemed to be male. But then again, he wasn't even sure of
that.

Cursing his stupidity – he should have foreseen this – McFadden
marched himself back down Broadview to Gerrard and asked the
translators to insert a clause saying that only *English* messages
could be returned. Then he made another run out to Mississauga
so he could pay a second time to have his piece reprinted. Again
he was struck by the odd mixture of politeness and disapproval
with which he was met, but again he put this down to his own
occidental insecurity.

In the meantime his voice mail had chalked up another thirty-
seven calls, each one as impenetrable as the last. For McFadden it
was a time of frustration mixed with outright fear; how was he to
deal with sixty clients? Even if he solved the language problem?
Playing them over, he could tell that several had rung up more
than once, probably wondering why no one was getting back.
And there were a surprising number of hang-ups. Still, the numbers overwhelmed.

The *Jia Hua Weekly* published Thursdays. That day being Friday, he had a week to wait before his notice hit the streets.

Thursday was a long time coming – and then he had to give his voice-mail apparatus another day to log whatever calls came through. Dialing in his access code, his brain was jumping with the possibilities.

This time there were eleven.

McFadden assumed the decrease was due to many of his first-time callers being inarticulate in English, which was as good a way as any of shortening the list. But when he played them back, he had to wonder if he'd accessed someone else's mail.

At first he simply didn't understand. He could follow the English all right, at least in most cases; he just couldn't take in what the words were saying. It was a case of expectation being so far removed from outcome that he failed to grasp what he was hearing.

Caller number one was saying something about needing to know daytime business hours – he could get away only in the daytime – and no way was he going to leave a message, but maybe he'd call back later. Caller two likewise declined to identify himself, but was this in-calls or out-calls? And how much?

When the third caller expressed curiosity about age and ethnicity, McFadden was beginning to suspect that he had wired into some kind of cultural cross-connection. But it was not until caller number seven specifically requested big big bosoms and yellow-coloured pussy hairs that he was able to confirm, beyond all doubt, that something had gone awry in his translation. Straightaway he cancelled the answering service, effective immediately; he didn't need the morality squad on his case before he'd even started.

McFadden sat for several minutes to compose an inward calm, then raced back down to Broadview wishing he could get his hands on a machete. At the door he paused a moment to control himself before bursting through and pressing his paper beneath the nose of the woman at the desk. It was the same wrinkle-faced matron he'd dealt with his first time round.

"What does this say to you?" he asked, in what he believed to be a tone of icy control while pointing to a column he had circled in vermilion ink and ringed with exclamation points.

The woman read it over calmly. "You sex seller," she said.

"I am not sex seller!" McFadden slapped his English version down beside the paper, jabbing his finger from one to the other. "Does *this* say what *that* says? It goddamned well does not."

The woman, now perplexed, called back into the office. A middle-aged man in a grey suit appeared and launched a rapid spate of inquiry, from which McFadden was excluded by the failure of his language. The man removed both copies and placed them side by side beneath a desk lamp. A weighty span of silence settled, McFadden standing, hands on hips, feet apart, rib cage rising; the woman adjusting her gaze from this stranger to the little grey man, whose own eyes flicked back and forth between the pages. At first his expression admitted nothing but detached annoyance, a certain tilting of the head suggesting there was nothing here to warrant his attention. Then something seemed to catch his eye, a quickening of interest that drew his brow a little closer to the page; a readjustment of his spectacles a trifle farther down the nasal slope. A tiny smile began to twitch around the corner of his lip, while a hand rose in valiant effort to suppress the snort of air that rushed into his sinus. The little man's shoulders began to tremble, and then to shake.

The woman stared, baffled now as much as McFadden himself, while her colleague began to produce a sound the like of which McFadden hadn't heard since his last rotation in a trauma unit during med school. She rose from her chair and hurried to retrieve the papers from this fellow, whose mirth was such that McFadden was beginning to wonder if he still remembered how to do a CPR. Then suddenly she saw it too – and now she was laughing, hiding her mouth and turning her face to the wall. Doors began to open and faces appeared. In a few minutes the room was filled with laughing orientalists, slapping one another on the shoulders and watching McFadden at a distance from behind their hands.

– – –

"They thought you were a pimp."

"How did you know?" He can't believe the girl has just poleaxed his punchline.

"Call it a sixth sense."

"Yes," he says, trying to hide his disappointment. "When they finally got themselves under control, the guy came over and told me whoever did the translation apparently misinterpreted my meaning. Very sorry. It seems that where I wrote 'Wild *Game*,' this person read 'Wild *Games*.' Plural. You can see that that would sort of change the slant of things." The girl's reaction is not at all what he was expecting. "Wild *games* . . . " he says hopefully, " . . . available for discreet –"

"I get it."

"The bastards hardly even apologized."

McFadden is crestfallen. He has amused himself so often with this story he couldn't help believing it should have the same effect on someone else. "Anyway," he sighs, deconstructing the remainder of his narrative, "the next go-round I got a little more into the Chinese spirit of things." He scratches his head, sorting through his scattered recollections. "Hold on." Now he's digging in his pocket for his wallet. "I kept this one too." McFadden is sorting through the several bits of paper he's extracted, scanning them quickly, then folding them back into place.

"Ever heard of a shoebox?"

"Hard to fit in your pocket. Here it is!" He begins to pass it over, then stops just as the girl is reaching. "You're driving," he says. "I'll read it out. And by the way, you're speeding."

The girl rolls her eyes; the needle is only vaguely to the right of where the law requires it.

In his hand are two folded bits of paper, bound together by a staple. "This one's the Chinese version," he says, blinking at a scrap of newsprint so crumpled it's begun to come apart at the creases. "I can't read it any better now than I could back then, and I'm still not a hundred percent sure it says what it's supposed to say. I guess it did the trick, though."

McFadden clears his throat with all the self-consciousness of a first-time author on the podium at Harbourfront. "This one's the English original:

```
GOOD HEALTH! Restaurant owners and other per-
sons interested in obtaining WILD DELICACIES
for banqueting purposes - RACCOON, SQUIRREL,
WILD DUCK, WILD GOOSE, WILD PIGEON, MANY
OTHERS! Finest Quality, Wholesale prices.
Please leave msg in English @ . . .
```

et cetera, et cetera . . . I think I asked them to put stars around the 'in English' part."

McFadden reads it one more time, then slides it back into his wallet, still chuckling. "You won't believe it, but they wanted to charge me translating costs for this one too – after holding me up for two weeks and possibly almost getting me arrested! The nerve still takes my breath away. We had quite a little haggle over that one, I can tell you." He is smiling again. "I think we settled on half price – and I made them fax it over to the *Jia Hua* office so I wouldn't have to drive out again. Three times in two weeks is more visits to Mississauga than should be asked of anyone."

"Did you remember to reactivate your voice mail?"

"Yes!" he says, pleased she's paying attention after all. "And of course I got them to assign me a different number."

". . . So what happened?"

"What happened –" says McFadden, still not certain she isn't just being polite but plunging on regardless, "what happened was Mr. Hu."

– – –

After placing the ad, McFadden had waited the usual week, then scratched his growing beard for the requisite one day extra – he had this down to a routine by now – and called in for his messages. The distant, disembodied voice informed him that this time there were none. Zero. He had already put himself through the ritual of ensuring the thing had made it into print; even as he keyed the numbers, he had the latest copy of the *Jia Hua* spread across his knee. The number printed was the right one, so he knew the word was out. But so far no one was listening.

The next day he called again: still nothing. And then again a day after that. On the third day it occurred to him that the problem might be technical; maybe something was wrong with the answering system. So he called and left a message of his own, then called right back to see if it was there, and presto: his own voice telling him he might as well move to Arizona and take up lawn bowling. Or maybe buy himself a loom on Saltspring Island.

By day five it was looking like things were definitely heading back toward the drawing board. Same again day six. What the hell, he said on Wednesday, and paid the good people at the *Jia Hua Weekly* to try again just one more time. Friday morning he called up as he drank his morning coffee, more from habit than from hope, and discovered that a Mr. Hu would like to get in touch.

"What kind of a name is Hu?"

"Chinese, I think, though I don't know if it's Cantonese or Hunanese or Kan or what have you. Come to think of it, I'm not even sure it *is* Chinese, or for that matter if it's even Hu. Mr. Hu and I conduct business on a strictly formal footing. We don't tend to chat."

"So this guy's some kind of middleman?"

"Mr. Hu is my client. He is not so much a middleman as a party with whom I deal exclusively."

"I guess that makes sense when you don't have any other clients."

"Mr. Hu, of course, is not aware of that. And that, as they say, is water under the bridge." McFadden knows he's talking far too much but has no urge to check himself. "Of course there were some initial differences. It took Mr. Hu quite a while to reconcile the relationship of supply and demand with the imperatives of conservation."

"Speak English."

"Mr. Hu had a little trouble at first coming to terms with seasonal shutdowns. Apparently *his* clients are more concerned with availability than renewability. And still he approaches me from time to time with a special order I cannot in all conscience honour."

Her posture indicates she has decided to ignore him. McFadden smiles and trails a finger out the window. "Take raccoons." He sighs. "A brilliantly renewable resource. According to the MNR – that's Ministry of Natural Resources – we have forty thousand of them in downtown Toronto alone." Here he looks deliberately crafty and winks. "And you can take it from me, that figure is significantly low. But whatever, it's in *my* best interest to keep those numbers up, you see? So that means maintaining a stable breeding population. Which of course means not interfering during breeding cycles. Even the Hudson's Bay Company recognized the logic of that way back in the seventeenth century, and you can't imagine a more rapacious, profit-driven bunch than that."

He pauses, smiling, content to note the girl is listening despite herself.

"One of the big advantages of live trapping – I did tell you I use only live traps, didn't I? – Fine. One of the big advantages of live traps is that I can release breeding females and harvest only males. Though it's my opinion that males of all species have things tough enough these days, so I don't trap any raccoons at all from mid-April to the first of June. Sort of like a holiday. After that, I admit, I take the males exclusively until late October, when the pelts are prime. Then it's open season while the market's at its best and the young ones are grown enough to take care of themselves."

"I thought you said furs had to be stamped, or something, by the government before you could sell them."

"Very good!" he says. "They do."

"Then how do you get yours stamped if you don't have a licence?"

"I don't."

"So how do you do it?"

"Mr. Hu, of course."

"*Who* exactly is Hu?"

"Between you and me, I think he smuggles them straight to China. There's an incredible luxury market developing. I suspect he finds a buyer for almost any grade he ships. He certainly buys up everything I'm willing to sell, though there's endless haggling over grades and pay scale. But it works out well for me, because it lets me sell my skins year-round, while conventional trappers get to market only two or three months a year."

"So you're a poacher."

"Technically, yes . . ."

The girl makes an impolite sound.

"But the bottom line is that the raccoon population in the city is as high or higher than it's ever been – I'm not even making a dent. Same with squirrels. And, wherever I can, I actually *do* observe the Game and Fish Act. For instance, section twenty-one, if memory serves, tells us it's an offence to allow the pelt of any fur-bearing animal to be destroyed or spoiled, which is exactly what I'd be doing if I took only the meat and didn't sell the fur on top."

The girl is quietly shaking her head. "The Reverend used to quote the Bible any way it suited him."

"The Reverend?"

She has straightened her back and tightened her hands on the steering wheel. "Nothing," she says. "I don't want to talk about that." He watches her fingers grip and loosen. "And anyway, he wasn't really a reverend, he just liked us to call him that."

"Who would that be?"

"I don't want to talk about it."

McFadden makes a mental promise to come back to this. "At any rate," he says, trying not to lose the thread, "Mr. Hu had trouble understanding the necessity of cutting off *his* clients during seasonal shutdowns. But that's the nature of business, isn't it? And I try to keep up a pretty much year-round supply of pigeons. Pigeons breed all year long; there's no off-season for them." He has stopped again. "Pigeons are quite an interesting bird, by the way . . ."

The transformation's astonishing. It's almost like she's left his presence. She is staring straight ahead, and he wonders for a moment if she's even following the road. McFadden shifts a little, ready to jump for the wheel if he has to. For want of any other option, he simply prattles on.

"Officially, pigeons are classed as migratory, you know, so they fall under the Migratory Bird Act, which is a federal legislation. But of course there's nowhere for them to migrate to; they're European transplants, like house sparrows and starlings, though in Europe – at least originally – they were migratory. After we brought them here, they had no idea where they were going, so they just stayed put."

"You're a real encyclopedia."

"Actually, the history of starlings is even better . . ." It's a relief to hear her speak again. "Did you know the starling just passed its centenary as a North American resident? No, of course you didn't. Well, in the 1890s an American named Eugene Schiefflin decided North America should have every bird ever mentioned in Shakespeare, so he started importing them. The Shakespearean reference, if you're interested, comes from one of the Henrys. Shakespeare gave us far too many Henrys, if you ask me, but that's neither here nor there. In any event, in *Henry IV Part One*, a character named Hotspur wants to teach a starling to nag the king, which is about as neat a harbinger of political lobbying as you could ask for – but I'm digressing . . ."

He wonders how he lets himself go on like this, yet something's warning him trivia may be by far the wiser course at present. She seems neither engaged nor particularly disengaged. McFadden clears his throat and sallies on.

"Anyway, this guy Schiefflin brought over a flock of European starlings and let them go in Central Park. He tried skylarks and nightingales too, as well as starlings, but it's hard to imagine a nightingale surviving long in Central Park. Starlings were the only ones to make it. Now there are millions of them, maybe billions. He was a drug manufacturer, which probably explains it."

"So what's *your* excuse?"

"I've been trying to develop a niche market for starlings, you know, but Hu won't pay enough to make it worth my while. They sell them by the crate at the big markets in Taipei, but for some reason there isn't a demand for them here. We'll see . . . Be that as it may, for the most part Mr. Hu and I have developed quite an amicable relationship. Though I still haven't been able to convince him that I don't do foxes."

"Sure," she says. "Who does?"

"That's just the point, isn't it?" He is delighted to permit the irony to pass him by. "But evidently certain parts of foxes are good at certain times of year for certain medical conditions – pertaining to eyesight, if I'm not mistaken. So he still pesters me for foxes. But I refuse."

"Bully for you."

McFadden lets a little silence grow, and is rewarded with her cautious glance to let him know she didn't mean to hurt his feelings.

"OK," she says, "tell me why you don't do foxes."

"Well," he says, "it's just that . . . I *like* foxes."

The laughter comes completely unexpectedly, like music from a hidden speaker.

"What a guy!"

"It'd be the same again," he adds, timing his delivery, "if we were talking about possums."

"*Possums!*"

McFadden hasn't played Diogenes long enough that he's forgotten how to read an audience. For that matter, neither had Diogenes.

"You're looking," he says with mock self-satisfaction grounded in a genuine sense of accomplishment, "at the collector of Toronto's first ever wild opossum. I would have said first recorded opossum, but of course I wasn't able to record it." He decides to risk another wink, but the girl is avoiding his eye. "It's been known for quite some time that possums have been expanding their range northward into Canada. I'm not sure why, but they are – though come to think of it, who can blame them for bailing out of Alabama. There have been several sightings down in the Niagara region, but so far none in Toronto. At least not until I caught mine. Of course I let it go." McFadden lowers his voice and affects a glance behind him. "I never mentioned the matter to Hu; something tells me there would be a strong demand for possum tails. But I'm hardly going to trap a species before it's even patriated."

"You did say *possums*?" she says. "Like in *The Beverly Hillbillies*?"

"The very same."

"Got you! You said you never watched TV!"

McFadden tries to stop himself from smiling. "*The Beverly Hillbillies*, my dear girl, dates from a time when television was still in black and white and nobody knew that it was dangerous. Like Walter Raleigh and tobacco."

"Whatever you say, Einstein. So what does he do with them?"

"What does who do with what?"

"No. What does Hu do with *possums*?" she says, with a giggle that makes McFadden wish that he had diamonds he could give her.

"I have no idea."

"What do you mean, you have no idea?"

"Just what I said. In an average transaction Mr. Hu will purchase, oh . . . I don't know . . . say a hundred or so raccoon, maybe two hundred pigeon and another couple of hundred squirrel. And however many geese – probably two or three dozen, depending on the weather – and likely half as many ducks. I show up wherever we've agreed to meet. We haggle, he pays. Then we load them in his truck and both of us drive away in opposite directions. That's the last I see of him until our next appointment. So I have no idea where they end up after that."

"They end up in some Chinese restaurant, that's where they end up."

"They may," he says. "Or Vietnamese, or Korean, or Polynesian or North African. I wouldn't be a bit surprised if some find their way into the plats du jour in Yorkville. There is no underestimating Mr. Hu. As I've said, we've been doing business long enough to respect each other's methods."

"Are you shitting me?"

"Everybody's got to make a living."

"You're really not shitting me?"

"Why would I?"

"But how do you get away with it?"

"I get away with it because I'm not really doing anything wrong."

The girl is shaking her head again in a way he can't interpret. Despite himself, McFadden is pontificating. He has thought about this far too much to let it go unjustified. "People obey laws because the laws make sense. When they don't make sense, we stop obeying. Game laws make sense; that's why people respect them. The Game and Fish Act is very good at doing what it's supposed to do almost everywhere except Toronto. Toronto's an anomaly. I sometimes wonder what the MNR would do if they knew about me. My guess is that they'd turn a blind eye. The overpopulation of raccoons in the city has got to make them nervous – especially with this new strain of rabies coming up from the south. I'd bet they'd love to see some trappers operating in Toronto, except the public would go crazy."

"So don't *you* worry about rabies?"

"I get shots."

"What do you mean, you get shots? You mean like rabies shots for dogs? People don't get rabies shots!"

"Of course they do. But I should advise you that your health insurance doesn't cover them – which is no concern of mine, since it doesn't cover me in the first place."

"Really. I didn't know that. But anyway, that wasn't what I meant. I mean, don't you worry about *people* getting rabies when they eat these, um . . . wild delicacies?"

"It cooks out. Rabies is a virus; it can't survive heat. So unless people are eating their raccoon at sushi bars, which I doubt, then it's not a problem."

"You have an argument for everything, don't you?"

"That's because there *is* an argument for everything."

There is an interlude while McFadden scratches his foot and sneaks a peak at the speedometer, which hasn't moved much since the last time he looked.

"Another dilemma," he says, "is the Beretta." He pauses here again, but the girl doesn't take the bait, so he carries on without her. "The main reason they don't allow trapping in the city is because of the prohibitions against discharging a firearm."

This gets her attention. "All right," she says. "Go on."

"Say you're the MNR and you've decided you *are* going to allow trapping in the city. Your biggest problem has got to be the practical logistics. Leghold traps are obviously not an option because they're prohibited in the first place. The MNR allows only the kind of trap that kills instantly, so there isn't any suffering. But of course you can't do anything like that in town, with people's cats and dogs and so on. So the only other option is live-catch box traps – which, as I've said, are what I use.

"So . . . ?"

"So the problem is, what do you do with the animal once you have it in the trap. I mean, you have the difficulty of how to –" He glances over, concerned in case she's squeamish, but if she is she isn't showing it. "– you know . . . dispatch it."

McFadden clears his throat. "The Ministry recommends a .22-calibre short into the middle of the forehead. They give diagrams of the ideal place to aim in one of their booklets. Which again is fine if you're out in the bush, but not too practical when you're on the other side of someone's fence in Lawrence Park. So it's a bit of a Catch-22, if you take my meaning." He checks to see if she has caught the pun, but apparently she hasn't. "A bit of a paradox . . . ?"

"Are you saying what I think you're saying?"

"Well, yes. The only way you can really do it is to bend the rules a little."

"You mean you actually go around shooting off a gun?"

"Well . . ."

"How can you do that! I mean, people must hear it."

"It has . . . ah . . . well at first I used a silencer."

"Holy shit! You're really not shitting me! James Bond meets the Mad Trapper!"

"I went over to Buffalo to get it. Cross-border shopping. I'll tell you, those Yanks will sell you a side arm for every occasion."

"You're serious, aren't you?"

"To be honest, I'd never even held a handgun before, never even had one in my hand. But stroll into one of those gun shops down there and they're hanging from the wall like ham hocks in a German deli. I told the guy I needed a .22 pistol with a silencer and he sold me my Beretta without so much as a bat of an eye. The silencer doesn't look anything like they do in the movies, much longer and clunkier. The really scary thing is that it wasn't even all that expensive. I mean, you could pay more for a good lunch. They're lunatics."

"*You're* the lunatic!" But she's smiling in a way he hasn't seen before. "What do you do, sling it from your hip? Or are you more the armpit-holster kind of guy?"

"Later I discovered I didn't even need the silencer. I was reading one of the trapping magazines – there are several top-notch publications, you know – and one of the articles talked about BB caps."

"BB caps?", she says. "*BB caps!* Where do you get this stuff?"

"I just told you, from a trapping magazine. Anyway, a BB cap is like a regular bullet cut down so it only holds a very small charge of powder. They sell them at the same places you buy regular ammunition; I just didn't know it. They're used mostly by trappers, and maybe the odd assassin who doesn't want to make a mess."

He knows he has her attention now. "There's enough velocity to kill something if you're holding the muzzle right up against its skull; but not enough to make much in the way of noise, or to send the bullet any distance. So in a sense they're quite safe. If you shoot someone with a BB cap from thirty feet, you likely wouldn't do much damage, maybe not even break the skin. I kept the silencer anyway, though – it lengthens the barrel and makes it easier to poke through the cage."

The girl takes her eyes from the road to stare at him full on. "So where do you keep it?"

"Can you watch where you're going, please?"

"I'm just asking. I mean, how do you hide it?"

"You can be very sure I keep it tucked away. And honestly, I do hate having it. But there just isn't any practical alternative. I experimented with lethal injection – you know, veterinary-style. But you can't go selling meat you've just pumped full of Euthanyl. And anyway, it isn't cost-effective. So the Beretta is the only way. But I definitely do lose sleep over it. It's not at all comfortable, I can tell you, violating a law you unconditionally support."

But the girl is not interested in moral dilemma. "Seriously," she says, "what do you do with it? Do you keep it at home? . . . Is it here on the truck?"

McFadden, however, is starting to feel he's been talking long enough. And for the last little while he's been noticing that the landscape has been changing. It's still forest, but the forest seems to be getting tamer somehow. And significantly flatter.

"What's the difference," he asks, "between a prairie and a plain?"

The girl studies him quietly, then shrugs. "All right," she says brightly. "What's the difference?"

He looks at her. "That's what I'm asking! You come from the Prairies – you should know. Why, for instance, do we call them the

Prairie provinces? Why don't we ever call them *Plains* provinces?"

"Oh."

"What do you mean, 'oh'?"

"I thought it was a joke."

"What?"

"A joke. You know, like what's the difference between a prosthodontist and a prostitute?"

"I see."

"So . . . ?"

"So?"

"So what's the difference?"

"Between a prosthodontist and a prostitute?"

"Yes."

"OK," he sighs. "What is the difference?"

"Two lines in the phone book."

McFadden is surprised to find himself chuckling. He has never much liked the dental types.

"Can I ask a stupid question?" she says.

"Shoot."

"What exactly is a prosthodontist?"

"Someone who rebuilds people's teeth."

"Oh well, that makes sense then. The guy who told me that joke offered to give me a cleaning for free . . . Well, not exactly for free. Anyway, I guess he was one."

"I suppose so."

"All right," she says. "Your turn."

"Hmm?"

"Your turn to tell a joke."

But McFadden is still engrossed in grassland semantics. "For that matter," he says, "why don't we call them savannahs, or steppes . . . or pampas?"

"Pampas?"

"That's what Argentinians call their prairies. What's the difference between a pampas and a prairie? Could we call Manitoba a Pampas province, and be etymologically correct?"

The girl, aloof to the challenges of geographic nomenclature, is staring out the window. "I'd call it mostly bush, myself."

"Right," he says. "The Bush provinces."

Several moments pass, but McFadden is reluctant to let the subject drop. "I don't think the real Prairies begin until around Winnipeg."

"How far's that?"

They have just passed a signpost saying *Winnipeg 49 kilo-metres.*

"I'd guess fifty kilometres," he says decisively, and reaches into the glovebox for his map. He has just remembered that he doesn't want to go through Winnipeg. McFadden has had enough of the Trans-Canada. The route over Lake Superior has only two possibilities, and the other's even longer. Now they're into Manitoba, there are other highways. "Pull over when you see a spot. I'll take over for a while."

"Think you can keep us on the road?"

"Let me see what I can do."

His foot is actually feeling fairly good; there is no pain now when he pushes the clutch. Wonderful what a bit of rest will do. It was one of his favourite prescriptions as a physician, remarkably effective even in his line of speciality, though it never did much for billing.

McFadden works his way boldly through the gears, unperturbed by pedals but mindful of his steering. He has been behind the wheel no more than ten or fifteen minutes when all at once the forest ends. Suddenly they're on the plains.

"Amazing."

Landscape stretches out before him as far as he can see. Up ahead he spots the exit he's been looking for, and he turns off the highway, heading south. If the girl is curious about the change in course, she keeps it to herself.

"Look!" she says, pointing to a narrow set of towers rising from the plain in candy-apple red. "The first elevators."

"So they are," he says, admiring the prairie postcard.

They both watch the odometer click.

"You want to hear something funny?"

McFadden contains his sigh. "Go ahead."

"I thought *you* had drugs."

"*What?*"

"Drugs or girls."

"What are you talking about?"

"When you picked me up. Remember when you picked me up and I got in your truck and we drove for a little while, and then you just pulled off the road and stopped. The truck was hidden behind all those logs, and you opened the door and got out. I thought for sure you were going to go for me . . . I remember thinking I could try running for the bush again if I had to. Or maybe I should just go along with it. I couldn't decide which was smartest. And then you were gone for a while and I still couldn't decide, so I just stayed where I was. Then you came back and got in and started up the truck like there was nothing the matter, and the next thing I know, we're on the highway again."

The girl has paused to order her thinking. McFadden keeps his mouth shut.

"But then a little while later you started talking about food, and then *food* was all I could think about. It was . . . oh, a long time since I'd eaten anything . . . I mean, with a knife and fork and everything. So when you stopped again and brought out those whatd'yacall'ems . . . "

"Squabs," he says quietly.

"Yeah, squabs. When you brought out those squabs, they just blew me away. I'd have eaten ten of them, you know, if I could have. So it started to look like maybe you were OK. But then that Winnebago thing drove in and you didn't breathe once until it was gone.

So then I think to myself, all right, so the guy is up to something. So naturally, I think it's drugs."

"Of course."

"But drugs didn't add up. When you were in the back I thought I heard you talking, and water running. What do you need to do that stuff for with drugs? I mean, if you're running drugs, you just want to get them to wherever they're going as fast as you can; you don't have to stop and talk to them. So *then* I think to myself, holy shit – this guy's running girls too. And then right away my head starts to spin and my stomach is boiling and I think, oh Jesus Christ, he's drugged me, now I'm done for. Oh God, please don't let this be happening again."

McFadden remains absolutely silent.

"And then you got me into that motel room and I was so out of it and everything was so – well, you can't blame me for thinking what I thought, and that's what I did think – but it didn't quite add up either. I couldn't see any signs of . . . you know . . . and then the rest of the day just got weirder and weirder. All of a sudden you were bolting out of the room and we were checked out and in that truck again. And I *still* didn't know, but I started thinking you might be a good guy after all. Then we went to that place for breakfast, that place where you bought your sign, and you were so nice – and there were those guys at the other table – so by this time I'm thinking you really are a good guy. But then you disappear again into the back of the truck, and I just couldn't stand it any longer. That's why, when I saw you couldn't move while you were gluing up that stupid sign, I just had to go see for myself."

She has her hands in her lap, shaking her head. "Rats!" she says. "Jesus, you could have knocked me over with a feather. I still haven't decided if you're OK or even weirder than I thought . . ."

She is chuckling to herself now, rubbing her thighs as she smiles. McFadden has followed this, more or less, until the last bit.

"Umm," he says. "I get the part about you thinking the rats might be cocaine or something like that. I guess that makes sense, under the circumstances. But I don't quite . . . umm . . . The part about the girls. How would . . . I mean, why would anybody smuggle girls?"

In the silence, the look she gives him makes the little hairs stand up all along the back of his spine.

"Yeah," she says. "Why would they?"

There is true quiet now.

McFadden holds his breath. "At the restaurant," he says, "when you took the keys and opened up the back – what were you going to do if it was . . . ah . . . girls?"

"I don't know."

He nods. There is nothing in need of any confirmation; the nod acknowledges the lack.

The girl is gazing out the window.

"What were you doing there, on that stretch of road . . . when I picked you up?" It has come out so softly he is afraid she hasn't heard. He needs to fill his lungs. "Where was it you came from . . . ah . . . How did you get there?"

From the corner of his eye he sees her blink. Her lips part, then close again. He hears her draw in air and then exhale. In a moment she tries again to speak. Her hands have left her knees to clench together down between her thighs. McFadden finds he has to look away.

"It's a long story," she says at last.

When he turns again, she is trying to smile. He matches her effort, smiling back.

"You have a long time." He has spoken even more slowly than before.

"I think . . . " she says. "I think I'll take that, then."

McFadden has decided he would like to play the radio, or perhaps just fiddle with the dials. But of course there is nothing he can do but concentrate as carefully as he can on steering straight between the yellow lines.

When at last he looks, he is appalled to see that she is blushing. Furiously blushing. Her face and cheeks are scarlet red, the well of crimson spreading, as he watches, down her neck and out beyond her shoulders.

"Oh," she says, and swallows.

McFadden feels his own ears burning. A humid wave of something prickles through the cab. His hand is groping for the door panel, cranking down the window. In a few moments the girl has rolled down her side too.

"So," she says, "know any other good jokes?"

– – –

Wyley McFadden has always been willing to concede his limitations with regard to colour. He appreciates colour, very much – sea of blue, field of green, golden sunsets and all that; he just doesn't understand their application to people's clothes. Generally speaking, he is competent in most areas of sartorial injunction. McFadden knows, for example, that polka dots should not be worn with stripes and that white shoes are taboo before the May long weekend. As to the origins of these canons, however, he has no theories. He is given to understand that certain individuals are reckoned to be gifted in this matter, that some are simply born this way, like redheads or autistics. McFadden understands that he is not among this group.

This is not to say he is a shabby dresser. Far from it. McFadden's wardrobe, in the days of his medical career at least, was uniformly adequate. Early on in life he made a point of memorizing which ties went best with which jackets. He alleviated the need for choice in shirts by always wearing white. What he sacrificed in pigment, he made up for in quality of weave: McFadden's shirts were handmade broadcloth, starched, with minutely monogrammed French cuffs. Indeed, his onyx cufflinks became something of a trademark. Over the years it had evolved into a ceremony, repeated many times throughout the day, for the doctor to remove his links, align them precisely on the corner of his table, then carefully roll up his sleeves before snapping out the fingers of his latex gloves. It often irritated the lesbians, this performance, but to his way of thinking it allowed his clients a few quiet moments to prepare themselves.

His shirts varied only in the relative width of their collars, which widened or narrowed according to his tailor's interpretation of current trends in fashion. Problematic colours, like yellow or red, he learned simply to avoid. Polka dots, of course, even as they might apply to neckties, were strictly proscribed. Socks, slacks, scarves and overcoats conformed to an orthodoxy of charcoal grey, navy blue and certain tweedy weaves of brown.

There are guidelines pertaining to the selection of clothing, and these McFadden has learned by rote, like multiplication tables or the conjugation of irregular verbs. He has always understood that there are some who have mastered these rules so intuitively as to break them at will. Although admitting a degree of envy, on the whole he holds these revisionists in aggrieved contempt, and fervently resents their complication of a system Byzantine enough as it is. According to McFadden, there are much more fertile grounds for contemplation than pondering every morning which belt to match against which shoe.

Most puzzling, though, are those people who have their own colours – people who *know*, absolutely, that they look especially good in certain shades of blue, or fuchsia, or what have you. McFadden himself has no personal colour, though he wishes he had; then he could simply stick with it, and that would be that.

Since changing professions, of course, the demands on his wardrobe have greatly diminished. A trapper, even of the urban variety, is under no obligation to alternate his outfits. McFadden now wears much the same thing from one day to the next, except when going to the theatre. He still thinks about it, though, from a distance. Now that he is relatively free of practical constraints, he finds himself more and more at liberty to study the matter of sartorial aesthetics in the abstract. Why is it that some clothes, even to his ignorant eye, appear more appropriate than others? From time to time he assesses the presentation of strangers; why do some seem elegant and others not? Aesthetics, evidently, are beyond him. Some people just look good in certain colours and others don't, and that's the end of it. He is angry with himself for dignifying trivia, but it bothers him that anything at all is beyond his grasp.

Take this girl, for instance. He can't properly identify the colour she is wearing. Not quite blue, but not really purple either; mauve, perhaps, or lavender. Maybe indigo – McFadden has never been sure of the distinctions. The overall effect is basically blue, but a fully ripened blue, like a summer night before the stars come out. He tilts his head to appreciate the simile. There *is* a certain cloudy, starry sort of quality to this blue, though now that he is looking he sees several other colours too. A definite yellow – or maybe gold – and an orangey kind of red. The pattern is something like paisley, though he knows it isn't paisley because paisley he can always recognize by the curly little spermatozoa. Whatever it is, it becomes her.

McFadden is confident he has correctly identified this as *her* colour. The girl, therefore, is one of those people with a personal colour. This does not surprise him. It's clear that this particular blue complements her skin tone, eye colour, whatever. He wishes she were driving so he could study the matter more carefully.

She is lovely this morning. He's been observing this since breakfast back at the motel. What interests him particularly is the compounded effect of her sexuality. It's mostly the dress. True, her hair is done up somehow differently, which lends its own effect, and the makeup has somehow made her eyes seem bigger and her skin shinier. But it's mostly the dress.

"What are you looking at?"

He coughs, then rallies with an honest version of the truth. "I was trying to decide what colour that dress is."

"Oh." She seems disappointed.

"What colour is it, then?"

The girl reaches to her thighs to lift it briefly, then lets it fall. McFadden feels himself moving with the air beneath.

"Blue," she says.

He digests this.

"Just blue?"

"Well, what does it look like to you, salmon pink?"

"No! But there are several other categories . . ." He lets the sentence trail away.

Now she's philosophical, examining the material. "Blue usually isn't my colour, to be honest. But then there wasn't a lot of time to choose." She has brought up her chin and smiled again. "It fits, though. You like?"

"Beautiful."

To put some distance from his solipsism, he shifts his thinking more directly to the matter of sex. It is, after all, a biological imperative, like eating or breathing. To be honest, though, the similarity pretty much ends there. From a biological standpoint its forces are disturbingly erratic: compulsive one day, forgotten the next. Why so irresistible when it does strike, while just the week before it might as well have not existed? McFadden is troubled with the urge to cross his legs. It could be she's ovulating. There have been several studies suggesting that human brains are just as susceptible to pheromones as anybody else's. Maybe she's sending them off and he's just innocently picking them up, unconsciously, as it were. But he still thinks it's the dress.

If he hunches his shoulders a bit, he can hide it, or at least camouflage it better with his clothes. He has been surreptitiously untucking his shirt so as to spread the tail across his lap. It's quite uncomfortable, but his options, while conducting a moving vehicle, are limited.

The girl sighs and slips a little further down her seat, the wisp of fabric riding higher up her thighs. She is gazing out the window. Or it could just be she's dropping off to sleep.

It's still early, and the sun is streaming through the windscreen. How strange that barely hidden flesh is even more distracting than the flesh itself. He's sure, if she were naked, this wouldn't be as bad. But the sun has made her dress a gossamer of twilight haze, bathing breast and belly in this dimpled, dappled blue. Not just the outline, but the breast itself. If he looks, he can clearly see the hollow of her navel. Sunbeams slide and dart along the crevices of her limbs.

"You know what . . ." he says, and clears his throat. "My, ah, foot is acting up." He bears down on the steering wheel to correct any slippage of his own, and coughs. "Do you think you'd mind taking the wheel again? Sorry about all this."

The girl has turned and swung one knee around, to tuck the other foot beneath her thigh – purple, now, with the change of tilt.

"Is it hurting?"

McFadden mutters something in his chin.

"Oh poor you. We have to do something about this."

The trick, he has discovered, is to take deep breaths, but through his nose so nothing looks out of the ordinary. And keep his elbows in.

"Any time you're ready."

"What? Oh, right."

McFadden shifts his foot from gas to brake, and the truck is bumping off the pavement. He unlatches the door and swings around onto the running board. Now his back is to her and he's standing on the highway. A tractor-trailer rumbles by, air horns blaring. McFadden scurries to the rear and lingers at the tailgate, hoping she will choose the route around the front of the truck, but she has come this way as well. He plumps down on the bumper and crosses his legs, making a show of inspecting his foot.

She has the most disconcerting habit of standing close. There is perfume, too, and a sudden vivid image of last night's blue and gasping room. She has her hand on his shoulder, rubbing in sympathy, her bare leg pressed against his knee.

"We should have done this sooner."

"No. No. I'll be fine in a minute." He feels her gaze, but he is staring hard at his foot. "Go ahead," he croaks. "I'm just going to, um, visit the bushes – too much coffee."

She squeezes his shoulder and passes by. A slight vibration as the door thuds closed. He is absolutely certain none of this has been intentional. At least he doesn't think so.

McFadden takes his time among the bushes. The girl has waited patiently.

"Better?" she asks.

"Yes, thank you."

Though he can't escape the feeling that he should be labelling a collection jar.

– – –

The girl is behind the wheel again, so McFadden can watch the landscape. What he wanted was the opportunity to rubberneck this vast expanse of Earth. He has been trying to restrict the scope of his survey to the windows in his half of the cab, but his eyes keep panning all the way around. If he lets them go too far they run against the girl, which has an immediate foreshortening effect. He peers briefly at a patch of sun-warmed thigh, then back out his window.

All in all, the countryside is holding fairly well against the competition. He has the feeling this isn't quite prairie in its fullest sense – neo-prairie, perhaps, exceedingly flat, but sprinkled here and there with clumps of forest like islands on a placid lake. McFadden doesn't know if this ground used to have more trees and has been cleared or if it formerly was plain but has since been intermittently forested. Most of the woods seem to be in little dips and gullies, where the farms and houses also tend to sprout.

At Steinbach they hitch west again, and then again south, McFadden calling out directions from the map across his knee. He means to angle down into the badlands. The smaller highways take them through a series of towns and villages. He is more at ease with his cargo. Now that they have some miles behind them, the rule of surreption has relaxed a bit. It would not be possible to avoid towns in this part of the route anyway; there are too many.

People being unavoidable, he switches his attention to demographics. Steinbach turns out to be as Teutonic as its name suggests; they stop for gas and hear German spoken all around. A little farther is the French town Saint-Pierre-Jolys; the next is overwhelmingly Ukrainian. The entire country's cosmopolitan, he tells the girl – though his pleasure is mitigated by the sight of two boys on bicycles wearing Chicago Bulls T-shirts. It seems to McFadden that if they wanted to objectify a bunch of Americans, they might at least have picked the Blue Jays, or for that matter the Blue Bombers. But then again, it's only marketing – which somehow only serves to make it worse.

Soon they are crossing the Red River, reminding him of breakfast cereal and Louis Riel. He wonders if Riel ate a hearty bowl before the scaffold, and then rebukes himself for gallows humour. Even so, he can't help speculating as to the legitimate history of Red River cereal. Was it actually eaten in the 1880s? Or is that just marketing too? He hasn't had Red River cereal since he was a boy. Maybe if they stop for breakfast somewhere, he'll order up a serving. It would be good for the girl as well.

They've been fairly quiet, the two of them, with all this prairie rolling by. It's the real thing now, any shadows of the forest burned away beneath these open skies. There is more starting and stopping now, the road shooting straight from one town to the next: Myrtle, Roland, Rosebank. A joke about the lack of palm trees in a little place that calls itself Miami, but wit has fled them. McFadden has been looking out across the landscape, thinking. The girl is staring through the windshield. When a coyote appears, nose down in a fallowed quarter to the right, it is he who has to point it out, although she clearly should have seen it first. She nods, murmurs something, and the coyote is behind them. Now he fiddles with the radio, but it's the news, and news here appears to be an endless round of grain commodities broadcast by the tonne. Durum wheat at two-eighty-six. Oats and barley holding well at two-sixteen and one-sixty-seven, five. Soya markets down a shade. Canola up. Yellow corn unchanged since yesterday. The land is very flat.

He asks if she is hungry and she turns her head, surprised, and tells him no. So lunch is skipped today and they drive onward in a straight line pointing west.

Around Pelican Lake the ground begins to show a little sinuosity. McFadden is intrigued with the notion of pelicans. He has never seen freshwater pelicans and is strongly tempted to detour from the highway in search of one. He doubts the girl would raise objections, but the thought of justifying ornithological meanderings somehow checks the impulse. So the girl is a catalyst upon his conscience, too – something else to think about. McFadden takes his conscience where he finds it.

Instead, he points them down a new road heading south, and goes that way a while, not long, then west again. It has begun to register that there isn't that much longer. Manitoba is two-thirds crossed already, then it's just Saskatchewan – and then Alberta. Saskatchewan is wider at the bottom, true. Still, they'll drive it in a single day. And then Alberta.

"Come to think of it," she says, "I *am* hungry."

His mind's still farther west. "That was miles back."

"Then I'm even hungrier."

One day's drive, he thinks, and then Alberta. If they push on overnight, they'll be there in the morning. He is startled to discover that he wishes he were driving, so he could ease a little off the gas.

"Do you think," he asks carefully, "do you think that it's likely to rain?"

The girl adjusts the rear-view mirror so they meet each other's eyes, then twists and cranes her neck behind it, squinting up.

"No."

McFadden squints a little too. There are random herds of cloud, scattered on a field of sky like migrants on the way to somewhere else. No suggestion of rain. Visibility lends itself to speculation. "How do you feel about bacon and eggs?"

"How do you feel about a campfire?"

"If we can find a place to camp."

She has both hands around the steering wheel, primly looking straight ahead. "Then good."

– – –

Though it turns out not to be so simple.

McFadden is mentally committed to bringing this day's travel to an end. The problem, though, is the windswept absence of places to halt. His woodland, urban nature balks at all this emptiness. McFadden requires trees and cover for a campsite to define itself. Now and then they pass a clump of poplar, rooting in the hollows of the Prairies' flank – sloughs, the girl has called them – but these are always in the distance, or too close to the roadway to be useful. Everywhere is empty plain.

They've been passing derricks, sometimes singly and other times in scattered flocks, ovoid heads dipping up and down like palsied birds. Under no circumstances will McFadden pitch his tent in the vicinity of one of these. Now and then the girl will indicate some little dip or dimple midway in the distance and McFadden, though he strongly wishes otherwise, vetoes these with what he hopes is visible regret. And so they pass quietly from Manitoba on into Saskatchewan.

He wonders if they have crossed another time zone. He'd had these sorted out before departure, but he's lost track again of which way the clock is meant to go. McFadden unfurls his map: they have not passed a time zone. There isn't one until Alberta.

According to his calculations it can't be more than seven or eight hundred kilometres. He measures his thumb against the scale, then counts the distance out again. No more than nine or ten hours, driving at the speed limit. Half a day – not even.

Of course he still has no idea where she's going once they get there. She has mentioned foothills, which argues at least for the far side of the province.

"Umm . . . " he says, making sure he doesn't hold his breath. "Where exactly do you want to go?"

"I thought," she says hotly, "that that last place was fine. It was *you* who made me drive right by without even stopping to look!"

"That was not a campsite!" He forgets himself. "That was a drainage ditch!!"

"It had trees."

"Shrubs, you mean, and that would be generous. I'm not about to roll my bedding beside a culvert. Anyway . . ." He has stopped. "That wasn't what I meant. What I meant was, where in Alberta do you want me to let you off?"

"Oh."

The girl reaches for the dashboard and flicks on the radio. He almost smiles to hear the same voice reading off the monotone of grain quotations: "Soybean still losing, durum wheat at two-eighty-six . . ." But she twists the dial and now the cab is a crackling fog of static. A new voice fades in, then out, then in again. The girl leans back into her seat while McFadden, inveterate, adjusts his ear by habit.

There is something familiar in this voice – not the voice itself, but the type. That distinctive whispery quality. English spoken with an accent, but not. A cadence characteristically slower. An undertone of distant French; *th*'s emerging more like *d*'s. Then another voice, orthodox and clipped, politely interjecting with a question . . . and the Indian speaker carrying on as if the interruption hadn't registered. *Aboriginal person*, McFadden reminds himself.

He doesn't recognize the speaker. It is someone without a national profile – a local man – representing, it would seem, one of the bands in northern Manitoba. But the message is familiar: treaties not respected, government funding insufficient, promises broken, promises not made. Resentment growing by the day; don't know how much longer we can hold the young men back.

The girl's arm has whipped out like a snake and struck the radio dead.

"Asshole!"

He is startled at the fervour, and when he turns, smiling, the shock is nearly overwhelming: a surge of malice so intense it's almost luminescent. He half expects to hear the speakers shorting out. *Feral* – the word has sparked of its own volition into his mind. If the girl could move her ears, they would be lying flat against her skull.

McFadden concentrates a little time on loosening his shoelace. "Mmm" he says, and then decides against. "Where," he says, "do you want me to take you?"

He watches, fascinated, as her spine uncurls along each vertebra. The hairs along his own neck have begun to settle.

She trails a long, hard breath, then shrugs. "Where are *you* going?"

"I told you, yesterday."

"No, you didn't. You said you'd be stopping at a bunch of different towns. You never told me which ones."

"Oh," he says, trying to recollect. "Let's see . . ." The nice thing about not driving is that it lets him close his eyes. McFadden tends to close his eyes to focus better. "The first stop is Lethbridge – no, sorry, Taber – then Lethbridge. Then it's over to Fort Macleod, then up to Claresholm, I think, and then I'm pretty sure straight up to Cowtown . . . Though it seems to me there's somewhere in between . . . Hold on." He opens his eyes and spends a moment fishing in the glovebox. "Here it is," he says, extracting what for many months McFadden has considered *The Map.*

It's a photocopied enlargement of south and central Alberta, sketched over with a shape vaguely like the outline of an Iroquoian war club – its head sitting flat from Taber to Fort Macleod, the handle curving north to Edmonton; angled in a tapered grip from Westlock down to Vegreville, then south again back down toward the heavy end. It's an Etch-A-Sketch, connect-the-dots kind of diagram, linking up his target towns in one long loop from top to bottom – starting south, running north, then south again – ending where it started.

"The Rat Trail," he says, smiling at his mischief, happy to be talking after all this quiet.

"Alongside of every target town," he says, smoothing the map out across the dash so she can see it, "you'll see numbers with an x beside them, circled in red ink. Those are the designated rat drops. If you look, you can see most are smaller communities ranked as $1x$. Mid-sized centres get a $3x$ or $4x$. Calgary and Edmonton rate $6x$ each."

McFadden has shifted the map across the steering wheel. The girl has had to push it back so she can see the road.

"Why don't I let you drive awhile?" she says.

"Oh, sure." It's just occurred to him that she has been behind the wheel for most of Manitoba. They pull over on a lonely stretch of highway floating straight across an empty sea of grass, McFadden pausing long enough to piss against the tire. The girl tells him she can hold out until they stop, which had better be soon. "I'm really hungry, you know. Any time now I'll be gnawing on your shoulder."

"The figures you see inside the red circles," he says briskly, "refer to the number of colonies designated for each town."

"Can we do this on the road?"

"*What?* Oh. Of course."

When he has them up to cruising speed, he leans and points with one hand tugging on the paper.

"Wait a minute," she says. "And keep your hands on the wheel. I can read, you know . . . Let me get this straight. Every one of these places you've got circled here, you're going to. Right?"

"Right."

"And at every one of them you're dropping off some rats."

"I wouldn't phrase it quite so casually, but yes, that's close enough." She studies his map until McFadden feels that he should speak again. "So if any one of those communities is the one you want, you just tell me. OK?"

The girl's still silent.

"It's a lot of places," she says, apparently counting.

"Twenty-six," he tells her. "All told."

"Twenty-six."

Another silence.

"I could probably take you somewhere else, you know, once I get the rats all dropped. I mean, if you want to go someplace that isn't there on the list, I could probably drive you there. After."

"What did you say these little numbers mean?"

"That refers to the number of colonies to be dropped at each location."

"Colonies?"

"Yes. For my purposes a colony is a unit of thirty-five, sometimes thirty-six individuals – I had some extras. But generally speaking, it's thirty-five rats per colony – nine males to every twenty-five or twenty-six females."

He glances over, but she's blinking at him as though she wants him to go on. McFadden sighs.

"Rats don't tend to get along so well together; you may have noticed that. They're very much like people. They need to live together, but they can't stand one another, so they're always splitting off and striking out, constantly expanding their range. I'm expecting each of these initial groups to break up into three or four smaller breeding populations. This should maximize their collective chances for survival. But anyway, as I was saying –"

"Why thirty-five? I mean, what made you come up with that number . . . instead of . . . forty-five, say?"

Now it's McFadden's turn to study her. "The usual ways. Research. Experimentation. Also, how many rats I could fit in the back of my truck."

The girl is very obviously looking for something to say.

"Have a look," he says, "down near the bottom of the map. You'll see a place called Taber. Taber's the first stop."

"I know Taber."

"Fine." He has leaned her way to point again. "You can see there, it's listed as a 1x. That means it gets one colony: twenty-six females and nine males, released all in one location." The girl bobs her head. "Now, if you look over at Lethbridge, you'll see that it's a 3x. Or is it a 4x?" He has taken hold of one corner of the page again and tried to shift it his way.

"It says four."

"Four, then. That means it gets four separate colonies, released into four separate parts of town. Calgary and Edmonton are big enough for six each – more if I had them. All in all there are forty units going into the province, divided, as I've told you, into twenty-six individual communities . . . I take it none of them is where you want to go?"

The girl is still examining the map. "How come you've left out Medicine Hat? And . . . almost everywhere north of Edmonton?"

"Is that where you're going?"

"I'm just asking."

"Geography," he says, pleased with the question, whatever its motive. "Also climate. And of course the Alberta government."

He lets the silence hang again. There is obfuscation here, no doubt of that, but he has sensed a prickling of interest beyond the conversational manipulations. McFadden is delighted. It's been ages since he's had a good manipulation.

"What are you smiling at?"

"I beg your pardon?"

"You were smiling. Did I miss something funny?"

"Oh. No. I was just thinking."

"What were you thinking about?"

"Umm . . . geography." He decides to experiment. "Speaking of geography," he says, "you were about to tell me where exactly you want to get off."

She tilts her head and grins right back. "No, I wasn't. *You* were about to tell *me* why you picked these towns and not others." She has rolled his map into a cone, and taps him with it.

"All right." McFadden recognizes rapprochement when it has come and tapped him on the shoulder. "But you'll have to endure a history lesson."

She pauses a moment.

"I've had worse," she says.

– – –

"The first thing you should know about *Rattus norvegicus* is that in our climate they need people to survive. They have to have buildings or sewers – any sort of man-made protection from the cold. Otherwise the winters kill them. You know, I'm not certain I should be driving for this. I think I'd do a much better job without –"

"You'll be fine."

"What if I told you my foot was hurting?"

"What if I told you I was getting a headache?"

He is not quite certain how he is intended to interpret this. Judging by that feral little smile, she means exactly what he thinks she means.

"Alberta is able to maintain its rat-free status for four main reasons, three of them geographical, one of them political . . ."

She is arranging herself on the seat, getting comfortable. He can't help noticing the dress again. Her movements entail a great deal of crossing and uncrossing of legs.

"Reason number one is the Rockies, which stop any natural migration from the west. Reason number two is the boreal forest to the north, which is just too cold. Number three is the desert – and I mean this more in a demographic sense than climatic. If you look at northern Montana on the map, you'll see there are hardly any people, which means there can't be any rats. Remember, rats need people, so the southern route's cut off as well. This leaves Alberta with only one gateway so far as rats are concerned: the Saskatchewan border – and as a matter of fact, only the lower half of it."

McFadden glances over, but the girl is looking out the window.

"So that's where you're taking them."

"Yes . . . The only way rats can migrate to Alberta is through

a six-hundred-odd-kilometre stretch of border between Cold
Lake and Montana. That's their one window of opportunity.
The fourth and final barrier, therefore, to the transmigration of
rats across this great dominion of ours is the government of Alberta itself, which works very hard to stop them dead before they
manage to get through."

"You're shitting me again, aren't you?"

McFadden puts a hand above his heart. "The first rats in
Canada appeared on the East Coast, by ship, like all the rest of us
immigrants –"

"You mean white people."

"Quite right. Your ancestors arrived a few thousand years
earlier. But as for rats, they showed up sometime in the seventeenth century, maybe even the sixteenth. And just like everybody else, they started moving inland. 'Go West, young Rat,' et
cetera . . . By the 1930s they'd made it almost all the way across
the Prairies, well into Saskatchewan . . . "

He peers at her face to see how she is taking this in. "It's all in
the history books. This is standard demographics. In 1950 the
very first Albertan rat was discovered on a farm in a little town
just across the border from Saskatchewan. No one in the region
had ever seen a rat before. People didn't know what it was. The
government had to send out stuffed rats as public exhibits so the
local populace would know what to look out for."

McFadden still has a hand on his heart. "The powers that be
in Alberta recognized a plague when they saw one coming, so
what they did was deputize crews of official exterminators.
Then they trucked in tons of arsenic and strychnine, thousands of traps, and canisters of poison gas – and established
this six-hundred-kilometre kill zone. And that's how they plugged
the gap."

The girl looks doubtful.

"By now they have it down to a system. Almost all of their efforts are concentrated along this strip . . . " McFadden has retrieved his map and spread it on the seat beside her, tracing a line

with his finger. "They've demarcated an area 29 kilometres wide by 520 long. That's the *zone*. All of Alberta's rat prevention efforts are concentrated right here." He's still tapping on the map. "Seven municipalities in all. Each one has a Chief Pest Control Officer in charge of his own turf. The Pest Control Officer is responsible for checking every single building in his area at least once a year, and has the authority to order them torn down and dug out if they find an infestation. They're also using better poisons now. Which reminds me, when we stop, don't let me forget to give the rats one last rolled-oats treatment."

"I don't think I even want to ask."

"What they use now is warfarin, an anticoagulant. They mix it up with rolled oats, then throw in some confetti as a warning, so Albertans don't forget and boil it up for breakfast. But it kills the rats all right. What I've been doing is training *my* rats not to eat it. I put in cayenne pepper and other terrible-tasting things, then try to trick them into eating some. Rats learn very fast. A couple of years ago in Paris they tried out a new poison down in the sewers. I don't know if you've been there, but Paris has a lot of sewers. The point is that within hours – *hours!* – the news had travelled so fast throughout the rat population that not a single rat would touch it, no matter where else in the network they tried to put it. Rats may not like each other, but they communicate. Again, just like people. I've got them so that if they even smell rolled oats, they're off and running. I'm counting on this giving them that much extra time to get established. By the time the pest control authorities figure out their baits aren't being taken, it should be too late. Rats can reproduce every fifty-one days: twenty-three day gestation, twenty-eight days to wean the litter – and then they're ready for another cycle. History teaches that once they're reproducing, it's virtually impossible to stamp them out."

"You're really serious, aren't you? I mean . . . how can anybody . . . Why would anybody even *know* this stuff?"

"They publish."

"*Who* publishes?"

"The Alberta government. They're so proud of their rat-free status they print up fact sheets and send them out for free. Just write to the Department of Agriculture. It's all there. And I have to say, I'm especially thankful for the rolled-oats ruse; that could really make the difference."

"You are so . . . *weird*!"

"Be that as it may, and in answer to your question, the reason I'm not dropping any rats into Medicine Hat, or Wainwright, or Lloydminster, or any place near the border, is that that's exactly where they're most expected. That's where Alberta's waiting for them. I'm about to outflank them, to come at them from behind, where they're least expecting it. Think of the Maginot line and what the Germans did in 1940 . . . Sorry – what they did was go around it. The soft underbelly of Alberta, at least so far as rats are concerned, is exactly the region represented on the map you're holding in your hands."

But the girl isn't looking at his map.

While he's been talking, the land has changed. Not changed, exactly . . . Yes, *changed*. Still arid, still tufted with a down of sage. But not flat. Not even close to flat. The transformation is dramatic.

"Wow."

McFadden has lost the line of his monologue. "It's beautiful."

"We're stopping here," she says.

He simply nods.

"There has to be a road."

"Yes," he says. "If there isn't, we'll make one."

Later, when he finds it on the map, he sees that it is called Moose Mountain River – euphonious even in name, though topographically unsuited to its title. It's like, he thinks, a piece of prairie curved into a woman's hip. A landscaped intumescence, rounded slopes, maternal hills – an arid sort of opulence. Everything about it speaks to him in female metaphor. He wonders what it could possibly have to do with moose.

The river is several hundred feet below the level of the highway. They find a way that takes them down, then a track insinuating deeper still. At last the truck is creeping over naked coulee, down and in and farther down again. They pull up in a place that might have been the same before there were such things as people. A scent of sage and stillness.

"No bugs," she says.

"No bugs."

To make felicity complete, there is a supply of wood to hand. The river must have borne it down from farther north and left it for them in its bed – smoothed and rounded by the elements, polished desiccation. Tinder dry.

The girl is dragging pieces to the hearth she's busy making. "Get cooking."

And McFadden does.

. . . for rats, all change
in social status is
downward.

JOHN B. CALHOUN
THE ECOLOGY AND SOCIOLOGY
OF THE NORWAY RAT
U.S. DEPARTMENT OF HEALTH,
EDUCATION AND WELFARE

McFadden is awakened in a hail of hands and feet. Sleeping at a depth he hasn't reached in years, the shrieks embed like hooks into his brain and fling him, bouncing, back against the wall. He feels a piece of tubing bend, pop; and the ceiling drifting down around him in a slippery fog. A tent peg slashes on its end of rope; a piece of framing drags against his cheek. McFadden scrambles back, trawling her along with him inside this winding shroud, burying his face to guard against the nails. He gets a hand around her wrist and holds, squeezing with his knees to shield his groin.

"Shhhh . . . Shhhhh . . . You're safe," he says. "You're dreaming . . . Wake up. Wake up and you'll be safe . . ."

In time the fury slackens, spasms ebb. Collapsed walls tremble, settle, flatten and lie still.

"Are you with me?"

"Yes."

They lie like this until their heartbeats slow, breaths condensing in the closeness.

"You can let me go now." A hand has snaked its way around the folds of Gore-Tex to his face. "Are you all right?"

"Don't ask about me. It's you. Are *you* all right?"

"I'm OK. I'm sorry."

"Shhhh. It's all right."

With arms and elbows they push away the rumple of their erstwhile roof. She is pressed against him, fingers almost touching in the hollow of his neck, trembling still – waves that ripple rib-to-rib beneath his palm. McFadden breathes her breathing. He smoothes and touches, moving with his hands; hair and throat and waist and thigh, trailing fingers through a crust of semen where it has dried against her skin.

"Whenever you want," he says. "Understand?"

"Yes," she says. "Not now. I don't want to talk about it now."

"Sleep, then . . . It won't come again tonight."

Morning finds them twined like this among the ruins of his red tent, McFadden's troubled heart still pounding.

– – –

A silent breakfast spatters in its skillet. Eggs today, this time scrambled unassumingly with cheese, and bacon. Stocks are running low again. McFadden tends the eggs while the girl, head down, is busy cauterizing toast. She is wearing another of his shirts, with nothing else. He has stepped back modestly into his shorts. They both could benefit from soap. The river flows too turgidly to bathe. No matter – by evening they'll be in Alberta.

He blinks into the morning light, still sifting through this dawn. Before the sunrise she had whispered in his ear again, swimming through the nylon, drawing up astride him; her narrow spine a ridgepole holding back the buckled roof, keening out her pleasure. McFadden is a trained physician, for many years a student of particularly female form and physiology. He's surely

reached a point at which these things should not surprise him;
yet they do. Lying just above the earth – only such a little while
ago – fingers splayed to guide her, observing from beneath, unable to retreat from earlier suspicions that these orgasms have
been real. He *wasn't* wrong the last time. McFadden is no adolescent to beguile himself with theatre. He's been in business
long enough to know a spasm when he sees it. Or feels it. In
spite of . . . ?

And these dreams.

He should be feeling ten feet tall, two feet long. He should be
chuckling, smugly scratching, clicking with his teeth and humming. Instead they sit here in this smoky and uncertain silence.
A labyrinth of questions.

"The toast is ready."

"Ah."

He prefers his eggs arranged beside his toast; she takes hers
piled on top. They chew, and chew some more, and swallow in
the silence.

"You said you were a doctor?"

He almost drops the fork. "Yes." Then quietly, "I used to be."

"That's what you haven't told me."

"I'm sorry, I –"

"That's the part you haven't told me."

"Ah." Now he sees where this is going, a theory more con-
firmed with every mile. The telling of McFadden's life appears to
hold her own at bay.

"Well . . . ?"

He pretends to groan, and tries his hand at levity. "You know
that *really is* a long story."

She starts to speak, then stops, gazing at the fire. He understands precisely every word that's left unsaid.

"All right," he sighs, scraping out his pan into the embers. This
will surely fill the distance.

– – –

The interning Dr. McFadden chose reproductive technologies as his area of specialty partly because he was good at it, partly because he enjoyed the company of women, but mostly because he had very wisely identified it as *the* field of the future, and one sure to make him lots of money.

"In those days," he says, "and this is not that long ago, barely twenty years – things were wide open. Every practitioner called his own shots. Not that it's changed much. It's still the most unregulated field in medicine . . ." McFadden's palm is resting on the gearshift, extrinsically connected to the powertrain. He lifts his hand to rub his eyes. "Now it's just more . . . technical. There are professional guidelines, but they're voluntary, and anything voluntary means by definition unenforced. There's been a Royal Commission looking into it for years, but no one has a clue what they'll come up with. Or if anyone's listening. But *que sera sera,* I always say. *I'm* out of it . . ."

He smiles and the girl smiles back, acknowledging herself as audience. Driving gives the sense of doing something more than merely talking.

"Are you sure you want all this?"

"Yes," she answers brightly. "So what kind of doctor were you?"

"A good one, I like to think. At least –"

"No. I mean, what *kind* of doctor?"

"Oh. An andrologist. I thought I said that. An infertility specialist."

"All right," she says. "Go on."

He finds himself intimidated with the weight of all this history. After several miles he's decided simply to begin at the beginning. There are seven hours to Alberta.

"In the last decade or so," he says, "a lot of high-tech bells and whistles have been coming in and out of vogue, but the first thing you should understand is that it still all boils down to egg meeting sperm. Most of the time it's just that simple. But then other times it isn't . . ."

This is the same patter he has used a thousand times to calm the jitters of a thousand patients. Delivering it here, in the wastes of Saskatchewan with a truck full of rats, is oddly disconcerting. He can't help drawing parallels – this talking has him thinking – between his old life and his new. Sperm then, rats now. How bizarre even to look for similarities. And yet they do share the quality of being migrants. It's not possible to think of either one in terms of stillness or passivity – tunnellers both, by definition. The girl is waiting.

"Stop me if this is getting boring."

She nods without speaking. McFadden drops his palm to rest back on the gearshift. It's habit; the schematics on the surface are worn away with contact.

"For roughly seven or eight percent of couples – sometimes the numbers go as high as fifteen, because even these figures are hard to establish – but in a certain number of couples it doesn't happen. Are you with me so far?"

Again the nod.

"Fine. Now, when it doesn't happen, generally speaking it's for one of two reasons. One is that the sperm isn't doing its job – which is what we call the male factor. The other, predictably enough, is the female factor, which can be any number of things pertaining to the egg and its environment. There are also times when everything on both sides seems to be working but fertilization doesn't happen anyway. From a professional standpoint those are the most difficult, but also, of course, the most lucrative."

McFadden is finding that to do this right he has to be specific. His fear is that he'll get caught up in this himself and won't know when to stop. All this pontification has been going to his head.

"People have known for centuries, for millennia in fact, that sperm is what makes babies – and of course a woman too," he adds, reminding himself of the perils of ignoring the obvious. "There are Talmudic injunctions against women sleeping in the same sheets, or bathing in the same water, as men other than their husbands, which suggests a lively awareness of sperm motility even in biblical times. In the late 1880s, or thereabouts, an Italian named Spallanzani published a paper describing success with artificial insemination in dogs. A decade later, in London, we get the first recorded instance of artificial insemination among humans. So, from the late nineteenth century on, if not sooner, people know that women don't need to have sex to have babies; all they need is sperm. And that, in a nutshell, is the genesis of reproductive technologies."

He glances over, but the girl, outwardly at least, is showing every sign of studious attention. It's distinctly eerie, this one-man seminar. McFadden sighs, and stretches out his leg as far as it will go behind the clutch.

"Flash forward, then, to the 1950s, when American researchers prove that human sperm can be frozen, stored, thawed, and still be viable – and now we have the birth of the modern sperm bank. But it's not until the sixties and seventies – around the time I got into the business – that assisted insemination really takes off as a growth industry. We use the term *assisted* insemination now, by the way, not *artificial*. Sounds nicer. *AI* for short."

"I have a question."

"Shoot."

"Why do they bother?"

McFadden smiles. "Why do who bother?" Although he's fairly sure he knows what she means.

"These women. I always wondered. Why do they bother?"

"Because they want to get pregnant."

"But if all they need is sperm, why do they need a doctor? God knows I've . . . often enough. Anyway, I don't see . . ."

He smiles again. "That's the big question, isn't it? What I think you mean is, if a woman isn't getting pregnant with her partner's sperm, why doesn't she just –"

"Go out and get laid. Yeah. That was the question."

"The short answer is, in most cases she probably does."

"Oh."

He permits himself a moment to savour her reaction. "There has never been a study deliberately undertaken with that particular objective – at least if there is, I haven't seen it – and no wonder when you think about how you'd have to phrase it on your funding application. But there *is* quite a body of evidence amassed, shall we say, laterally. You'd be surprised how many geneticists over the years have had to quietly shelve their projects because their incidental findings have been just too . . . embarrassing."

She makes a twirling motion with her finger, expressing her desire that he move on to his point.

"The numbers range from five to as high as thirty percent," he says, "depending on who you read. But I'd say ten percent is safely arguable. As I mentioned, nobody to my knowledge has ever *deliberately* examined it, but study after study looking into other matters have turned up the uncomfortable and largely unreportable fact that some ten percent of children born in North America are not biologically related to the man they think of as their father."

"Oh . . ."

"That's what I mean. Let me put it another way. This country's population is nearly thirty million. Statistically speaking, then, some three million Canadians send Father's Day cards to the wrong guy."

The girl lets out a long and surprisingly musical whistle. McFadden is pleased with his decision to present this material up near the front of his delivery. He reminds himself again to keep his tongue from running away with itself.

"Another good indicator," he says, "is all those Abraham and Sarah stories. The ones about the couple who've been trying years and years and all of a sudden, out of the blue, *bingo*. It's a miracle! In my experience it's less likely a miracle than Sarah's having looked at her options from a somewhat wider perspective. You understand I say this as a clinician, not a cynic – however related the two positions might be. I'll also say, though, that you should never discount the miraculous. *Anything* is possible in the field of reproduction – in fact, by definition it's miraculous. We still have only the haziest understanding of how the whole thing works. That's what attracted me to it most in the first place."

"I thought you said it was the money."

"That too." McFadden pauses to regroup his thoughts. He is more secure now in the feeling that he has her attention. "In answer to your question: it seems likely that the majority of women *are* solving a lot of their fertility problems on their own. There haven't been anywhere near three million clinically assisted inseminations here in Canada, I can tell you that for free. Though no one can say that exactly, because hardly anyone keeps records."

"Who doesn't keep records?"

"We practitioners."

"You don't?"

"No. But we'll come back to that; that certainly enters into the story."

"All right. But I still don't see –"

"I'm coming to that."

"OK."

"That being said, there are still plenty of reasons for women to approach the clinics. The most obvious is female-factor infertility."

"You mean when it's the woman's fault."

"We don't like to use the word *fault*."

"What do you mean, *we*?"

"I mean fertility practitioners."

"I thought you said you weren't one any more."

"For the sake of argument . . ."

"Go ahead."

"When a couple have gone a year or more trying to have a baby and still haven't conceived, they tend to start thinking there must be something wrong. But they don't know for sure – or, if they do have a problem, whether it's a question of male-factor infertility or female-factor –"

"You mean whose fault it is?"

"It might also be a combination of the two factors."

"Like when it's really nobody's fault."

"So at this stage all the couple knows is that they want a baby but so far, despite all their trying – and let me tell you, when people try, they really try; I mean ovulation charting, temperature taking, calls in the middle of the day to get home quick because it's *now*, sometimes hormone –"

"Can I ask another question?"

"Certainly."

"Why do you always keep talking about couples? What about women who just want to have a baby?"

"*That's another reason!* That's another very big reason for fertility clinics. I should know that better than anyone. Yes, of course, single women and lesbians are a very large component of the client profile, larger every year. *That's* what got me into all the trouble." McFadden has quickly put up his hand to ward her off. "I'll get to that, I promise. Where was I?"

"Single women and lesbians."

"Before that . . . I was trying to explain about female-factor infertility."

"That's when it's her fault."

"People go to the clinics," he says, "at least to start with, in order to find out why they aren't conceiving." He pauses. "To find out whose fault it is . . . It could be the woman, it could be the man. Quite often it's a combination of both. Male infertility, by definition, has to do with sperm. Either there isn't any or there isn't enough, or there's a problem with delivery."

"You mean when the guy can't get it up."

"For starters, yes, but mostly, we deal with problems in the sperm itself. Oligospermia is the name for when there isn't enough; azoospermia is when there isn't any at all."

"*Zoo?* Did you say *zoo!* Like where they keep the animals?"

"Same word, yes. In this sense it means *life*. Though I have to admit, I've always liked the word too for its association with the animal world – or rather for its reminder that we belong to that world too. But I digress. In reproductive terms it means simply life. No sperm, no life. Straightforward.

"As long as the man is producing live sperm, he's got a chance at fatherhood, even if for whatever reason it isn't getting where it wants to go – namely, up the Fallopian and into the egg. If there's no sperm, though, that's the end of the line for his particular genes. If it's a case of oligospermia, or if it's a motility or morphology issue – morphology refers to the size and shape of sperm, and motility relates to its movement – then there are things we can do . . . I know this is technical, but I'm trying to keep it as simple as I can."

"And I'm just a simple girl."

"I didn't say that!" That was unfair. McFadden has to push aside a growing wish that he should stop this altogether and go back to watching the Prairies. "As I was saying, there are things we can do now to help the sperm. Diagnostics, if you like. Semen analysis can show several things, for instance if the sperm can benefit from washing, or a swim-up, or maybe a jolt of caffeine."

"You're kidding!"

"Not at all."

"Swim-up . . ." she says. "What could that be? And here I always thought the only thing to think about was whether you should swallow."

"The density of sperm – its concentration of parts per millilitre – is of course highly significant. The more sperm present per ejaculate, the greater the likelihood that one will make it all the way to the egg. The reverse, of course, is also true . . . If this is boring you, I can stop right here. There are lots of other things for us to talk about."

She puts her hand on top of his, where it's resting on the gearstick. The extra pressure has enhanced the oscillation. "Don't be a spoilsport," she says, trailing fingertips along his knuckles. McFadden resists the urge to turn his palm.

"If a sample shows poor motility – if the sperm are just not good swimmers – then we can soup it up a bit with various treatments. Forward motion, that's what we're looking for. Anything enhancing that, enhances the odds."

He is suddenly embarrassed by the placement of his hand, though to move it now would be to call attention. "Morphology refers to the sperm's shape," he says. "Abnormal morphology tends to slow it down, which tends again to decreased fitness. So we do what's called a swim-up. That's covering the semen with a filter of protein; the most motile sperm will swim up and through it. Or we can do a washing, which concentrates the sperm into a smaller volume . . ."

She has removed her hand. "Sperm washing," she says, almost in a whisper. "What an idea. Pavlov and Skinner would have liked the sound of that."

Perhaps he shouldn't be, but McFadden allows himself to be surprised. "Pavlov?" he says. "Skinner?" Her awareness of these names is unexpected. "I don't see the connection."

The girl's shock is absolute. "*You know them?*" It's as if she's touched a burning element.

"Well, it's been a while . . . but . . ."

"Oh my God. *You?*"

She has tucked her legs up like a spider and scuttled as far back as she can. She's choking. Her jaws are working up and down. Hyperventilation. Christ, he thinks, not again.

"Oh my God oh my God."

"What's going on?"

Once again he's utterly at a loss. This sudden panic's so intense it's gripping him as well. He can't think straight.

"Wait a minute!" he says, struggling to sort this through. "Just wait a minute . . . Something's . . ."

He has put his hand out reassuringly but pulls back when he sees she's tearing at the door latch. There's hardly been time to get his foot off the gas.

"Wait! Calm down! *Please. Something's gotten all mixed up!*"

The hand's still hung out in the air between them, like an out-of-order traffic signal. He checks the road, then pleads again for calm.

"Just hold on. Hold on. What is it we're talking about? . . . Ivan Pavlov and B. F. Skinner were behaviourists. I'm a little rusty, but if I remember right –"

"You *know them*?"

"Not personally. How could I? I mean . . . they've been dead for years. But –"

"They're *dead*?"

He takes a moment to sort out his own surprise. "Of course they're dead. Pavlov, at least, has been dead for half a century. Skinner was later, I think, but he must have died sometime back –"

"What are you talking about?"

"What are *you* talking about? OK. OK, let's just wait a minute . . . We've got ourselves on different wavelengths. Listen . . . bear with me. *I'll* tell you what I know and you tell me if it fits . . . OK? Just please close the door." He starts talking before she can think of reasons not to listen. "Pavlov was one of the first of –"

"But you say he's *d-dead*?"

"Long dead."

She has closed the door. He can hear her breathing in and out, squeezing her hands between her thighs.

"All right," he says. "All right." McFadden has the truck back up to highway speed. "I'll tell you what I know, all right? And you match it up against what you do . . . Everybody studies these guys in first-year psychology. Let me think . . . They were both interested in behavioural conditioning. Condition and response – something like that. Pavlov was famous for his dogs. He wanted to prove these dogs could be trained, conditioned, to repeat certain behaviours automatically. He used a combination of reward and punishment – sorry if I'm not up to scratch on this – and got them so they'd salivate every time he rang a bell. He had them isolated, somehow, so there was no external stimuli except him. And every time he let them have food, he rang a bell. The whole point was to get them to salivate even if there wasn't any food, just the bell. That proved they could be taught to produce certain physical reactions to completely unrelated stimuli . . . or something like that . . . It's been a long time."

"Oh, God."

"What?"

"Oh my God."

"What?"

"So you're telling me Pavlov is some dead scientist."

"Forty years dead at least. What did you think . . . ?"

"It doesn't matter."

"Umm, well . . . " McFadden has the feeling he should just keep talking. "Skinner was into the same sort of thing. I think he taught pigeons to play the piano. But his specialty was rats. He's best known for this thing called the Skinner box –"

"What did you say?"

"The Skinner box. It's . . ."

But the girl has gone into convulsion.

– – –

"I was thinking we were past that."

"Sorry."

"Please don't say that."

They have walked a little distance from the truck. It stands behind them, silhouetted in a sea of prairie, like a ship becalmed. The girl has drawn within herself, though as he watches he can see her, piece by piece, extrude herself back out. Remarkable. She walks a pace or two beside him, shaking out her arms and legs.

Cleanup wasn't all that bad this time. She had held the vomit long enough to crank open the window. Nothing a little rain won't wash away. He has found a towel, drawn some water, dug her out a toothbrush.

"Thank you," she says. "You put up with a lot."

There is nothing to be said to this.

"Since we're stopped already, I'll just take a minute seeing to the rats."

She nods, though her eyes tell him she is grateful for this little time apart.

It's only been an hour since last the rats were tended, but McFadden takes his time, and then remembers his intent to give them all a final oatmeal treatment. So an honest twenty minutes pass, McFadden dosing each compartment with a measure of coarse rolled oats steeped in Louisiana hot sauce.

The girl is nowhere to be seen. When he climbs back down and shuts the doors behind him, it takes a little while to spy her out, seated in the prairie grass, a thousand miles around her. She is brushing out her hair. He wades out to her, and she turns and smiles a smile that dazzles even in his incredulity.

"I think," she says, "that when we left off you were just explaining how to wash a batch of sperm."

And this is how it goes.

– – –

"The interesting thing about male-factor infertility is how often we end up treating the *female* for it."

"Why is that?" she answers prettily, easing her foot off the clutch. The girl has indicated she would now prefer to drive.

He has resumed his strangely therapeutic self-disclosure. Therapeutic – he wonders, to whom . . . ? She has made it very clear she will not talk. McFadden, obligingly, reinserts himself into the silence.

"Once you've enhanced the sperm," he says, "you still have to bring it into contact with the egg – and that almost always involves some degree of intervention with regard to the woman." He's always hated expressions like "with regard to"; why did he just use it? The girl, still gearing up, nods encouragingly.

"Artificial insemination is generally described as a treatment for male infertility, which at one level is perfectly accurate – and at another, not at all . . ." As he's feared, he's warming to the subject. "If it's using the husband's sperm for insemination in his wife, that's a fair enough assessment. The man involved is still passing on his own genetic material, which you'll have to ac-knowledge is a definitive feature of reproduction, and the woman *is* submitting to at least some degree of medical intervention. But if it's a case of *donor* insemination – in other words, if the woman is using sperm from someone other than her husband – it's clearly inappropriate to describe the process as a treatment for *his* problem. *He's* still sterile; there's no cure in this for him. It's just circumventing his sperm with someone else's. The wife ends up ensuring *her* genetic continuity by marrying her chro-mosomes with the donor's, but at the end of the day the hus-band's genetic future is still non-existent. Is this making any sense?" McFadden's own head is beginning to hurt. He wonders how the girl's holding up.

"Fine. But I still don't get why you're talking as if it's brain surgery or something. I mean, there can't be that much to it, is there?"

He sighs. "You're right, of course, in many cases. But in oth-ers the level of intervention is significant, up to and including surgery. To give the sperm a better chance, we often move it higher up into the reproductive track. It's a bit of a simplifica-tion, but generally speaking, the higher we put it, the greater the level of intervention. Intracervical insemination is pretty basic; all you need is a syringe, or even just a cup – basically anything at all to squirt in the sperm. But Fallopian insemina-tion involves laparoscopy, which in turn requires general anaes-thetic. And of course with in vitro you have to go right in and get the egg, and once you've fertilized it, go back in again to rein-sert it. On top of this there are all the drugs for timing ovulation. It's true, you know: when women argue over-medicalization, they have a point."

"All right," she says. "I admit half of what you just said was way over my head. But still you haven't told me why all this stuff happens."

"You mean what causes infertility in the first place?"

"Yeah . . . I guess so."

"That's the big question, isn't it? And very often we just don't know. In my own practice I saw hundreds of cases in which, so far as I could tell, everything should have been working fine, but wasn't. And no one, including me, could tell these women why. It's incredibly hard on the people involved. My wife, I should tell you, was infertile. So I know whereof I speak."

"You said you weren't married!"

"No, I didn't. I said I was divorced."

"No, you didn't."

"Yes, I did. Or if I didn't, that's what I meant to say. Anyway, I haven't had a wife in years. But *I* don't want to talk about *that.*"

He knows he's just descended into theatre. That's the problem with the urge to reciprocity. McFadden carries on as if this last has been unsaid.

"There is always a percentage of congenital causes, people who are born with malfunctions we can identify. But by and large you could probably get away with saying infertility usually comes down to a blockage of one kind or another. That's an oversimplification, I know, but after all, we haven't got all day."

More and more he is alarmed at how fast the day is fleeing. They are well past Estevan already – quite a bit past, he thinks. This may even be the fringes of the badlands. Certainly the landscape's changing. It's becoming more dramatic; windswept, low-shouldered hills marching off into the distance. He wishes he could just shut up and watch the scenery.

"When I say blockage, I mean exactly that: something stopping either the egg from getting down to the sperm or the sperm from getting up to the egg; anything that scars or damages those narrow little passageways. With male factor it can be as far removed as a bad case of the mumps. Even a few degrees of elevated temperature can badly damage sperm. Or varicose veins in the testes –"

"Varicose veins in the nuts? I've never seen that!"

"Or too-hot baths, or too-tight shorts –"

"That I've seen."

"More commonly, it can be traced to drug abuse or alcohol, and of course sexually transmitted diseases."

The girl says nothing.

"Female factor is fairly similar. Again, it comes down to blockage – endometriosis, for instance, or prior ectopic pregnancies. Then there are the same factors as for men: drinking and smoking. Alcohol and nicotine seem to affect the Fallopian tubes' ability to transport the egg."

McFadden pauses for a moment to organize his thoughts. Yes, he thinks, this must be the beginnings of the badlands.

"But STDs are the biggest. Twenty, twenty-five percent of female infertility comes down to that. It's amazing how often a woman can pick one up without even knowing that she has it. If a simple case of gonorrhea or chlamydia goes undetected, it can get right into the Fallopian tubes and scar them to the point that the egg can't pass. You'd be surprised how many Granite Club ladies have showed up on my doorstep just because of a little case of chlamydia they got way back when they were still in pleated skirts. Gonorrhea's not as bad, but it has its share of repercussions . . ."

McFadden doesn't know if it's his own words or the girl's reaction that suddenly has alarm bells going off like cluster bombs inside his skull. Certainly she is looking anywhere but at him. He struggles to complete his thought, but the thought has vanished. McFadden's mouth falls open; this terrifying shift in perspective has killed whatever might have been intending to emerge. Is she thinking what he thinks she's thinking?

Dear Sweet Fucking Jesus could he have been this stupid! He's supposed to be *a doctor!* McFadden is frantically recomposing their encounters, but there isn't any solace there. The girl is keeping very still and staring out the window. Jesus. How *could* he?

"While we're on the subject . . . " she says.

Oh, no . . .

"Just so you know . . . " Her face is to the window. "In case you were worrying about . . . you know . . . Don't. You don't have to."

"*What!*"

"You don't have to worry . . . I just want you to know you don't have to worry."

"Oh. Oh, well of course I wasn't . . . " McFadden is strangling himself trying to think of a polite way to inquire how she can be so bloody certain.

"I don't blame you for worrying." Even in his terror her voice comes to him as buckling under the weight of its intentions. "It's just that . . . I can promise you . . . I don't have anything."

"Um . . . " he says. He can hardly bring himself to ask it. "How do you know?"

The girl is blushing. Not merely blushing, but flushed so violently a hand has risen to her face to leach away the heat. McFadden's own condition isn't any better.

"I don't mean to . . . " he says. "But . . . realistically . . . how could you . . . know for sure?"

"They *tested* me! *All right?*"

The force of this has nearly silenced him. If this weren't so important . . .

"Who tested you?"

"They did blood tests. All the time. Blood tests, urine tests, you name it, they did it. They were very very careful. So I can tell you . . . The thing is . . . I can tell you for sure . . . "

"Who's *they?*"

The girl has twisted her face again into the corner of the cab. "Shut up! Shut up! Just leave me alone!"

"*Who* tested you?"

"Shut up!"

"Who tested you?"

"Pavlov and Skinner!"

"Who the hell are Pavlov and Skinner?"

"Leave me alone!"

"But that's not fair!"

"Nothing's fucking fair!" She has spun back with that serpentine agility. "Nothing's fucking fair. Nothing. All right? I just told you the important thing, and now that's all I want to say."

"I'm sorry."

"It's all right," she says heavily. "You have a right. I just wanted to settle your mind."

"It's settled," he tells her quickly. "You know, I never even thought about it until just that moment . . . which itself is very strange. You'd think that me, of all people . . . I mean, you wouldn't think . . . Who's Pavlov and Skinner?"

– – –

"They're not really antelope," he tells her, stretched across her lap with his binoculars propped against the window. "Actually, they're more closely related to sheep. *Pronghorn* is the better name." He has counted seventeen, scattered over half a mile of prairie. McFadden has always longed to see a pronghorn.

"Why don't we go out there and join them?"

"What?"

"It's way past lunchtime," she says. "I'm hungry. Let's have a picnic out there where they're grazing."

McFadden looks up from his lenses. "Is it that late already?"

"Time flies when you're having fun."

The landscape has been rolling these last miles, and this place is rolling too. As the girl and he lug their bundles and a blanket from the truck, they startle up a pair that must have bedded down in a defile below the sightline.

"This is the spot," she says, while McFadden watches bobbing rumps recede into the prairie.

"Maybe they'll come back."

"I'm going to get the mattress," she tells him, while he stretches on the grass.

The scene is so much like the day before it's almost an excess of metaphor; all that's missing is the driftwood fire and a trickle of the river intermingled with the wind. McFadden closes his eyes and scans this last half-day; twelve hours, fourteen hours. Time does fly, even when it's standing still: charcoal in the fire, crickets in the sage; his offer of a glass of wine, her refusal, his belated recognition that drink is not an ally to this girl. And then her unbuttoning, as if she has been born to loose these buttons. And then these savage dreams . . .

"Have you gone to sleep on me?"

He opens one eye to see her standing by his shoulder, trailing his deflated mattress, air pump dangling at her side. "How do you work this thing?"

"The ground is soft," he says, and pats the turf. "If it's good enough for antelope . . . "

Common wisdom would inform him that a girl of her profession should not take pleasure in the act. It would tell him such a history would freeze out these faculties, bar the doors against delight. And yet, when it begins, her zeal is more than equal to his own. He still can't shake the feeling of an almost supernatural exuberance, an escalation so symmetrically intense it seems beyond their authorship alone. As if their movements are the rostrum of some libidinous divinity, a *dea ex machina*, intent on staging an exactly perfect pitch of pleasure. What astounds him is how obviously it's worked this way for her as well; and more to the point, why this leaves him so uneasy. McFadden finds himself unequal to his senses.

They are lying, facing the sky, watching the sun pry holes into a bank of cloud, pouring slanted shafts of light in pools on the horizon. They've been so still, the pronghorn have forgotten them. He can hear one, molars grinding somewhere in the nearby distance. And then, with an embarrassment of poetry, a rainbow sparkles into being. He could swear one leg is anchored somewhere just beyond the truck. These empty heavens leave themselves so open.

"The Bible says that God put out the rainbow as a promise that He wouldn't screw us over any more," she tells him out of nowhere.

McFadden brushes the dust from his trousers. "Then we'd better get a move on," he says, disinclined to trust a covenant so clearly unenforceable. "I didn't know you were a student of divinity." He has taken her hand, drawn her to her feet.

"What?"

Stupid. Why does he do this? He tries again. "I didn't know you had a religious background."

The girl snorts. "I've swallowed my share of God's Glory," she says, and will say no more.

– – –

They're definitely now in the badlands. Sometimes a name just suits, like *foothills* or *tar sands*; it speaks its definition. *Badlands* is perfect, a word interpreted in texture. This is cowboy country. Rodeo arenas in every little town; streets so wide they have to shout to reach the other side; false-front clapboard, peeling paint. Even tumbleweed. They pass a town called Big Beaver; the girl purses her lips but makes no comment. It's like stepping back another century, a film set built on one dimension. A little farther on, in Coronach, they stop for gas. McFadden has to interrupt his seminar on sperm collection. While waiting for his change, he checks the map. Almost half the province gone already.

He has been behind the wheel since lunch. A little stiffness in his backside tells him that perhaps they should have changed again. Too late. Distractions of the highway afford a little time to rearrange his thoughts.

The girl repeats her question. "So they really have to do it by themselves?"

People just can't stop themselves from asking this.

"Strictly solo, I'm afraid. You'd be surprised how often they're expecting otherwise. I bet half my donors show up expecting Ursula Andress in a nurse's uniform standing by to help them tickle out their samples. But it doesn't work that way . . . Plastic jar, dab of mineral oil, and maybe a back issue of *Penthouse*. It isn't particularly time-consuming. Some of the regulars get good at it, though once in a while you get one that misses. I remember a guy from Halifax trying to tell me he should still get paid. But what good's it doing anybody on his pant leg? If it isn't in the jar, it counts as recreation. I know they're used to transfer payments down there, but I thought that was taking things a little far . . ."

Political satire, however, is not of interest at the moment.

"How much do they get?"

"Per donation?"

"Yeah, per donation."

"Standard these days is about a hundred dollars, but it depends how earnestly you need it. I paid a man ten thousand once for a total of two samples. But that was under special circumstances."

"Ten thousand *dollars*?"

"And I had to make two trips to England to get them. But we'll come back to that."

"Ten *thousand*? I mean, a hundred is more or less call-girl standard, but ten thousand for one date . . . That's L.A. money!"

"Actually, it was for two . . . dates. As I said —"

"But ten grand! Who was this guy, the Pope?"

Since their stop for lunch, McFadden has been intermittently looking out for pronghorn. He hasn't spotted any, but he has caught sight of two coyotes. Coyotes are too familiar back at home to warrant much by way of comment, although he admits these westerners are somehow more in keeping with the image of coyoteness. He would also dearly love to spot a badger. Authenticated badger sightings are a rarity where he comes from; McFadden himself has never been so fortunate. Since crossing into Manitoba he's been on the lookout, circumspectly scanning while he talks. He levers up his seat to get his elevation as high as he can manage, maximizing his periphery, and begins to scan a careful arc from one side window to the other, and then more slowly back again. So far nothing but a Swainson's hawk soaring over on the girl's side.

"Will you please keep your eyes on the road?"

"Will you please stop interrupting?"

She executes a mock obeisance, then does that twirling with her finger. But McFadden's honestly forgotten where he was.

"It's just I think it's funny you pay a guy to jack the same as johns pay me to jack them." The sentence catches in her ear and sends a peel of giggles through the cab. "Sorry," she says, patting his knee in a way he knows this time is quite devoid of sexual intent, "you'll get it out eventually . . ." Which sets her off into another round.

"Now then," McFadden says, and clears his throat. "Let me first say a lot has changed since when I started . . . "

– – –

It was the Parsee, really, who changed it. But of course this isn't accurate. Not changed, so much: inspired. Facilitated. This won't be easy. What he remembers best are not the parts that lend themselves to brevity. Names, for instance. Did they ever get so far as that? Funny that he can't remember. Certainly the Parsee knew *him*, or at least his occupation. But of course it couldn't work the other way around.

Ten thousand dollars. Seed money, if ever the term was appropriate; all the more so as it wasn't his money. And what about the woman? Something amusing . . . something incongruous . . . Smith! Yes, of course. Smith. How could he forget an alias like that? He remembered at the time accusing himself of stereotyping. After all, the British were in India long enough to have left a legacy of surnames; no reason for there not to be a smattering of Smiths in the pages of the Bombay phone book. But this one wasn't one of them.

Mrs. *Smith*.

He has a perfect picture of himself, listening through the door, as Mrs. Smith appeared at his reception desk, without appointment. "I am sure the doctor will find time for me," she said. And the doctor did.

So much to explain. How much time left? he wonders, but doesn't interrupt himself to glance at the odometer.

Clients of an ethnic background were often very hard to match. It was necessary, at least it was usually necessary – he could certainly provide exceptions – to pair them with a donor of similar ethnicity; presuming of course that donor insemination was the required course of treatment, which in those days at his clinic would have been statistically most likely. This wasn't always easy. The sperm of Caucasian males – Wasp milk, as he called it when he was sure no one was listening – was fairly easily obtained, other variants much less so. Is this degree of detail necessary?

He finds he has to edit out so much of what remains most clear. The textures, the non-essentials: the rustle of Mrs. Smith's sari that first day in his office – was it red or purple? – the hint of hair along her upper lip, above the gloss of lipstick. Red, he thinks, perhaps this argues red. Non-essentials.

Mrs. Smith, it turned out, was twenty-eight, married five years, three months. And childless. Physicians had assured her *her* reproductive system was perfectly in order. This was how she phrased it. Mrs. Smith's husband, on the other hand, was more advanced in years, though not inclined to give consideration to the possibility that their union's lack of issue might have anything to do with him. This too was how she phrased it. Evidently the situation was causing grave concern to families extending several generations on both sides of the marriage bed. There was also, as she made clear, a quantity of trans-Pacific equity increasingly in jeopardy unless things were soon taken in hand.

"So you see," she told him, "what I need is to be pregnant."

Already McFadden was assembling his catalogues. It seemed to him that there was nothing in his present stock, but he was sure one of the bigger banks could ship him something. He never liked to go this route; McFadden was a nationalist, whenever possible, when it came to sperm selection. However there was only so much latitude for protest in economies of scale. The larger sperm banks in those days were all south of the border.

"I should tell you," he said, by way of preparing for the financial implications of a case like hers – health insurance covered some things but not others – "I must tell you that sperm from Indian donors is sometimes rather hard to get . . ."

Mrs. Smith stopped him with a subtle yet commanding tap of fingers on McFadden's desk. "Perhaps I haven't managed to explain myself," she said. "I don't require *Indian* sperm. What I need, specifically, is sperm from a *Parsee.*"

McFadden, to his shame, had only the vaguest notion of what a Parsee was. It seemed to him they belonged to one of the religious groups in India, as distinct from Hindus, Sikhs or Muslims. At that time this was the limit of his understanding.

"I imagine you know nothing at all about Zoroastrians," said Mrs. Smith, and when McFadden refused to react: "I should first tell you that there is a distinct Parsee community here in Toronto, but that it is very small and highly interwoven. Everyone here knows everyone else."

McFadden answered with something like a noncommittal nod.

"What this means, of course, is that it will be absolutely impossible to recruit a donor in this city."

"Of course," he said, thinking he was beginning to see where this was going.

Mrs. Smith examined him minutely, then shrugged. "Parsees," she told him, "are Zoroastrians, originally from Persia." To his credit McFadden managed to prevent himself from displaying any semblance of surprise. "They escaped religious persecution in the seventh century, eventually migrating to India. Most Parsees settled around Bombay, though in the last century communities like this one have grown in other parts of the world."

What he remembers most distinctly was her refusal to unlock his eyes. "Parsees have been described as better understood in terms of caste or race," she said, "rather than religion. It's essential that you understand this. Some of these restrictions have loosened, but the fact remains that the child I intend to conceive, with your help, must be a Parsee; which means that its biological father *has to be a Parsee too*. Do you understand?"

McFadden hastily assured her that he did. What he was thinking was that nowhere in the catalogues of donors, anywhere, had he ever come across a listing under Parsee.

"Naturally, the donor must physically resemble my husband. The procedure is to be accomplished with a minimum of dishonour to all parties, including the donor, who must of course remain anonymous."

McFadden moved his head and pursed his lips. He'd been in business long enough to know the virtues of a meditative silence. Mrs. Smith opened her valise and handed him a sheet of paper.

"There is the original community in Bombay," she said. "This would be the likeliest source. As well as Karachi, Singapore, Hong Kong, Sydney, and London, England." McFadden obligingly ticked off each entry as she read. "Toronto, Vancouver, Montreal, New York, Boston and Washington are all out," she said, watching to be sure that he had followed. "The farther away the donor, the better. These last are just too close for safety."

McFadden, feeling very much the schoolboy hoping to be overlooked until a question comes along that he can safely answer, kept his own eyes lowered to the page.

"You leave it to me to find the donor," said Mrs. Smith. "What I need from you is to collect the sample once the donor is located, and then inseminate me."

"I see," McFadden said, because now he did.

"Will you do this?"

He had received a strong impression that, while cost might not be irrelevant, it was secondary to objective. "Yes," he answered without hesitation.

"Good," said Mrs. Smith. "Then I'll be in touch."

"Wait!" His tone stopped her, mid-rise from her chair. "There are several factors you need to consider."

The conversation had been a little too one-sided for McFadden's liking. For the most part his patients tended to fall into categories. On one extreme were those so shockingly ignorant it often pained his civic conscience, knowing he was helping them to reproduce. At the other were the women who understood the workings of their bodies much more intricately than he could ever have hoped to do himself. Mrs. Smith, very much so, had struck him as belonging to the latter group. Still, there were things to discuss.

"You understand," he said, "that timing in these matters is necessarily precise."

"Yes, of course."

"Your own window of opportunity, in terms of fertilization, is narrow, a matter of two or three days. First, we have to know precisely when you're ovulating before we can proceed with the insemination. That's presuming we have the sperm to begin with, and that it's viable, and that it's safe."

Mrs. Smith appeared to view all this as wasted breath. "Yes, yes," she said. "I'm like clockwork. My cycle has always been predictable. That's another reason I know it isn't me. You forget, I have been paying very careful attention to this for some years now. Anticipating ovulation will not present a problem."

"That's good, that's very useful. But it's still only half the equation. You are aware, for instance, that even if we were to locate a donor tomorrow, we would not be able to proceed with the insemination for a minimum of six months."

"Six months! That's out of the question!"

The change in tone was disconcerting, more so than he expected. McFadden had intended this to be a jolt; her poise was just a little irritating. But facts were facts.

"The use of fresh semen is no longer medically sanctioned," he said as gravely as he could, then paused to let this settle. "For several years now the standard has been to freeze it for a period of six months, testing before and after for the A.I. virus, hepatitis B, herpes simplex, chlamydia, gonorrhea, syphilis, and so on." This was not strictly true, as McFadden well knew. Many physicians still routinely used fresh semen if they were confident of the donor's background, despite the regulations. But Mrs. Smith had no need to know that.

"Six months! That's impossible!"

"I am sorry to tell you that the Ontario Ministry of Health guidelines require six months of cryopreservation before we can proceed."

But Mrs. Smith was quick at thinking on her feet. "All right," she said, "all right. Then it won't be in Ontario. In fact, it won't be anywhere in North America. I was hoping you could go and get the sperm and bring it back to me, and we could do the procedure here. But if that's not possible, I'll go with you. How long should it take? I suppose that depends on where I find the donor – say a maximum twelve-hour flight, then twelve hours back, that's twenty-four. Even with time for stopover I should be able to get back within thirty-six hours. I'll come up with a reason. You and I fly to wherever we find the donor, you collect the sperm and then you can inseminate me on the spot, and then we both fly back together. The only reason I need you in the first place is as a go-between. I don't want to ever see the donor and I don't want him ever seeing me. Otherwise I would take care of this myself. But if you're worried about Ontario regulations, none of it will happen here. So you needn't be."

This was more familiar. This sort of thing he'd seen before. Infertility, he tells the girl, has repercussions far beyond the body. Very far beyond. He's seen clients on the verge of nervous breakdown, sometimes past it. It gnaws upon a woman's sense of place and balance, driving out caution, even common sense. Mrs. Smith's particulars, to say the least, were quite unique; but not the force behind her visit.

"Mrs. Smith," he'd said as gently as he could, "this is not a question of bureaucracy or geography. It's a question of disease. Viruses do not stop at borders."

"But malpractice suits do. So if that's what you're worried about, don't. There is no danger to you if we do this offshore."

In fact, McFadden was not the least concerned about malpractice. There were very few malpractice suits in his field of medicine – still aren't, as far as he knows – because so very much of it goes undocumented.

"It's not my safety we're discussing," he answered evenly, "it's yours," and pressed his point before she could evade him. "Even if we waived that protocol, there are just too many others. The logistics are simply too complicated. Remember, you have to think about this from both sides of the equation: sperm and egg, egg and sperm. They both have to be brought together in peak condition at exactly the right time, and even then the odds are still against you.

"Please think about this! Even if we manage to time your cycle exactly, even if we get you on an airplane to wherever it is you've located your donor at precisely the time your egg is descending the Fallopian – and that's assuming all the stress associated with the trip doesn't throw off your cycle, which is more than probable – even if you manage all of this, you still have to have your Parsee donor willing to drop everything and be on hand to produce a specimen once you've got yourself through customs. It's too much to expect. You understand that, in the most relaxed circumstances, conception rates are only about twenty percent for any given cycle. And less than sixty percent of zygotes make it past the first few cell divisions even *after* fertilization. It takes the average woman months of trying before she actually gets a pregnancy, often five or six or more.

Sorry, but these are the statistics. How many months can you fly to Karachi or Sydney – or wherever? And how often will you have this hypothetical donor standing by to oblige you when you get there?"

This last bit may have been unnecessary, but McFadden had warmed to his work. On this matter he was inflexible.

"All this presupposes my willingness to expose you to the fluids of a complete unknown," he said. "And this, I am sorry to say, I will not do."

"Oh, please!" she said. "You just don't know . . . " Mrs. Smith was on the verge of more than tears. "You just don't know how –"

"Wait!" McFadden did know. "I have a proposal. Let me tell you that, even if you accept my suggestion, your chances are slim at best. First I advise you to find a donor as near as possible. If you insist on going overseas, pick London; it's the shortest flight. Much better, Boston or New York. Fresh sperm does not live long outside the body, a matter of hours. But let me do some thinking about that . . . If we retrieve it safely, it still must be divided into straws, then frozen, which typically will decrease its viability further still. On top of all this, I'm going to have to find some way of getting it back and forth through customs . . . " The more McFadden thought about this, the less he liked the odds; on the other hand, the more attracted he was to the challenge.

Perhaps an undercurrent of enthusiasm had crept into his tone. Mrs. Smith revived a little. "You can do this?"

"I will meet with the donor twice," he said. "Two meetings, six months apart. This is non-negotiable. On both occasions he must be willing to provide me with a specimen of semen and at least two vials of blood. If both samples pass the screening process, we should have plenty of material to get you pregnant – *if* all the cells concerned are viable. It's a long shot. But theoretically, not impossible . . . "

– – –

"So?" she says. "What happened?"

McFadden is uneasy with the girl's expression. It reminds him too much of his former wife's when she was watching certain programs on the television. His answer is succinct.

"I went to London," he says. "Twice."

"And?"

"What do you mean, *and*?"

"Did she have her baby?"

McFadden pauses, surprised by the question, then shrugs. "I couldn't say."

"What do you mean, you couldn't say?"

"I told you, I don't know. It was not my job to follow up on post-conception. I can tell you that the zygote was successfully implanted. That's it. After that I never saw her . . . But anyway, that's not the point. The point of the story isn't Mrs. Smith, or whatever her real name was. It was the *man*, the donor. The man who changed my life."

McFadden is not a fan of melodrama, and this last statement was once again precisely that. He wishes he could take it back. It was not as if this man actually changed his life; more like precipitated little clouds of alterations that eventually produced for him a brand new climate. Which is tantamount to change, he supposes. All right.

The Mysterious Parsee was waiting, as arranged, in the lobby of the London Delta Chelsea. McFadden, with seven hours onboard thinking time behind him, was distinctly ill at ease. At the airport in Toronto, Mrs. Smith had handed him a Blue Jays baseball cap. "This is how he'll know it's you," she said. McFadden was a fan of Blue Jays baseball, but he would never dream of wearing one of their moronic caps. Standing in the lobby of the London Delta Chelsea, dressed appropriately for time and place and season, beneath a royal blue hat, McFadden battled with his self-composure. Passersby would gaze at him and then pretend they hadn't seen.

"Dr. McFadden, I presume."

First impression was of what good fortune Mrs. Smith had had in this, her toss of chromosomal dice; the man was handsome. McFadden's height, perhaps a little taller. Smooth skin, clean features – somewhere in the Omar Sharif school of bearing, though he knew Sharif was supposed to be Egyptian. Still, the likeness stood.

The second thing to strike him was that this man knew how to dress. McFadden's own attire was appropriate – once he'd whipped away the baseball cap – but the Parsee was downright elegant. On top of all this was the voice: that smarmy, plummy Oxford drawl. Cultured – not a word he'd often had occasion to apply to people.

The two men silently shook hands.

"Follow me," said the Parsee, and led them to an elevator.

A room was booked upstairs. It was understood that McFadden would settle the bill when the time came, but the Mysterious Parsee had checked them in already and was fishing for the key. McFadden maintained a lofty silence as the door swung open. "After you," he said.

"Thank you. Drink?"

On the sideboard stood a distillation McFadden often had to wait for months on special order to obtain at home, and two square-cut crystal glasses. He made a mental note to browse the duty-free, time permitting.

"Please." Though grateful for the whisky, his obligation to his client required him to intercede. "I must ask you," he said, "to limit your intake. Alcohol, as you may know, debilitates sperm." The Parsee threw back his head and laughed. "Damage done already, I'm afraid," he said, then sobered. "Well then, down to business?"

Replacing his glass, McFadden passed an envelope. "Five thousand dollars," he said. "Canadian." Mrs. Smith was adamant that any extra costs for currency conversion must fall to the donor. "The balance, as agreed, is to be payable six months from this date, barring complications, of course."

"Of course." The Mysterious Parsee nodded and slipped the envelope into his pocket. "Well," he said, for the first time showing signs of discomfort. "Which would you prefer, the blood first, or . . . "

McFadden consulted his watch. His return flight was not for several hours. Until then, he intended the Parsee's fluids to remain precisely where they were. It took a moment to explain as much. "The shorter the transit, you understand, the greater the viability."

"Oh . . . I hadn't . . . Well then." McFadden and the Parsee regarded one another from across the room. "Do you do this often?"

"Actually, no."

"I see. Quite."

"And you?"

"Hardly."

Another silence, after which the Parsee settled back into his chair, and then leaned forward. "I assume," he said, "that I have your personal assurance my genetic material will never be used in any other context outside of that for which it has been contracted."

McFadden blinked. He was unprepared to make any such assurances. If there were straws left over, and typically there would be, it was fully his intention to add them to his cryo-bank. "I don't quite follow," he said, by way of stalling.

The Parsee narrowed his eyes. "It is very simple." He had risen to his feet. "I require the same safeguards for my genes as your patient – their recipient – has required for hers. Otherwise the arrangement is nullified."

"Please sit down."

The Parsee returned to his chair.

"Am I permitted to ask," said McFadden after a moment, "how this *arrangement* was arrived at?"

"You are not."

"I see . . . "

Another span of silence, after which the Parsee appeared to reconsider.

"It was through an intermediary," he said. "An advertisement was brought to my attention which your client, evidently, had registered at this end. Cleverly worded. It directed me to the intermediary – a go-between – who in turn was in touch with your client, wherever she may be. Judging from your accent, I would assume America." McFadden was careful neither to confirm nor to deny. "The intention, of course, was to assure each other total anonymity."

"Of course," said McFadden, and nodded. "The turkey-baster shuffle."

"I beg your pardon?"

"My apologies. It's a familiar process. Or should I say a more complex version of a familiar process, though much less common now than some years back. Practised mostly in the lesbian communities. A woman would enlist the help of a friend, who would in turn be aided by another friend. Three removes, you see. This third party would locate a sympathetic male, often also homosexual, willing to provide the sperm and turn it over to the intermediary – the go-between, as you say – who then would convey it to the first woman in the hope of generating pregnancy. The name relates to the household appliance favoured as the agent of insemination."

"Good Lord."

"Motive, of course, was essentially the same: donor anonymity, recipient anonymity. After AIDS it became too dangerous, particularly in that community, as I'm sure you can imagine. So you seldom see it practised now. May I help myself?" he said, moving to the sideboard.

"I'm terribly sorry. Please do."

"Yours?"

"A little, yes. Thank you. I had no idea . . ." The Parsee rose again and paced the room. "In any case," he said, "I still require unconditional –"

"I'm afraid I don't see the importance."

The Parsee stopped and stared, and then retrieved his glass. "Do you mean to say it's typical for men to provide you their sperm for use in *just anybody*?"

McFadden's own astonishment left him somewhat disadvantaged. He sipped his whisky. "Yes," he said.

"But that's . . . revolting!"

A painting hung above the sideboard, slightly off-centre. Horses, done in oil, with very small heads and very long legs. McFadden pondered the perspective.

"I'm sorry," said the Parsee, sitting down again. "It may be that I am misinformed. My knowledge of this subject comes from the little I've read in the news publications. But I've been given to understand your *female* clients are offered quite a latitude in terms of choice . . ."

He had paused expectantly. McFadden, evidently, was supposed to carry through this line of reasoning, but he hadn't grasped the point.

The Parsee was shaking his head. "Are there not catalogues?" he asked. "Data banks? Donor profiles?" While not precisely ruffled, he seemed genuinely disturbed at McFadden's lack of comprehension. "In other words, is it not true these women are encouraged to pick and choose? Blue eyes to match the husband's; dark complexions here, heavy eyebrows there? A cleft chin just like Uncle Jack's. Oh look, this one's a barrister! Polish sperm for Polish patients; redheads with freckles laid in for the Highland market? This donor is a Roman Catholic, all those on page sixteen are Pentecostal. I'm quite certain I'm not mistaken. I understand the donors must remain anonymous, but surely you provide your patients information about what *kind* of men they are. Don't tell me it's some blind-chance lottery, not revealed until the nursery?"

"No," said McFadden, "of course not." Though he'd seen occasions where it might as well have been: Latino couples ending up with blue-eyed, blond-haired babies because the doctor just assumed that's what they'd be happy with. But that seldom happened these days. Selection wasn't quite as detailed as the Parsee seemed to think, but essentially he had it right.

"And the donors, do *they* have equal say?"

McFadden shook his head, less from denial than perplexity. "But how could they?"

"How could they *not*?"

It took a moment to digest this. Returning to the sideboard, McFadden used the opportunity to refill his glass.

"Cheers," replied the Parsee, with some degree of petulance. "Forgive me," he continued. "I don't mean to be didactic about this, least of all with someone of your profession. But as I understand it, we humans are composed of forty-six chromosomes. I assume I am correct in this."

McFadden moved his wrist to make the whisky swim around the glass.

"Twenty-three of these come from the egg cell, while the other twenty-three are provided by the sperm. They combine during conception, do they not, to produce a person?"

"Syngamy," said McFadden, quietly nodding. The implications of what the man was driving at were beginning to come home.

"Fine, then, syngamy. The point is that the twenty-three chromosomes coming from the egg are of no more or less importance than the twenty-three deriving from the sperm . . . "

This was, admittedly, a bioethical conundrum he had not before considered.

"But if I am correct in understanding the situation as you present it, the practice is completely biased in favour of the *female's* chromosomes – in terms of selection, I should say – at the expense of the male's."

McFadden returned to his chair. "I'm not quite clear on what you're saying," he said. Although he now believed he was.

"Forgive me, Doctor, but it's obvious. From what you are telling me, your clients come strolling into your office, along with their chromosomes, and go shopping for a set to match. They pick the ones they like, reject the ones they don't. But the chromosomes they're browsing over have no such right of refusal. If I understand this correctly, once *you* get your hands on them, they're captive. *They* don't have a choice. Any creature off the street can walk in and say, 'I want that one,' and that's the end of the matter. You've denied them their right to *their* share of selection."

In all these years McFadden had never thought of it in quite this light. "From a practical consideration," he said, "how could I?"

"From an ethical consideration, how could you not?" The Parsee had worked himself into a pitch of genteel indignation. "Anything less is reprehensible. And certainly from a personal standpoint . . . " He was on his feet again. "I arrived here today prepared to entrust you with *my* chromosomes because – and I will candidly admit this – I need the money. But only under the terms of this agreement, and no other. I would never do this otherwise, not for any sum." He placed the envelope on the bed between them. "If you tell me there is the slightest likelihood of you selling my genes to anyone else, then I must bid you good day."

McFadden's mind was reeling with the implications of this wildly new perspective. What upset him most was that *he* had never thought of it. Even so, there were practical matters to be dealt with.

He jumped to his feet and took the Parsee's hands in his. "I give you my word," he said fervently, while the Parsee put the envelope back into his pocket. "It's unusual, of course, but I can see it means a lot to you –"

"*Unusual?* You really mean to say this isn't standard practice? You are actually telling me you find men willing to sell you *carte blanche* authority over their progeny? Jews who would not object to you using their sperm for insemination among Gentiles? Scholars who would yield their sperm to imbeciles? Muslims providing sperm for Christians?"

"We don't get a lot of Muslims –"

"That's not the point!"

"Or scholars either, for that matter. But I understand what you are saying . . . I just hadn't ever thought about it quite that way."

"I am truly shocked. How can one set of chromosomes abase themselves so completely to another?"

"I don't know," said McFadden. "They just do."

"Deplorable. I'm sorry, Doctor. Please don't take this in any way personally. It's simply that I assumed all along there would be some kind of protocol . . . some formal sort of agreement . . . an element of choice presented to the donor, that's all. The same respect for male chromosomes as for female. Surely *they* demand it."

"Yes," said McFadden, "they do."

"Have a drink, old man. You seem a little out of sorts."

– – –

"So what's the big deal?"

They changed seats a few miles back and once again the girl is driving. Far from speeding now, McFadden has to keep reminding her to pick it up a little.

"What do you mean, what's the big deal?"

"I don't see what was so important. You got pissed in some hotel room. What's to change your life?"

"Well, nothing really changed until –"

"Hold on a minute. Before you go on about that part, I want to know what happened. Did you get the cum through customs, or were you too drunk to catch the plane?"

"I was not drunk!" McFadden is offended. "It all worked out. The medium worked; the sperm stayed alive. I kept it in a bubble taped against my stomach so the temperature remained at constant. No one stopped me at the border. It survived the freezing too. The Mysterious Parsee passed all the blood work. After the 180-day quarantine I flew back to London for the second round, but you know, all he wanted to do was watch soccer – football they call it there. It was some big match. Six months I'd been thinking about the things this man had said, and all he wants to do is watch a bunch of Brazilians running up and down in knee socks. He really was just in it for the money. Anyway, everything worked."

"So? Did Mrs. Smith get her baby?"

"I *told* you, I don't know. Presumably she did, since I never heard from her again. But I couldn't say for certain."

"And you never even *tried* to find out?"

"No."

"How could you?"

"Don't *you* start."

"I'd just think you'd be curious . . ."

"I leave that to the obstetrician. As I've been telling you, Mrs. Smith's travails are not the point of this. The point –"

"One more question."

"Go ahead."

"What's a straw?"

"A straw?"

"Yes. You keep talking about taking this Parsee guy's sperm and dividing it up into straws. So what's a straw?"

"Oh. Sorry. A straw is basically a measurement of sperm. I mean that in a quantitative, not qualitative, sense . . . Sorry, it's an *amount*. A healthy donor produces four or five hundred million sperm a pop. When you consider that only one of them is necessary for fertilization, you can see it's a bit more than you need, especially when you can save it the trouble of racing up to the egg. So we take the ejaculate and divide it into smaller quantities, and store them in tiny glass tubes called straws. Then we freeze them in liquid nitrogen. I should have explained that too. That's what we mean by cryopreservation. *Cryo* comes from the Greek word for frost. It freezes and thaws very fast so the cells stay alive. An average donor yields about eight or ten straws per ejaculate. Once they're frozen, you can store them indefinitely."

"And how much do you charge your clients for these straws?"

"Clever girl. Prices vary, but let's set a ballpark figure at about $125 a straw. That's for regular, pasteurized Wasp milk; ethnic minorities are more expensive." He can see the girl is calculating.

"Ten times $125 comes out to $1,250, then take away the hundred you paid the donor. That's a nice little profit."

"There's more. A lot of clinics charge for six cycles, in advance and non-refundable. I should have explained that too. A cycle just means your monthly cycle. If someone charges for six cycles, he's charging you for six months of treatment, often at two or three inseminations each month. It can get incredibly expensive. If the client happens to get a pregnancy right away, she still pays the whole six months. Mrs. Smith, for example, took three cycles, if memory serves; so if I was one of those doctors who charged for six, she'd have paid me twice as much as she needed to. It's this kind of thing that gives the business a worse reputation than it already has. Some of these women, you know, completely lose their minds. You almost have to see it to believe it. They get so desperate they'll do anything, and their husbands feel so badly they go along with it. Sell the car, sell the house. You'd have to have a black hole for a heart to take advantage of that."

"How much did you charge Mrs. Smith?"

"You don't miss a trick, do you?"

The girl is amused, though McFadden's only just realized what he's said. "Sounds like neither do you."

"All right. Mrs. Smith paid through the nose, but only because she could afford to. You don't get those all that often. Believe me, there are just as many I've had to do for nothing. I told you, some of them go crazy. If you turn them away because they can't afford it, you just know they'll do something dangerous. The Mrs. Smiths of the world help subsidize the others."

"I believe you," she says, though by the looks of her she has her mind on something else. "So what about the Mysterious Parsee?"

"What about him?"

"You say he donated – you've gotta love that word, *donated* – you say he *donated* twice. That would be somewhere between sixteen and twenty straws, total. But then you said Mrs. Smith only took three cycles, at three straws per cycle. So that would be – what? – only nine straws used up. Which means you must have had between seven and eleven straws of Mysterious Parsee sperm left over. So the question is, what did you do with them?"

"Quite the little head for math," he says. McFadden is labouring to catch up with her calculations.

"You're stalling."

"No, just thinking. My mind is not as nimble as yours . . . Actually, your numbers are slightly inaccurate, but that's not your fault. I inseminated Mrs. Smith *four* times each cycle, not three, if memory serves, just to be certain; which would have used up twelve straws. But on the other hand, the Mysterious Parsee was a better producer than you've given him credit for. Eight to ten is just the average; some men produce a lot less, some more. This guy was well into the upper percentiles. I remember him exactly because his numbers were the same as mine. The Mysterious Parsee was a twelve-straw man, which is exceptional. What that means is that the Parsee would have produced twenty-four straws over the two donations. Quite remarkable, actually. Which therefore would have left a twelve-straw surplus."

He's hoping this quantity of detail might distract her. She has that look again.

"Hold on a minute," she says, "hold on just one minute! Did you say . . . ? You *did* say!" She has taken up a handful of his shirt. "Why would *you* know how many straws *you* produce?"

McFadden twists a finger through his beard, which reminds him it could use a little trimming. "You didn't happen to get a pair of scissors while you were shopping, did you?"

"Shut up about the scissors."

He juts his chin a little to present a formal profile. "Isn't it getting a little bit ratty? No pun intended."

"Shut up about the beard."

McFadden sighs. "If you'd ever stopped interrupting, you'd have known by now that *that* has been the whole point of everything I've been trying to tell you . . ."

The girl has let go of his shirt.

– – –

They are in Alberta. Suddenly it's just appeared, a sign on the road saying *Welcome*. They've pulled off and set up camp. This time the girl is cooking so McFadden can go on talking. He's been sitting on his hands, watching her assault upon his cooking gear, to say nothing of the raccoon ragout he's quite certain she is burning. If he makes any gesture to assist, she glares him back into his place and tells him to shut up and keep talking.

"The only person I really feel sorry for," she says, "in this whole story is your wife."

McFadden nods, and forces his eyes from the copper-bottomed pot he can smell beginning to singe. It's true. His ex-wife is the only person in the whole story *he* has any sympathy for. Still does, though he's fairly confident she would spit on him if she ever met him in the street.

"It was more like the final straw," he tells the girl, "to be honest. Things hadn't been going well for years. That's a cliché, I know, but then most truths are." Normally he avoids even thinking about this, much less discussing it. But it takes his mind off how badly he wants her to lower the flame.

"It must have been awful for her."

"Which part?" he says, mindful of the irony.

"Not being able to have a baby. I mean, in the first place; all that stuff about you later would have made it worse. But I bet it was terrible all along. Of all the guys she could have married, she had to pick the one who helped *other* women get their babies."

"Thanks." But in her usual way the girl has abstracted things precisely. A sterile woman coupled with a fertility specialist was not a recipe for happy marriage.

THE DOMINION OF WYLEY McFADDEN

"And there was nothing you could do . . . ?"

"No egg, no pregnancy. Simple as that. At least we knew early on. Diagnosis in her case was unequivocal. In an odd sort of way that was almost a blessing – knowing for sure, I mean. It's the women who don't know who have it especially hard, who think they should be fertile but aren't, or who end up with serial miscarriages. They're the ones who tend to really lose it. We only had eight months of uncertainty before the verdict came in. Some couples go on like that for years, and still never know."

"Was it you who did the, um . . . testing?"

"No. I knew already it wasn't me, but we thought it was better that she consult another specialist, for her side of things."

"How come you never adopted?"

"My fault. In hindsight I know that's what we should have done. But that was years ago and I just didn't . . . I can honestly say that if the problem had been on my side – I mean, if I had been infertile and not my wife – I would have advocated donor insemination. How could I not, in my position? But adoption isn't reproduction. Reproduction means reproducing. It means repeating your genes and your forebears', not just having a baby in the house. An adopted baby would have been unrelated to either of us. I didn't see the point."

"What I don't get," she says, "is how you knew it wasn't you? You said before you even started testing her you knew it wasn't you?"

She has that gleam again that tells him she knows he's holding back. McFadden has swallowed enough embarrassment today not to be too much bothered by another bite.

"All right, but it was only the once. And that was *years* before I ever thought of getting married, way back when I first opened the practice. I was curious. Anybody would be."

He knows there's no way out of this and so he hams a bit, playing up the hesitation. The girl taps her fingernails against her spatula, and he notices again the oddness of the calluses around her knuckles. McFadden sighs a sigh that isn't altogether artifice.

"I'd been wondering about it, I admit. Curiosity is the donor's second biggest motivation, you know, behind cash. Some studies show it's even more important. I guess I was just as curious as anybody. In those days the donor profiles were fairly rudimentary: height, weight, skin colour, hair colour, profession, personal interests, do you have any lunatics in the family? That was pretty much it. I made up a donor profile matching myself and temporarily added it to the file. A nice couple came down from Timmins and picked mine."

McFadden has placed his hand above his heart. "I swear I did nothing to influence their decision. I even left the room. But they pointed to my profile and said this is the one – or should I say the wife pointed; the husband, as usual, was looking like he wished he was someplace else. He was more or less the same build as I am, which probably accounted for the choice, though I suspect the 'Medical Doctor' entry beside the reference to profession might have had something to do with it. The only thing I lied about was in the hobbies category: I put down chess and archery. So maybe it was the archery. They probably have a big demand for archers up in Timmins."

"So you got this woman pregnant with your own sperm while she thought it was from an anonymous donor?"

"It *was* from an anonymous donor. I can be as anonymous as the next guy."

"And did it work?"

"As far as I know. I was curious, that's all. The semen was just as carefully vetted as any other she would have received. My curiosity was satisfied, and I never did it again. Not for fifteen years, anyway. Not until that damned Parsee wiped out my bank."

"It was *not* the Parsee. You can't blame him. It was *your* doing. Nobody forced you."

"Yes, yes. All right." McFadden is a little touchy, now the story's out.

"So on top of all that with the lesbians, you have a grown-up kid in Timmins, too?"

"*I told you!* I never follow up beyond conception . . . *Jesus Christ, get out of there!*" McFadden has leapt to his feet with a stick from the fire in his fist. He is shocked to see the girl curl herself into a ball and try to roll away behind the upturned chair.

A very flat and triangular animal is prying at the back end of his truck, standing on its hind legs like a bear, scrabbling with very credible claws at the hinges of his tailgate.

"A badger!" he shouts in a confusion of emotions. "Look at him. He's trying to eat my rats! Hey, you! Badger! Piss off!"

Another part of him is appalled at the girl's reaction, but the efforts of the badger permit him not to think of this. He pulls her to her feet as if this hasn't happened, shouting maledictions.

"Leave my rats alone, you Vandal! You Goth! They'll have problems enough with two-legged Albertans! Go on! Git! Get away from there!"

All the while he's being careful not to get too close. Badgers, according to his understanding, are merely wolverines that dig. The girl has composed herself. She gives a look of uttermost contempt and then advances, stamping her feet and clapping her hands. McFadden, his masculinity compromised, hastens to her side, but the badger is already retreating, shuffling back toward the prairie.

"A badger!" he says excitedly.

"A mental case," replies the girl.

– – –

The problem with the Parsee was that he got McFadden thinking. Usually McFadden's fairly good at thinking. The Parsee having thought of something he himself had not, somehow strangely disconcerted his perceptions. As a matter of personal policy McFadden viewed his donors with as long a lens as possible; not to say they were a particularly scruffy lot, as donors went. Suppliers – this was how he thought of them, like the men who came by twice a month to drop off latex gloves and cartons of cervical swabs.

In the early days, fertility clinics operated out of hospitals. This is what's given rise to the notion of sperm donors as medical students. At least that's McFadden's theory. His own clinic was free-standing and private, and never once – unless he counts himself – had a medical student of any stripe volunteered to drop by in the morning with a fresh deposit. The closest he can think of was an unemployed ambulance driver from Cape Breton who stayed on the books for years until a string of mine disasters sent him home in hopes of work.

Finding donors was always one of the profession's biggest headaches. Rejection rates were a steady seventy to eighty percent. Not to say that altruism didn't sometimes play a part, but a bit part at best. Those men who enlisted out of genuine public spirit tended to be fiftyish, balding, and given to Hush Puppies and bifocals. He might get twenty million parts per millilitre, if he was lucky; more often their counts were just too low to bother with. The real producers were the eighteen-year-olds, the ones he could slot in twice a week for beer money. At least he hoped it was beer money. If they happened to be hard-to-get minorities, McFadden was sorely tempted to overlook a needle track or two. He wouldn't ever use the word degenerates, but there weren't too many Nobel laureates either.

Whatever thought he gave to his donors was by and large reflective of his own attitudes to *them*. McFadden has always had an ear for ambiguity, but this transcended the enigma: an antithetical contempt, on his part, for the underpinning of his entire operation. In truth, he never really came to terms with motive in his donors, or more precisely, never sanctioned it – merely paid. These Esaus could trade away their patrimony for a hundred-dollar pottage, though Esau, at least, might claim deception. McFadden's donors consented to the sale with eyes as open as their wallets. Or did they?

This was the question that disturbed the doctor's sleep through the twilight of that fateful flight from Heathrow: the intemperate disparity between consent and *informed* consent.

The Parsee's point was carried home. To be informed required *in-formation*, and this was offered to one group of gametes much more than to the other. Most of his recruits were hardly past their teens; how could they be expected to step back and take the long view? *Information*, insofar as they received it, amounted merely to what McFadden chose to tell them. Which wasn't much.

The more he contemplated the Parsee's radical objection, the more he saw its moral merit.

A document, not just an information packet, more expansive in detail than the standardized consent form. Something closer in spirit to the database he laid out for his paying clients. This had never been done. This was uncharted territory.

McFadden kept a pad of paper in his briefcase. He raised his seat, drained his Scotch and snapped the folding table back in place. It turned out much more complicated than he'd expected: columns of consent cross-referenced against demarcations of refusal, homologies and heterologies tabulated and defined. Long before he landed, he was forced to switch to coffee. The final version extended into many pages. In the end he had to sit an hour with each and every donor merely to explain it.

The intention was achieved, though putting it into practice took him months of organizing. When all was said and done, McFadden could boast the only sperm bank in the country based on chromosomal reciprocity. All his donors, from this point forward, had the opportunity to designate precisely where they thought their sperm should go, and where it shouldn't.

"And they all ruled out dykes."

McFadden winces. Even in his private contemplation he tries to avoid these grosser terminologies. Not so the girl.

"To a man," he says. "Not even one. Not *one* initial beside the 'single women and lesbian' category. *Nada*. Some did later, but I had to disqualify them because *they* were gay. That's CFAS requirements, by the way, nothing personal. The Canadian Fertility and Andrology Society rules out homosexual donors because of

AIDS. The problem was that lately I'd been specializing more and more in lesbian clients. I was filling a genuine niche."

"That's the part I don't get. Why exactly were these lesbians always coming to you?"

McFadden looks some more into the fire. He's skipped a little of this part deliberately, for brevity. Trust her. And he's dying for a drink. He keeps glancing over at the truck in case the badger sneaks back again to run amok among his rats.

"The rats are fine," she says. "The truck's locked."

McFadden's still uneasy. The girl, on the other hand, seems perfectly recovered. "I want to hear about the lesbian connection."

He forces the bottle of Macallan back into the locker where he knows it's waiting. "Most doctors in the early days refused to treat them. I shouldn't say treat – a lot of fertility specialists declined on principle to inseminate lesbians and single women. That's more accurate."

"Hard to believe anybody could prefer a turkey baster to an honest cock."

Since the badger incident she seems to have taken on some kind of edge. He hopes that if he ignores it, it will go away.

"So they started coming to me."

"And you did it for them?"

"If I hadn't, they would certainly have resorted to something much less safe, and what agenda would that have served?"

"So you took on the dyke market?"

McFadden bites his breath. "You may dispute the benefits of children raised without a father, and your objections might have merit. But how much worse if they come into the world with a terminal disease?"

"I thought you said you never looked beyond conception?"

"You're wasting your talents, you know. You should have been a lawyer."

"You liked my talents well enough a little while ago."

"So there I was," he says, "with a waiting list of special patients and not a single straw to give them."

"And so you started using yours."

"And so I started using mine. But just for lesbians. Some of the white donors said they didn't want their sperm going into black women or Jews, and some of the Jews were very clear about proscribing Gentiles – all that whole Pandora's box I cursed myself for ever opening – but at the end of the day there was always enough to go around for everybody – except the lesbians. For some reason everybody ruled out the lesbians. I had no idea."

"Why didn't you just get lesbian sperm from one of those mail-order banks you were talking about?"

"That would have defeated the whole point of the exercise. Just because it came from somewhere else, the donors still weren't given right of refusal. Anyway, I always hated importing American products. We get enough Walt Disney as it is."

"So you used your own sperm for the lesbians."

"What do you want, an affidavit?"

"And how long did this little orgy carry on?"

She's jealous. It has only now occurred to him – the girl is jealous. At least there's no other explanation for this bizarre hostility that comes handily to mind. The mysteries of human emotions will never cease to entertain him.

McFadden shakes his head. "Fortunately, not that long," he says, "or I'd have never made it out alive."

"What are you smirking at?"

"The strange thing is, I never found out how they knew."

"*Yes!* I wanted to ask you that too. How did you get caught?"

"I don't know. Believe me, I sweated bullets trying to figure it out, but I never did. It couldn't have been blood analysis; I was never actually required to submit one. The best theory is that someone on my staff leaked it out, although how *they* knew is still a mystery. But honestly, I don't know."

"What the hell you smiling at?"

"All I know is that a letter arrived telling me they knew what I was up to, and that as soon as they subpoenaed me for blood tests, everybody else was going to know it too. Two weeks later I was on the way to South America. I told you that part, remember? I had to make it look like I'd run away for good. So I never got a chance to launch my own investigation."

"What did you do with the letter?"

"I showed it to my wife."

"You *idiot!*"

"No choice in the matter, by that stage."

"And what did your wife do?"

"She showed it to her lawyer."

"And what did her lawyer do?"

"She discussed the matter with the lesbians' lawyer."

"So the lesbians got themselves a lawyer too?"

"Oh, yes. A marquee one at that."

"And what did *your* lawyer have to say to all of this?"

"I didn't need a lawyer."

"What?"

"I needed an accountant."

"An accountant?"

"And a damned good one. Not cheap either, though none of the lawyers were, for that matter. But I never would have made it without him. Do you want to know a secret? I think by that time I was glad it happened. Things were starting to get out of control. Not just me, I mean – the whole industry. It's past understanding, what they can do now, even in the few years I've been out. Ten years ago you could argue it was still mostly a matter of fixing what you could fix and surrogating what you couldn't. You could still believe you were assisting nature, not thwarting it. If the man's sperm was no good, you swapped in somebody else's. As you pointed out, women had been doing that without benefit of medical intervention since the beginning. Then we got the first test-tube baby, but it still wasn't all that big a deal. In vitro was designed to get around blocked Fallopian tubes. If the egg couldn't make it through, you just went in and removed one so it could be fertilized outside. It was still a question of healthy sperm meeting healthy egg – still arguably natural. *Then* we started being able to take *unhealthy* sperm, cells that never would have had a chance in nature, and enhance them so now they could be combined with the ova in vitro – meaning, literally, 'in a glass' – did I explain that? yes? – the ova itself having been manipulated to make it as easy as possible for the sperm cell to penetrate. But do you know what they're doing now?"

The girl looks about to answer, but McFadden doesn't want to break his train of thought.

"This is just since I've been out; that's how fast technologies are coming on stream. Now they can take sperm that's so badly deformed it can't penetrate the egg even *after* the shell's been punctured to make the entry easier – they can take this wonky sperm now and *inject* it into the egg. Did I tell you that only about one sperm in every million is strong enough to make it all the way to the egg under natural conditions? One in a million! That's how rigorous the process of *natural* selection is meant to be . . . But now they can retrieve a sperm that's so badly misshapen it doesn't even manage to get itself ejaculated – it can be salvaged from urine, for God's sake, after retrograde emissions – and they can take that sperm, which in the world outside the lab was never meant to spread its DNA, and make it fertilize a living ovum. You have to wonder what kind of people a procedure like that is going to end up making."

"I thought you said you never looked beyond conception."

McFadden has to pause to catch his breath. "Maybe you should have been a psychologist instead of a lawyer."

"You keep trying to weasel out of telling me about the lesbians."

"You know, you seem to be a little fixated on these lesbians."

"*I'm* fixated? You're the one knocking them up."

It's dark by this time, and the stars are out, a billion of them in a sky so low he wonders that the moths aren't tempted. And no mosquitoes. There were no mosquitoes last night either, just a silent breeze and the odd coyote yelping somewhere off in the distance. He hopes coyotes are out again this evening, though he's not certain if badgers fear coyotes or whether it works the

other way around. Geographically, this is well beyond his area of
expertise. Come to think of it, he's not even sure if badgers are di-
urnal. Maybe they stay at home after dark and he has nothing to
worry about. Though on a night as bright as this . . . ?

"Stop obsessing about badgers and talk to me about the
lesbians."

"Even if they don't get at the rats, they could scratch up the
paintwork."

"It's a truck!"

"It's not a truck. It's a camper van."

"Well, it's got plenty of scratches already. It's not like it's a
Porsche, you know."

"When the letter came," he says, "I knew that was that. And
I'm not sure I was too much broken up about it. So it was mostly a question of doing what was right while trying to keep as
much of my own skin as I could salvage. The lesbians got
themselves a gynoraptor of an attorney, a real politico. This was
a career-making case for her. I think at one point she even suggested she was doing it pro bono. There was just no precedent,
not in Canadian jurisprudence. It could easily have made it to
the Supreme Court if we'd all decided to go that route. Of
course it would have wiped me out, whatever the outcome.
Oddly enough, that's what saved everybody. I think you should
turn down that heat."

"It's fine."

"No, really, I can smell it. And all you're doing stirring it like
that is churning up the burnt parts."

He tries to take the spoon away, but she pulls it out of reach.
"You just can't leave anything alone, can you?"

"But you're *burning* it!"

"All right. All right." Scowling, she lowers the flame and
McFadden's anxiety. "You were telling me what you did with
the letter from the lesbians."

"Right. I showed the letter to my wife because I had to give
her time to file divorce proceedings and get *her* lawyer into the

loop. There was no hope, by that time, of saving the marriage. And anyway, by that time it was clear enough I'd have to disappear. So I hired my accountant. It all came down to money. The lesbians' counsel indicated they were pursuing, oh, several counts of paternity. And my wife, of course, had her support claim. It was obvious that the most sensible thing was to concentrate on dividing up the assets rather than waste time defending them, which would just have swallowed everything in legal costs. So I hired the accountant to add up exactly what I was worth, less the gold."

"The gold?"

"Less the gold. I didn't tell him about the gold. But I gave him carte blanche on everything else: all my banking, the complete books to my business dealings. I put him in touch with my stockbroker and real-estate agent, turned over the deed to the cottage and the keys to the Mercedes. I even handed in my bank card. The idea was for him to come up with a statement of my total worth, which surprised even me. Then we set up a meeting between him and my wife so he could show her the numbers and explain how much the lesbians were going after. Then he met with the lesbians so he could do the same with them, except to let them know my wife stood just as good a chance of winning as they did. After that, he arranged a meeting between my wife *and* the lesbians, where he was able to document how much their *lawyers* would end up getting if they didn't settle this amongst themselves. Which I'm glad to say they did. I always wished I could have been a fly on the wall for that little get-together.

"Once in a while," he says, "the thing that makes the most sense is the thing that actually happens. It wouldn't have done anybody any good, except the lawyers, to turn this into a media circus. My ex-wife, bless her, was quick to see the logic there. Some of the lesbians wanted to get militant, but my diplomatic accountant quietly pointed out how their children could hardly be said to benefit from smaller settlements, as well as all the harassment that would surely go along with public hearings. He was a great accountant; I still send him Christmas cards I get postmarked down in Paraguay. And he didn't make out so badly himself: I gave him a percentage of the total based on what he could pry back from the vultures. If there's a class of people I really hate, it's lawyers – lawyers and dentists.

"Anyway, he went to them with what must have been very neatly calculated personal gratuities, which helped persuade them they were acting after all in their clients' better interests. The lawyer for the lesbians wanted to make sure I'd never practise medicine again. She said it was essential to the well-being of society, which I thought rather self-evident at that point. She drafted a letter to the College of Physicians and Surgeons and had me sign it. The College was all too happy to revoke my licence quietly; a show trial would have opened up a hornets' nest for them as well. I made a big point of insisting on a few thousand dollars for myself – basically enough for a one-way ticket out of the hemisphere and some resettlement money – just to make sure no one suspected the gold. And then I disappeared."

The girl is staring at the quarter moon. "I don't even want to know what all this has to do with where we are right now," she says. "But you might as well tell me about the gold."

"It was buried in the backyard, or most of it. I told you that my clients often preferred to pay in cash. That means those funds were never reflected in my OHIP billings or, of course, on year-end revenues. Non-existent money. Every year I converted part of it to gold for portability – though I don't know why people use that word, because it's the heaviest stuff imaginable – and buried it. When the time came, I dug it up and buggered off. But before you get all dewy-eyed and mercenary, let me tell you it wasn't any fortune; just enough to hide behind and keep me going until the trapping business started generating income, which I'm proud to say it has."

"So if I understand this right, you're telling me your wife and – what was it you said? – *several* lesbians and their children still live in Toronto, and *you* still live there too? And nobody ever sees you?"

"They might. But I keep a low profile. I've gone to quite a lot of trouble changing my identity, and Toronto is a very big city. Theoretically, we could all spend the rest of our lives there, and never bump into each other. I said before that my wife would spit on me if she saw me on the street, but that probably isn't true. What she'd far more likely do is pretend she *didn't* see me. She's still a well-bred girl from north Toronto, after all. Controversy isn't as big a thing in real life as it is on television; most people tend to avoid it. As for the lesbians, who knows? If they discovered me again, they might get bees in their bonnets, but what good would it do? All they'd see now is a broken-down rat catcher. If not, it's still a wide world, plenty of room for new beginnings."

McFadden yawns. He's finished.

It's astounding that he's finally got the story out, but even more so, it's exhausting. Perhaps that's the true nature of catharsis – more fatigue than release. He wonders dimly what Aristotle would have said to this.

"So what are you going to do?"

"What do you mean?"

"When you finish letting loose your rats – what are you going to do then?"

McFadden yawns again. For the present, the past is too fatiguing to impose itself upon the future. And besides, his foot is acting up.

"Are we going to eat that," he asks, "or is it your intention to carbonize it absolutely?"

*And the muttering grew to a
  grumbling;
And the grumbling grew to a
  mighty rumbling;
And out of the houses the rats
  came tumbling.*

ROBERT BROWNING
FROM "THE PIED
PIPER OF HAMELIN"

H e had prepared himself. At least, he'd warned himself the dreams would come again tonight, and come they did, the moon still barely a quarter-way across the dome. In the hours afterwards he lay and watched it, a vaguely whitish presence sliding inch by inch along the ceiling of his tent, until he had to crane his neck and roll his eyes to see in the gloom behind.

He's begun to register a pattern: an inverse relationship between wakefulness and sleep. The better the day, the worse the night. This has been the worst by far. Not just the thrashing, now, but sounds as well to leave his own mind gutted. A hollow in the darkness, reciting the unspeakable. For McFadden it's a form of willing torture, this voyeur's private haunt: fascinating and repellent both. The empirical observer, he; detached in his unequal light, archivist of gaping mouth and bobbing throat, flying hands and heaving hips. And recorder to the voice itself. He wants to lift his palms and shut his ears, and yet he wants to listen. Fighting with himself to act or counteract – impose or interpose – McFadden settles with himself at last, and listens.

In the course of time it ends as it began, a shift in pressure, a change in rhythm. The spine relaxes; conscious hands renew themselves. They lie awhile in silence, the girl reassembling, McFadden with open eyes upon the filtered moon.

"It's just that everybody's always had to fuck me."

For a moment he's not certain which side the voice has come from. He feels her lift a hand to touch her face. So it's the girl herself. McFadden blinks into the shadows, biting back his breath. For a while it seems as if she's finished. He listens to her breathing, then she speaks again.

"In those days we lived in a house the band council owned, my mom and me. I remember that because they always had the keys. Even when I tried to lock the door, they just walked right in because they always had the keys. They'd bring along a case of beer or a bottle. When she drank enough, she'd start to cry before she fell asleep, and that's when they'd come into my room and fuck me too. I used to wonder if they came for me or for her. I guess she used to wonder too. When the Children's Aid showed up, she never even tried to stop them."

He understands, now, what's happening. His own story finished, the girl has decided to assume her own.

"How old were you," he asks, "then?"

"Old enough, I guess. That's what brought in Children's Aid, when it started showing. They said I was too small to have a baby, and they must have been right. Because the baby died."

"Oh, God." He reaches through the gloom to find her hand. She lets him keep it, then withdraws it to fold it with the other in the hollow of her neck.

"After that, they put me into foster houses. I don't know, five or six, I think. None of them for long. Not until the religious people."

Her hands are primly folded at her throat. She is silent for so long he wonders if she's changed her mind.

"Where was this?" he asks.

"Where?" The question puzzles. "I don't remember. Some town. It doesn't matter. They were very well respected in that town, though. They used a fixed-up school bus to drive around in, because they had so many kids. And it had to have one of those wheelchair elevators because a lot of them were cripples. They had a church set up in the basement, with an altar and crosses and everything. All of us went down there every day to pray. The bigger kids had to carry down the little ones who couldn't walk. And every day he'd read us stories from the Bible and we'd all say prayers together and then he'd bless us all . . ."

She has rolled her wrists and joined her fingers, pressing palms to make a silhouette against the vault of murkish light.

"But he must have thought I needed extra blessing, because he started taking me down there by myself. Just me. He liked to put his hand on my head when we were praying, but it never stayed that way. Always after that it ended up with me down on my knees, praying faster and faster, and him hard up behind me until he wanted me to say *amen*, the way he liked, stretching out to make it last. But even if I did it right, he'd call me names after, bad names from the Bible, and tell me I was going to burn. Most of the time he let me go then, but other times I had to stay there with him, praying even louder, and then I'd know I was in for sore knees. We'd stay there, sometimes him crying, telling God how bad I was – him praying a line and me saying it back. If he was tired, that would be enough, just the praying. But if he got up and stood in front of me and made me close my eyes again, I knew I was in for really sore knees."

"Oh, God."

If the girl has heard the irony, she shrugs it off. McFadden himself is unaware of what he's said. All he knows is that he's wishing he had never asked.

"The funny thing, you know," she says, "is that I always knew it was me. For everybody else he was exactly what they said. The newspaper in that town had him in it all the time. He coached hockey, took kids camping, adopted all those cripples – all that stuff. Like I said, it's me. Men just have to fuck me."

McFadden understands how exactly this applies to him as well. A moon-bathed arm reaches out to touch him. "Not you," she says, and stops his heart with charity.

Above, a tent flap ripples as a little breeze disturbs the membrane. Outside, crickets, a warbling coyote, the rumble of a heavy truck somewhere in the distance. Prairie farmers rising early too.

"Tell me," he says, "about the Skinner box."

The girl removes her hand.

Now he knows what he's been hearing, he thinks it may have come out earlier as well, but certainly the last time. *Skinner box*, she'd said, repeated again and again like the mantric notes of a hymn. And then the slow and rhythmical beginnings of the movement itself. McFadden is unhappy with analogy but finds he needs it. It helps to keep him distant, allows him to concentrate on cause instead of effect, prevents him from being swept up in the performance. These dreams torment him. Patron or player? *Skinner box, skinner box, skinner box*, she whispers, like a Dionysian chant. And then the hips begin to heave . . .

"How did you know?"

"You say it," he tells her gently, "while you're sleeping. Over and over . . ."

She has moved as far away as space permits.

"What does it mean?" he asks. "We both know . . ."

She shifts again, nearer this time, and takes his hand. "You don't want to know."

McFadden sighs and clears his throat, wary of the truth in this. "What does it mean?"

"You don't want to know." She has placed his hand across her lips. "You don't. You don't."

He feels her teeth against his skin. "All right," he says, repositioning. "It's up to you."

Outside, he sees it's very nearly dawn.

– – –

And so they speak of rats instead.

Falling back on custom, McFadden has redirected the conversation toward himself, or more precisely this time, to his rats. They lie beneath the sleeping bag, the girl in preterition, McFadden conscious of his own chest moving slowly up and down. He draws in deeply, then expels again in shortened, shallow drafts of concentrated effort.

"What are you doing?"

"Breathing," he says. "How well do you know Calgary?"

Calgary is far away at present. By force of concentration McFadden moves it nearer. He's been there only twice, flying in and out for conferences, living out of his hotel room. Edmonton he's never visited at all, nor any of the other places on his list. He has his maps, of course, but these are short on detail.

At first the girl misunderstands his motives. "I know the hotels," she says, "if that's what you're asking."

"That's not what I was asking. I mean geographically, the town itself. The best places for the rats."

She turns over on her side and touches him, strokes his cheek. Beneath the sockets in this partial light he sees the eyelids blink. She has understood, now, what he's about.

"You're a nice man."

"Ah."

"What exactly are you looking for?" Now it's his turn to flounder in degrees of meaning. "I mean about the rats," she says, and takes his hand again and kisses it.

"Oh, the rats. What we're looking for," he says, pausing to confirm the change in subject, "is the kind of place that suits –"

"The rats."

"Yes. The rats." He can see the stencil of her chin against the curve of wall, angling toward the ceiling. "What they need is somewhere there is food and water, protection from the cold. A place to spread out, dig in . . ."

"Like the rest of us."

"I guess that's it." He takes a moment to consider. "The problem, though, is with reconnaissance; meaning to say, I haven't done any. So of course the guidance of someone more familiar with the local terrain would be . . . of great assistance." He can see the white of partly smiling teeth. "Therefore I repeat the question, however awkwardly: how well do you know Calgary? Or Edmonton, either?"

"Well enough," she says. "But like I told you, when it comes to cities I'm a downtown kind of girl. If you want to settle your rats out in the suburbs, I don't know if I can be much help."

"Is Calgary anything *but* suburbs? I wasn't aware . . . " But his mind has focused. "Downtown, you know, might have its merits."

McFadden's approach to rat resettlement, until this very morning, has been largely theoretical. He has reduced the proposition to its basic principles, of which, according to his reasoning, there are two. One: *Rats like the kind of places people live.* Two: *People don't like rats.* On these two commandments, he tells the girl, hang all the Law and the Prophets.

"Aren't they kind of opposite?"

"Of course. But all good principles are; that's what gives them substance. And certainly, in the case of rats, they're reconcilable. Nearly every place around the world where you find people, odds are you'll find rats too. Alberta's an anomaly. So in theory it should be easy. But in practice the other side has a big head start. It all boils down to evolution."

"I don't know why, but I really like it when you talk that kind of bullshit."

"Bullshit is the basis of reason," he says, comfortable with more familiar territory. "In most cases – in terms of modern history, at least – rats and people colonized the world together. Wherever people went, rats went along with them. So we're pretty much used to one another from the start. But that didn't happen in Alberta. By the time rats caught up, Alberta was ready. It's had many years now of rat-free borders. We've just changed that, you know. Here we are, already behind the lines. But that's just manoeuvres – the real battle is patriation. Now we have to defy the paradox. We have to get our rats right in there where the Albertans live, but without them noticing."

"But I just bet you have a plan."

"As a matter of fact, I haven't."

"I thought you *always* had a plan."

"Not this time. At least not one I'm very happy with. I've picked the towns, of course. I know I'm on solid ground in terms of region. And the rats themselves are ready. I'm very pleased with how well the rats have travelled. But where exactly they should go *within* each town is something I haven't sorted out yet. I mean, I haven't been able to, have I? There's no way of determining that until I get there. That's why I'm asking about Calgary and Edmonton, though the same question applies to any of the other towns on the list. So . . . ?

"So what?"

"So can you help me with location?"

"I have to admit, I haven't been thinking too much about what would happen once we got here."

"I have. But then again I haven't."

"I sort of thought you'd just *dump* them."

"It's not that simple," he tells her. This is what he'd thought about the girl as well. "They have to be positioned somewhere they can get themselves established. Once they've dug in and started breeding, they'll be fine. If we pick the spots right, they'll spread out from there. But they have to survive long enough to get the process going. It's like they say with any other real estate: location, location, location. You know, the more I think about it, though, the more downtowns make sense . . ."

Having put aside the past, McFadden shifts toward the future, at least as far as tomorrow. *Today.* It must be close to dawn by now; his watch is somewhere underneath the bedding. On this day he'll begin releasing rats. Hard to believe he's really reached this point. He likes the girl's suggestion. Downtown locations – by definition city centres – certainly have the virtue of being the ideal place from which to populate outlying regions. Rats, he tells her: are like people, as soon as they can, they move out to the suburbs. But typically, downtown is where they're found in highest concentration. On the other hand, the risks of detection . . .

"Can I ask something?" she says.

"Sure."

"If I get this right, what you're looking for is the kind of place where there's lots of people, but also the kind of place where you find the kind of people not too likely to notice your rats."

"I guess that sums it up."

"So what kind of people are those?"

"I'm not sure it's a question of . . ."

"What kind of people are the kind of people who aren't likely to notice any damn thing? Unless it comes and sits on their face?"

"Umm . . ."

"Drunks!"

For a moment he wonders if he is meant to take this personally.

"And where are you sure to find drunks?"

"Is this a rhetorical question?"

"Bars. Where else? So maybe I wasn't so wrong in the first place. Maybe downtown hotels *are* what you're after. And let me tell you, if you want a personal guide to bars and cheap hotels, I'm the girl for you."

McFadden is so taken with the logic he nearly misses its conclusion. He gives himself a moment to let the implications settle.

"It's beautiful," he says. "It's perfect. The more I think about it, the more beautiful it is. It works for the big places as much as for the small. Every town, no matter what size, has a main street. And every main street has to have its own hotel. It's perfect. Bars usually have restaurants, don't they, where they serve up burgers and fries?"

"Sure."

"So there's our food supply. Whatever people eat, rats will eat too. Places that serve food probably put their garbage out every night, so it's a constant source. Perfect. And of course they'll have washrooms and kitchens that use up lots of water, so there has to be extra sewage capacity, which means there must be manholes handy – which takes care of harbourage as well! And they back onto alleys, too, for deliveries? It's almost too good. You know, you're brilliant!"

She is looking at the moon, now almost down behind their heads, her eyes rolled back to see it. McFadden tries to dampen his enthusiasm, but ideas keep pressing.

"Another thing, you know, is that they're easy to find. We won't have to waste time driving around. Just figure out the neighbourhoods and then locate the bars. For the smaller towns it's even better; all we do is cruise down Main Street . . . "

"You have maps, you said, don't you?"

"Yes."

"I mean of the towns."

"Yes."

"Then just look for railway lines. Wherever the train tracks and main street come together, that's where you'll find your hotel. They built them for the railwaymen in the old days. Other people use them now. Guys from the oil patch, jughounds, survey crews, sometimes the girls who work there. But everybody's from some-place else. Nobody's going to give a shit about your rats."

"You're brilliant," he says again, though more and more aware that this is not enough.

"It's because of people I thought of it. What you said. Those places, only reason anybody goes back into the alleys is to puke, or maybe if they're working. But nobody's going to give a shit about your rats; nobody gives a shit about anything except get-ting drunk and getting laid. Either that or you're working. Then you see enough rats inside not to care about the difference."

It's too much now to leave alone. McFadden takes his hand and lays it flat across her stomach. "You . . . ?"

"Yeah, me. Before I started up seriously. Later too, until I learned better. After that I moved to the cities."

"Is that . . . ? Is that where you ran into this Pavlov and, um . . . Skinner?"

The girl removes his hand. "What time is it?"

McFadden gropes for the flashlight. She winces in the sudden glare and looks away. He finds his watch among the creases of the sleeping bag. In her thrashings she had torn it from his wrist. "It's nearly four," he says.

"Then it's morning."

– – –

The first lot goes down a manhole behind a strip bar in Taber. McFadden leans against his pick to pry the grate, the girl tips in the rats. Before he's even kicked the lid back on they've disappeared into the pipes. Ninety seconds, start to finish. It's 6:06 a.m. By seven-thirty they'll be done drops two and three in Lethbridge, and be en route to number four.

At Fort Macleod they stop to buy matching coveralls – municipal blue – and a pair of hardhats. Now they are invisible. McFadden has devised a box in size and shape like any ordinary tool case, except it opens from the end instead of hinging from the top. They park beside the alley and load the rats – nine males, twenty-six females, all sorted out and caged by sex before he left Toronto – then stroll out at a workman's pace, the girl with a clipboard tucked beneath her arm, McFadden carrying his tool box. The scent of rotting garbage guides them, the rows of refuse bins; close at hand they find the sewer. McFadden lifts the grate, the girl flips back the hinge and tips the box. A Genesis of rats spills and clamours down the piping. Ninety seconds, start to finish. So far no one's even looked at them, much less presumed to interrupt. It is just past nine a.m. and already they have planted half a dozen units, covered hundreds of kilometres.

By noon they've finished Claresholm and High River. Calgary is next. He's been nervous of the city, knowing he will have to find his way around by trial and error – but with the girl as guide they now expect to finish there before the day is out. He's surprised, already, how quickly this is going. While he drives, the girl is studying his map.

"It has a six beside it," she says.

"Calgary?"

"No, Honolulu."

"That means it gets six separate colonies. Two hundred and ten individual rats."

"I guess you want them kind of scattered?"

McFadden nods and checks the fuel gauge. "They should be separated, but not too far apart. The idea is for each colony to expand outward from its point of origin. If and when they reach the stage they're overlapping, they've won. Nobody's going to eradicate them after that. Once they're breeding, it should only take a year or two."

The girl is squinting at the map. She has fished a pencil from the glovebox and seems to be drawing lines and jotting numbers.

"What are you doing?"

"Organizing. Just let me think."

McFadden minds his silence as the miles elapse.

"All right," she says.

"All right what?"

"Six, you said, didn't you? Then all right, I know where we're going."

As they near the outskirts, she directs him to a turnoff. They drive a little distance along a multi-laned thoroughfare – Calgarians for reasons of their own prefer to call their highways *trails* – then off this to a smaller street. It seems to be a residential district, but the downtown skyline looms nearby.

"Here!" she says. They have passed a drooping building with a pair of neon cowboy boots blinking from the rooftop.

"Here?"

"Yes, here! Unless you have somewhere else in mind?"

"No! I mean, I just didn't expect it to be so . . . soon."

The next five drops go by in rapid sequence. He can't quite come to grips with how smoothly this is going. When he glances at her sketches, he's amazed at how precisely she's divided up the city: six interlocking regions blocked out according to geography; six neatly designated drop-spots, clearly marked, with routes laid out between them. There's no denying his own deployments would never have been so quickly or comprehensively achieved. According to his own forecasts, he shouldn't even *be* in Calgary until tomorrow. It was guesswork at best, but McFadden had calculated that if he averaged one drop every hour, he could get all the units out in forty hours' driving, not counting time to sleep and eat. Realistically – taking into account delays – he thought he'd be lucky if he finished inside a week. It's hardly four o'clock yet and already Calgary's behind them. That's fourteen drops completed, and the day – according to the girl – barely half over. She has said she wants to finish Edmonton before they sleep.

At this rate, they'll be done tomorrow.

He should be delighted, but somehow he is not. Whatever time she cost in transit, she has more than made up now they're here. Yet he's having trouble with this . . . finality. Furthermore, what with all these bars, he's been working up a thirst. Twice now he's proposed they stop off for a drink, but the girl won't listen. She's completely taken over. Even when it's his turn to drive, he has the feeling that *he*'s now the passenger.

The country's flying by: a town, a stretch of prairie and then another town. They've done so much already he's losing track of order. He has to ask to see the maps to place their whereabouts. It's gratifying, of course, and yet there's something almost manic in this pace they've set, the pleasure of achievement lost in the haste of action.

"What's with all these little outfits?" he asks.

"What?""These things I see people wearing. I'd never noticed."
"What are you talking about?"

McFadden has the feeling he can slow things down with a
dose of levity, get things back on track with an injection of
comic relief. Besides, he never really *has* noticed how absurdly
these Albertans dress.

"Those great big hats," he says. "And the enormous belt
buckles. To say nothing of the high-heeled boots. I mean, they're
kind of fancy, aren't they, when you look at them? More like
ladies' pumps with ankle reinforcements." He glances over,
but the girl is not to be drawn out. "I'm seeing them on grown
men," he tells her. "All over. You must have noticed. Even
right downtown in Calgary, and not a cow in sight. It can't be
these guys are actual cowboys, can it? More like dentists
and CAs."

He is giving this his best, but the girl is not responding. She's
absorbed in maps and watching out for road signs. McFadden
settles back in his seat and shakes his head. "Only in Alberta," he
sighs, "would people take their fashion cues from Texas."

"You're not exactly Gianni Versace yourself," she says, then
reminds him the turnoff for Carstairs is coming up straight
ahead. McFadden shrugs and switches on the turn signal.

The drop in Carstairs takes barely twenty minutes, then Olds,
and then three more in Red Deer, which she tackles with a special zeal. She's behind the wheel again for this leg, and by this
time has set aside her maps. It's very clear she knows exactly
where she's going. McFadden's seen a lot of rundown bars already, but the place in Red Deer wins the prize so far. He's
been watching her, when he can, recording clues to her emotions.
As the rats go down a grate behind the bar, he steps aside a little
to see her face. It's glowing. Not with pleasure or even satisfaction, but with a bruised and bleak ferocity. He has the feeling
she'd prefer to see them swarming through the lobby. It's un-
canny, this familiarity; all the more so as these places are so
much the same.

McFadden is no innocent of taverns, but he has never been so struck before with how alike they are, exactly as the girl described. All of them with rooms for rent above, peeling paint, rotting mortar, a fetid, omnipresent air of stale neglect. Each alley has its reek of urine. Even the clotted mats of vomit seem like remnants of the same collective meal. Already he can't remember if the screenless window with the pigeon roost was Calgary or Carstairs. This place, though, seems to hold some particular significance. He puts his theory to the test.

"Why don't we stop here," he says, "for a drink?"

In other circumstances he would have found her shock amusing. "Are you crazy?"

"Just thirsty." To say nothing of hungry. McFadden leaves it there. Nevertheless, it's after seven p.m. by this time – a full day already – and he's pushing for some rest. He tries an alternate approach. "What town is next, after this?"

"Ponoka."

"Ponoka. All right. Before we get to Ponoka, let's stop somewhere quiet and I'll set up the stove. It won't take long. I'll warm us up some soup." He has a jug still in the freezer, summer squash and carrots, simmered in a gamy broth. "Maybe we could make some sandwiches?"

"No time."

"Aw, come on! You must be starving – we haven't stopped all day. I know *I* am."

"There's a McDonald's on the way out. We can take the drive-through."

"McDonald's!"

"Take it or leave it."

So McFadden eats a Big Mac for the first time in many, many years. It's not as bad as he expected, though he's astonished he's permitted this. "That's what happens," he says, "when you go too long between meals, you'll settle for anything."

She looks at him, briefly, and then looks away.

– – –

And so it goes . . . Ponoka, Wetaskiwin, a quick jog west to Thorsby and then on up to Edmonton itself. Edmonton is slated for another full six units; the girl goes about it with the same methodical intensity she brought to bear in Calgary. Even so, it is hours after midnight by the time they're finished. McFadden is sleeping. He feels the truck bumping to a halt before the cadmium glow of a roadside motel. They are somewhere on the outskirts of Edmonton, though it takes a little while to recognize the fact.

The girl yawns. "Twenty-eight done," she says, then smiles. "Twelve to go."

McFadden summons up the energy to speak. "Incredible," he says, and rubs his eyes. Exhaustion has truly got the better of him. He's been dozing on and off since dark, rousing himself to assist with the drop, slipping back into unconsciousness the moment the truck is on the road again.

"We'll be done tomorrow," she says.

Dismounting, he's reminded that his foot started throbbing somewhere back near Thorsby. No matter. He is also starving, but too tired now to care – though the girl by his side revives a trace of the physician. He takes her by the elbow and studies her face in the neon light. "This was stupid," he says. "You must be totally used up."

She smiles wanly. "Never mind."

While he's checking in, she stumbles back to feed and water the remaining rats. Just over four hundred left, give or take. Close to a thousand delivered in just one day. Impossible.

McFadden has no recollection of finding his way to the room. As his head drifts toward the pillow, it occurs to him that he is sleeping in a province that is now just like all the rest. *Rattus* has come to Alberta. But the revelation floats away before the much more deeply satisfying feel of sinking down into the mattress. He is only vaguely conscious of her standing by the bed beside him.

"This is where they got me," she says.

But he's too far away to bridge the gap. McFadden's final waking image is the girl, standing still and naked by the bed, staring into the motel mirror.

– – –

He has no idea where he is. His eyes have opened to the sounds of traffic and a room of unremitting brightness. A greenish globe hangs from the centre of a textured ceiling sprayed in stippled plaster. The bed covering is orange, as is the shade of the lamp across the room. A radio is playing, though he has not located its position. He remembers now he is somewhere in the vicinity of Edmonton, in a room in a suburban motel.

The girl is absent.

A glance into the shower stall confirms this. It seems to him that last night they parked the truck beside the door, but when he shifts the blinds to look, there is no truck. McFadden steps into his pants and leans against the sill. The truck is absent. He puts on his shoes and his shirt, closes the door behind him and checks the rear of the building. The truck is definitely missing. When he gropes among his pockets, he confirms that the keys, of course, are missing too. And now he realizes he does not have the room key either.

The man behind the check-in counter looks him over sadly.

"I just went out to buy a newspaper," says McFadden, "but I forgot to take my key." As a show of authenticity he would have bought a paper on the spot, but his wallet, evidently, has disappeared as well.

"What's your room number?"

"I don't know." Then, wishing to be helpful, "It's one of the ones on this side, though." He is oddly relieved to find his watch still ticking on his wrist. "Is that really what time it is?" He has pressed the face against his ear. "Is it ten a.m. already?"

The man nods without looking. "What name?"

McFadden flinches, but the man is busy at his ledger. "McFadden," he says, hoping this is true. He has only the dimmest recollection of checking in.

"McFadden . . . McFadden . . . Yes, here you are."

Apparently there is some confusion as to which room he has actually been occupying. It is unclear to the day manager if his replacement on the night shift wrote 11 or 17. "Idiot," he mutters, and withdraws grimly to the telephone. "Serves him right if he wakes up."

McFadden listens to an exchange of heated accusation and denial. Even after, there remains a doubt. The day manager's hand hovers uncertainly above the key rack before descending, with misgivings, on number 17. "Checkout time's in half an hour," he says, as McFadden drops the key into the pocket of his still-unbuttoned shirt.

The truck is parked before the door of room 11. McFadden knocks.

"Where were you? I was getting worried!"

"Where was *I*? – *I* was not the one who ran away with the keys!"

She is unloading several articles wrapped in greasy-coloured paper. A not unpleasant smell has filled the room.

"Oh no! Not again?"

"You're an ungrateful son of a bitch, you know that?"

"But twice? . . . In succession?"

She has handed him a Styrofoam container big enough to drown a cat. "Shut up and drink your coffee."

The coffee is just as bad as he expected, but the rest, he has to admit, is not the disappointment he'd anticipated.

"I hate to say it," he says, poking through the wrappers, "but those were surprisingly good. Are you going to eat that last one?"

"Don't even think about it. If you're still hungry, we can stop again on the way out."

"Damn!" He has looked at his watch. "I forgot. Checkout time's in fifteen minutes."

"What? I haven't even showered!"

"Then you'd better hurry."

"You're just trying to get your hands on my breakfast."

"That's completely untrue."

She stands, unbuttons, and the dress falls around her feet. McFadden is interested to note that this time she is wearing mauvish little panties.

"Go ahead then," she says, "eat your Egg McMuffin."

– – –

Vegreville is an hour east of Edmonton and home to the world's most impressive Easter egg. McFadden insists on driving by it on their way through town.

"It *is* big, isn't it?"

The girl is unmoved. "It's hollow on the inside."

"Structurally, I guess, that would make sense. You know, though . . . I've been thinking."

She shrugs.

"It's occurred to me that you didn't have your dreams last night."

"Yes, I did. You just stayed asleep."

This disheartens as much as it surprises him. "Then either they were milder than the last time or I was really out of it."

"I couldn't say."

But he has remembered something else. "Just before we fell asleep last night, didn't you . . . say . . . something?"

"I don't remember."

"Yes, you did. You said . . . *This is where they got me.* I think I remember you saying that – or was I dreaming as well?"

Her silence tells him it was not just his own imagination. Something in the way she's sitting, too, has slowed and hardened. His own hands tingle on the steering wheel. McFadden feels his heartbeat quicken, his senses flicker into high alert.

"Who got you?" he says, breathing softly through his nostrils. The hairs along his neck are pressing at his collar. "Was it . . . who I think it was?"

She rolls down the window, rolls it up again. Then nods her head.

McFadden lets the air inside escape. "Pavlov?" he says. "Skinner?" The names seem so ridiculous.

Again she nods.

"Do you want to tell me . . . ?"

Her hands are folded in her lap. This time she shakes her head.

"Not to worry . . ." he says. "Not to worry . . ." To give them both some breathing space, he steers one-handed and switches on the radio. "You know," he says, "I don't even know your taste in music."

For her sake he is quite prepared to find a country station, though country music never fails to turn his mind to contemplation of eugenics. But she does not answer. He moves the finder click by click along the dial, watching for reaction. Nothing seems to strike her fancy, so he switches to the FM band and pauses when he grasps a strand of something recognizable. It's *Le nozze di Figaro*, somewhere near the final movements. Her head is turned away from him, and so he leaves it. Figaro believes he is betrayed, he has followed Susanna to the garden . . .

She reaches up and turns it off.

"Not an opera buff . . . ?"

But she isn't smiling. She has both hands against her knees and presses, squaring off her shoulders, widening her ribs. "It was right in that motel."

"You mean the one we just left?"

"Yes."

"Jesus," he says, then collects himself. "Only if you want to . . . you know. I don't need to know anything you don't want to tell me . . ."

"I had to see if I could do it. Go back there. And I did . . . So now I know I can."

"Do what?"

She doesn't answer.

"Do what?" And when she does not speak: "You know, it doesn't matter even if you . . ."

She looks, eyes wild, and veers away.

"Tell me," he says.

She swallows. Her head bobs and again she swallows. "A guy calls," she says. "On the phone. He says he wants to meet me at this motel. He's been with me twice already and he's good – but downtown, where I usually work. He's good with the money, I mean. And he's *easy*. So I say OK, as long as you pay the cab. He laughs and says I'm worth it. And so I go."

"When was this?"

The question stops her dead. "What is it now?" she says, swinging her head, sucking in her lips. "I mean, what's the date?"

"The seventh, I think, or the eighth."

"*No!* I mean the *month!*"

"It's June."

"Oh my God! It was *winter!*" She is counting on her fingers. "February! *And now you say it's June!* Oh, God! Four months! I was on that island *four months?*" Again she's wrenching down the window.

"What island?" he says. "All right, then . . . Let's go back, we can talk about that later." Her hands are pressed against her chest to force the air. "Tell me about the motel. Who was the man at that motel?"

"*Pavlov.*" The word has come out almost in a whisper. "It was just a name . . . you know. I mean, I knew it wasn't real. But nobody's is. It didn't mean a thing."

"Why would it?" he says softly. "Of course it wouldn't."

"I get there and he opens the door. It's not until I'm in I see he has another guy. So I stop. The other guy is sitting on the bed. Pavlov says this is his associate, Mr. Skinner. That name doesn't mean a thing either, but it's smart to start polite, so I go over and I shake hands. But this guy Skinner won't let go my hand. He's staring at me, looking me up and down. I'm in my working clothes, you know, so he can see pretty much everything he wants to see. Then Pavlov says, 'Well?' Like a question. He's behind me. The other guy still won't let go my hand. 'She's perfect. Well done,' he says, and then he nods. And I know something's happening, but before I can move, Pavlov slams me and I'm face down on the mattress. One of them has me by the legs and there's this jab. I can hear someone counting, but already I can't move. They roll me over and I see Pavlov holding up the needle and Skinner yanking down my nylons, but I can't move. The next thing I know, I'm on the island."

"I guess," he says slowly, "the next question is – what island?"

"I don't know."

McFadden nods. It's very flat here. Flatter than flat. Nothing but these open fields. He wishes there was something here to help perspective.

"At first I didn't even know it *was* an island. I didn't know anything. All I knew was a room. Wooden walls, wooden ceiling, concrete floor. There were rings and hooks attached; later on I found out what they were for. But at first I never left the corner because they had this rubber rope around my waist, and if I tried to pull, it just tightened up and snapped me back."

McFadden, not knowing what to say, says nothing.

"And then they'd come in. There was never any light except what they brought, so you never knew if it was day or night, but you knew they came a lot because you were getting tireder and tireder, and they never let you sleep, never long enough to rest. It was always one or the other – Pavlov or Skinner, Skinner or Pavlov, like shift work. Whoever it was would carry in a chair and set it down so I could just reach it if I stretched. And then he'd open up his fly and say, 'Begin.'

"At first I told them they could fuck themselves, but they just laughed and said fucking came later, when I was a good girl. And then they'd go away.

"Then more time would go by. And they never let me sleep. And they never let me eat . . .

"I don't know," she said, "how long. Long enough I started licking at the wood. If you licked it wet enough, you could get a taste. Then they started bringing in the food. Always something warm that smelled so good it made my mouth fill up so I had to swallow. They'd sit right there in front of me. And they'd eat it. And when it was done, they'd get up and they'd go. They'd come in sometimes and put a cup of water to my mouth, but never food. 'Food is for good girls,' they said. And then they'd go."

She has stopped talking. He knows that she is hardening herself to tell him what she has to tell him next, so he locks his eyes upon the prairie, taking in her horror from behind himself in profile.

"And so I was a good girl.

"The first time it was Skinner. He came in with his bowl of something that smelled so incredible and just said, 'Well?' And this time I said, *Yes*. But he wanted me to say it. 'Yes what?' *Yes, I'm going to be a good girl* . . . So he puts the food down, and he sits in his chair, and then he said 'Oops,' like he's forgetting something. And he gets up again and leaves. But he's back right away with this metal thing. He walks up to me and smiles and touches me with it, and I think he's killed me . . . I mean, it hurt so much I thought I had to be dead . . . He said it was a cattle prod, adapted for good girls when they're bad, and then he smiled again and said 'Get up.' When I got up, he touched me again, and this time I couldn't get up. So he sat there watching me, and he ate my food. Then he threw some water on me and told me how much better it works with water. So I got up. And he sat there on the chair again, with me down on my knees, and he said: 'Let's try again' . . . This time, though, he held that cattle prod up between my legs and he said if he even felt a scratch of teeth . . . you know . . . So I was very careful. 'Now wasn't that nutritious,' he said . . . Then he left.

"Next time it was Pavlov. Then Skinner, then Pavlov . . . They started giving me little bits of real food if I did everything right. Never enough, never near enough so I could think of anything else . . . I was always so hungry. Around this time they were teaching me to do it without using my hands, so they tied them up behind my back. I didn't care about that, because all I could think about was the pieces of food they'd put into my mouth. It got so whenever they'd come in I'd be nuzzling their crotches like . . . like a dog who knows its master has a biscuit in his pocket."

McFadden holds up his hand. "You know what?" he says. "I'm just going to pull over for a minute. I can't –"

"Keep going!"

So he swallows hard, eases off the clutch and points the truck on down the yellow lines like ribbons trailing off into the plain.

"They were giving me pills every day," she says. "I guess they were vitamins, to keep me going, because I didn't get sick. Also they gave me needles. I thought it was drugs of some kind, but they laughed and said they were professionals – narcotics were for little-leaguers – this was just a bit of penicillin. In case I had any . . ."

McFadden nods.

"One day they both came in and said, 'Congratulations! You're clean.' What they meant was that all my blood tests had come back and now they knew I didn't have AIDS or . . . anything else. After that they started fucking me.

"Though I guess it's fairer to say I started fucking them, because that's what they wanted. They wanted *me* to do it. If I did it right, I got that little bit of food. If I didn't . . . still hungry. You learn to do it right. You learn to pay attention. Pretty soon you're trying to think of what they want before they want it. You teach yourself never to stop thinking. If you blank out just a second, you might miss picking up on what they want, and then they don't put any food in your mouth.

"It must have been around this time they started with the Skinner box, and that must have gone on for . . . oh, I don't know how long . . . Then one day I realize I don't even have the rope around my waist. And my hands aren't tied. And when I think about it, I remember it must have been off a long time already, because I've been needing my hands for things I'm doing. *And I didn't even notice!* I never even saw the difference. That's the day I must have started waking up. That's when I understood that what they wanted was *my brain* to be their fuck. And that's how I *was* fucking them. *I* was their fuck; the rest of me was just accessories. It must have been some accident, you know, like maybe an hour's sleep I wasn't supposed to get. I don't know. But it got me back. I was different after that."

She is drawing circles with her fingers on the glass. McFadden stretches out his neck and swallows.

"But it was harder, after that. If they ever saw what you were thinking, they'd just start you back at the beginning, and I knew . . . it was so close. So close already. So I had to *pretend* I wasn't there, never let them know.

"They started doing little tests. One day I saw the door was open. Maybe they left it open other times and I just didn't see. Maybe they were doing tests like that all along. When they had you that way, you didn't *see*. Only *them*. It was only with *them* that anything good happened. When they weren't there – it was being in the dark, and hungry. You were so *happy* to see them. And if you did everything right and they fed you, you were happier still. All you wanted was to be a *good girl*. But the door was open, and there was daylight. There was *daylight* coming through, and for such a long time I never even thought about the difference."

She has stopped again, and shudders. McFadden feels her shoulders shaking, though he has not brought himself to look.

"When I think about how close I was, right there – I can hardly even breathe. I almost got up. I almost got up and looked out the door. And they'd have been watching, of course. They'd still be testing, to see how I was doing. And if they saw that there was still enough of me for that, they would know that what they should do was go back to the rubber ropes and the hands behind the back and the blindfold and all that stuff before the Skinner box. And that would have done me, I know. But I didn't . . . I just stayed there in my corner like the door was closed. When Skinner came in, I was *so happy*, on my hands and knees with my eyes always on his eyes so he could tell me what he wanted and I wouldn't miss it. I was a *good girl*."

McFadden wills himself to turn his head, but she doesn't see him. She's staring straight ahead, at where the sun has tricked a pool of shining water on the pavement.

"He closed the door that time, after he left. But when Pavlov came in next, he left it open. And it pretty much stayed open after that. But I made sure I didn't notice. All I ever saw was Pavlov. Pavlov and Skinner. Skinner and Pavlov. Then one day Pavlov was moving me around the room the way he sometimes did, and he took me right *outside* the door. That was *so* hard! Because I couldn't notice any difference. I couldn't act like I could see that anything was changed. The world wasn't any different, inside the room or out. All I could see was Pavlov. I did everything exactly like I did it *inside. Because there wasn't any outside!* After that, they started working with me outside more and more. And I started getting more sleep because *they* started relaxing and sleeping longer too. And I was getting more food now, because sometimes they'd let me wait beside the table when they were eating, or sometimes they'd want me to be the table and they'd let me lick their fingers and lap up little bits of food. That was one of the things they did: all the time I was there I never ate except what they fed me with their hands. That was a rule they never let up on. But as time went by, they started treating me more and more like I wasn't something they should be worried over. Like I was . . . trained.

"In some ways that was harder, because Skinner really liked that cattle prod. But he wasn't supposed to use it in the Skinner box, so he had to wait until Pavlov wasn't looking. He liked the feel of the electricity, up inside, after the shock, and Pavlov was always giving him shit about *negative reinforcement.* But mostly it was better because it was things like that that got them talking overtop of me, like I couldn't hear them. I'd just stand there or kneel there or lay there getting wet and never taking my eyes off their eyes, so I could do what they wanted whenever they wanted it. But I could *listen.*

"That's how I found out I was on an island. Pavlov came in one day cursing about the bugs – about how there could be so many bugs on an island this goddamned small in the middle of a lake this goddamned big. I must have been there a long time already, if the bugs were out – but I never even thought about that. I was thinking about the bugs, though. I knew they didn't like the bugs because they were always complaining when they had to go outside. And whenever Skinner got a bite, he'd have me lick the spot to take away the itch. Pavlov said there was no way that could have a shred of medical validity, but Skinner said he didn't care, he just knew it worked. So after that, Pavlov tried it and then they were arguing about whose bites needed licking the worst. But it was bad for me, the bugs. If you're naked all the time, they can crawl in everywhere. While I was still locked up in the room the bugs never bothered me, but when I was out they could get me pretty bad. And I could never slap at them, or scratch, because that would have meant I was paying attention somewhere I wasn't supposed to. Skinner was always getting onto Pavlov's case for forgetting to latch the screen door and letting in the bugs. And who was going to pay good money for someone puckered up in blackfly bites? . . . That was how I found out what they meant to do was sell me."

"*Sell you?*"

"Yeah. That's what it was all about. That was these guys' job."

The girl is looking at him now, and McFadden feels his own eyes drawn into hers and then released, back out onto the prairie.

"They'd get an order and then they'd find a girl exactly like the order wanted. And then they'd do her like they did me. And once they had her ready, they'd sell her. I think it was a lot of money. I heard them talking numbers like a hundred thousand. And they

sure worked hard at it. Some oil guy in the Middle East somewhere wanted Pocahontas. So they picked me."

With the logic of a reeling mind McFadden fixes on a detail.
"But a hundred thousand . . . ?" he says, trying to pinpoint a horizon in all this decumbent earth. "Why would anyone . . . I mean,
it's so . . . "

The girl shrugs. "For what? You hear all the time people fork-
ing out a million dollars for those horses they play polo with."
And then she makes a noise that in other places might have felt
like laughter. "But let me tell you, a horse isn't going to –"

"Oh, God."

"This is Holden."

"What?"

"This is Holden!"

"What are you –"

"This is the turnoff for Holden! If you don't slow down,
you're going to miss it."

"Oh . . . "

"Turn here!"

– – –

Holden has its rats and now the girl is driving. McFadden's
going through the motions. It's as if their histories are reversed
and he's the one in tatters. Camrose is next. The day is barely
moving. Now and then they'll pass another of those clever bits of
prairie art: a tin man welded out of tailpipes; a tractor built from
bales of hay; a rusted wood stove with its lid turned up and a
sign saying *Open Range*. The girl has started up again.

"I'm not sure," she says, "but I think sure they only pick off
hookers. When hookers go missing, who notices, right? And
also, they're . . . partly trained already. I found other hairs on
the pillows they used in the Skinner box. Long blond ones. Not
mine. So before me they must have had an order for a blond."

"I have to ask," he says, though another part of him does not want to, "what would happen if this training didn't . . . What would happen if you didn't pass those tests?"

She looks at him without a trace of pity. "It was Lake *Superior*. They don't call it that for nothing. Lots of water. The island was way out, two or three miles from shore. They could do whatever they wanted." Her eyes are on the road again. "Not that I knew it was Lake Superior . . . I still thought it was Alberta. There's lots of lakes up north from Edmonton; I figured it was one of those. I almost lost it on you right at the start, you know, when you told me you were going to Alberta. I thought that's where I was already."

"*That* . . . was *then*?"

"Yeah. But I didn't know it at the time. There was this little boat launch on the mainland, so I pulled out there. And a road that went off into the woods. I left the canoe and started running up the road, listening for cars, but no cars came. Then I couldn't run any more, so I walked. Miles, I guess. Then all of a sudden there was the highway, and a truck coming. And that was you. I must have been a sight."

The banality of the statement, the irony, brings him close to idiotic laughter. McFadden waves his hand. "How did you get a canoe?"

"Sorry," she says. "I'm jumping ahead."

Again the evenness of tone has dazed him. "Jumping ahead . . ." he says.

"Like I said, it was an island, but the funny thing was that it was like an island *on* an island. They called it a cottage. The room they kept me in was special, but the rest of it was just like you'd imagine a cottage: screened-in porch, wood stove, big glass windows. But no one could go outside. I mean *I* couldn't go outside, but *they* couldn't either. Because of the bugs. In the wintertime they must have gone by snowmobile – I never saw one, but that's the only way – but I don't remember anything at all about the winter. I was in that room till spring, and by that time the bugs were out too. That's why they never went outside either.

"But I guess they had to get supplies. One day I was with Pavlov. He'd brought me out of my room so I could rub him while he read this book, and he was concentrating on the book. Then he lifts his head like he's listening, and then I hear it too . . . a sound like a motorboat. I think he's going to send me back into the room, but then I feel him shrug, like he isn't going to bother. And in a few minutes Skinner comes banging through the door, slapping and swearing, and tells Pavlov to come and help him unload the goddamned boat, because the goddamned bugs are murder. And Pavlov says, 'Why not just get her to do it?' And Skinner looks and says, 'Yeah, why not?' And then he tells me to go and unload the boat. But I know this is another test . . . so I smile and walk out the door like I'm dreaming. There's a path, and a dock, and a boatful of groceries, and cans of gas and propane tanks. And I pick up as much as I can carry and walk back up to the house. I know Skinner's done something to the motor. The bugs are all over me, because I'm naked, and when I get up to the porch they're discussing whether it's such a good idea to let me get all covered up in bites like that, when I'm expecting company. And Pavlov says no, it probably isn't, so they make me wait in the corner while they finish the unloading, and I just sit and smile and smile, and keep my lips wet, and wonder what they meant by that . . .

"A few days later I find out. Pavlov has to go somewhere, and I don't know what's going on. They're both excited, cracking jokes, and finally they tell me Pavlov is going out to get another girl. And you can tell he's looking forward to it. He keeps on telling me this is the very best part. 'This is graduate level,' he says. 'You'll like this part.' I don't know what he means, but he's always smiling and telling me how much fun it's going to be. Even more, I know that Skinner can't wait for Pavlov to go, because he likes to do things to me when Pavlov isn't there. I think Skinner would have understood that word of yours."

It takes a few moments. "Sorry, *what*?"

"Your sign," she says. "That word on your truck."

"What are you –"

"Your *sign*. The one you got at that restaurant!"

"Paradox, for God's sake?"

"Yeah. Skinner would have understood that. He would have known where you were coming from." Her fingers drum against the steering wheel while McFadden gropes for shreds of meaning. "The whole point of the Skinner box was to make me like it. That's what I'm trying to tell you. It's like that dog you were talking about . . ."

"Dog?"

"Yeah, the one you said the real Skinner worked on, or Pavlov – I forget which one you said. But that dog you said they trained to be hungry when it wasn't really hungry. I've been sitting here, figuring this out."

"Listen," he says. "I don't –"

"That was like the Skinner box. Only it wasn't food, it was sex. It wasn't supposed to make me – what's that word you used? For what they wanted that dog to do?"

"Salivate? You can't be talking about –"

"Right. Except it wasn't supposed to make me salivate, it was supposed to make me come."

"What are you saying?"

"I figured it out. Of course I didn't understand it while I was doing it, but I understand now: it was to make us girls come on command. I guess they had buyers who liked having that . . . button to push. Everybody likes the girl to come, don't they? I mean, everybody in the business knows *that*. But if you can really *make* her come –"

"This is too much!"

"Anyway, the problem was that Skinner was one of those guys that *didn't* like the girl to like it – even though that was exactly the opposite of what he was supposed to be doing. See what I'm saying? That's why he always had to wait for Pavlov to be somewhere else."

I can't believe this, he thinks. There's a surge of vomit rising in McFadden's throat. *I can't believe this.* For a moment he isn't sure if he has said the words aloud. He gulps and swallows and forces back the bile. Never once, in all his professional career – this nausea.

She's going on as if nothing's happened. "Sure enough," she says, "Pavlov is barely in the boat before Skinner's dragging me into the room."

McFadden feels the truck decelerating and realizes with shock that they are turning. Camrose is on another highway. A signpost says *Camrose 48 kms*. At least that's what he thinks it says. He can hardly believe what's happening. Why are they going to Camrose?

"The only times I ever wore clothes," she says, "is when they had me put on special outfits. They had this buckskin thing, with feathers and beads and leather thongs around me. That was Poca-hontas, I guess. And sometimes they'd spend hours drawing de-signs, because they hadn't made their minds up yet about tattoos – and I'd have to keep still while they drew things on me with a Magic Marker. But the rest of the time the rule was no clothes. Except when Skinner thought that Pavlov was asleep – then he'd have me wear his little outfits. What does UCC stand for?"

"What?" McFadden has to try to focus. "What?"

"UCC. He had this shirt he liked to wear when Pavlov wasn't looking, and those were the letters."

"I don't know. Maybe it's an acronym . . ." He can't think. His mind is quite incapable of moving anywhere beyond the high-way straight ahead.

"Anyway," she says, "Pavlov's barely out of sight before Skin-ner's got me in his tennis whites. Little white top, pleated skirt – he even had the Reeboks and the socks with pompons, the whole getup. And then he asks me if I would care to play some tennis, and I'm supposed to tell him no – I'm never, ever, sup-posed to tell them no to anything, but this time that's what I'm supposed to say. So I say it. And now he gets to bend me over the net and hit me. And he counts that tennis way: 'Love-fifteen, love-thirty, love-forty. Game!' Then he starts all over again. Usually he hits me with the flat part, where the strings are, so it doesn't leave marks – because that's another one of the important rules. But this time it's the metal and he keeps on aiming for the same spot, but I don't whimper and I keep calling out *'Your point!'* until he says 'Set!' Because I know if I whimper, what comes next is going to be a lot worse.

"When he's done, he asks me if I'd like to play a different game, and I'm supposed to say no again. And right away I'm on my knees and he's in his chair, but now he has the cattle prod. He likes to poke the cattle prod all over me – on my lips, up my skirt; and I know it's only a question of time before he lets me have it, and that's the worst part, waiting for it . . . So finally he zaps me, and I flop like a fish; but I'm so used to it now it doesn't take long to get over it. So pretty soon I'm on my knees again, wetting my lips like I just can't wait. And Skinner can't wait either, because he loves that cattle prod. He says, 'Begin.' And I take him in my mouth – but this time I bite down as hard as I can."

McFadden is so mesmerized it takes a while to register. "What did you say?"

"Hard as I could. Of course he still has his hand on the trigger, so it was only a second before he let me have it. But it must have been quite a shock – a double shock, come to think of it. Hey, I just made a joke!"

McFadden can hardly stomach what he's hearing.

"What Skinner was forgetting," she says, and this time she *is* laughing, "what he was forgetting was that, with him in my mouth like that, any electricity that went into me went into *him* too . . . So Skinner goes flying back with his arms out and flips over backwards in the chair, but I'm more experienced than he is in this, and I'm ready for it. Before he's even got his eyes half open, I'm through the door and slamming it closed and throwing all the bolts that kept me locked in all that time.

"And then I'm running. It's hard, running after all those months – they've been training other muscles, and my legs keep giving out – but I know that underneath that porch there's a canoe, because they fucked up big and let me see it. And I'm praying, please please *please* God, let there be a paddle too, and thank God! Thank God, there is! The canoe has a hole in the side, but I get it dragged down and into the water before Skinner's even half awake. And I'm off that island."

She is breathing hard, and McFadden with her.

"Still, it almost killed me. It was real old, with the canvas peeling, and it kept on taking in water. If the wind was higher, I wouldn't have made it, or even if it was coming from the other way. But it was blowing into shore instead of out, and the waves were huge, but that way you could tuck right in between them. So they just pushed me in. It was a long time, though, and I was so scared he was going to find some way of coming after me. The hardest part was when I got to shore. There were rocks all over and the waves kept wanting to smash me onto them, and now they were coming at me sideways. The water was up around my knees by this time, and there wasn't any way for me to bail it out, and any time they'd be swamping me. Then all of a sudden, around this point there's the landing, and I only have to swim the last few feet and there's gravel screening to crawl out on. And still no sign of Skinner. I crawled out and started running."

McFadden can't believe how fast his own heart is racing. It's like . . . he doesn't know what it's like. "You mean it was a *boat* landing – for boats?"

"*Of course* it was a boat landing. What other kind of landing is there? And a boat was on it, the same boat they brought the groceries in, an old aluminum outboard. I must have found the spot they used for getting on and off the island. It was an old logging trail, not much more than a path, but there were tire tracks that had to be Pavlov's. I just started running up this road, ready all the time to dive into the bushes if I heard anybody coming. But I can tell you, after a few hours, if Pavlov drove up I'd have jumped right back into his car. Because the bugs were so bad. I really thought they were going to kill me. After all that, I thought, after almost drowning and everything else, I'm going to die from the mosquitoes. You know, I was so crazy with them I almost walked right across the highway and kept on going down the other side. I was in the middle of the pavement before I noticed I was on it. And then I saw this truck coming – it didn't matter, you could have been Pavlov and it wouldn't have mattered, I just had to get out of the bugs. Funny, eh?"

Funny is not the word he would have picked. McFadden has returned to his senses. "I just can't *believe* you! You're the most . . ." He doesn't know exactly what he means. But what he means is that he *does* believe her – this is not the point. What he can't believe is how she can be so . . . *resolute.* All of this was only – dear God, was it only just a week ago? He tries to count exactly but gives up because the time just isn't recognizable.

"So that's the story," she says, and sighs.

"Jesus Christ!"

"This is Camrose coming up."

"Camrose?"

– – –

A pair of magpies swoop low and bank into a grove of cottonwood, black on white, then disappear. He wonders what keeps magpies west of Manitoba, and blue jays east. They seem to occupy more or less the same environmental niche, but there are no magpies in Ontario – or none that he's aware of – and he's fairly certain blue jays don't cross over to Alberta. What prevents them from expanding into one another's ranges? Or perhaps they do. For all he knows, they do it all the time. Ebb and flow. Territories shifting back and forth, like borders in the Balkans.

They are just a little south of Stettler. Daysland and Bashaw are finished, along with conversation. They've been operating in a vacuum these last few stops. Talked out. He knows there's more to say, but neither one is saying it. So they keep to the essentials: scouting out locations, conforming to the pattern; he loading the rats into his tool box while she reconnoitres down the alleys. In Daysland there isn't any sewer, so instead they pick a building with a sunken roof, abandoned to the birds and broken bottles, and let the rats go there. Six towns to go – so close to finished. It all seems so remote. McFadden tries to think of what he should be doing, now the rats are almost gone. The exercise is futile.

He has managed to persuade her to allow a break for lunch, and has the Coleman going in a little gully down out of the wind, warming up his squash and carrot soup. They have bought a dozen bagels – McFadden doesn't associate bagels with a place like Bashaw, but that's what she came back with while he waited, motor running, parked against a curb – bagels and a square of Philadelphia cream cheese. She is toasting bagels while he stirs the soup, bending from the waist to turn them, blowing on her fingertips. From the corner of his eye he sees a breast demurely peeking through a gap between the buttons. What about her now, he thinks, beneath her coveralls? It all seems open as these prairie winds. He is itching to get back into the subtleties forest. Five hundred kilometres, give or take. Six hours' driving, say, and all of this is finished. *Skinner box*, he thinks, and pushes that aside.

McFadden tries to catch her eye but she is busy with the bagels. He clears his throat, coughs, but finds the nerve has failed him. So he drops his head and fiddles with the gas feed, trimming down the flame. It would not do to burn the soup.

His reaction to her story has been strangely staggered over time: an apostatical stage of shock, right at the beginning, then a shabby lapse into resentment at his own reduction to banality – but over all, this wrathful, wilful grief. He is awed to silence by the girl's composure, her integrity. *Skinner box*, he thinks, his mind revolving like a bubble in the eddy of a drain.

She is, in every way, a refutation of everything she ought to be. That's the other thing that he's been thinking, these last hours, measuring the words for what he means to say. But when he tries, it comes out in a pulp of bad analogies and impotent allusions. She listens, with an almost stolid patience, then takes his hand.

"I'm still breathing," she says, and draws his hand toward her mouth and kisses it. "And so are you." Behind her lips he feels the stillness of her tongue.

"Just don't think about it," she says. "That's what I do." She touches his hand with her lips again. "They can fuck me," she says, "but they can't fuck me up."

McFadden takes his hand away.

"Here's your bagel."

"Thank you." He passes her a bowl of soup.

"Listen," she says. "I want to ask you something."

He waits.

"Remember when you said you'd take me wherever I wanted to go? Remember?"

McFadden's memory is not as steady as it ought to be, but he remembers this.

"Yes," he says. "It was back . . ." He has raised his arm and waves a hand toward the prairie. "Anyway, I remember . . ."

"Will you still?" They understand the lack of any need to answer this. "I know where I want to go."

McFadden waits.

"But I want to take some rats as well."

"I see," he says, quite undismayed. The information bears no more or less significance than any of the other fragments strewn across his thoughts.

"I've been counting. There are six stops left to go. That's 174 rats still on the truck. If we took two or three from each of the six – what do you call them, colonies?"

McFadden nods. "Yes, colonies," he says.

"If we took some from the others and made up a new one – a seventh colony, I mean – would that hurt anything?"

He doesn't know what kind of answer there should be to this.

"I mean, there would be two or three less in each one, but then we could make up an extra one, an extra colony, for me to take with me."

"What's the last stop?" he asks. It does not strike him in the least unusual that it is he asking this question of her. "According to the map," he says, "the last stop?"

"Vauxhall," she replies without hesitation.

"Vauxhall. Then we can just skip Vauxhall."

"Are you sure?"

"Yes, I'm sure. You can have Vauxhall's rats. Vauxhall can do without its rats. Why not? After all . . . " He lets the sentence trail away.

"That makes Brooks the last stop, then," she says. "After that you take me and my rats and drop us off, like you said you would."

"All right."

"Are you sure?"

"Of course I'm sure."

"Good."

"Now I have a question for you."

"What?"

"What's your name?"

She studies his face.

"Your name," he says. "I want to know your name." He is surprised at her surprise. "In all this time," he says, "I've never known your name."

"Names," she says, "are just what people call you."

"Yes," he says, considering, "that's true. Let's say I want to know what people call you."

She is staring out into the prairie, holding her bowl in her hands. A flicker of breeze has blown a strand of hair across her face.

"You can call me Fida," she says without moving.

"Fida," he says. "An interesting name . . . " He supposes it must be of Aboriginal origin. Cree, perhaps, or Blackfoot or Assiniboine – he has no idea. Perhaps sometime he'll inquire.

"So you're going to take me with the rats?"

"Of course," he says. "Of course I will."

But in a sieve I'll thither sail
And, like a rat without a tail,
I'll do, I'll do, and I'll do.

WILLIAM SHAKESPEARE
MACBETH,
1.3.8–10

They have chosen a motel at random and checked in in time to catch the restaurant before it closes. McFadden has no idea where they are, and little sense of how they've got here. After eating, he removes himself to feed the rats – all thirty-six remaining – while she showers. Then he takes his own turn. The water feels peculiar, as if it's not absorbing as it should. He dawdles through the shaving, trimming his beard, paring his nails, flossing his teeth. She is waiting in the bed, a paragon of something that he cannot quite identify: bruises healed, skin smooth, limbs without blemish. Her hair is tucked behind her ears; she smells of soap and body lotion.

"I can't, you know," he says, and holds the towel around his waist.

She has the strangest way of smiling at unsmiling times.

"If I can," she tells him, "then so can you."

– – –

Later he has given up on trying to drink himself to sleep. He knows what's coming, and when it happens he intends to be prepared. He's brought the bottle into bed with him and sips it, glass by glass, until the liquor's done away with taste. This motel has come equipped for drinking: a bottle opener screwed into the door frame, a plastic bucket with a lid for ice, two glasses vacuum-packed in sterile wraps. The other one's still standing upside down inside its paper sheath. Propped against the pillows, McFadden bides his time, sip by measured sip, until the pattern of her breathing alters and the dream begins.

Now that he knows exactly what he is seeing, he can watch in conscious detail. At first she shows a brave resistance, but in due course she's responding. The mattress starts to heave, and McFadden has to look away while her tongue begins its grope among the pillows. Still he soldiers on, until the denouement approaches, then excuses himself to go and stand beneath the shower so the sound is deadened in the water that he cannot feel. He has forgotten what it's like, this taste of absent tears.

By the time he's back, it's nearly over: movement much more rudimentary – a monoglot of groan and whimper – then silence. He waits a little for the muscles to relax, while her pupils narrow their acceptance of the light that filters through the room. He can see the eyes grow wide again, then close. He pours another drink and waits. The bottle is half empty.

"Are you there?" she says.

McFadden coughs in answer.

She rises from the waist and folds her legs and sits beside him, holding out her hand. He passes her the bottle. She takes it, gracefully, slides the neck by inches like a phallus down her throat, and with a single, fluid tilt decants what's left without a trace of sound or motion. He has heard of this, though never seen it done.

"What time is it?" she asks when she has swallowed.

"Two-thirty," he says, grateful to look at his watch. "Quarter to three."

"Then it's time to go."

– – –

The night is open, the sky a brilliance of stars, and the darkness gleaming in an undertone of astral light. He knows by now where they are going – not where, precisely, she has told him this is not important – but now he knows the place.

"But why there?" he asks, "I mean, why there, instead of . . ." What he means is, with so many other claimants, why single out this one?

"Because that was where it started," she answers simply. "That's the one place anybody's ever owed me. That's where they started fucking me instead."

After this he keeps his questions to himself.

He watches out the window through this weirdly mitigated gloom, light and dark so finely balanced in obscurity. The open landscape casts no shadows. In time the road begins to undulate, he senses hills beneath the tires; the emptiness of plain gives way to random tracts of scrub. Underbrush begins to close in on the highway, and now the shadows reappear. McFadden willingly assumes his ignorance: when road signs emerge in the headlights, he shades his eyes until they've passed. She has let him know they're headed for the place where she was born.

They turn off onto gravel and drive for miles on secondary roads, the girl behind the wheel with steady, silent competence. McFadden feels the pebbles strike the undercarriage. The roadbed degenerates to washboard, then begins to wind and narrow. Now a scattering of buildings appear and disappear beyond the verges: squat and squalid shacks with scraps of metal littering the yards; light from windows framed in shards of broken glass.

"This is where the ordinary people live," she tells him. McFadden looks away from the window. "The ones who don't have connections." He nods as if he understands. "The band council," she says, "owns all these houses, but council members don't live here." There is a jolt, and then the ride is smoother. "We're coming up to the office," she says. "They keep this section paved."

The smooth new roadway takes them in a bend, and then another, then delivers them into a flood of artificial light. A huge stone and timber structure rises from the centre of a parking lot, ringed in glowing street lamps anchored in the asphalt. The brightness of the place alarms him.

"Don't worry," she says. "Anybody still awake will be passed out by this time of night."

"But you do intend to let them go *here*?"

The place is so fantastically imposing, the only thing he's certain of is that he wants to be away from it. A tepee – or at least something modelled on the tepee, but distorted to gargantuan proportions and hung with coloured lights. A concrete cone, he thinks; a Christmas tree five or six storeys high.

"They could never get the elevators to work," she tells him, "so they closed off all the top floors. Not here," she says, "there's a barn out back."

The driveway circumscribes the council office like a European traffic circle with an exit leading off into the bush. Once beyond the ring of light, the road degenerates into a mass of cracks and seeping potholes. The girl slows the truck as they bump along, then stops beside a dark, dilapidated building – indeed a barn, as he can see now in the headlights – clearly left to ruin. A mountain of weather-blackened hay moulders against the nearer wall.

"When I was a kid," she says, "after the oil money came in, somebody thought we should get into horses. So they built this barn and bought a string of thoroughbreds, but then I guess they got tired of having to feed them." She turns off the ignition and pats him on the knee. "Your rats," she says, "will know exactly what to do."

When they leave the silence of the truck, a pack of dogs begins to howl and McFadden freezes.

"Don't worry about the dogs," she says. "They stay chained. People here believe that dogs are part of our heritage, but nobody needs them, what with snowmobiles and ATVs. The dogs stay chained."

McFadden wishes she would keep her voice down. "Can we just get on with this?"

She shrugs and unlocks the back of the truck. He can't get over his uneasiness. The dogs step up their baying; he can hear them lunging, choked off by the chains. McFadden scrambles to the back and lifts down the rats. He hurries to the pile of fetid hay and, without ceremony, dumps them to their fate.

"Show 'em your stuff," she whispers, watching.

McFadden steers her back toward the cab. "I'll drive," he tells her.

She shakes away his hand. "I told you, you don't have to worry. It's only their own they're any danger to."

"Get in," he says, and starts the engine, drowning out the dogs.

– – –

It isn't more than five or six kilometres before the headlights appear in the mirror.

She tells him to relax. "It's just some of the warriors out for a cruise. They'll be piss-drunk though, so give them lots of room to pass."

"*Warriors?*"

"They're always either warriors or elders; that way everybody gets to be somebody. Don't worry."

"You keep saying that."

McFadden slows the truck and eases over, but the car behind them does not pass. Then the horn begins to honk, at first in rapid pulses, then more and more insistently, until it settles into a steady blare.

"Now what?" He watches in his mirror as the heads and arms begin emerging from the windows.

"I don't know."

"Should I stop?"

"No, I don't think so."

The road is narrow. Wherever there is space McFadden offers room to pass, but the car stays honking right behind them. "They'll get bored," she tells him. "They'll turn off when we get up to the highway."

McFadden drives on in an envelope of noise. The car is now so close his mirror isn't registering headlights. Then suddenly, a jolting thump, and the truck skips and slides in the gravel.

"Jesus!" he says, "they're ramming us."

High beams spray across his mirrors, and before McFadden has decided whether to brake or to accelerate, the other vehicle is beside them. He has a fleeting image of hands and leering faces, and then the bright red flash of brake lights straight ahead. It's not possible to stop. The crunch comes, loud but not hard – and then a sudden stillness.

"Shit."

"A BMW," she says, "so it has to be someone connected."

McFadden begins rolling down his window as the men spill out, but changes his mind when he sees that some are heading for the girl's side. He steps out onto the gravel and locks the doors behind him.

"You rear-ended us!"

"Didn' hear us, asshole?"

"Who the fuck you think you are?"

McFadden has raised a hand for calm, but someone pushes hard against his chest.

"Didn' you hear us honking?"

"Of course I heard –"

"Well . . ."

"What do you mean, *well*?" McFadden is fighting with himself for calm.

"You say *honk if you're horny* – and we're horny."

"What?"

But another hand has slammed into his chest. His arms are being pinned. McFadden tries to shake them off, but someone kicks his feet out and he's down in the gravel. He is being dragged to the rear of his truck.

"*There!*" they say, jerking back his head. "*There!*"

Hands are pointing at the bumper.

"*What?*"

A chorus of laughter: "It says it right there." They are pointing to the bumper of his truck. "It says *Honk if You're Horny*. And we're horny."

His bumper sticker, a peel-and-stick he'd bought with the rest of the decals, applied and then forgotten.

"You guys are a barrel of laughs."

This time the blow is to his face. He tastes blood, but somehow he is back on his feet.

"*What's in the truck?*"

One or two detach themselves and clamber up the running board. "*Hey! A girl!*"

McFadden has an elbow loose and smashes it into the face beside him. He gets hold of a jacket and mashes a nose with his forehead. There is hardly room to kick, but his knee has found a groin. After this the blows begin to tell against him. He hears the grunts of effort and tastes the liquor in the air. A high, sharp whistle pierces through the din.

The girl has stepped out onto the gravel and stands in the light of the open door.

He has to spit the blood before his voice will come, and more of it obscures his vision. When he blinks, he sees the girl's hands rise and level, in her hands his own Beretta. The long, absurdly foolish barrel circles in the air, and then a short bright spurt of flame and a man beside him screams and falls. Things move much more slowly now, and happen all at once. The extended barrel swings toward another target and the targets scatter, crashing in the underbrush beyond the light. He can hear the sound itself retreating – snapping branches, thrashing underbrush growing dimmer with the distance. Then silence. The man on the ground is silent too, and then begins to scream.

"Fida!" shouts McFadden through the blood.

He has his feet again and she moves toward him, then stops and kneels by the side of the man she's shot. The shot man's eyes are wide and open.

"You . . . !" he says.

But the girl has slid the gun into his mouth.

"Fida!"

The girl withdraws the barrel and points it at McFadden's chest. "That's not my name," she says, and then returns the muzzle to the shot man's mouth. "Are the keys in the car?"

"What?" McFadden says. *"What?"*

"The keys, you idiot. Never mind, I hear the engine running. Go move the car off the road. And bring me back the keys."

The man she's shot has tried to move his head. She pushes the gun in deeper until he chokes and lies still.

"Fida!" McFadden takes another step, spitting out blood.

"I told you! That's not my name! Just move the car!"

He does as he is told. McFadden steers the BMW off the road and into the ditch, then returns to where the girl is kneeling, and holds out the keys. She rises, the gun still pointing at the shot man's face.

"Throw them into the woods," she says.

He hears the keys deflecting through the undergrowth, then nothing at all as they land.

"If you so much as move," she tells the man she's shot, "if you so much as open your mouth, I'll put a bullet in your brain."

The man acknowledges with a scuffle of his head against the gravel.

"Let's go."

— — —

"BB caps."

"But Christ, what if they *weren't?*"

"I checked."

"What do you mean, you checked?"

McFadden has no doubts about her presence of mind, but he still can't believe she could have had quite so much sang-froid as all of that. They have pulled off the highway; McFadden is tending to his injuries. It seems to him that lately he's been taking quite a lot more beating than he honestly deserves.

"You missed a spot," she says, pointing to a patch where the blood still oozes from behind his ear.

It's almost morning. The sun is not yet over the horizon, while the moon has disappeared around the other side. There is enough half-light to see. McFadden wets his ear with alcohol and rubs. The nerves connected to his face are still anaesthetized with shock; he can poke and prod without much pain, like a dentist before the freezing's out. He should count himself lucky: so many fists were flying, they got in one another's way. He has no broken bones or even serious contusions, which is, he notes with private satisfaction, better than can be said for the other side. On the other hand, his side was better armed.

"There's no way you would have had time to check what kind of bullets –"

"Not *then*, stupid. A long time ago. Back when you first told me."

Early on in his trapping career McFadden had devised what until this moment he'd believed to be a deviously clever hiding place, cunningly sewn into the passenger-side upholstery. It's where he's always kept the Beretta.

"All right," he sighs. "At any rate –"

"You're going to be a mess tomorrow."

He can feel the crushed capillaries leaking blood beneath the skin, and resists the temptation to strongly agree. "Not as bad as that guy you shot."

"He'll be fine. You said yourself, those BB caps won't even break the skin."

"That was from a distance! You were barely ten feet away!"

"I aimed for the one with the heaviest jacket. It was leather. I bet he hardly has a mark."

Sang-froid. McFadden considers introducing the term, but decides he isn't up to it. The shakes have started up again – nerves, he knows, minor shock compounding with nervous exhaustion. But he's got the chills and his hands are trembling, and he doesn't want her seeing this. He lets the yawn come through. He can't prevent the yawns.

"What if they come after us? What if they got the licence number?"

"You're joking, right? I promise you, they're asleep in the woods right now. By the time they wake up and start trying to figure out what to do with the car, you'll be long, long gone. They won't remember anyway."

McFadden nods. He's not even sure why he asked. Another chill settles in and he has to press his aching shoulders back to stifle it. He's seldom felt so disconnected.

"Go to sleep," she says. "I'll take the wheel from here."

– – –

When he returns to himself, it's morning. He blinks in the sunlight and gropes for his watch.

"What time is it?" His watch was broken in the scuffle. "Where are we?"

"It's almost open."

They are parked against a curb in what appears to be a residential side street. She points through the window to the building across the boulevard.

"What's almost open?"

"The library. The sign says it opens at eight. It must be close to that by now."

"What are we –"

"I want to go to the library."

"But, Fida . . . Sorry, you said that's not your name."

"Don't worry," she says. "Nothing to worry about."

"What's that supposed to mean?"

"It's just a name they gave me – Pavlov and Skinner – while they had me. It's nothing important."

"Of course it's important!"

She has put her hand across his mouth. "Look!" she says. "It's open!"

McFadden follows her into the building. It's a single-storeyed, small-town kind of book room. Light slants through a window, catching the dust in the air. The space is trimmed with bits of prairie iconography: Indian feathers, buffalo horns, odds and ends of cowboy tuck and tackle. On a shelf against the wall stands a stuffed coyote, posed with a prairie dog dangling between its jaws. The place feels empty, though there must be an attendant somewhere. McFadden has no idea why he's here.

Born of the generation that still finds it difficult to speak out loud in public reading rooms, he whispers as he points to the coyote. "There you have it," he rasps, "plains ecology in still life. Prairie dogs were the absolute foundation of the food chain. There used to be millions of them, hundreds of millions. Albertans killed them off." The silence is oppressing him. "That's why they need my rats," he tells her. "They've created a vacuum . . . "

"*Prairie dogs* have nothing to do with it."

She has spoken this with such asperity he finds he has no wish to probe it further. It's morning now. McFadden is awake and falling back on habit.

"I don't think any eastern squirrel ever attained the same degree of ecological importance," he says. "Did I ever tell you about my experiment in Mimico?"

She's ignoring him. He has no thoughts on what is happening; all he knows is that his head hurts. She is stalking restlessly from shelf to shelf, scanning titles, trailing fingers down the bindings, abruptly moving on. McFadden simply follows, whispering as he goes.

"Did I tell you black squirrels and grey squirrels have the same biology? I did, I think. There's no difference, you know, except colour. The interesting thing is that in Toronto the *black* phase dominates; you hardly ever see a grey one. But in other places it's the reverse. Some cities seem to have mostly *grey* squirrels. I have no idea why. Anyway, I always wondered –"

"You don't have to *whisper.*"

"What?"

"There's nobody here. You don't have to whisper."

"There's got to be someone. Anyway . . . "

She has turned her back again and disappeared behind a wall of shelved encyclopedias. McFadden hurries after, speaking from the middle of his throat.

"Anyway," he says, "I started wondering if it was just chance evolution that favoured blacks over greys, or whether some sort of natural selection was at work. Then I wondered if I could change the colour distribution artificially. Squirrels mate twice a year, you know, so it wouldn't take very long to start seeing changes in the breeding stock. There's a spot out in the west end, just off Lakeshore, where a little point of land sticks out into the water. It's not very big – just a few acres maybe – but there's lots of old houses and big trees, so it's got good squirrel density. It has a narrow neck to it, which makes it almost an island, so I was able to go in there and trap out all the black squirrels and release all the greys, and record what happened."

He had no idea, until this girl, how he prattles. It must be the setting.

"Why?"

"What do you mean, why?"

She hasn't stopped, but has slowed her pace a little to let him catch up. It's a relief to McFadden's larynx.

"*Why?*"

"I told you, to see what would happen."

"You like to play God, don't you."

"Well," he says, "somebody has to."

She has stopped now and turns to face him, staring. Her arms hang poised mid-air, motionless. The stillness is strikingly effective after all this motion. She seems about to speak, then stops and drops her hands against her sides.

"Well, *do something useful*, then," she says. "At least you can help me find a fucking book!"

"What fucking book?"

But she's off again, pacing down the aisle. As far as he can see, there isn't any pattern to this prowling search, this aimless rummaging from shelf to shelf, running her hands along the spines as if she hopes to find the thing she seeks by feel.

"*What* book?"

She has stopped again and whirls to face him. "On *Pavlov*," she says. "What did you think? And *Skinner*. The real ones. I just want to know."

"I see."

And he does see. He is surprised, in fact, he hasn't seen it sooner.

"Well?"

"Sorry, I . . ."

"Are you going to help me find my book?"

He's had to take a moment, readjusting. "It might be, you know . . . more than one book. It might be two or three books, or more. I don't know . . . We'll have to look and see."

"Then look."

McFadden starts with the reference shelf, widening the search from there. The problem is not finding material; he's surprised, in fact, how well stocked this place turns out to be. The problem is separating out the texts that are . . . acceptable. He is fearful of the things this search will bring to light. And he has no idea of her reading level. He finds himself leaning on this pretext, discarding certain texts as too obscurely technical, telling himself she's unlikely to understand the language anyway. In truth, his mind is reeling with the prospect of what will be disclosed. He doesn't want her seeing this.

She shadows him from shelf to shelf, arms folded, arms dangling by her sides, fingers twisting, tapping against her hip – as if she senses his temptation. He's never seen her quite like this. The search takes time, his own eyes lingering over certain passages, going back to read them again and then again, hairs rising on his neck. He tears a scrap of paper into strips, noting pages, identifying passages, marking bits of clinical notation *she herself has lived through.* His imagination has rebelled. There are moments when the implications strike with such ferocity he has to stop and rub his eyes, pretending that the light here in the shadows of the stacks is insufficient. He doesn't want her reading this.

"Can I have some money?"

McFadden glances up from where he sits, cross-legged, stomach churning. He starts to ask, then stops.

"Ten will do," she says, "five."

He gives the girl a twenty.

"I just realized," she says, "in all the time they had me, I never had a smoke. Pocahontas doesn't smoke. There's a 7-Eleven up the street."

"Ah," he says, and lowers his eyes to the book in his lap that he wishes he could burn. In all his life he's never dreamed of such a thing. She turns to go, then turns again and touches his face. He feels her fingers trace the swelling.

"It's all right," she says. "Don't worry, it'll be all right."

He watches her pacing up and down before the window, inhaling one after another, burning her fingers with the paper match. When he has found as much as he can tolerate, he beckons through the window. She grinds her butt into the sidewalk and returns.

"Hello!" she says brightly.

It takes a moment for McFadden to understand that it is not to him she's speaking. A man has appeared – the librarian, of course – in a woollen cardigan with a stub of pencil poking through. "I just thought you should know," he tells them, "that there are study tables over there." He gestures to the books piled about them on the floor, taking in McFadden's battered face. "It might be more comfortable . . ." he says, and lets the sentence trail away.

"Thank you," says the girl.

"Yes," says McFadden. "Thank you."

They follow the librarian to the tables, McFadden clutching his citations. The girl has taken a seat with her back to a window, and McFadden arranges his material before her. He places them in the order he believes they should be read, marking the pages, highlighting pertinent passages. The librarian has disappeared again, and McFadden finds his tongue.

"It's not as much as it looks," he says, "it's just spread out over different books. Start with this one" – he has handed her the first, opened to the proper page – "then just read the parts I've marked and go on to the next."

The girl watches, then takes the book into her hands. The light is pouring in behind her, and she moves the page into her shadow, softening the glare with the shade of her body. Seated opposite, McFadden has to squint to see. She reads slowly, from one word to the next, tracing the line with a finger, creasing her brow in concentration. From time to time a tiny pink edge of tongue slips out between her lips and he wonders how often it is possible for this girl to break his heart.

"I can read," she says. "Don't look at me like that."

McFadden excuses himself and goes about a research project of his own. He is amazed at how easily he has come to this decision – as if it had all been decided on much earlier. He combs the stacks and comes back to examine the proceeds of his own reconnaissance. The girl does not acknowledge his departure or return. Sometime later he gets up again and finds the librarian, who points him to a set of wooden filing cabinets tucked away behind the circulation desk.

McFadden quietly removes himself to another table, where the light is better shaded, and studies his ordinance. In a remarkably short while he has done as much as he can do, amazed that this can be so easy. He returns to her table and tells the girl he's going for a walk. She looks up, nods and goes back to her reading.

It's the kind of prairie town that trails off into farmland. Empty spaces widen; vacant lots give way to pasture; town cars re-conform to pickup trucks, clapboard garages devolve to metal drive sheds. Here and there McFadden spies some chickens, pecking in the weeds. Each house seems to have a dog tied up beside the driveway; hounds, mostly, baying until he passes out of sight. He has always felt sorry for these animals, kept only for the hunting season, chained to their stake for the rest of the year.

McFadden stops. He bends, reaching for support, and vomits on the road. *Oh, the bastards,* he thinks, *oh the fucking, fucking bastards.*

The significance of her name has dawned upon him: *Fida,* feminization of *Fido.*

McFadden wipes his chin and corrects his breathing. Walking back, he reminds himself that his decision had been made already. He wonders what this says about him, though, that this sophomoric play on words incites him more than anything so far.

The girl is waiting for him at her table by the window. The sun now pours in so brightly he can hardly make her out against its glare.

"I have some questions," she says.

He had intended to come around the table and sit beside her, but something in her voice advises him to leave a space between them, so he sits across from her, shading his eyes against the sun.

"Shoot."

"I've been thinking," she says. "I've been wondering . . . " The books are stacked neatly now, in a single pile; she lays a finger against the bottom volume and pushes the whole towards him. ". . . if you could tell me what these guys were trying to do."

"Um . . . "

The question vibrates with its own intentions, but has no feeling yet for what. McFadden is unsure how to answer. He wonders briefly if perhaps she hasn't understood, if the mass of information has been too much. But then he sees that of course she has. There is understanding in her expression, and this is what he does not understand.

"I suppose you could say," he says, "if you wanted to sum it up –"

"That's it!" she says. "That's exactly what I want. What was that thing you said? . . . *In a nutshell.* Give it to me in a nutshell."

"They were behaviouralists. That's the simplest way to put it. They studied behaviour –"

"Whose behaviour?"

"Ah." Despite himself, despite the terrible tension he feels at this table, he can't suppress a tiny smile of pleasure. "I know you've read that part," he says, "so I know you know the answer. It was animals they studied, but of course it was human behaviour they were after – drawing parallels with human nature."

"Human nature, or just nature?"

He pauses, feeling for her meaning. "I don't follow –"

"You're just the same as they are! Aren't you?" She speaks this in a whisper, as if the arid temperance of this place has after all impressed itself. *"You're no fucking different!* All your playing God with squirrels and rats and lesbians. You're just the same! *Aren't you?"*

So this is where she's going . . .

"Here's what I want to know," she says. "I don't get you! You said you were a doctor. That's what you said! And *these* guys"– she gives the books a violent shove –"*these guys* were doctors too, weren't they?"

"Yes . . . but an entirely different –"

"You shut up! It's me that's talking. It's the same – it's the same thing! Doctors have to go to school. And *that* means they have to have money. And that means they can do what they want. You can do whatever you want, and you chose this. You *chose* this! Same as them. You start fucking around with your lesbians, just for fun, just so you can dick around; *these* guys start fucking around with animals, just so *they* can dick around. It's the same! It's the fucking same. Because you didn't *have* to do that. You could have done anything! But that's what you *wanted* to do. Then you screw up, and now you can't be a doctor any more. But you don't care, you still have the money, and *now* you decide you want to be your stupid trapping thing."

"Urban . . ." says McFadden softly. "Urban trapping."

"But you *still* have the money to do whatever you want." She holds up her hand to stop him. "Don't start! I know what you're going to say. You're going to make a big deal about telling me it's not *very much money* – that's what people with money always say."

McFadden closes his mouth. He has to hold his hand above his eyes so he can see.

"You said it yourself – all that about the gold. *You had the money!* You didn't have to be a fucking trapper. You did it because you *wanted* to."

McFadden bends his knees and grips his armrests, hoping that perhaps he can move his chair around the table.

"And *then, that's* not enough either. Now you decide you're going to take rats to Alberta. Why? *Because Alberta doesn't have any!*"

He can see her arms move up in agitation to pass her fingers through her hair. He watches the light as it's trapped in her hair. But he cannot see her face.

"This is what I don't get," she says. "This is what I don't understand! I've been sitting here all afternoon, trying to figure it out. I've read your books, I've read the things you said to read, hoping that in there somewhere there would be something to tell me you were *different*. But there isn't. So this is what I need to know: what kind of a person does this?"

She has turned her head to look away. In the unexpected shadow McFadden is aghast to see her face streamed with tears. His shock is such that he very nearly challenges. He very nearly asks, *Why does anyone do the things they do?* He very nearly asks her: *Why do you?*

Then he stops. Because of course he knows.

He's hoping she will speak again and give him time to think, but she does not. McFadden holds his hand against the sun, appalled to watch these tears.

"You're right," he says at last. "You said it. I just like to dick around. It's what we do. As a species. It's what we do. Put it down to human nature. It's what defines us. We dick around."

"I don't."

"No," he says, acknowledging the truth of this. "You don't."

"It's *men*. It isn't human nature. It's *men*."

McFadden drops his hand and closes his eyes to the dazzle. "You would have a better perspective on that than I." Because he cannot see, he does not know how she reacts. "But you may be right," he says. "*Insemination* – it covers quite a lot of ground, when you think about it. Neatly Darwinian. But as for me, I think it's more. It's *human* nature. I can't speak for the differences between men and women, because I think the sum's the same. We're perverse, together or apart. Look at me. Look at you."

He hears her stir and draw a breath, but McFadden now has things he needs to say.

"We pretend that what we want is simple, but that's not what we want. That's the opposite of what we want! Human nature is the search for *complications*, not simplifications. The only reason we try to simplify our lives is to make room for the complications. *That*'s what distinguishes us as a species. We *like* turmoil. That's the root of the human psyche – the same things Pavlov and Skinner were after. Once you know you're perverse, you can deal with it. That's why good so often ends up bad. People who try to do good just don't get it; they try to operate on simple principles. They try to simplify things, but nature's against them."

"Which one are you?"

McFadden wishes not to answer.

"Good or bad? Which one?"

He smiles toward her silhouette. "I dick around," he says.

"I thought I was in love with you . . ."

She has let this out so softly it's as if she hasn't spoken. McFadden opens his eyes and lets his pupils take the glare. He blinks, unseeing.

"Never, *never* . . . in all this time," she says, "with *anyone*. And I thought . . . *Fuck you!* Fuck you and your *complications!*"

There are footsteps. McFadden turns in time to see the librarian, stock-still. "Sorry," the man whispers, "sorry," and backs away.

The girl makes a sound that seems like laughter. "He was coming over to tell us to be quiet," she says, and makes the sound again.

"*Let me tell you something about love.*" McFadden's voice has cracked against the strain. "Love is the worst of them, the worst of *all* of them – religion, politics . . . It's just another ideology, another way to make things simple. It goes against the very heart of human nature. Intelligent people can't be in love any more than they can be Baptists. Love is for the stupid."

"So now you think I'm stupid."

"Oh, no! Oh, don't you try that. How dare you try to say that! How *dare* you even think about that line of argument!"

He needs to see if she is seeing, so he cups his hands around his eyes to watch her through his fingers. She watches back, her expression now impossible to read.

"You're the word man," she says at last. "Come on, let's have it again."

She's lost him.

"The one you're always going on about. The one on your truck . . ."

"*Paradox*," he sighs. Once again she's whipped him into smiling. McFadden raises his hands in surrender. "There's something else for us to talk about," he says. He has reached across the table to his own tidy gathering of data. "There's something here I want your help with." McFadden moves his chair around to where they both can see. "This is an enlargement of the eastern shore of Lake Superior," he says, smoothing his maps against the polished wood. With the index finger of one hand he indicates a spot along the shoreline. "The highway runs just over here." He places a second finger just below the first. "Somewhere on this stretch of highway is where I picked you up. Remember, that first day?"

It's as if the rest has vanished. She stares at him now, wide-eyed, hands pressed against the high bones of her cheek.

McFadden moves his fingers a little distance to the left. "Somewhere in this stretch of water," he says, "is your island. There are quite a few of them, though most I've been able to eliminate. That still leaves these," he says, "here, here, and here, as possibilities. So now I have to ask some questions –"

"Why are you doing this?"

McFadden smiles, and shrugs. "I dick around."

The girl has risen from her chair and backs toward the window. Her fingers twitch behind her until they touch and grip the sill.

"I'm not going," she says very softly. "I'm not going there."

"Of course you're not." McFadden says this gently, almost with a smile. "Of course you're not." He swivels in his chair and, like a lover, lays his hand against her cheek. "You have to tell me now," he says. "It's time. You have to tell me where you want to go."

– – –

It's nearly dusk when they arrive. They've driven several hours west toward the foothills, down into a valley and up again the other side. McFadden long ago has ceased to pay attention. The girl calls directions, he follows. They have left the highway well behind, bumping down these discontinued logging roads, the girl forward in her seat to scan for landmarks. Things have changed, she tells him; rivers altered, clear-cuts grown again. But she finds her way. It's nearly dusk when they arrive and build their camp.

The place is indeed beautiful. But it's difficult for McFadden to separate this beauty from the one that occupies his mind.

"It hasn't changed," she says. "Here at least it hasn't changed."

McFadden smiles and nods his head.

Tonight he cooks her roast of pork, braised among the embers, with applesauce – as promised all along. She wears another of his sweaters, and the wool absorbs the smoke.

"Take the sweater," he says, and gestures to the rest. "Take what you need. I don't want you being cold. I only want you . . . safe."

She closes her eyes for a moment as a pocket of sap bursts into a sky of sparks. "Thank you," she says. "But you . . . you're the one who should be careful. They're dangerous, you have to know that."

McFadden smiles again and nods. He knows in which direction dangers lie.

When it is time for bed, they go, and afterwards she sleeps, then dreams. McFadden lies awake until the dream is over, consuming it like fuel. He will not sleep. As the hours pass, he listens for the wolves – real wolves, here in the timber – howling from the high ground. The sound and omen please him.

When he awakes, the girl is gone.

A few small things are missing – hardly anything. He wishes she had taken the Coleman stove, at least. Or the axe . . . But these he finds neatly stacked away inside the truck. He finds his sweater too, stretched to air against the wire of the cages where his rats were housed. The smell of girl and rats and smoke combine. McFadden leans his head into the wool and lets the scent absorb in memory. She has broken camp while he lay sleeping, built the morning fire and stacked things neatly here, against the rows of empty cages.

He waits an hour while the fire dies, in case there has been a miscommunication. But of course, there has not.

McFadden busies himself with bucket and soap, peeling away the bumper stickers and scrubbing off decals, which now serve no purpose. With the flat blade of his knife he pries the wooden sign from where it has been glued beside the door. Dabs of dried adhesive mar the paint where it was glued, and won't wash off. No matter. He tosses it in with the rest of the junk, and closes the door.

The truck bounces several miles and bumps its way toward the highway – smoother going as the roads bear east, then flat and temperate asphalt all the way to Lake Superior. When she feels the way has eased, the girl extrudes herself from where she's wedged beneath the cages. The wire mesh has pressed its pattern deep into her skin. She finds McFadden's sweater, puts it on, then lights a match. A flashlight has been laid to hand, and now she finds this too.

When the blood has flowed into her limbs again, she stands, braced against the motion, and begins to organize – folding out the sleeping bag, pumping up the mattress, tidying the litter. She knows he will not stop for many many miles, perhaps not until he gets there. No matter. This means that there are many miles before he finds her. There is water. There is food. And the plastic bucket, there, when needed.

Enough.

She has cleared a little space to make room for the chair, and sits, then smiles and stands again. The girl has spied McFadden's wooden sign. She scans the rows of cages. Opening the door of one, she sets the sign inside – *Paradox*, it says – where she can see the letters through the mesh, and carefully closes the door.

ACKNOWLEDGEMENTS

Many thanks to my editors Anne Collins and Stacey Cameron for choosing, shaping, and so sweetly refining this book. Thanks also to my wife, Rennie Renelt, for remaining so during its long stages of writing, and to Paul Harper for his keen understanding of *Ratus Albertanus*. I'm grateful also to Doug Fagg, trapping instructor, for showing me the perils of nicking the gut, and to Diane Allen of The Infertility Network who led me so patiently through that labyrinth. Heartfelt gratitude to the province of Alberta and its stalwart leaders.

Both the Ontario Arts Council and the Toronto Arts Council provided grants in support of this novel. Let me acknowledge here how deeply welcomed these were.

Scott Gardiner's writing has appeared in several publications, including *Toronto Life, Canadian Geographic, The Globe and Mail* and *The Toronto Star.* He has worked as a deckhand on the Great Lake freighters, a wall-plasterer in Spain, a soap salesman in Germany, a fact-checker at *Maclean's* and an education consultant in Labrador. He lives in Toronto. *The Dominion of Wyley McFadden* was shortlisted for the Commonwealth Writers Prize 2001, Caribbean and Canada Region's Best First Book.